D0710629

The time between those two dates in January is the focus of a fascinating political suspense story in which radicals working outside the government and politicians working within combine unwillingly to make Washington an armed camp and the Act of Succession a travesty of justice.

On January 3, Clifford Fairlie, president-elect, was in Paris on his way to Spain on a special goodwill mission. His chances for success were high: not since Kennedy had the United States possessed a leader who commanded such personal admiration.

On January 3, at noon, as Congress was being sworn in, five bombs went off in the Senate and House; by January 4 the toll stood at 143 dead.

On January 10, ten days before he was to be inaugurated, Clifford Fairlie was kidnapped in Spain, taken to a deserted farmhouse in the Pyrenees, and from there on an intricately planned voyage. To David Lime of Protective Intelligence fell the job of tracing the kidnappers' route.

And the radicals were not through: they had plans to eliminate others, plans that would result in the president-elect's being succeeded by a man who stood for everything Fairlie was against. The option became—find the president-elect or break the line of succession.

Brian Garfield combines the political excitement of the Washington scene with the strategic suspense of a worldwide hunt to give us one of his most engrossing novels.

LINE OF SUCCESSION

Books by Brian Garfield

BRIAN GARFIELD

DELACORTE PRESS / NEW YORK

LINE OF
SUCCESSION

Library of Congress Catalog Card Number: 78–38897
Manufactured in the United States of America
Second printing—1972
Library of Congress Cataloging in Publication Data
Garfield, Brian Wynne, 1939–
    Line of succession.
    I. Title.
PZ4.G2315Li [PS3557.A715] 813'.5'4 78–38897

DESIGNED BY *Julian Hamer*

For John
and
Gunilla Jainchill

1700737

"The terms of the President and Vice-President shall end at noon on the 20th day of January, and the terms of Senators and Representatives at noon on the 3rd day of January . . . ; and the terms of their successors shall then begin.

"The Congress shall assemble at least once in every year, and such meeting shall begin at noon on the 3rd day of January. . . ."

Article XX
Constitution of the United States

LINE OF SUCCESSION

FIVE BOMBS

SUNDAY, JANUARY 2

10:45 P.M. EST   The girl's body was found by a man in a raincoat. It was in an alley near the intersection of Euclid and Fourteenth Street Northwest—a black neighborhood of brick row-houses and urban ferment.

At first the man in the raincoat shrank from the body: he stood against the wall breathing shallowly, blinking, but in the end he knelt by the girl and began to search near and under the body, although there was little hope. If she had been mugged there would be no handbag.

A car was going by slowly. The man in the raincoat ignored it until it stopped, but then it was too late. The spotlight swiveled onto him and pinned him against the wall.

He threw up an arm in front of his eyes and heard the car door open and chunk shut. There was a voice:

"Turn around. Hands high against the wall."

The man in the raincoat obeyed. He knew the routine. He splayed his feet a yard out from the base of the wall and leaned against his palms. The patrolman frisked him and found nothing and moved with a crunch of shoes to the girl's body.

The second cop got out of the squad car. The first cop said, "DOA. Send in a squeal—we'll want the wagon."

The man in the raincoat heard the first cop get up and take two steps forward. The cop's voice had changed: before it had been weary but now it was taut, angry. "What in the hell did you do that with?"

"I didn't do nothing."

He felt a sudden grip on his shoulder and the cop pulled him upright from the frisk position and cracked the handcuffs against his wrists.

"Now sit down."

He slid down with his back against the brick wall. The drizzle ran down inside the collar of his raincoat and he hitched around on his buttocks to free enough cloth to cover the back of his neck. The spotlight was in his eyes and he kept them squinted almost shut.

"You vicious bastard," the cop said, very soft.

When the boot caught him in the ribs he was half expecting it and he managed to ride with it, toppling over on his side; it hurt but it hadn't broken anything. He stayed on his side with his cheek in the gravel. He had learned submission a long time ago. If you showed any fight at all they would kick the guts out of you.

The cop's feet shifted and the man in the raincoat got ready for another kick but then the other cop came from the car. "Take it easy, Pete."

"You didn't see what the son of a bitch did to her. Take a look."

"Just take it easy. Some lawyer sees him all black and blue they'll turn him loose and hand us a reprimand."

"Since when can anybody see black and blue on that spade hide?" But the cop didn't kick him again.

The other cop went over to the dead girl. Breath whistled out through his teeth. "Sweet Jesus."

"Yeah."

"What'd he do it with?"

"Beats me. He must have ditched the knife."

"Took more than a knife."

"I'll have a look around."

The first cop started to prowl the alley, and the second cop came over to the man in the raincoat. "Sit up."

He obeyed. The cop was above him and when he looked up he could see the cop's fleshy white face in the hard beam of the spotlight. The cop said, "You got some identification? Move your hands real slow."

The man reached inside his raincoat and took out the little plastic case. The cop took it from him and lifted it, turning, to get it in the light. All it contained was a numbers slip, a welfare card, Social Security and a single dollar bill.

"Franklin Delano Graham," the cop said. "Jesus Christ."

11:20 P.M. "I think he's telling it straight," the lieutenant said.

The sergeant propped himself against the hip-high partition that delineated the lieutenant's corner of the detective squad room. "Hell, he's a junkie. He wouldn't know the truth if it kicked him in the face."

"Then what did he do? Mangle the girl like that, grab her bag, go away somewhere and hide the bag and the stuff he mangled her with, and then come back and hang around waiting for us to pick him up? I can't buy that."

The sergeant looked across the squad room. A dozen desks, men sitting at half of them. Franklin Delano Graham was on a bench against the far wall, guarded by the patrolman who had brought him in. Graham's black face was closed up with the singular bleakness of a junkie who knows he's not going to get his next hit in time.

The sergeant said, "I guess that's right. But I'll book him anyway."

"Send him over to the methadone clinic."

"What for?" But the sergeant went to his desk and sat down to type up the forms.

The lieutenant was on the telephone. "Have you got a make on the dead girl yet?"

11:35 P.M. Alvin stood just inside the window keeping watch on the street. The sill was a half inch deep in dust and there was a large white-painted X across the outside of the panes. He could see through it past the front steps to the sidewalk where Linc and Darleen stood under the street lamp in tight vivid colors, both flaunt-it-baby black and lean, looking too casual to be sentries.

The bombs lay in a row on the table, and Sturka worked on them with studied concentration. The five people from California sat on wooden boxes in a little circle at the far side of the room. Peggy and Cesar were near the table watching Sturka work on the bombs; Mario Mezetti was in the corner on the floor, absorbed in rereading Ché's diary.

Alvin looked out the window again. The air was misty but the drizzle had quit. When cars passed, the wind whipped away white exhaust spumes from their tailpipes. A few black people moved along the street and Alvin looked at their faces. Probably tomorrow wouldn't change their lives at all. But you had to try.

Sturka was hunched over the long refectory table. No one spoke; it was a silence of discipline and sweat.

The room was broken plaster and splintered floorboards. Mario had cellotaped the photo of Mao on the door and beneath it one of his humorless posters, *Long Live the Victory of the People's War.* The Californians' suitcases were stacked neatly by the table and Peggy was using one for a seat, smoking a Marlboro and watching Sturka build his bombs. There was a gooseneck high-intensity lamp with an extension cord which Sturka moved from mechanism to mechanism as he worked on them. A pile of lumpy knapsacks on the floor, a scatter of ashes and dirt and empty styrofoam cups, and a stale sense of abandonment: the block was marked for demolition and that was why there were whitewash crosses on the windows.

Everything was laid out with professional neatness as if for a display—the five handbags and briefcases, innards exposed; the plastic gelatine and the wires and batteries and detonators and stopwatches.

Peggy was restless: she came to the window and looked out past him at Linc and Darleen on the curb. She touched his sleeve. "Bad vibes, Alvy?"

"No. Why?"

"You look tight."

"Well it's a heavy thing."

"They're not exactly homemade Embarcaderos."

"I didn't mean that."

They had spoken low but Sturka's head lifted and the intense eyes pushed against Alvin. He turned his shoulder to the room and Peggy went back to her suitcase and lit another Marlboro. Peggy was a sad tough girl and Alvin liked her. Three years ago in Chicago she had been demonstrating against the war—just standing in the crowd, not carrying a sign, not doing anything, but cops had charged into the crowd and a pig had dragged Peggy across the curb steps by her feet, bouncing her head on the concrete; they had manhandled her into a wagon and rousted her into a precinct station, and they had called that resisting an officer. Now she was twenty-three, angry, dedicated, rootless, and one other thing: she was a registered nurse. Sturka surrounded himself only with professionals.

Alvin had come down from New York on Monday night with Sturka and Peggy and four others after Sturka's private meeting with Raoul Riva. The five who had volunteered to carry the bombs had arrived in Washington Thursday from the West Coast; Alvin hadn't seen any of them before and they kept to themselves, so that he still knew very little about them beyond their names and faces. That was the way Riva and Sturka always worked. The less you knew the less trouble you could cause.

The five volunteers sat drinking coffee, two men and three women. The men were short-haired and clean-shaven, quite well dressed; the women looked middle class, the girl in a long-sleeved wool dress and the fat girl in sweater and skirt and the small black woman in a tweed suit. They didn't look like terrorists and of course they weren't supposed to. The little black woman was middle-aged: she had lost two sons in Indochina. She had been teaching at UCLA but they had dropped her contract because of her radical activities. She had a third son somewhere in Canada and a fourth in the Panthers in New York.

Cesar had recruited them. He had gone out to the Coast and hung around the fringes of the radical groups until he had found people who would suit Riva's purposes. Cesar was persuasive as a recruiter: it was Cesar who had brought Alvin in. "Revolutions are made by professionals, not schoolchildren. Look, you've had it with soft-head protest, demonstrations that don't mean nothing. And there ain't no point to the crazies, that's just random violencing. Corby, you got combat experience, you know about tactics and planning and being professional—you want to join an organization that knows where it's at."

The group had no name, no set of initials; even Sturka went under a false name—he was Stratten to everybody he didn't trust, and he hardly ever trusted anyone.

There was no visible coalition but Raoul Riva was somewhere on the fringe—a part of Sturka's operation but not a member of this cell. Possibly Riva had a cell of his own; Alvin wasn't sure— he had seen the Cuban only once and at some distance. It was a taut cell and alliances were not discussed. Riva existed somehow on the periphery—an old warrior brother of Sturka's, a shadow-figure.

Sturka seldom spoke to any of them; he had no small talk and he wasn't a speechmaker. Indoctrination sessions were chaired by Cesar. Sturka remained aloof from the study groups; he absented himself often when Cesar was guiding them through the teachings of Marighela and Mao and Ché. At first Alvin had taken Sturka's indifference badly: a revolutionary had to remember *why* he was fighting. But he soon learned Sturka had forgotten nothing: his memory was absolute and he required no refresher courses in the philosophy of liberation.

Sturka had no personal charm, he made no effort to light angry fires. He had no striking mannerisms, no habit movements, no interest in what impression he might be making. Alvin had never even heard him complain about injustice or the pig Establishment. Sturka's leadership depended on his competence: he knew what had to be done and he knew how to do it.

Sturka was between forty and fifty, bigger than he looked—he seemed sick-chested because he tended to hunch his shoulders. His face was bony, long-jawed, pitted by the scars of some old skin affliction. He was dark for a Caucasian; he had straight black hair and a vague foreign accent that Alvin had never been able to place. According to Cesar, who had been with him longest, Sturka had fought with Ché and the Palestine guerrillas and in Biafra and Guyana and, fifteen years ago, in the Algerian FLN. From a few things that had been let drop Alvin had the impression Sturka had learned his professionalism as a mercenary in the Congo and in Indochina.

Sturka had an expert's contempt for explosives. He knew the science of demolition and he had the concentration of a monk. Now he was hawked over the bombs, shaping them. The plastic gelatine had been manufactured in the United States but Mario had flown out to Singapore and bought it on the black market—it had been stolen from an arms dump near Da Nang. The stuff was malleable as modeling clay; Sturka was distributing it along sheets of lead foil inside the false bottoms of the three handbags and the two briefcases. The Number Eight detonators and battery packs were pressed into the plastic against the stopwatches that would trigger the detonators. Sturka had machined tiny combination levers, actuated by the lock fittings on the outsides of the cases, to push the start buttons of the watches. The lead-foil sheaths would prevent metal detectors from discovering the concealed mechanisms, and the use of stopwatches would avoid detection by listening devices which otherwise would pick up the ticking of a time-clock detonator.

The preparation of the watches had been delicate and Alvin had watched with interest. Each watch crystal had to be unscrewed; the tip of the minute hand had to be bent up, and a metal prong soldered to the watchcase so that the minute hand in its circle would touch the prong, completing the electric circuit that would detonate the explosive. The watchcase was screwed to the housing but everything else was imbedded in the soft clay of the gelatine, so that the entire apparatus lay flat and looked a bit like a printed electronic circuit. Flattened neatly across the leaded bottom of each case, the bomb was no more than half an inch thick, but each case carried eighteen ounces of plastic explosive and that was enough.

Above the false bottoms the handbags and briefcases contained a variety of journalists' commonplaces: pencils, pens, spiral notebooks, odds and ends of paper secured with paper clips, small pocket pencil sharpeners, ink jars, pocket combs, cosmetics, keys, cigarettes and cigarette lighters, banded packets of three-by-five index cards. Sturka had selected the items for their shrapnel value. A hurtling paper clip could pierce an eye; a cigarette lighter could kill.

Sturka was fitting sheets of lead foil across the tops of the molded bombs now; he was almost finished. It only remained to fit the false bottoms into the cases.

Cesar stood up, pressed his fists into the small of his back and stretched, bending far back; he windmilled his arms to loosen cramped muscles and came across the room to the window. Glanced at Alvin, glanced at Darleen and Linc outside, and peeled back his sleeve to look at his watch. Alvin followed his glance: almost midnight. D Day. Alvin looked around the room and after a moment he said, "Where's Barbara?"

"Gave her an errand to run," Cesar said very offhandedly.

It bothered Alvin. Sturka and Cesar had gone out three hours ago with Barbara and had returned without her twenty minutes later. Alvin made his voice very low because he didn't want to disturb Sturka. "Shouldn't she be back by now?"

"No. Why?"

"Getting kind of close for time. We don't want our people wandering around on the street where they could get picked up and maybe talk."

"She won't talk to anybody," Cesar said, and moved away toward the table.

Alvin looked down at his hands, and turned them over and looked at his palms—as if he had not seen them before. It bothered him that they still didn't trust him enough to tell him things.

MONDAY, JANUARY 3

2:10 A.M. EST The Assistant Medical Examiner had just settled gratefully into his chair when the phone rang. "M.E.'s office, Charlton speaking."

"Ed Ainsworth, Doc."

"Hello, Lieutenant." The Assistant M.E. put his feet up on the desk.

"Doc, about that girl they brought in DOA from Northwest. My sergeant seems to have kind of a garbled report on her from your office. Maybe you can straighten it out for me."

"Garbled?"

"He says you told him somebody'd cut out her tongue with a pair of pliers."

"That's right. I did."

"A pair of pliers?"

"The jaws left clear indentations on what's left of her tongue, Lieutenant. Maybe I phrased it badly in the report. I said they'd cut out her tongue. 'Pulled' would have been more accurate."

"Good Christ." After a moment the lieutenant resumed: "You did the autopsy yourself?"

"I regret to say I did."

"And there's no sign she was sexually molested?"

"None. Of course that's not conclusive, but there's no sign of vaginal irritation, no semen, none of the usual——"

"Okay. Now the cause of death, you've got 'heart removal' here. Now for Christ's sake what——"

"Read the whole thing, Lieutenant."

"I have. God help me."

"Heart removal by probable use of ordinary household tools."

"Yeah. You mean kitchen knife, that kind of thing?"

"That's a utensil. I said *tools*. I suspect they used a hammer and chisel, although I can't prove it."

The lieutenant didn't speak for a little while. When he did his voice was very thin. "All right, Doc, then tell me this. If the cause of death was a hammer and chisel against the breastplate how in hell did they get her to hold still for it?"

"I wasn't there, Lieutenant. How should I know? Probably a few of them held her down and one of them did the job on her."

"And she didn't scream?"

"Maybe she screamed her head off. You know that neighborhood—they mug you on the street in broad daylight, nobody lifts a finger."

Another pause. Then: "Doc, this has got the stink of some kind of ritual to it. Some hoodoo voodoo thing."

"Was she Haitian or anything like that?"

"We haven't got a make on her yet. I don't know what she was."

The Assistant M.E. had her face in his mind. It must have been a pleasant face before. Young—he had put her at twenty-one or -two. The proud Afro haircut, the good long legs. The telephone moved fitfully against his ear. He said, "I admit it's one I haven't come across before."

"God forbid we ever come across it again. Listen, just for the record, if we come across a bloody pair of pliers can you match them up to measurements or anything?"

"I doubt it. Not unless you find tissues adhering to the pliers. We could set up a circumstantial case on the basis of blood type, I suppose."

"Yeah. All right. Look, anything else you didn't put in the report? Anything that might give a lead?"

"Up in New York and Chicago they seem to have quite a few mobster killings where they rub out somebody who squealed on them and leave the corpse lying around with a big plaster of tape over the mouth, or they pour a jar of acid in the mouth, that kind of thing. It's a warning to other potential squealers—you know, see what happens to you if you open your mouth to the wrong people."

"Sicilian justice."

"Yes. But this girl wasn't Sicilian, that's for sure."

"Maybe the killer is."

"Maybe."

The lieutenant sighed audibly. "With pliers and a hammer and chisel? I don't know."

"I'd like to help, Lieutenant. I'd love to put it all in your lap for you. But I'm all gone dry."

"All right. I'm sorry I bugged you, Doc. Good night."

3:05 A.M.   The make on the dead girl came into the detective squad room on the wire from the FBI fingerprint files and the sergeant ripped it off the machine and took it to the lieutenant's desk in the corner. The lieutenant read halfway into it and went back to the beginning and started again.

"A Federal snoop."

"From Justice."

"It's an FSS number. She was Secret Service." The lieutenant sat back and spent ten seconds grinding his knuckles into his eye sockets. He lowered his hands into his lap and kept his eyes shut. "Cripes. I was starting to get a picture."

"What picture?"

"I had it worked out. She was a hooker and she rolled some capo from the Mob, not knowing who he was. So the capo sent some of his boys out to take care of her. But this blows it all to hell."

The sergeant said, "Maybe we'd better call Justice."

3:40 A.M.   A telephone was ringing, disturbing David Lime's sleep. He listened to it ring. He had never fallen victim to the compulsion to answer every telephone that rang within earshot; anyhow this was not his own bed, not his own bedroom, not his own telephone; but it disturbed his sleep.

He lay on his back and listened to it ring and finally the mattress gave a little heave and a soft buttock banged into his leg. There was a clumsy rattle of receiver against cradle and then Bev said in the dark, "Who the hell is this? . . . Shit, all right, hold on." Then she was poking him in the ribs. "David?"

He sat up on his elbow and took the phone from her. "Uh?"

"Mr. Lime? Chad Hill. I'm damned sorry to have to ——"

"The hell time's it?"

"About a quarter to four, sir."

"A quarter to four," David Lime said disagreeably. "Is that a fact."

"Yes, sir. I——"

"You called me to tell me it's a quarter to four."

"Sir, I wouldn't have called if it wasn't important."

"How'd you know where to find me?" He knew Hill had something to tell him but first he had to clear the sleep from his head.

"Mr. DeFord gave me the number, sir."

Bev was getting out of bed, storming into the bathroom. Lime dragged a hand down his jaw. "Bless Mr. DeFord. Bless the little son of a bitch." The bathroom door closed—not quite a slam. A ribbon of light appeared beneath it.

"Sir, one of our agents has been murdered."

Lime closed his eyes: a grimace. Not *Smith's dead.* Not *Jones has been killed.* No. "One of our agents has been murdered." Like a fourteen-year-old imitating Reed Hadley's narration for a Grade B Warner's picture: a mausoleum tone, *One of our aircraft is missing!* From what plastic packaging factory did they obtain these kids?

"All right, Chad. One of our agents is missing. Now——"

"Not missing, sir. Murdered. I'm down here at——"

"*What* agent has been murdered?"

"Barbara Norris, sir. The police called the office and I was on night duty. I called Mr. DeFord and he said I'd better get in touch with you."

"Yes, I imagine he did." Grandon Pass-the-Buck DeFord. Lime sat up, squeezed his eyes shut and popped them open. "All right. Where are you now and what's happened?"

"I'm at police headquarters, sir. Suppose I put Lieutenant Ainsworth on, he can explain what they've got."

A new voice came on the line: "Mr. Lime?"

"That's right."

"Ed Ainsworth. Detective Lieutenant down here. We had a DOA tonight, a young black girl. The FBI identifies her as Barbara Norris and they gave us an FSS service number for her so I called your office. You're in charge of her section, is that right?"

"I'm the Deputy Assistant Director." He managed to say it with a straight face. "DeFord's the Assistant Director in charge of Protective Intelligence."

"Uh-huh. Well Mr. DeFord said she was your agent. Do you want the details by phone or would you like to come down and see for yourself? I'm afraid they made a mess of her."

"Definitely a homicide, then?"

"You could say that. They ripped out her tongue with a pair of pliers and they dug out her heart with a hammer and chisel."

The door opened and Bev walked naked across the room, sat down in the chair and lit a cigarette and blew smoke at the match. She didn't look at him: she stared at the floor.

Lime said, "Sweet Jesus."

"Yes, sir. It was pretty God damned vicious."

"Where did this happen, Lieutenant?"

"An alley off Euclid. Near Fourteenth Street."

"What time?"

"About six hours ago."

"What have you got?"

"Next to nothing, I'm afraid. No handbag, no visible evidence except the body itself. No evidence of sexual molestation. We found a junkie searching the body but he claims he found her that way and the evidence supports his story. I've had people combing the neighborhood but you know the way things are in those parts of town— nobody saw anything, nobody heard anything."

"Any possibility she was killed somewhere else and dumped there?"

"Not likely. Too much blood in the alley."

Bev stood up and padded to the bed. She handed him a freshly lighted cigarette and an ashtray and went back to her chair. Lime dragged suicidally on the cigarette. Choked, coughed, recovered, and said, "Do you need me down there to identify her? I seem to recall she had no next of kin."

"Mr. Hill here gave us a positive identification on her. It won't be necessary. But if you can give us a lead—if I knew what she'd been working on. . . ."

Lime ducked it: "She was on a security case—I can't give it to you. But if we come across evidence that might help in a criminal prosecution we'll pass it on to you."

"Sure, that's okay." A voice of resignation: the lieutenant had known the answer before he'd asked the question. But you had to go through the motions. Everybody has to go through the motions, Lime thought.

"Tell Chad Hill I'll be in the office as soon as I get dressed."

"I will. Goodbye, sir."

Lime rolled over on his side to cradle the phone. Light in the room was weak, splashing in through the open door of the bathroom. He thought about the dead girl and tried to remember her alive; he smashed out the cigarette and climbed off the bed.

Bev said, "I don't know about the other guy. But your end of that conversation was right out of a rerun of *Dragnet*."

"Somebody got killed."

"I gathered." Her soft contralto was deepened by the hour and the cigarette. "Anyone I know? Knew?"

"No."

"Now you're being strong and silent."

"Just silent," he said, and climbed into his drawers. He sat down to pull on his socks.

She got back into bed and pulled the sheet and blanket up over her. "It's funny. No two men get dressed in the same order. My ex used to start from the top down. Undershirt, shirt, tie, *then* his shorts and pants and socks and shoes. And I knew a guy who refused to buy tight slacks because he always put his shoes on first and couldn't get them through leg-huggers."

"Is that right." He went into the bathroom and washed his face with cold water. Used her toothbrush and glanced at the lady-electric shaver on the shelf, but decided against it; he had a shaver in the office. In the mirror there were bags pendant under his eyes. *I can't possibly be as old as I look.* He looked like a big sleepy blond Wisconsin Swede gone over the hill and a little seedy. A little bit of office paunch, a fishbelly whiteness about the upper chest and arms. He needed a couple of weeks on a beach in the Virgin Islands.

He gargled mouthwash and went out into the bedroom and reached for his shirt.

Bev looked as if she had gone back to sleep but then her eyes drifted open. "I thought you'd got yourself out of the dagger end of things and confined yourself to cloaks."

"I have. All I do is keep the papers moving."

"I see. You send girls out to get killed for you."

He cinched up his trousers and reached for his tie. Bev sat up, making a face, the good breasts lying a bit askew. "You'd better have a bite of breakfast, I suppose. It wouldn't do to go ogling corpses on an empty stomach."

"I could do with toast and coffee."

She wasn't tall but she stood tall: a straight-up girl with long legs and high firm hips and a fair amount of mischief in her face. Playful, tawny, good-tempered.

She was the woman he would love if he could love.

She went out to the kitchenette, belting a terrycloth robe around her. She wanted to be useful to him: it was part of her character to be useful; she was a widower's daughter.

He got into his hairy brown sports jacket and his cordovan loafers and went into the kitchenette after her. Kissed the back of her neck: "Thanks."

10:35 A.M. Continental European Time   There was a knock at the door and Clifford Fairlie looked up from his newspaper. His eyes took a moment to focus on the room—as if he had forgotten where he was. The sitting room of the suite was quite grand in its *fin-de-siècle* elegance: the Queen Annes, the Cézannes, the Boulle desk, the expanse of Persian carpet to the heavy double doors. It was a suite to which President-elect Fairlie had admitted few reporters because he had found that most journalists detested any politician who seemed to know the century in which the furniture around him had been crafted.

Knuckles again; Fairlie shambled to the door. He was a man who opened his own doors.

It was his chief aide, Liam McNeely, slim in a Dunhill suit. Behind him the Secret Service men in the anteroom looked up, nodded, and looked away. McNeely came in and pushed the door shut behind him. "Morning, Mr. President."

"Not quite yet."

"I'm practicing."

The smell of expensive aftershave had come into the room with McNeely. Clifford Fairlie settled on the Queen Anne couch and waved him toward a chair. McNeely collapsed as if boneless: sat on the back of his neck, long legs crossed like grasshopper limbs. "Lots of weather we're having."

"I spent a winter in Paris once, a long time ago. I can't remember the sun shining once in the five months from October to early March." That had been the year he'd lost the Senate race for reelection from Pennsylvania. The President had twisted the knife by sending him to Paris as peace-talk negotiator.

McNeely uncrossed his legs with a getting-down-to-business sigh.

The notebook came out of his pocket. "It's about a quarter to eleven now. You've got the Common Market people at noon and lunch here in the hotel at one forty-five with Breucher."

"Plenty of time."

"Yes sir. I only mentioned it. You don't want to show up at the meeting in that outfit."

Fairlie's jacket had leather patches at the elbows. He smiled. "Maybe I ought to. I'm Brewster's emissary."

McNeely laughed at the joke. "Press conference at four. They'll mainly be asking about the plans for the trip to Spain."

That was the nub, the trip to Spain. The rest was window dressing. The vital thing was those Spanish bases.

McNeely said, "And they'll want your reactions to Brewster's logorrhea last night."

"What reactions? For Brewster it was damned mild."

"You going to say that? Pity. It'd be a good chance to get in a few digs."

"No point being inflammatory. Too much anger in the world already."

"A lot of it incited by that pisspot Napoleon in the White House." McNeely had a Yale Ph.D., he had been an Oxford fellow, he had written eight volumes of political analysis, he had served two Administrations—one in the Cabinet—and he persisted in calling the incumbent President of the United States "this flimflam fuehrer" and "the schmuck on Pennsylvania Avenue."

It was an attitude not without some justice. President Howard Brewster was a man who specialized in answers, not questions; he had the kind of mind to which Why-not-victory? oversimplifications were very attractive. Brewster represented to uncanny perfection that large segment of the populace which still wistfully hoped to win a war that had been lost a long time ago. To quick-minded sophisticates he stood for Neanderthal politics and nineteenth-century simplemindedness. Brewster was a man of emotional outbursts and political solipsism; to all appearances his attitudes had ceased developing at about the time the Allies had won World War II; and in the age of celebrity, when candidates could get elected because they looked good on a horse, Brewster's total lack of panache made him a genuine anachronism.

But that view of Howard Brewster was incomplete: it did not take into account the fact that Brewster was a man of politics in the same way that a tiger is a creature of the jungle. The pursuit of the

Presidency had cost Brewster almost thirty years of party-climbing and fund-raising dinners and bloc-wooing within the Senate in which he had sat for four consecutive terms. Yet the unresponsive Administration of the unresponsive Government, which McNeely deplored with vigorous sarcasms, was not really of Brewster's making. Howard Brewster was not so much its architect as its inevitable and typical product.

It was no good condemning Brewster out of hand. He had not been the worst President in American history, not by a wide margin, and the election results had shown it: Fairlie hadn't so much won the election from Brewster as avoided defeat, and by an incredibly small margin: 35,129,484 to 35,088,756. There had been a madness of recounts; Brewster supporters were still crying foul, claiming the Los Angeles machine had delivered to Fairlie the bloc votes of Forest Lawn Cemetery and the Pacific Ocean, but neither election officials nor Brewster's campaigners had been able to furnish proof of their allegations and as far as Fairlie knew they weren't true anyhow—the Mayor of Los Angeles wasn't that fond of him, not by any means.

In the end Fairlie had eked out 296 votes in the Electoral College to Brewster's 242, carrying the big states by small margins and losing the small states by large margins. Brewster's support was in the South and in rural America and the confusion of party allegiances had probably cost him the election because he was nominally and loyally a Democrat while his Republican opponent was in fact somewhere to the left of him.

"Deep thoughts, Mr. President?"

McNeely's voice lifted him from reverie. "God. I simply haven't had enough sleep. What have we got laid on for tomorrow morning?"

"Admiral James and General Tesworth. From NATO in Naples."

"Can you move it back to the afternoon somewhere?"

"Hard to do."

"I've got to get some rest."

"Just hold out a week, Mr. President. You can collapse in the Pyrenees."

"Liam, I've been talked to by too many admirals and generals as it is. I'm not doing a big-stick tour of American military bases."

"You could afford to touch a few. The right-wing press likes the idea that you're doing a world tour of leftist capitals to cement relations with Commies and pinkos."

London. Bonn. Paris. Rome. Madrid. Commies and pinkos? But Fairlie did not laugh. America's cross to bear was its simple minds: the ones who saw no distinction between England's socialism and Albania's Communism.

McNeely said, "Now the L.A. papers are speculating you're on your way to Madrid to give away the Spanish bases."

"That's a pretty good one." Fairlie made a crooked smile.

"Uh-huh. We could have cleared some of it up, you know. But you've insisted we're not to comment on that to the press."

"It's not my place to comment. Not yet. I'm here unofficially."

"As Hollerin' Brewster's goodwill ambassador. Which is really, you know, quite rich."

There *was* a point to it. Europe had taken on the aspect of an American sandbox and United States presidential elections had become quadrennial paroxysms of anxiety throughout the Continent. A shift in stance which Washington regarded as minor might well upset the entire equilibrium of Common Market affairs or NATO's economy or the status of the Russian Mediterranean Fleet vis-à-vis the American Sixth. The idea had come up three weeks ago during the White House state briefings through which Howard Brewster had conducted Fairlie: to reassure "our valiant allies"—it was a Brewster phrase, typically irrelevant and typically outdated—of the continuity and goodwill of the American Government, wouldn't it be a good idea for Republican President-elect Fairlie to call informally on half a dozen heads of state as the personal representative of Democrat President Brewster?

The idea had the kind of grandiose theatricality one had learned to expect of Howard Brewster. But Fairlie had agreed for his own reasons: he wanted to meet Europe's heads of state face to face and an informal pre-inaugural series of meetings might find them more relaxed and natural than had some of the hurried Presidential visits to the same capitals earlier. Unburdened by administrative chores Fairlie would have time to get to know them.

But the Spanish upset had exploded against them all. The bloodless pre-Christmas takeover: Perez-Blasco had wrested Spain from Franco's indecisive successors and Howard Brewster had growled to Fairlie, "God damn, we got a whole new ball game." Even now the ink was hardly dry on the junta's proclamations. Perez-Blasco was feeling his way, trying to shore up the first populist government in forty years. Spain was still the key to the Mediterranean, launch pad for the American nuclear structure in Europe—and Perez-

Blasco's spokesmen had sent up trial balloons in the Spanish press: should Madrid nationalize the nuclear bases and evict the Americans? Nothing was settled: no one knew which way Perez-Blasco would jump.

"You can charm the big bastard, Cliff." Brewster had rolled the cigar in his mouth. "Use all the rational arguments, but lean on the son of a bitch too. Tell him you're just as liberal as he is but God damn it Moscow's got all those boats out in the Med and ask him if he really wants to see them turn the thing into a Russian lake."

It was a good thing Brewster was going out. His brand of gunboat diplomacy would lose the Spanish bases. Brewster's premise was right: you were in competition with Moscow, that was no myth. But it wasn't the kind of competition you won by frightening the customers. Perez-Blasco had to be shopping around for aid; he had already confirmed diplomatic recognition of the Soviet Union and even McNeely had pointed out that where Egypt had gone Spain could easily follow. Perez-Blasco was by no means a far-leftist; nevertheless he was markedly to the left of the old Franco regime. He was a proud man who had come up from poverty, and you did not wave guns under a dignified man's nose. Intimidation was not a very useful tool in modern international relations—not when the customer could get miffed, turn his back on you, and go to the competition.

You had to be cool. You had to go to him, but not in a hurry and not as a beggar.

Clifford Fairlie stood up, a Lincolnesque figure with a tall man's stoop. Thirty-one years ago he had won a seat on the Media town council. In less than three weeks he would be President of the United States.

7:00 A.M. EST   At his desk in the Executive Office Building David Lime was half through his second breakfast of the morning. His eyes were focused wearily on the Barbara Norris file.

The documents and photographs were scattered over the desk. Chad Hill, on his feet at the corner of the desk, was running his finger across them: an unassailably pleasant-faced young man packaged in a blue suit and striped shirt. "This one. Stratten. He seemed to be running the show, from her reports."

The blurred photograph suggested a rangy man with deep-set

eyes overhung by dark brows: a somehow European face, between forty and fifty.

Stratten, no first name, no initials. The active files of Lime's Protective Research Section included some quarter of a million cases and according to the print-outs from the computer none of them mentioned anyone named Stratten or anyone who had ever used the name as an alias.

It was an obvious case: classic and tiresome. Barbara Norris had infiltrated the group, had found out something she wasn't supposed to know, and had been killed to guarantee her silence.

The Stratten blowup showed a face full of latent violence. The Norris girl had snapped the picture a week ago with a Minolta concealed in the folds of her leather handbag.

He reached for the phone. "Get me somebody over at NSA. Ames if you can get him."

He cupped the mouthpiece in his palm and looked up at Chad Hill. "Call the New York office and have them send some people over to that apartment this bunch was using on West End Avenue. Have them give the premises a good toss."

Hill went out to his own desk and the phone came alive in Lime's fist. He put it to his ear. "Ames?"

"No, this is Kaiser. Ames won't be in till nine. Maybe I can help out, Mr. Lime?"

Another of those pitchless voices, uninflected, sounding like some electronic contrivance programmed to imitate human speech. Lime closed his eyes and leaned back in the swivel chair. "I'd like to run a make on a character through your R & I machines."

"Mind if I ask the nature of the case?" It was spoken by rote. Agencies didn't do favors for other agencies unless a reason was supplied.

"It's a protection case. Some hints about an assassination attempt. One of our people was working on it and they seem to have taken her out."

"Then she was onto something." The observation was less redundant than it might have been: Lime's department investigated thousands of assassination threats every season and virtually all of them proved trivial.

"Nothing on your man from FBI?"

"Nothing from any domestic files. We've run him through all of them."

"What have you got? Fingerprints?"

"Fingerprints and a mug shot." Barbara Norris had lifted the prints off a water glass Stratten had used: she had sprinkled it with talc and taken it off with masking tape, and washed the glass afterward.

"Well that ought to be easy enough. Send them over."

"I'll get a runner to you. Thanks."

He hung up and looked at the photo again while he buzzed for a messenger. The straight black hair was bushy at the back, not a distinctive cut, and he wondered what had persuaded him Stratten was a foreigner. Perhaps the set of the mouth or the slight lift to the right eyebrow. But there was something more than that and it still eluded him when the messenger came for the photo and fingerprints.

Then Lime found it in Norris's December 28 report: *Slight accent, indeterminate, possibly Balkan.* The notation was sandwiched into the center of a single-spaced paragraph but he'd read that report at least three times, the earliest five days ago and hadn't caught it consciously until now.

It was a bomb plot, an assassination attempt of some kind. Bombs were always surer than bullets. The one called Mario—they hadn't known her long enough to trust her with full names—seemed to have thought they were planning to bomb the White House. But it was all very vague and Lime hadn't been ready to buy it right off the shelf because the White House was isolated and heavily guarded and virtually impossible to attack with anything less than an armored combat division. The White House Detail had been alerted and Norris had received instructions to stay with Stratten's group until she learned whether their intentions were real or only the idle bluffing of a handful of radicalized screwheads freaked out on bravado and drugs.

But now it was time to leash them. Three hours ago Lime had put out the order to pick them up: Stratten and Alvin Corby and the others identified by FBI computers from information fed to Lime's office by Barbara Norris.

The initial tip had come by way of the FBI from a Panther plant they had in New York, a citizen whose mother had informed him vaguely that she was involved in an attempt to assassinate someone in Washington. The citizen had tried to dissuade his mother but it was all long-distance telephoning and very little could be said on an open line; he had failed to talk her out of it and so he had alerted the FBI because he wanted to protect his mother from the consequences of her foolishness. The FBI had passed it on to Secret Service Director B. L. Hoyt, and Hoyt had passed it on down the line through channels to Lime. Assassination threats were Lime's bailiwick.

The Secret Service was a sub-agency within the Treasury Department. It was charged with two distinct functions between which there was what could be called a "connection" only with some serious abuse of the word. It was B. L. Hoyt's duty to apprehend counterfeiters and to protect the lives of politicians. The logic of it was on a par with most Washingtonian logic and it hardly even annoyed Lime any more.

The ball was in his court and he had to play with it. He had makes on five of them: Alvin Corby, twenty-six, black, an Indochina veteran, a former member of several black radical groups; Cesar Renaldo, thirty-one, born in New York of Puerto Rican parents, arrested twice for possession of hashish and once for assaulting a policeman during an antiwar demonstration; Robert and Sandra Walberg, twenty-four, twin brother and sister, both former SDS-Weathermen, both carrying records of arrest and conviction for possession of marijuana (sentence suspended) and disorderly behavior during campus building occupations at the University of Southern California (six months probation); and Beulah Moorehead, forty-one, the mother of the FBI's Panther plant.

There was partial information on some others but none of it was hard. A black couple named Linc and Darleen. The one called Mario whom Norris had described as "their banker, I think." Two more recent arrivals from the West Coast called Claude and Bridget. And the Stratten item.

Norris's last report was three days old. She had included half-frame 16mm negatives of Stratten, Corby, Renaldo and the five who had arrived that afternoon from California. There were fingerprints on Corby and the Walberg twins and a set on Stratten which had proved useless since they didn't match any prints on file in Washington or St. Louis. Norris had not obtained a set of Renaldo's fingerprints, but the New York police had identified his photograph by comparison with their mug books.

The Walberg twins had histories of marijuana arrests; Renaldo and Corby had narcotics records. It was possible they were junkies. If you followed that reasoning you could assume they might wake up and realize what they'd done: the Norris murder. They might be terrified, they might run for it, disband, scatter, go to ground individually. They might forget any grandiose assassination plots in the rush to sanctuary.

It was a comforting theory but it was no good. The hole-in-the-wall they'd been using on R Street Northeast was empty now—very empty and very clean. Clean enough to indicate they weren't just a bunch of frightened addicts who had cleared out. Someone with presence of mind was directing the operation.

What had she known? What had she discovered? Lime had long ago been disabused of the notion that you could rely on premonitions and portents; but this thing had all the telltales of a major professional assassination job.

11:20 A.M. EST   The car decanted Dexter Ethridge and his Secret Service bodyguards below the West Portico of the Capitol and Ethridge looked up past the crowd to the dome where the flag was going up the staff to indicate that Congress was convening: that the Ninety-fifth Congress was about to gather for the first time.

He recognized many faces among those moving toward the doors. Most of the members would be entering by subway from the Senate and House office buildings but there were those like Ethridge who made a point of coming here to absorb the effect from outside before going in. Architecturally it was a *faux pas* and parts of it were endlessly in danger of falling down—some of the basements were shored up with clumsy brick walls and propped massive timbers—but if you were a politician you were very likely a sentimentalist as well and the great dome always instilled in Ethridge a properly sober respect and reverence.

Dexter Ethridge had sat, listened, spoken, and cast his vote inside this building thousands of times: he had entered the House twenty-four years ago, served two terms, run for the Senate and lost, run again two years later and won, and served three full terms—eighteen years—as United States Senator from Michigan. In that time he had cast many votes for winning causes and many votes for losing causes, but he had never to his knowledge cast a deciding vote. From this day forward he would cast no vote that was not a deciding vote: Dexter D. Ethridge, Vice-President-elect of the United States, would be allowed to vote in the Senate only when his vote was required to break a tie.

He climbed the steps, uncomfortably aware of the Secret Service men who never seemed to hurry but always managed to be within arm's length of him. The agents in various shifts had been covering Ethridge and his family since the Denver Convention five months ago but he still wasn't sufficiently accustomed to them to be able to ignore them; he found himself wasting altogether too much time exchanging small talk with them. But that had always been his weakness. From childhood he had been a buttonholer; he loved to engage people in conversation. Among his colleagues it was hardly a unique characteristic.

At the head of the steps he stopped and turned a half circle on his heels to look down along the Mall. There was a small demonstration down there—a cluster of radic-libs carrying signs, girls in dirty Levi's and men with self-consciously hirsute faces. From here Ethridge couldn't read the placards but there wasn't much doubt of their message: they wanted Freedom Now, they wanted the defense budget cut to a trickle and the highway program killed and a hundred billion for welfare and health and ecological cleanups.

Clifford Fairlie might accomplish a few of those things, although there would be a great deal of harrumphing and pettifoggery because no Democratic Congress could afford to pass a Republican President's programs without going through the motions of loyal-opposition resistance: Fairlie's programs would be amended wordily, but that was window dressing. The interesting thing about Fairlie's election was that it was going to force the Democrats to move even farther to the left, if only to enable them to continue berating the Republicans as obstructionist reactionaries.

Fairlie had offered the running-mate slot to Dexter Ethridge because Ethridge was a Republican Senator from a big industrial state (the liberals had tried to pin on him the epithet "the Senator from General Motors"); Ethridge could be counted on to help attract the support of Big Business, and in the farm states he could be billed as a conservative candidate. Yet he had never in his life described himself as a conservative. "Moderate" was the word he liked, and it was only because he stood somewhere to Fairlie's right that he had been regarded by the press and at least some of the voters as a rightist. But that was all politics—electioneering.

Fairlie had been quite candid about it: "I'm too liberal to suit a lot of them. If I'm going to get wholehearted support from the party I've got to show my sincerity by picking a running mate they'll approve. Ideally I suppose I ought to pick Fitzroy Grant or Woody Guest, but frankly that would tie my hands—I need a running mate who looks more conservative than he is. The right-wingers associate you with Detroit industrialists so I think they'll approve. . . .Me? I think you've got a lot of common sense and a good conscience. How about it?"

The thing was, he liked Cliff Fairlie. If it hadn't been for that he might have refused the nomination: the Vice-Presidency was ordinarily a thankless job and for a man as inclined toward real political activity as he was it didn't have irresistible appeal—a Senator with eighteen years' seniority could wield considerably more power on the Hill than could a minority-party Vice-President. But Ethridge believed Fairlie could win and he allowed Fairlie to convince him that he could help Fairlie win.

Now at the top step of the portico he looked out across the Mall and discovered, a bit to his surprise, that he did not regret it. He had no trouble recalling the excitement that had attended the arrival of the Kennedy Administration—that had been during Ethridge's first Senate term—and he had the heady feeling this morning that Clifford Fairlie would bring the same kind of magic to Washington. It was an important if not vital event for the country at this point in its history: Kennedy had not been a particularly good administrator, he had been a bad politician really—in his handling of Congress he couldn't hold a candle to Lyndon Johnson—and some of his decisions had been disastrously wrong. But the important thing about the Kennedys and the Fairlies was their quality of visible leadership. Not since Kennedy had the United States possessed a leader who commanded personal admiration, who stirred the imaginations of Americans and foreigners alike, who owned the aura of style and grace that made it possible to forgive their errors and to hope. Fairlie inspired that kind of hope.

The sky above the Capitol was bleak with the threat of snow; Ethridge stood in the wind in his topcoat, his cheeks stinging a little, but he had been raised on Michigan winters and the chill did not drive him inside. Tourists and journalists gave him covert stares and filed past him to observe the ritual swearing-in of the houses of Congress on this day of convening. Down on the Mall the pathetic little circle of marchers continued, virtually unnoticed, to trample the brown grass with their picket signs lifted high. Ethridge nodded and smiled and spoke briefly to friends and colleagues and acquaintances who went past; but he kept his place, somehow reluctant to break the feeling of this place and time, this moment of anticipation and hope and half-realized thrill. It was seventeen days yet to the inauguration but today, this noon, marked the real beginning of the Fairlie years, for this Congress that first met today would be Fairlie's Congress and everything they did in the next seventeen days would reflect that, regardless of Brewster's lame-duck occupancy of the White House.

11:40 A.M. EST David Lime strode the corridor toward the Seventeenth Street exit of the Executive Office Building, consulting his watch and shooting his cuff. Chad Hill kept pace with an athletic effortlessness that would have been commendable if it hadn't been for his youth: he could spot Lime twenty years.

"But shouldn't we stay in the office?"

"What for?"

"Well some central location at least. To coordinate everything."

"Nothing to coordinate," Lime said. "We've got a radio in the car."

They batted out through the glass doors. Lime pulled his coat collar up; the wind was a hard fast one, coming up from the Potomac, and the temperature had dropped sharply in the past few hours. Snow soon, he thought, and ducked to slip into the back seat of the plain green four-door Chevrolet that pulled to the curb to meet them. Hill slid in beside him and Lime said to the driver, "Right over to the Hill—the west steps, it'll be faster."

The driver checked his mirror and waited for a line of cars to go by and then slid gently out into the traffic lanes. Chad Hill said, "You'd better speed it up. Use your siren."

"No," Lime said. "There's time. And I don't need a traffic snarl of rubberneckers paralyzed by the siren." He sat back and closed his eyes and wondered if his face reflected the inner scowl.

Chad Hill said, "I hope to God you're wrong."

He probably was wrong. But it was a possibility.

The timing was what suggested it. Stratten's group had arrived in Washington about a week ago; the reinforcements from Los Angeles had arrived a few days later. When you moved into an area and you had it in mind to do violence, you didn't spend any longer than you had to setting things up. So whatever they planned to do, they planned to do it soon.

Killing Barbara Norris had been an act of desperation; if they'd had sufficient time they'd have done it more dramatically or more quietly. One or the other. The job they'd done on Norris was the kind of thing you did when you didn't have time to do it better. If the vicious mutilation had been intended as a message then its delivery had been hasty: with sufficient time they'd have planted the body where it would have attracted more attention. The front step of a newspaper building or the side door to a police station or the foot of the Lincoln Memorial.

So they were in a very big hurry now. That meant it was probably on for today.

They had a sense of dramatics. You could tell that by the arrogant set of Stratten's head in the photo, if not by what they had done to Norris. So it was a good bet their master plan would involve something public, something big, something not merely violent but catastrophic. Because of the odds you had to rule out the probability of an attempt on the President's life. The President only had seventeen days left in office: he hardly made a priority target.

What was left? The President-elect was junketing in Europe. They weren't likely to go to all this trouble merely to plant bombs in the Pentagon or the Library of Congress; Stratten didn't look the sort who would take much satisfaction from the anonymous bombing of symbolic buildings.

So it wasn't far fetched and it wasn't even unlikely that they planned to set off bombs in the Capitol Building during the hour when the new Congress was being sworn in.

11:50 A.M. EST　The Vice-President-elect was about to turn and enter the Capitol when he felt weight beside him and looked around to see Senator Fitzroy Grant at his elbow. Grant gave him the benediction of his lifted cigar and extended his hand, and they shook hands formally because they were in public. The Senate Minority Leader said, "Too bad about those young people down there with their picket signs. Spoils a flavorful day, doesn't it?"

"Oh, I don't know, Fitz. I think if they weren't down there we'd miss them. You get so used to them."

Fitzroy Grant had a dewlappy face and bassett eyes set in deep weathered folds; a sly figure, full of insinuation and Edwardian gallantry; an engaging grin and the vanity of polished shoes and good clothes and cared-for hands. He ran a palm over his head carefully, not dislodging the neat wave in his senatorially white hair and waved genially to a passerby. When Ethridge glanced that way he saw that the passerby was Senator Wendell Hollander of Kentucky, elderly and bowlegged, coming up the steps like a crab. Hollander was puffing; he didn't look at all well, but then he hadn't looked well in the eighteen years Ethridge had known him. Hollander was the picture of the seedy, rheumy, larcenous and crafty Southern politician, but of course that was only the surface stereotype perpetuated by the press: underneath Hollander was as sober as a Jersey City judge and as gentle as a school of piranha.

Hollander came forward busily disposing the muscles of his face toward lines indicative of pleasure. He was a little deaf and shouted. "Mr. Vice-President-elect, suh! Mr. Senator!"

"Hello Wendy." Ethridge almost managed to make his voice sound cordial. There was the ritual of handshaking. Ethridge hated Wendell Hollander and he was certain Hollander hated him, but neither would ever admit it; their hostilities were covered by a warm surface pleasantness which if anything had intensified since the election because they were now members not only of opposite parties but of separate branches of the government. Wendell Hollander was Chairman of the Senate Appropriations Committee and President pro tem of the Senate, and it was unquestioned that the club would reconfirm him in both posts today. Hollander's seniority was impeccable; he had sat in the Senate since 1937.

Hollander extracted a gold chain from his vest pocket, consulted the snap-lid gold watch, made a loud remark about not wanting to be late, and crabbed his way into the Capitol building. Fitzroy Grant's eyebrows cocked upward in amusement and Ethridge said, "If there was ever an unimpeachable argument for demolishing the seniority system, Wendy is it."

"You can put that in the bank," Grant said. "I've spent twenty years trying to argue with him and you just can't do it. He only raises his voice and talks right through you. Nobody can match Wendy's inane oversimplifications and half-truths and downright absurdities. Now and then I get in a word and one-up him, and he rears back on his dignity and leaves the room."

"He's a dangerous man, Fitz. We can't afford to go on condoning these old crackerbarrel fossils who see Communists in every phone booth and want to make Asia into a desert."

"Well I suppose. But he's hard to dislodge. The man's a hero in those regions where it's known as fact that the nation is in the final stages of Communist subversion."

"Funny," Ethridge murmured, "I seem to remember you expressing the same sentiments back around the time of Joe McCarthy."

It made Senator Grant smile. "I thought the campaign was over, Mr. Vice-President—or would you like to compare voting records?"

"Mr. Minority Leader," Ethridge said with a feeling of happy comfort, "I believe it's time we went inside and attended the formalities." And the two old friends turned to enter the Capitol.

As they did, a big yellow-haired man in a coffee-stained topcoat intercepted Ethridge's Secret Service detail and began to talk swiftly into Agent Pickett's ear.

Ethridge was about to walk past the men when Agent Pickett took a sidewise pace which courteously barred his path. "Excuse me sir. This is Mr. Lime from our headquarters."

The big blond man nodded. "Mr. Vice-President." A cigarette hung in the corner of Lime's wide flexible mouth. He had an amiable bulldog face and a cheap haircut and big hard violent hands.

Lime said, "I don't mean to cause alarm——"

"But you're about to," Ethridge said, smiling to take the edge off it. "Whenever a man starts out by saying that it means he's about to kick you in the guts."

It made Lime smile a little before he said, "These things almost always come to nothing. But you need to be advised—we think it's possible a radical group plans to bomb the Capitol."

"When?"

He saw Lime's eyes narrow with quick respectful scrutiny and it wasn't hard to tell why. Ethridge had brushed past all the obvious and commonplace reactions— *What? Bomb the Capitol? Why that's outrageous! You can't let them get away with that! Who are they? What makes you think anything like that's afoot!* No: "When?"

Lime said in answer, "We've got no hard information. But if they do it at all they'd be likely to do it with both houses in session."

"In other words right now?"

"It's possible," Lime conceded.

"Do you want to clear the building?"

He saw Lime hesitate. Ethridge said, "Of course I have no way to advise you—I don't know how serious the threat is."

"That's the trouble," Lime admitted. "We don't know that there's any threat at all."

"Have you got your people inside searching?"

"Yes, of course."

"I assume you don't suspect any members of Congress of being a party to whatever it is you suspect?"

"No. It appears to be a small group of radicals."

"Well they won't get onto the floor of either chamber then. They'll be in the visitors' gallery if they're in the chambers at all, is that right?"

"Yes."

"And your men are searching there? Posting themselves there to prevent anyone from throwing things?"

"As much as possible, yes."

"Then I think we'd better proceed with things on schedule," Ethridge said. He looked at his watch: eleven fifty-seven. "I don't mean to seem callous but we've been bombed before. It's never done much injury or damage. The Constitution requires that this Congress convene at noon today, and unless you have something very strong to go on, I don't think we should attempt to evacuate the Capitol."

Agent Pickett, always conscientious, said in his Alabama drawl, "That's what Mr. Lime said to me, sir, but for the sake of your safety I think I ought to recommend that you not go inside until we've checked it out."

"That may take an hour," Ethridge said. "They'll be starting the proceedings in two minutes' time."

"Yes sir," Pickett said. "I still think it might be a good idea for you to wait, sir."

Lime said, "We'll have to leave that to you," and turned to hurry into the building.

Ethridge looked around. Fitzroy Grant had been buttonholed by someone else and had already disappeared inside. Ethridge touched Ted Pickett's sleve. "Come on, then, I don't want to be late," and walked in under the high doorway.

12:05 P.M. EST The Washington press corps numbered more than two thousand accredited correspondents from the United States and thirty foreign nations. Armed with press cards which Stratten had obtained from a source he hadn't divulged, Bob Walberg and his sister and three others had gained entry to the Capitol and its two press galleries half an hour before. It had gone just as smoothly as Stratten had predicted. Yesterday the Walbergs and the others

had shaved their beards and trimmed their hair and fitted themselves into the Establishment clothes they were now wearing; Stratten had filled their wallets with all manner of false ID.

And Stratten had briefed them thoroughly. The Capitol had been
bombed twice before. In 1915 a German instructor from Cornell
University had protested American arms sales to the Allies by setting off an explosive device in the Senate reception room; it hadn't
done much damage. In 1970 radicals had exploded a bomb in the
Senate wing—a powerful explosive planted in a men's lavatory on
the ground floor. Only one bomb, but it had damaged seven rooms:
knocked down walls and blown doors off their hinges. The plastic
explosive Bob Walberg carried was considerably more potent than
that—and his companions carried four more like his. And this time
it was for real: the 1970 explosion had gone off in the small hours of
the morning when there had been almost no one in the building.
Today Congress was in session and Stratten had both wings covered: three in the House chamber, two in the Senate. It was going
to do one hell of a job on the Establishment.

Right on, Bob Walberg thought. Reporters milled around him,
getting in and out of seats, squeezing along the aisles of the press
gallery. It was a cinch to spot the Secret Service agents in their
business suits, giving everybody the eye. He kept a straight face
while he lifted the briefcase onto his lap and snapped it open. He
knew the guards were watching his movements but they had poked
through the briefcase down at the door before they'd admitted him
and they hadn't found the bomb then so they weren't going to spot
it now. Nobody was going to find it until it was too late.

Along the back row of the press gallery stood a few men in
uniform but Stratten had said not to worry about them. They were
the Capitol Police Force and most of them were patronage appointees—students, part-timers.

He took a notebook and pencil out of the case and snapped the
case shut. As he did so he glanced at his watch: ten past noon. The
proceedings were late getting started, but then it was always like
that. As he set the briefcase down under the seat between his ankles
he touched the rivet under the brass catch to start the time mechanism. It could always be stopped—that was the advantage of using
a stopwatch for a time device. But it was ticking now and Bob
Walberg knew he had thirty minutes to get away and his nostrils
dilated and he began to sweat.

The galleries were settling down. At the far end of the press gallery he saw Sandra, looking professional with a pad in her lap and a pencil poised over it.

Below him Congressmen were getting settled in their semicircular rows of chairs. The Speaker of the House, Milton Luke, emerged from a door behind the Speaker's rostrum. The Doorkeeper was ushering in dignitaries, bringing them down the center aisle and seating them. Bob Walberg's seat was in the third row of the press gallery, above the rostrum and a few yards to its left; he judged the distance critically and decided the bomb in his case would take out a good part of the left-hand section of Representatives' seats.

Somebody was tapping a microphone, blowing into it to test it; the sounds were echoing over the loudspeakers. The Chaplain of the House was at the rostrum and Bob Walberg heard his aged voice crackle over the PA system: "Blessed is the nation whose God is the Lord. . . ." And Bob Walberg thought automatically *Psalms 33:12* and had a moment's image of Sabbath School at Temple in Culver City, the rabbi talking in gentle reasonable words about the goodness of God and men. It made him remember his *Bar Mitzvah* and the Schwinn bicycle his father had given him. Stupid middle-class phony liberal with his smelly delicatessen and his NAACP contributions and his sickening hypocrisy.

"Almighty God," the Chaplain intoned, "we pause at the beginning of this Ninety-fifth Congress to thank Thee for Thy providential care over us. . . ."

The summer of Bob Walberg's *Bar Mitzvah* they had had the riot in Watts and he remembered his father loading the shotgun: *Those bastards come down my street we'll see what happens, hey?* His father with the socialist platitudes and the color TV that was the first in the neighborhood, the slave wages he paid the black and Mexican workers who mowed his lawns and cleaned out the deli and kept house for the Walbergs while the Walbergs spent weekends in Las Vegas and sent Bob and Sandra to camps and schools for middle-class problem children.

". . . Thy wisdom and Thy grace unto this new Congress as we climb this holy hill of our nation's life and pray that Thou endow all those who serve Thee in this place with nobility of spirit and character. In the Redeemer's name we pray. Amen."

The Reverend Mosley stepped down and the Clerk of the House approached the microphone. Bob Walberg looked at his watch.

"Representatives-elect to the Ninety-fifth Congress, this is the day fixed by the Twentieth Amendment of the Constitution and

Public Law nine-four-dash-six-four-three of the Ninety-fourth Congress for the meeting of the Ninety-fifth Congress of the United States. As the law directs, the Clerk of the House has prepared the official roll of the Representatives-elect. Credentials for the four hundred and thirty-five districts to be represented in the Ninety-fifth Congress have been received, and are now on file with the Clerk of the Ninety-fourth Congress. . . ."

It was no good telling him what a hypocritical old klutz he was. He wouldn't know the truth if it kicked him in the teeth. Sending contributions to Israel and keeping his accounts in a bank that did business with South Africa and you just couldn't make him see.

"The reading clerk will call the roll."

"The state of Alabama. Mr. Price. . ."

Sixteen past noon. Another eight or ten minutes, and out. The thing was not to look like you were in a hurry. Ask the guard on the way out where the men's room is.

"The state of Mississippi. Mr. Bailey. . ."

He could almost feel it ticking between his ankles. His watch: twelve-nineteen. It was due to go off at twelve-forty; all of them were. Get out at twelve-twenty-five, he thought. That'll give me fifteen minutes to get clear. Linc will have the car ready by the corner of the New Senate Office Building, and Darleen's got the Oldsmobile parked up on Tennessee Avenue so we can make the swap: if some idiot gets the license number of the first car we'll still be away clean. By the time they start setting up roadblocks we'll be on our way through Baltimore, heading for the Jersey Turnpike.

Martyrs are cheap, Stratten had drummed into them. *Any stupid head can be a martyr. We've got to prove you can do it and get away with it. That's the whole point, isn't it. Not just that you can attack the Establishment, but that the Establishment's powerless to do a thing about it.*

The bird next to Bob Walberg was giving him an odd glance. Bob straightened his face and pretended to jot a shorthand note in the pad on his knee.

"The roll call discloses that four hundred and twenty-seven Representatives-elect have answered to their names. A quorum is present. Now the next order of business is the election of a Speaker of the House of Representatives for the Ninety-fifth Congress. Nominations are now in order. . . . The chair recognizes Mr. Breckenyear of Louisiana."

"Mr. Clerk, as chairman of the Democratic caucus, I am directed by the unanimous vote of that caucus to present for re-election to the office of Speaker of the House of Representatives of the Ninety-fifth Congress the name of the Honorable Milton C. Luke, a Representative-elect from the State of Connecticut."

"The chair recognizes Mr. Wood of California."

"Mr. Clerk, as chairman of the Republican conference and by authority, direction, and unanimous vote of that conference, I nominate for Speaker of the House of Representatives of the Ninety-fifth Congress the Honorable Philip Krayle, a Representative-elect from the State of New York."

"The Honorable Milton C. Luke, a Representative-elect from the State of Connecticut, and the Honorable Philip Krayle, a Representative-elect from the State of New York, have been placed in nomination. Are there further nominations? . . . There being no further nominations, the Clerk will appoint tellers. The Clerk appoints the gentleman from Ohio, Mr. Block, the gentleman from Illinois, Mr. Westlake, the gentlewoman from California, Mrs. Ludlum, and the gentlewoman from Vermont, Mrs. Morrison. Tellers will come forward and take their seats at the desk in front of the Speaker's rostrum. The roll will now be called, and those responding to their names will indicate by surname the nominee of their choice—Luke or Krayle. The reading clerk will now call the roll."

"The State of Alabama. Mr. Price. . . ."

Bob Walberg looked at his watch and looked up across the gallery. Sandra was watching him.

It was time. He stood up, apologizing *sotto voce* to the lady beside him; he placed his briefcase on the seat, as if to save it for his return, and made his way out into the aisle past the lady's knees, and turned up to the back of the gallery. The uniformed guard watched him approach. Bob Walberg whispered in the guard's ear and the guard pointed and whispered something which Bob Walberg didn't catch, but he nodded and thanked the guard and slipped out.

12:30 P.M. EST   The East Portico afforded the best exit from the Capitol because you could head right out Maryland or Pennsylvania Avenue without getting tangled in the tortured traffic patterns of the Mall. With that in mind David Lime had posted himself beside the radio car on East Capitol Street immediately below the Portico where he could watch the faces of those who emerged from the building. It was a long shot; of course it was a long shot—everything was.

He kept fighting the impulse to reach into the car and snatch up the microphone and bleat into it: has anybody found anything? They would let him know if they did.

He looked around again, turning a full circle on his heels, and now he began to develop an interest in the spruce-green Plymouth that had pulled up at the curb below the New Senate Office Building. It had a young man in a self-conscious Afro at the wheel and white wisps of exhaust flailing from its tailpipe. Lime automatically noted the license number in his pocket pad and this time he succumbed to the urge to reach for the microphone.

"Dispatch, this is Lime."

"Go ahead Lime."

"Have you got a squadrol on Maryland Avenue between here and Stanton Square?"

"Hold on. . . . Car Five Niner, you on Maryland? Whereabouts? Okay, stand by. . . . Hello Lime?"

"Right here."

"Affirmative your query."

"Request you hold your car on Maryland until further notice from me."

He heard Dispatch relay the message to Car 59 and re-experienced the irritation he always felt when dealing with vehicular patrols: you had contact with Dispatch but not with other cars and therefore everything had to be relayed through Dispatch. It was the only method that made real sense but nevertheless it was annoying.

Lime said into the microphone, "Convey this to Car Five Niner, please. A 'Seventy-two Plymouth four-door, blue-green, license New Jersey Samuel Bravo Dog Three Three Four. If that car comes north on Maryland with more than one person in it, I want it stopped."

"Affirmative Lime. . . . Car Five Niner——"

Lime handed the microphone to the driver and turned to look up at the Capitol steps. Chad Hill was coming down two steps at a time, not out of any visible urgency but simply because that was the way he liked to move. When Lime had asked for his transfer out of NSA and they had shunted him over to Secret Service he had not succeeded in bringing any of his own people with him and he had been forced to pick an aide from among strangers. Having hired Chad Hill he was able to find no plausible reason to fire him; but Hill had an uncanny capacity to irritate him right up to the breaking point: *God save us from eager beavers.*

Chad Hill reached the car and gave him a pained look. "We've eyeballed everybody in the visitors' gallery and the uniformed boys have done a second go-round on packages and handbags."

"Nothing?"

"Not a damn thing."

"What about the press gallery?"

Hill's head jerked back. "My God. I never thought of that." *Neither did I until just now.* Lime said gently, "Do it then."

"Yes sir."

Chad Hill turned to trot away and Lime's glance rode up past him to the top of the steps. Lime said, "Never mind, Chad."

"What?" Hill was swinging back.

A middle-aged black woman had emerged at the Portico and Lime had a feeling that was Beulah Moorehead from Los Angeles, and he was sure of it when the Walberg twins loped out behind her.

Lime talked fast. "Get inside—tell our people to get to the PA mikes and clear the building. I'm calling the bomb squad. On the run, now."

Lime put his hand into the car window and the driver slapped the microphone into it. Two more people emerged at the Portico and trotted down the steps behind Mrs. Moorehead and the Walbergs. They were slanting north as they came down the wide steps—heading generally in the direction of the green Plymouth—and Lime barked into the mike, "Bomb Squad, Dispatch. Make it fast. I've made five suspects leaving the building. Tell Bomb Squad to start looking in the press galleries in both chambers. I'm having the building cleared now. Tell Car Five Niner to remain on station to pick up that green Plymouth if it gets away from me. Out." He tossed the mike in past the driver and wrenched the door open. "Come on with me."

"On foot?"

"Does your union prohibit it? Get your hand near your piece." Lime was in motion, heading across the soggy dead grass with his plunging stride, a fresh cigarette dangling unlit. The driver panted to catch up. Ahead of them the five people were moving straight toward the Plymouth, walking very fast. Lime began to run, sweeping back the side-vented coat that accommodated his service revolver. He raised his arm overhead; his hand described a quick arc and Secret Service men began to converge from several points.

Now the five were piling into the Plymouth, still unaware they had been made. The agent from the Senate Office Building doorway reached the passenger side of the car and showed them his gun. Lime, on his toes and running full out, couldn't hear anything with the wind slapping his ears; the agent was talking into the car and then a burst of white exhaust puffed from the car's pipe and the car was squealing out into the avenue. The agent spun all the way around, knocked off his feet.

It was about forty yards: Lime got down on one knee and braced his shooting arm in the open palm of his left hand and shot for the tires, cocking the revolver with his thumb and firing single-action, six very rapid ones; then he was on his feet and running again, searching his pockets for fresh ammunition.

He had exploded a rear tire but the Plymouth was still going, lumping along on the rim. Probably doing thirty miles an hour, with Lime and his men running after it. It was a block ahead when the squadrol, its red and blue lights flashing, came in sight on a collision course and slewed across the Avenue, blocking traffic in both directions and sealing off the Plymouth.

Lime kept running, his coat flying, plugging cartridges into the side-swung cylinder of the S & W, and beyond the Plymouth the uniformed EPS cops were pouring out of the cruiser and clawing for their .38's—it was not yet certain the Plymouth wouldn't ram the squadrol. There was a great racket: the cruiser's blockage had caused a rear-end chain collision in the far lanes of the avenue and there were bangs and squeals and grunts of metal. The Plymouth was lurching toward the curb and when Lime saw that they were trying to drive it up on the sidewalk to eel past the cruiser he dropped to his knee again and began to shoot with care. The EPS cops followed his lead and almost instantly someone's bullet exploded a front tire and the Plymouth rocked over against the building wall, narrowly missing a terrorized pedestrian. The Plymouth dug its bumper corner into the building and it wasn't going anywhere after that. Its doors popped open on the near side but the EPS cops had it enfiladed and Lime was coming in on the dead run, and when the six people climbed out of the car they had their hands in the air like victims of a stagecoach robbery in a John Ford movie.

Lime pushed past the uniformed cops. He was puffing, and angry with himself for it: he hadn't run more than three blocks' distance. In college he had done the four-forty with no effort at all. He swept his glance over the six from the car, trying to single out the leader, but he couldn't pick a spokesman by looking at them—so he made an arbitrary choice: he selected the weakest-looking face and went to work on Robert Walberg.

The crowd from the wrecked cars in the avenue was making so much noise Lime could barely hear himself. He waved a couple of cops toward the incensed civilians and addressed himself to the Walberg boy. A muscle worked at the back of Walberg's jaw. Lime kept talking to him: "Where are the bombs, boy? Where'd you leave them? Come on, let's have it. Where'd you put the bombs, Bobby?"

If you know the name, use the diminutive; it helps break them down, it makes you Authority. Maybe they'd called him Robbie or Bob-o but Bobby was most common, most likely. "Come on, Bobby." Lime had a cigarette between his lips; he struck a match but did not stop talking so that the cigarette pumped up and down violently while he tried to light it; he succeeded only in blowing out the match, and tried another.

Walberg's eyes mirrored his terror and Lime didn't even give him time to answer: he mentioned Stratten and Alvin Corby and made it very clear to Walberg that he knew everything: that he knew a great deal more than he did in fact know; and finally he let himself run down and waited for Walberg's answer.

It might have worked but the big black one in the Afro butted in and none of the cops had the sense to stop him. "Don't tell the pig nothing, boy. You go get fucked, honkie. We don't tell you mothers nothing."

Lime made an angry gesture and his driver whipped past and yanked the big Negro away. It was probably too late after that but Lime kept pushing Walberg: "Come on, Bobby. Where are the devices? When are they set to go off? Come on, Bobby." He had the gun in his fist and he allowed the terrible rage to leak out through his eyes; he was right up close against Walberg, breathing smoke into the boy's face, and the boy's jaw was juddering with fright.

Then Lime heard the muted chug of the first explosion, like a hard-cued break against a rack of pool balls, and his face changed with the realization that his questions were too late.

12:40 P.M. EST   In the Senate the two bombs went off about seven seconds apart.

Dexter Ethridge had watched Gardner, his successor, go down

the center aisle to be sworn in, and then take his place at Ethridge's old desk on the Republican side of the aisle.

And now before Ethridge had time to move, before he had time to react at all, the wall behind the rostrum began to tilt and heave: the shock wave hit him, pressed him back into his chair.

He saw the partition begin to crumble behind the podium, bringing the lower seats of the right-hand half of the press gallery down toward the Senate floor, as reporters shrieked and clawed. Chunks of masonry and wood shot through the air and choking dust filled the chamber and the overwhelming noise echoed and reverberated. A shoe, incredibly intact, hit the arm of Ethridge's chair and lodged there. It grazed his fingertips, no more. Ethridge drew air wildly into his chest in panic. There were bodies, *human bodies in clothes,* hurtling through the air like projectiles. Pieces were cracking out of the high ceiling. Plaster andsawdust made an immediate dense stink.

And now Ethridge was moving, sliding out of the chair, seeking blindly for shelter with the intuitive response of a man who once had heard 77mm shells coming in and knew how to dive for cover.

Down on his face: he shoved his head under the seat of the chair and wrapped his arms around his face and he was like that when the second bomb exploded. The floor jumped, bashed his chest; debris rained on his exposed rump and the backs of his legs. He found himself thinking he was going to have a hell of a bruise on his hip from that one and he might be limping for a few days. . .

Someone was screaming insistently close by, loud enough to drown out much of the other racket. Objects were slamming against walls and furnishings and something in this madness collapsed the chair above him: it broke off at one side and he felt the jarring blinding blow against the back and top of his head, and then he was sputtering and shoving with his arms and scrabbling with his feet to get out from under the weight of the thing that was on him.

This is a hell of a position for the Vice-President-elect of the United States of America. He was giggling a little, backing out of the trap, his butt way up in the air, on his chest and knees, backing out, giggling. . . . He pulled his head out and up and saw that the chair had broken only on its left side; it had tilted over, rather than flattening straight down, and it had left a triangularly tent-shaped opening which had saved his skull the direct crushing smash of the enormous chunk of plaster that had fallen on it.

His head stung with an awful pain and he lay facedown again, feet lodged against the base of some other chair. His eyes were closed against the pain. The cloudburst of debris had tapered off; things were cracking now, pattering like gravel, splitting and splintering and settling, but the overwhelming noise now was from human voices—the voices of terror and the voices of agony, and a man somewhere very nearby saying over and over again, "Lord Jesus, Lord Jesus, Lord Jesus, Lord Jesus."

There was a long splintering crack, and a momentary silence, and a shuddering crash afterward: a wall coming down, or a section of gallery. Someone yelped like a small dog and the voice nearby was still moaning, "Lord Jesus, Lord Jesus," and Ethridge squinted his closed eyes tight against the pain in his head. In the distance he heard a long rising human scream and he had heard a scream like that once before from the throat of a man eviscerated by shrapnel on a dismal battlefield, but this was no battlefield this was the Senate of the United States and this could not possibly be happening here, it was unthinkable.

When he opened his eyes virtually all the lights had gone out. Ethridge heard the moans and cries and had to check to make sure he wasn't uttering sounds himself. He sat up slowly on his knees, bracing his hands against the remains of furniture but then his right hand slid against a resilience of flesh and he recoiled.

His head whipped around and the sudden movement blinded him with pain; he pressed his palms to his temples and slid fingers toward the top of his head, half expecting to probe into a pulpy mush at the top of his skull: but it was all normal hair and scalp, and chunks of plaster. He felt no softness, not even the dampness of blood. Now he moved his head with slow caution and in the very bad light he saw only a slow-swirling fog of dust and smoke.

He stayed on his knees until moving beams of light began to play through the wheeling mist and he began to catch the voices of whole people, the ones using the flashlights. A small fire burned somewhere across the room. In the uncertain visibility Ethridge caught sight of a figure sprawled broken across the wreckage of a chair: he moved close and recognized the dead face of Allan Nugent who had been the senior Senator from Indiana.

Ethridge climbed across Nugent's corpse and made his cautious way down toward the worst destruction, looking for survivors to assist. He had been buffeted and slammed and abraded by the violence but he was on his feet and moving, and in the old Army if you were an officer capable of movement you helped.

The dense dust settled faster now and more flashlights appeared;

in the growing light he saw people making their way by ones and twos toward the exits, some walking unaided, some dragging themselves, some dragging others. One man was running, until someone stopped him with a stiff-armed block. No one was screaming any longer but the ruins were filled with groanings.

He found Alan Forrester, the junior Senator from Arizona, sitting with his back to an overturned desk, rubbing his eyes with thumb-enclosed fists like a small child who has just been awakened. Ethridge knelt by him and pulled Forrester's hands away from his face. "Are you all right?"

"I—uh."

"Are you all right, Alan?"

Now the eyes came open and Forrester blinked, squinting. His eyes were incredibly bloodshot but he didn't look injured. Ethridge reached for his arm. "Come on."

Forrester let Ethridge assist him to his feet. "Dex? Dex?"

"Yes, it's me."

"Christ, Dex."

"Head for the lights, Alan. Can you find your own way?"

Forrester was shaking his head violently as if to clear it. "Never mind. I'm all right—I just came apart for a minute there. I'll help you look."

"Good man."

The two of them prowled down into the incredible rubble. At once they fell upon a heap of debris and began to claw at it because a human arm protruded from it but when they had pawed the rubble away they saw that the arm was severed: the young Arizonan looked up at Ethridge and his voice went rusty and almost soundless: "Oh my dear God, Dex."

Ethridge made a careful point of not looking at the fabric of the sleeve or the shape of the hand. He climbed over the pile and went on until he found a man slumped across a desk with one hand under his forehead and the other dangling at arm's length. He lifted the man back in his seat by the shoulder and recognized young Gardner, his own successor in the Senate, who had been sworn just before the explosion, and for one terrible instant Ethridge thought Gardner was dead too but then the eyes fluttered open and rolled sightlessly.

"Concussion, I think," Ethridge said. "Can you carry him out Alan? I'm going to keep looking."

The flashlights were close by, moving fitfully; men were calling back and forth. Forrester got Gardner up on his wide back in a fireman's carry and heaved him away, calling back over his shoulder: "Watch yourself, Dex."

Ethridge intended to. You didn't help anyone by falling down and breaking your own ankle. He probed into the wheeling dimness and found a mangled body half-buried in shattered cords of wood. Nobody he recognized; probably a reporter; and now he began coming across bodies in great number, many of them mutilated but some of them uncannily natty in repose, and of the six or seven he tested for respiration and heartbeat he found only one member of the Senate—March of Idaho.

Now the rubble stirred just ahead of him, somebody trying to dig himself out; a hand thrust out through a hole and Ethridge scrambled toward it and began heaving chunks of stone and plaster away and finally he had exposed the tunnel under a pair of adjacent senatorial desks—a tunnel which by some curious caprice had remained inviolate and had sheltered its occupant although the gallery partition had fallen right across it.

It was Fitzroy Grant and he was quite alert and conscious.

And Fitz Grant demanded in a voice like an Indiana hog caller's, "Jesus God damn Christ what in the hell is all this?"

"Are you all right?" Ethridge said in awe.

Grant's sad drinker's eyes focused slowly upon him.

The slow splendid deep voice rolled out with full strength: "When I've made an inventory of my bones I'll let you know, Mr. Vice-President. But in the meantime how in the hell did we get here and what in the hell is this? Limbo, by the Lord! The ninth circle? My good Faust—lead me the hell out of here!"

8:10 P.M. Continental European Time The four Secret Service agents rattled around the sitting room of Fairlie's suite, restive and suspicious and angry, and his aide Liam McNeely for once in his life was sitting up straight in a chair, with his slim boudoir face poked defiantly toward the radio and the booming voice of the BBC Home announcer.

Clifford Fairlie walked across the room and his hands reached up to draw the drapes against the misty chill darkness of the Parisian night but his eyes were not focused on anything much at all; he was listening—to the droning radio and for the telephone's bell.

He shambled to the highboy and poured an ounce of Dubonnet into a crystal aperitif glass with the hotel's monogram on it. Walked to the radio and fiddled with the tuning dial but effected no improvement in the background static. The French radio was carrying the story as well but Fairlie did not want to concentrate on translating in his head.

He prowled the room now, too eruptive to sit still, sipping the Dubonnet until it was gone, after which he carried the empty glass around with him, rotating it between his palms. McNeely's head kept turning, indicating his attentiveness to Fairlie's movements, but neither McNeely nor the Secret Service agents spoke: either they were too stunned by the news or they were awaiting a cue from Fairlie.

" . . . complete listing of casualties has not yet been released, as it is understood the authorities are still sifting through the rubble of the two legislative chambers of the American Congress which were bombed little more than ninety minutes ago. Of course the President-elect, Mr. Fairlie, was not in Washington, and his Vice-President-elect, Mr. Ethridge, is reported to have escaped serious injury although he was present in the Senate when the powerful devices were detonated."

It penetrated Fairlie's consciousness that the British Broadcasting announcer was winging it: tossing out time-consuming bits of background information to fill the time because he had run out of hard news to report, then swinging back into the bits and pieces that had come in on the international newswires and recapitulating the story which by now everyone in the world had heard.

"It was announced officially by the White House Press Secretary, Mr. Hearn, that swift action by the United States Secret Service resulted in the capture of six suspected terrorists almost immediately after the explosions in the American Capitol. According to Mr. Hearn five of those arrested actually planted the five explosive devices, and the sixth was the driver of their escape car. Names and descriptions of the six have not been divulged, but Mr. Hearn did reveal they are three men and three women. Whether the Government suspects that more than these six were involved in the. . . . One moment, please. We have only just received this. The Director of the FBI, who has been placed in charge of rescue and investigative operations at the bombed Capitol building in Washington, has authorized the release of a preliminary list of casualties. We are advised the list will be read out by the President's news secretary, Mr. Hearn, in just a few minutes' time. BBC is now preparing to switch us via satellite to live coverage of Mr. Hearn's briefing in Washington."

There was an obsequious knock. McNeely rose with alacrity and two of the agents went with him to answer the door. It was the hotel manager, wheeling a large television console. Fairlie thought irritably that it had taken the hotel almost three quarters of an hour to locate and deliver the television set to his room—probably the same set he had had removed the day of his arrival because he detested television and found French television to be a particular abomination.

The hotel manager backed out of the room after whispering something in McNeely's ear. The agents turned to stare at the warming TV screen, and McNeely said to Fairlie, "He says the place is crawling with reporters and the rumor's around that you're going to make a statement."

"Not just yet."

"I hope they don't think of bringing a battering ram." McNeely didn't smile; he only flopped into his chair and brooded toward the screen.

The telephone.

McNeely bounced up and Fairlie watched him with care. He had left instructions with the switchboard to connect no incoming calls except from President Brewster, who had called an hour ago and asked him to stay on tap.

McNeely covered the mouthpiece with his palm and gave Fairlie an unreadable look. "It's the girl on the switchboard. She's holding a call for you from Harrisburg."

"Jeanette?"

"Yes. Evidently she's been trying to get through to you for more than an hour. I gather she's blistering the corns off the poor girl on the board."

That wasn't hard to credit. Fairlie approached the phone, moving awkwardly sideways to keep the TV screen in view. It was French television of course and the sound was down very low; he could hear the BBC radio announcer introducing Perry Hearn and on the screen he could see the satellite picture of the White House Lawn, gray on a misty cold afternoon with a thick crowd waiting, breath pouring like steam from their nostrils.

"Jeanette?"

"One moment please." An American operator's voice.

"Cliff darling?"

"Hi sweet."

"My God what trouble I've had reaching you. I finally had to pull rank—the President's wife is calling, I told them. It sounded God-awful to me."

"How is it there?"

"It's madness, Cliff. You can't imagine it. I think the whole city's glued to their television screens as if they were bleeding to death and the tube was their transfusion bottle."

"There hasn't been any trouble, has there?"

"Outside of the Hill, you mean. No. I don't think anybody's thought of making trouble. We're all too numb." It was a good clear connection but she was pitching her voice high and loud as if to span the intercontinental vastness.

The TV had gone to a tight closeup of Perry Hearn's amiable bland face and the radio carried Hearn's voice but they were somewhat out of sync, the radio voice anticipating the movements of Hearn's lips on the screen by a half second. *As of now thirteen Senators and twenty-eight Congressmen are still missing. . . .*

"Are you all right, sweet?" He had turned his shoulder to the others in the room and spoke low, confidentially into the telephone.

"Oh I'm all right, Cliff. Just overwrought. The little one's kicking inside me—I guess he can sense my excitement."

"But you're all right."

"I'm fine. Really, darling."

"That's all right then."

. . . list as of now includes ten United States Senators and thirty-seven members of the House of Representatives, whose bodies have been identified. . . .

"I suppose I've been trying to call you because I don't know what else to do. I needed your voice, Cliff."

"Have you got people there with you?"

"Oh yes of course, everyone's descended on me. Mary came over the instant she heard the news and the children are both with me. I'm very well looked after."

. . . Speaker of the House Milton Luke escaped injury and is with the President at this moment. Senate Majority Leader Winston Dierks suffered a leg injury but is listed as being in satisfactory condition at D. C. General Hospital. Senate Minority Leader Fitz-

roy Grant will probably be released from Walter Reed Army Hospital within a few minutes. . . .

". . . wish I weren't preggers, Cliff, I wish I were there with you."

She had lost a baby two years ago and this time they had decided she would stay at home and not travel with him. Fairlie said, "Do you want me home?" and hated himself for it, knowing his decisions couldn't be based on her wishes.

"Of course I do," she replied; the softness of her voice was freed of sentimentality by its flavor of affectionate ridicule: she knew as well as he did that he wouldn't drop everything and fly straight home on her whim.

. . . ter Ethridge will remain in Walter Reed Army Hospital overnight for observation and tests, but he appears to have nothing worse than a few contusions, and his physician says he's in the very best of health. The Reverend Doctor John Mosley, Chaplain of the House of Representatives, is on the critical list at. . . .

". . . but I couldn't very well ask it of her."

"What?"

"Oh darling you're not listening, are you. It doesn't matter. I was only saying Mary's offered to pack an overnight bag and move over here for a few days to help look after the children."

"Might not be a bad idea, you know."

"I think I'd rather bear my grief in private, Cliff. We've lost an awful lot of friends today."

"Yes," he said. "Yes."

. . . brunt of the casualties has been borne by Washington's press corps, for which the President is deeply grieved. At present it is known that seventy-one reporters lost their lives in the disaster. . .

He said, "Do you have the television on?"

"Yes, I'm watching it with one eye."

"Doesn't Perry Hearn look terrible?"

"I know. Midge Luke called me a little while ago, just to say Milt wasn't hurt and she was so glad you weren't there, and Milt told her the President looks like the last survivor of an Infantry patrol in some muddy trench. My God, Cliff, how can it have happened?"

. . . Capitol Building. Emergency crews under the direction of Capitol Architect James Delaney are already shoring up the chambers, but until a thorough survey has been made we're assuming the entire building is unsafe, and all individuals and offices are being evacuated into temporary. . . .

Jeanette's voice continued on the wire and he wasn't really listening to her words but he heard her voice, her tone, the soft warm nesty feeling she created so easily; it occurred to him that her real reason for calling him was not so much to reassure herself as it was to remind him of their unbroken romantic communion—to give him that to lean on; so that suddenly he felt a quick welling in his throat of gratitude and adoration.

. . . President will speak to the nation this evening at seven o'clock eastern standard time. . . .

"I'd better ring off, sweet. I'm expecting word from President Brewster."

. . . ordered flags to fly at half-mast until further. . . .

"Do you think he'll ask you to come home?"

"I don't know. We talked about it and he said he'd get back to me."

"What do *you* think you should do, Cliff?"

"If they'd hurt Dex Ethridge at all of course I'd have had to come right home, but he appears to be all right, and since they've caught the perpetrators I doubt there'll be any need for me to——what?"

"I couldn't hear you for a minute. The connection seems to be fading. I guess I'd better get off the line now. But call me when you've got it decided. Love me?"

"Love you," he said very soft into the phone cupped against his shoulder. He heard the click and the static of the transatlantic cable.

. . . list of the dead includes Senators Adamson, Geiss, Hunter, March, Nugent. . . .

His hand rested on the cradled phone as if to retain the thread of contact with Jeanette. He looked up. *Ordway, Oxford, Robinson, Scobie, Tuchman. . . .* Perry Hearn's mouth, moving not in synchronization with his radio voice, was an evil ugly thing and Fairlie wrenched his eyes away from the screen and carried his glass to the Dubonnet bottle.

Jeanette: soft lips and upswept hair. Not that much different from the girl he had courted back in the medieval days when you still courted girls: she had been a psych major at Vassar in pleated skirt and saddle shoes and for six months she had returned his weekend invitations unopened because when a Vassar girl received anything with a Worcester postmark she knew it was from a Holy Cross man and Vassar girls did not date Holy Cross men. Finally a classmate had informed Fairlie of this and he had had the presence of mind to drive over to Cambridge to mail the next invitation. She must have received that one: at least it was never returned to him. But there was no reply. That summer he wrote two invitations from his home outside Cheyney, Pennsylvania. These she had regretted with formal little notes. Finally in the fall he had prevailed upon a botany professor who was going off on sabbatical. The professor had taken the sealed envelope and agreed to post it. A week later Fairlie won: a phone call from Vassar—"What on earth were you doing in Alaska?"

After his first year at Yale Law she had agreed to marry him. After his second year she had married him. After the bar exams he had moved her to Cheyney and she had fallen in love with the place, the great trees, the rolling hills, the struggling Negro college and its eagerly tutorable students.

Young with childless zeal she had become compulsively tidy and organized. She took to making lists of things to do and things for Fairlie to do; she posted them on the refrigerator door, boldly penned in her expansive hand. Finally he had cured her by appending an item to her itemized list: *9) Check likelihood of obsessive list-making on part of* second *wife.*

They were an idyllically and atypically happy couple. The children had come soon—Liz was now fourteen, Clay was going on ten, which was to say he was more than six months past his ninth birthday—and the pressures of twenty-four-hour politics had had inevitable effects on the fabric between them, but their respect for each other's individuality and their private sense of humor had secured them pretty well: once last fall he had got up early to dress for a campaign breakfast and when he was ready to leave the hotel suite he had crept into the bedroom where she was half asleep, and had nibbled her ear and caressed her breast and when she made a low smiling throat-sound he had whispered in her ear, "Where's Cliff?" and she had shot bolt upright and yelled. She had scolded him for weeks about that, but each time with laughter.

"President Brewster."

He looked up. It was McNeely, holding the phone out toward him. Fairlie hadn't heard it ring. At least McNeely hadn't said, "It's the pisspot Napoleon."

He took the receiver from McNeely and said into the mouthpiece, "Fairlie here."

"Hold on please, Mr. Fairlie." Brewster's secretary.

Now the President came on the line. "Cliff."

"Hello Mr. President."

"Thanks for waiting." An unnecessary courtesy: where would Fairlie have gone? Howard Brewster's flat Oregon twang sounded very tired: "Bill Satterthwaite's just talked to them over at Walter Reed. Old Dex Ethridge is fine, just fine."

"They're releasing him, then?"

"No, they want to hang onto him for a day or so, run him through that damned battery of tests they like to do." He could almost hear the President shudder over the six-thousand-mile telephone wire. "But there's nothing wrong with Dex, he's fine and dandy. I always said it'd take more than a whap on the head to do any damage to a Republican."

Fairlie said, "It's that elephant hide we all wear."

There followed Brewster's energetic bark of laughter and then a ritual clearing of throat, and Brewster said in his matter-of-fact voice, "Cliff, I'm going to talk to the people tonight. It'll be pretty late your time but I'd appreciate it a whole lot if you'd hold off on making any kind of statement until after I've made mine."

"Of course, Mr. President."

"And then I'd be truly obliged if you'd step out and back me up. We need to have a pretty good show of solidarity on this thing."

"I can see that," Fairlie said—cautious, not wanting to commit himself to a blank-check promise. "Do you mind if I ask what the substance of it will be?"

"Don't mind a bit." Brewster dropped into his man-to-man confidential voice:

"I'm going to talk tough, Cliff. Very tough. There's a lot of screwballs out there with loud voices and I don't think we can afford to give them time to start broadcasting conspiracy alarms and sniping at us the way they did when JFK was shot. There's a risk of panic here, and I mean to head it off."

"By doing what, Mr. President?" Fairlie felt the fine hairs prickle at the back of his neck.

"We've just had an emergency meeting of the National Security Council together with various interested parties—the Speaker, some others. I'm declaring a state of national emergency, Cliff."

After a moment Fairlie said, "I thought you'd captured the bombers."

"Well, we've got some pretty damn fast T-men and thank God for them. They nailed those degenerate savages before they'd got two blocks from the Hill."

"Then what emergency are we talking about?"

"There's some others mixed up in this thing—five or six that didn't get caught, maybe more."

"You know that for a fact?"

"Yes. I do. We do know there were more people involved in this than we actually caught at the scene."

"You're declaring a national emergency mainly to hunt down a handful of co-conspirators?"

"Well, we don't know how many they are, but that's beside the point, Cliff. The thing is, we've been rocked by this. Warshington's out of kilter. Now God knows how many other groups of vicious animals we've got out there in the woodwork—suppose they decide it's time to jump on the bandwagon and whip up this big revolution they're always yelling about? What if they get the violence stirred up until we've got riots and snipers and bombs crawling out from under rocks in every city and state across the country? We've got to forestall that, Cliff, we've got to demonstrate that this government's still vigorous enough to react speedily and decisively. We've got to defuse the savages, we've got to show a little muscle."

"Mr. President," Fairlie said slowly, "I'm beginning to get the feeling you're talking about a wholesale nationwide roundup of suspicious characters. Is that what you mean when you talk about a national emergency? Emergency powers?"

"Cliff," and now the voice was deep and filled to overflowing with sincerity, "I think we're all together on this, I think the people are with us. Liberals and moderates and conservatives alike, all of us. We're saturated with this damned violence. We're all grieved and sickened by these atrocities. Now's the time, Cliff—we've all got to join forces to freeze out the extremists, the violent animals. And if we *don't*, then God help this country. If we don't stop them right now then they'll know for a fact nobody's ever going to keep them from kicking over the pail."

"I see."

"Now at the same time," the President continued briskly, "I mean to set an example of speedy justice with these bombers we've caught, because if we intend to deter other animals from trying the same kind of thing we've got to show that punishment can be immediate and complete. Now I don't mean to try the case on television, mind you, but I'm going to make it clear to the people that there's absolutely no cause for alarm—that we've taken the steps necessary to preserve the peace, that we've already got these murderers behind bars and we're going to have their guts for guitar strings. I'm going to give them tough talk, Cliff, because I think it's what the people need to hear, and I want to get in there ahead of the bleeding hearts before they start drowning the newspapers with crocodile tears about these poor unfortunate misunderstood children and how if they're guilty then we're all guilty, it's society's fault, all that crap." The President drew a shuddering long breath to continue, "Before they can get up steam to do that I'm going to put these animals on trial in a public courtroom quicker than you can say Jack Robinson."

"Well I don't see how you can do that overnight, Mr. President. They've got to have a fair trial. They'll have to be defended—the attorneys will have to have time to prepare their case."

"I recognize that, Cliff, but I don't mean to let any water flow under the bridge. I think you ought to have a little talk tonight with your Attorney General designate, because he's going to have to pick this thing up in the middle and we need to make sure he's not going to be wishy-washy."

"I'll talk to him," Fairlie said. "But I'd like to come back to this national emergency you're declaring. I still need to know the exact boundaries of it."

"Well Cliff, you named it before. A roundup."

Fairlie sucked breath into his chest and took his stand. "Mr. President, I don't agree with the wisdom of that. I think it's premature."

"Premature? My God, Cliff, they've slaughtered dozens of the best people in the American Government. *Premature?*"

"You can't very well blame the slaughter on every individual in the FBI's files of suspicious radicals."

"The point is we've decided not to let them take advantage. We intend to put them on ice and keep them there until this case has been tried and we've demonstrated our toughness by executing these bombers." Then, into Fairlie's stubborn silence, President Brewster added, "I don't hold with killing, you know that, but there would be one thing worse than killing these savages, and that would be not killing them."

"I haven't disputed that part of it, Mr. President."

"Cliff, I need your support on this. You know that." The President breathed hard into the phone. "The Establishment protects us, Cliff. We're obliged to protect it."

"I think a roundup at this point would have a terrible effect on the country. It could only be interpreted as the overreaction of a government in panic."

"Not at all. It would demonstrate our self-respect. To ourselves and to the rest of the world. That's damned important right now. How can any society expect to hold together without self-respect? It's a matter of showing muscle, Cliff, and that's something we've been too reluctant to do."

"Maybe with good reason. I think a roundup right now would give the radicals exactly the kind of provocation they want. Oh, keep surveillance on the really suspicious ones of course, but let them alone. Mr. President, the radicals have been trying for years to goad the Government into violence. If we start herding them into camps it'll be exactly what they've been waiting for—there'll be outraged cries of police state and fascist suppression and we can't afford that now."

"Cliff, I think you're more concerned about their outraged cries than you are about their bombs."

"I haven't heard of any bombs since the Capitol, Mr. President. There doesn't seem to be any chain reaction."

"They've hardly had time yet, have they." The President was getting curt now; he had been long enough in power to get out of the habit of conciliatory argument.

"I'd like to give it a little time, Mr. President. If we see a chain reaction starting in the next day or two—if the snipers and bombers start coming out from under those rocks you mentioned—then I'll cooperate with you right up to the hilt. But if we don't see any sign of that kind of trouble then I'm afraid I'm going to have to fight you on this."

An attenuated silence, and Fairlie could all but see Brewster's agonized face. Finally the President said in a lower tone than he had used before, "I'll have to get back to you, Cliff. I'll have to consult with my people. If I can't get back to you before my broadcast I suppose you'll get my answer from that. If we decide we must go ahead with the program as I've outlined it to you, then you'll do as you see fit, I guess, but I'd like to remind you this is a damned precarious time for all of us and there's nothing we need quite so badly right now as a show of undivided solidarity."

"I'm very aware of that, Mr. President."

The courteous goodbyes were distant and chilled. Fairlie sat by the telephone and brooded at it. He realized that if he were in Washington today it would be much harder for him not to be swept up in the urgent sense of horror and the unreasoning emotional demand for reactive vengeance.

It had been up to him to support Brewster, but his refusal reversed their positions. Brewster was the Chief Executive and had the right to make final decisions but only for the next sixteen days, after which the decisions would be Fairlie's, and Brewster had to worry about that now because this decision wasn't the kind he could present to his successor as a *fait accompli*. If Brewster arrested thousands of people and Fairlie quickly turned them loose, it could give Brewster and his party a terrible black eye; at the same time it could put a libertarian luster on Fairlie's administration—perhaps not enough to convince the radicals that Fairlie could be trusted, but certainly enough to persuade them to postpone any full-scale anti-Fairlie warfare for an interim while they sat back and watched to see how Fairlie performed.

These considerations had to be coursing through Howard Brewster's mind right now in the White House and they were considerations not easy to dismiss. Brewster was almost singularly aware of history and his place in it; given time to reflect—and Fairlie's brake had surely given him that—Brewster might decide to recant because the alternative was to risk condemnation for one final reckless act.

There was no sure way to predict which way Brewster would go but Fairlie had offered him a way out—and Brewster, the political animal, would avail himself of it if he could.

This was not the time to fly back to Washington. The President's televised address would take place before Fairlie's jet could get him farther than the west coast of Ireland. If Brewster ordered the roundup Fairlie would have to return to the States at once. But if Brewster softened his approach there would be no need to break off the planned visits to Rome and Madrid, and the announcement a few hours ago that Perez-Blasco had granted diplomatic recognition to Peking made it all the more important that Fairlie complete his schedule and resolve the question of the Spanish bases. In the meantime, in the next few hours, there was nothing to do but formulate his own statement and wait.

6:35 P.M. EST   The chill rain fell in a soup of drizzle and mist. It threw foggy halos around street lamps and the lights of cars that hissed past on the wet paving. Guards stood in yellow police slickers and hoods at the steps of the Executive Office Building.

David Lime crossed to the White House side of the drive and

walked along the fence to the gate. At intervals inside the fence he could see the dripping shadows of alerted guards—members of the Executive Protective Service, formerly the White House Police Force, and of the White House Detail of the Secret Service: the first group to protect the building and grounds, the latter to protect the President and other persons.

A knot of troubled people stood in the night rain outside the main gate. Lime threaded his way through them and presented himself to the guards, and was admitted.

He invaded Brewster country by the low side entrance and had only just entered the press lobby, filled with reporters standing tense under the large formal paintings, when Halroyd, the Special Agent in charge of the White House Detail, drew him to the corridor again. "Mr. Satterthwaite said he'd like a word, sir."

Lime lifted his eyebrows inquiringly and Halroyd took him along toward the basement offices which Satterthwaite and the other Presidential advisors used.

The office was very small and unspeakably cluttered with paperwork. Satterthwaite, resident White House intellectual, had no interest in appearances; the disordered piles on his desk reflected the impatient brain. Of the five or six straight chairs only two were not heaped with papers; Lime chose one, following the command of Satterthwaite's flapped hand, and sat.

"Thanks very much, Halroyd." Satterthwaite spoke in his high abrasive voice and the Special Agent withdrew; the door closed out the noises of voices and typewriters and teleprinters. "The President asked if I'd get a firsthand report from you before the broadcast. It *was* you who ran them down? One hell of an adroit piece of work. The President keeps talking about 'that genius over in Secret Service who saved our bacon.' "

"If I'd been a genius," Lime said, "I'd have thought faster and we'd have got the bombs out before they went off."

"From what I've heard, based on the tiny bits of information you had not one man in ten thousand would have guessed there was anything going on at all."

Lime shrugged. He wasn't insensitive to the fact that Satterthwaite's words were at odds with the expression on his face. The face was marked by an indelible arrogance, the hauteur of a brilliant but tactless mind contemptuous of lesser brains. Satterthwaite was a forty-one-year-old mental machine who wore thick glasses that magnified his eyes to a startling size and dressed himself with studied indifference, a challenging lack of grace. The black hair was an untidy tangle of electric curls; the blunt little hands were perpetually in motion. He had the nimble aggressiveness of his diminutive size.

"All right," Satterthwaite said. "What have you got?"

"Not too much from the bombers yet. We're working them over."

"With rubber hoses I trust."

It seemed rhetorical; Lime didn't rise to it.

Satterthwaite said, "The NSA files identified the leader for you—the one behind these six. You know who he is. Julius Sturka."

Lime couldn't altogether keep the anger out of his face and Satterthwaite jumped at the admission but Lime headed him off: "I never met the man. Fifteen years ago he was working the same part of the world I was, that's all."

"He was an officer in the Algerian FLN. You were in Algeria during that nonsense." Satterthwaite pushed it aside. "This man Sturka—who exactly is he?"

"Armenian, I think—maybe Serbian. We never knew for sure. It's not his real name."

"Balkan and obscure. That's all rather Eric Ambler."

"I think he fancies himself that way. Soldier of fortune, trying to overturn the world order singlehandedly."

"But not a young squirt."

"Not unless he was a babe in arms when he was a light colonel in the FLN. As I say, I've never seen him. He's supposed to be in his late forties roughly. We've got one bad snapshot—I don't know of any other photographs. He's camera shy. But name a war of liberation in the past ten years and he's probably figured in it. Not at the top, but not as a menial either."

"A mercenary?"

"Sometimes. Not usually. It's possible he was just hired to do this one but we've got no evidence to indicate it. More likely it's his own caper. Sometimes in the past few years he's worked with a Cuban named Riva, but there's no sign of Riva in this case. Not yet at least."

"Does he have much of a following? If he does it's odd—I've never heard of him."

"He doesn't work that way. He'll put together a little cell or two and concentrate on the vitals of the government he's trying to break. In Algeria I don't think he had more than twenty soldiers, but they were all crack professionals. Did more damage than some regiments."

"For a man who's never met him you know him pretty well, don't you."

"I was supposed to nail him. I never did."

Satterthwaite licked his upper lip, like a cat washing itself. He pushed his glasses higher on his nose and watched without expression as Lime lit a cigarette. "Do you think you'll get him this time?"

"I don't know. Everybody's looking for him."

"You've alerted the other agencies? Other countries?"

"Yes. He's probably still in this country—at least we have reason to believe he was here until late last night."

"Here in Washington, you mean?"

"He left a calling card."

"That agent of yours who was killed."

"Yes, that one."

"What makes you say that's his calling card?"

"He seems to have been one of the people who stirred up the rebellion in Ceylon a few years ago. The government cracked down on that one hard—infiltrated the rebels and singled out the leaders and had them killed.

"The Ceylonese insurgents had to take strong measures to protect themselves. According to NSA it was Sturka who took out the government infiltrators—butchered them dramatically, left them to be found in public buildings with their tongues and hearts ripped out. It was a warning—see what happens to informers who infiltrate us."

"Now I see what you mean by calling card." Satterthwaite shook his head. "My God these people are of another species." He removed his glasses and wiped them clean and held them up to the light at arm's length, squinting at them. His eyes, Lime saw with surprise, were quite small and set too close together. The glasses had left red dents alongside the bridge of his nose.

Satterthwaite gave the glasses a pained look and put them back on, hooking them over one ear at a time. It was the first time Lime had had personal contact with him, and one of the few times he had seen the man at all; Satterthwaite was not a frequent appearance-maker on television or in any public places. He was the President's chief advisor and he cast a long shadow but he was one of those invisible figures usually described by the press as "a high White House source."

"Well." Satterthwaite was reflective. "Shall we just stand here in outraged dignity? It's a furious mess, isn't it. The world's most powerful system, and they can get us over a barrel so easily. Small groups can tyrannize simply by finding a pressure point. These terrorists use any weapon they can lay their hands on; they recruit any fool who's willing to sacrifice himself in the name of some vague negative cause, and they know we're handicapped because we can only fire the second shot."

"That deters most of the professionals," Lime said. "The professional doesn't mean to get caught. Terrorism's usually an amateur occupation—they rarely get away free in the end, they tend to end up martyrs, and it's the amateurs who go for that. They don't care about the second shot—they don't care if the second shot blows them in two."

"And here you've got the worst of both, haven't you. A group of sacrificial amateurs commanded and operated by a professional who's pulling the strings. To tell you the truth," Satterthwaite said, "I think we've got our ass in a crack."

When Satterthwaite talked he had the disconcerting habit of fixing his stare against the knot of Lime's necktie; but now the enlarged eyes lifted, the abrasive voice hardened, the jaw crept forward. "Lime, you're a professional."

Lime wanted no part of what he saw coming. "I'm pretty low on the totem pole."

"It's hardly a time for blind obeisance to seniority and the chain of command, is it? We need a professional hunter—a man we can rely on to get the job done while the politicians keep hands off."

"The job of nailing Sturka."

"Yes. I'll be frank: we'd decided to throw a net, bring in everybody who's got a file folder, but something happened and we had to ditch that scheme. This is confidential, you understand—it doesn't leave this room."

"All right."

"Everybody wants this thing wrapped up and sealed. Fast, and no loopholes. Get Sturka, and if there's anyone behind him find out who or what it is."

"Suppose it turns out to be a foreign government?"

"It won't. I can't buy that."

Lime didn't buy it either, but anything was possible. "Let me ask you something. Are you suggesting we make Sturka a calling card?"

Satterthwaite shook his head. "That would be playing their game. I don't want him butchered. We've got to get the case packaged airtight and nail the son of a bitch and pin him up against it by the numbers. Arrest, trial, conviction, execution. It's time to quit letting these radical prigs hector us—it's time for us to start hectoring them for a change. But we can't do it *their* way—we can't ignore our own rules. They attacked the Establishment and it's the Establishment that must bring them down, by Establishment rules."

"It sounds all right," Lime said. "But you still want someone bigger than me."

"I like the way you size up."

Lime dragged on his cigarette and jetted smoke. "I've retired. I push papers around, that's all. A few more years and I go out to pasture."

Satterthwaite's smiling headshake was dubious. "Don't you see? All the people higher up than you are political appointees. Hacks."

"It's an FBI case, really. Why not let them run it?"

"Because FBI smacks of police state in too many minds."

"Nuts. They're the ones who're equipped for it."

Satterthwaite rose from behind the desk. He really was short—not more than five feet five in his shoes. He said, "We'd better get along to the proceedings. Thank you for indulging my ignorance."

They threaded the busy subterranean corridor and arrived at the press conference somewhat ahead of the President. At least it looked like a press conference: photographers prowled the room restlessly, reporters were collaring people and the TV crews had taken over with their logistical preponderance of equipment and manpower. The lights were hot and painful. Technicians were making loud demands for microphone voice levels. A cameraman yelled, "Get your damn feet off that cable," and lashed the heavy cable like a bullwhip. Somebody was being the President's stand-in at the podium behind the Great Seal and the TV people were setting up their camera angles on him.

One of the monitor screens was alight with a fill-in network broadcast. There was no sound but Lime didn't need commentary to follow the pictorial coverage. A forecaster's lighted pointer traced a schematic drawing of the Capitol's interior structure, singling out points where damage had been sustained by the substructures under the House and Senate chambers and the brick supporting arches of the building. Now the screen cut to an exterior long shot of the Capitol—the police had set up portable floodlights to illuminate the scene; officials and men in uniform were milling around and a reporter was facing the camera, talking. The scene shifted again, hand-held cameras following people through the shattered building. Smoke still hung in the colonnaded halls. People were sifting and winnowing through the rubble and dust. By now it was assumed all the bodies, living and dead, had been found and exhumed from the piles of wreckage; they were searching now for pieces of the bombs.

A knot of journalists buttonholed Lime. "You're the one who nailed them, aren't you?" "Can you tell us what happened down there, Mr. Lime?" "Can you tell us anything about the bombers you arrested?"

"I'm sorry, no comment at this time."

Across the room Perry Hearn had answered a ringing telephone; now he put it down and spoke, demanding attention; he made arm signals and everyone sought seats in the miniature amphitheater.

Talk diminished from roar to hubbub to mutter, and then silence. Satterthwaite caught Lime's eye and beckoned; Lime moved forward and took the chair Satterthwaite indicated, behind and below the presidential podium. The Vice-President and the Attorney General and several other dignitaries filed into the room and took seats on either side of Lime. Attorney General Robert Ackert gave Lime a tight brief smile of recognition; he looked tense and wary like a pugilist who had been hit too hard and too often in the head.

They all sat in a row behind the podium, facing the reporters below. It made Lime distinctly uncomfortable. He kept crossing and uncrossing his legs.

On the monitor screen he saw one of the network anchormen, talking with earnest sincerity into the camera. Now the scene cut to the unoccupied presidential podium and Lime saw his own face in the screen; it startled him.

"Ladies and gentlemen, the President of the United States."

President Brewster's leather heels clicked on the hard floor. He came in from the side and immediately seemed to dwarf the room: eyes looked Brewsterwards and the President gave the reporters his grave nod as he stepped up behind the Great Seal and touched one of the microphones with his right hand while he laid a small sheaf of papers on the slope of the podium in front of his belly.

The President looked into the television eye for a silent moment. He was a very tall man, rangy, tan, his face not unattractively lined —a big face, deep square brackets creasing it right down past the mouth into the big dependable jaw. He had a full bush of hair, still a deep rich brown—dyed, probably, for his hands were veined and beginning to show age spots. Flesh was heavy under his big jaw but he had a muscular way of moving which bespoke hours in the White House pool and steam room—an expensively taken-care-of body. He had a beaky nose and small well-set ears; his eyes were paler than their surroundings. He always dressed impeccably. Mute, as he was now, he projected warmth, looked sincere and intelligent; but when he spoke with his rough-edged twang he somehow seemed, regardless of the words he spoke, inarticulate. The accent was folksy, right for overalls on a sun-grayed clapboard porch with a jug of corn and a hunting dog.

It was mainly sham—both the polished appearance and the down-home voice. You had the feeling Howard Brewster really existed only in public. It occurred to Lime that ever since the election Brewster's face had turned steadily and remotely bitter, the outward sign of his rage and disappointment at the nation's failure to drink from him.

The President began to speak with the customary My-Fellow-Americans-let-us-suffer-together eulogy over the towering and distinguished Americans who had been lost. Lime sat with dismal detachment listening not so much to the words as to the rise and fall of the President's voice. Brewster was not a master rhetorician and his writers conformed to his own style; there were no ringing truths, no soaring aphorisms that might crystallize this moment in a phrase. Brewster's talk was soothing with the old familiar vagaries; it was calculated to give people an antidote to shock and rage—a speech of warm regret, quiet sorrow, and the promise that in spite of tragedy there was well-being ahead. There was a call for sorrow but not for alarm, a need for reappraisal but not for reactive fury. Let us not lose our heads, he said. Calm, he said, and the rule of law. The perpetrators have been captured, thanks to the alert initiative of Deputy Assistant Director David Lime of the Secret Service . . .

Momentarily the lights were fixed on Lime; he squinted into them and nodded into the cameras. The President gave him the benediction of a paternal sad smile before he turned back into the cameras and the lights swiveled away from Lime, and that was that for his part of it except that he had to remain in his seat for the duration of the President's talk.

It was so easy to give the people heroes nowadays, he thought. You strapped a man into a seat and shot him to the moon, and made him a hero. You put him on a horse in front of a camera, or you hired a dozen keen wits to write his speeches. Heroism was a packaged mass-market commodity, the ultimate cynicism.

People needed their myths, their heroes, and there was no room left for the real thing so you had to contrive fakes for them. It simply wasn't possible for a new Lindbergh to emerge: technology had gone beyond the individual. Those who persisted in facing individual challenges—the ones who rowed singlehanded across the Atlantic, the ones who climbed mountains—were relegated to the status of harmless fools because what they did was fundamentally meaningless, technology had demeaned it: you could always fly the Atlantic in three hours, you could reach the mountaintop by helicopter in a painless swoop.

The President was talking tough now, carrying a big stick. The perpetrators were in hand, they would be tried, the trial would be a firm example for the world and for those who sought to impose anarchic violence upon the freely elected governments of the world. Justice and law would be served. Our equanimity was not to be taken for equivocation; our tranquillity should not be mistaken for submission, our coolness for passivity. America's patience had been sorely tried, it was at its limit.

"Let our enemies, within and without, take warning."

The President concluded his address and left the room without opening the floor to any questions. Lime gave the reporters the slip and made his way back to the Executive Office Building. The streets were quiet; the drizzle continued, very cold, and beyond the curtailed pools of street lamplight the shadows were oppressively opaque. Street scene from a Sydney Greenstreet picture, he observed, and went into the building.

TUESDAY, JANUARY 4

5:15 A.M. EST Mario was grinning. "Man we have gone and filled the *New York Times* from the headlines right through to the classified section."

The newspaper rattled like small-arms fire when Mario turned the pages. "We really trashed them. Listen here: 'At midnight the toll stood at 143 dead, of whom 15 were U. S. Senators and 51 were Congressmen, and at least 70 journalists. Approximately 500 victims have been admitted to hospitals and emergency clinics, but nearly 300 of these sustained superficial injuries and have been released. At latest count 217 men and women and four children are hospitalized. Twenty-six remain on the critical list.' " Mario took a long breath and let it out with a nod of satisfaction. "Now talk about off the pigs!"

"Keep it down." Sturka was in the corner of the motel room with the radio turned down low. He sat within reach of the telephone, waiting for it to ring. Alvin wearily listened and watched; Alvin felt wrung out, pain throbbed between his ears, his stomach bubbled sour.

Sturka looked like a television gangster, stripped down to his shirtsleeves with a shoulder holster strapped tight around his chest. Cesar Renaldo was asleep in his clothes on the couch and Peggy lay across the bed smoking a Marlboro and drinking coffee out of the motel bathroom's plastic cup.

Big trucks snored by; the occasional semi-rig gnashed in and out of the truck-stop café in front of the motel. Peggy looked at Sturka. "Don't you get tired?"

"When I get tired I hear Mao saying a revolution is not a tea party."

Alvin slid back in the chair and went limp, eyes drifting half shut. Cesar on the couch was eyeing Peggy with a slow carnal stare. He kept his eyes on her too long: it made Peggy roll her head around, look at him, get up and go into the john. Its door slammed; Cesar smiled lazily. Cesar had moved in with Peggy two weeks ago but they had ended it quickly at Sturka's command. The privatism of establishing *couples* inhibited total collectivization. It was counter-revolutionary. It was an oppressive relationship, it led right back into everything they were struggling against: the capitalist orientation toward bourgeois individuality. The pig philosophy of separating one person from the next, encouraging the individual to assert himself at the expense of his brother.

You had to fight all that. You were the oppressed black colony. You learned the frustrating impotence of nonviolent resistance, sit-ins, demonstrations: self-defeating Custerism—bourgeois games encouraged by the Establishment, kids playing at revolution. Deliberately putting yourself in jail was immature and counterproductive. It did not help end the white-skin privilege of capitalism.

The Third World struggled against imperialism and the time to smash racist tyranny was now, while the momentum was there. Put the pigs up against the wall, increase the cost of empire, open new fronts behind enemy lines to smash the state, goad the pigs into reprisals which would awaken the masses to the fat fascism of the demagogues. People had minds like concrete—mixed, framed and set—and if you meant them to listen you had to blow things up.

The phone.

Sturka picked up. "Yes?"

Alvin fixed his insomniac eyes on Sturka hunching forward. "Where are you, a phone booth? Give me the number." Sturka scribbled on the flyleaf of the Gideon Bible and ripped it out. "I'll go to a phone and call you back."

Sturka cradled the telephone and reached for his jacket. "Everyone stay inside." He opened the door and went. It was probably Raoul Riva.

Peggy was lighting a cigarette from the burning stub of the old one; she stood just inside the bathroom door, stood there for a stretching interval and finally crossed to the front window. Parted the drapes and looked out. "I don't know."

Alvin said, "What?"

Peggy sat down on the floor and tipped her head back against the sill. "It was an uncool getaway."

Cesar rolled his head around. "So?"

"They got six of our people. We'd have to be stupid if we thought they'd all keep quiet. I bet they've given us away by now."

Cesar said again, "So?"

"So why are we sitting here? Waiting for the pigs to rip us off?"

"Gentle down." Cesar lay back. "Ain't nothing to fret about."

Peggy gave a sour bark of laughter.

Mario said, "Hey," whipping toward the radio.

The announcer: " . . . arrested less than an hour ago by police who had been staked out to watch the Harlem tenement. Identified as Darleen Warner, the woman is alleged by the FBI to be a member of the conspiracy to bomb the Capitol. This arrest brings to seven the number of bomb-plot conspirators apprehended so far. . . ."

"Oh that's sensational." Peggy closed her eyes.

"Get off it," Cesar said. "You want to push that stuff out."

Alvin gave them both bleak stares. He didn't want a push-out session, he was too tired. They had spent days in self-criticism sessions, Sturka and Cesar leading the harsh group therapy inducing them to exorcise their bourgeois conventionalisms and their individualized fears. They had lived taut, studied intensely, learned to accept discipline; now Peggy was backsliding and it was a bad time for it.

Shut up, he thought.

Perhaps the edge of the thought struck them all because Peggy closed her mouth to a pout and did not speak. The radio droned faintly and trucks went snarling by, Mario brooded over the *Times*, Peggy chain-smoked, Cesar dozed.

Sturka returned so silently it chilled Alvin. He was inside closing the door before Alvin knew he was there.

"We'll go out tonight. It's arranged." Sturka went around the room passing out documents.

Alvin had a look. Forged seaman's papers, a Venezuelan passport, entry visas for Spain and France and three North African countries. So that was why Sturka had needed the photos.

Sturka hitched up his trousers with the flats of his wrists. "We'll board ship tonight at Port Elizabeth—four of us, not Mario. She's a tramp under Anguillan registry. Going to Lisbon." His eyes, hard and colorless as glass, shifted toward Mario. "You'll fly over—book a flight to Marseille on the eighth. We talked about it before. We're still agreed?"

"Well I'm scared shitless, if you want to know the truth."

"I don't think they've made you, that's the point. We've got to know."

"But if we're wrong they'll grab me at the airport. They'll throw away the fucking key."

"We all admit it's a risk, Mario."

"Well I guess we've got to try it," Mario muttered. All through the development of the plan Mario was the one who had stayed in the shadows of the group and maintained his contacts with the pig world. Mezetti Industries thought he was engaged in market research among people his own age. It was something Mario had proposed to his father; his father had put the company's facilities at his disposal. Every week or so Mario went home, showed his face for a few days, kept his psychological alibi polished. Now it was necessary to make sure he was still free to move about. The group needed a member who could show himself openly.

Sturka was still talking to Mario: "We'll have to get you to a bank today."

"How much you need?"

"A very great deal of money."

"What, just to get the four of you on a tramp freighter? You figure to *buy* the fucking boat?"

"That's not what the money's needed for." Sturka smiled his chilly anger: Mario's resistance was undisciplined.

Sturka folded his arms across his chest and his rough pitted face became sleepy as it did when he had Cesar lecture them on doctrine. "Our people are in jail. They'll be arraigned Monday morning. The politicians will bellow about law and order, there will be waves of horrified indignation across the country. If they don't find enough evidence to execute our people they'll manufacture it, but they can't afford not to execute our people. A few of the underground newspapers will try to make heroic martyrs of them, but there's a very long list of martyrs who've been destroyed by the capitalist Establishment—martyrdom means nothing any more."

Alvin listened intently because Sturka was not given to philosophical ramblings. Sturka was getting to a point.

"And perhaps we need reminding that this operation wasn't conceived to give them martyrs." Sturka's eyes went from face to face and Alvin was chilled. "We had a purpose. I hope we remember what it was."

It was a mannerism: a cue, and Mario Mezetti obeyed it. "To show the world how much you can do even if you're only a small group, if you're dedicated to retaliation against the fascist pigs."

Sturka said, "We didn't finish, did we. The purpose wasn't merely to sabotage the Capitol, the purpose was to get away with it. To show the people we could get away with it."

"Didn't work," Cesar said. His voice was hard, high-pitched, nasal. He was digging around his mouth with a toothpick. "And the reason it didn't work was because——"

"The people are sitting." It was as if Sturka hadn't heard Cesar. "They're waiting, they haven't begun to move. They need a sign. Encouragement. The revolutionaries in this country are waiting for us to prove the time is right for revolution."

Peggy blew smoke from her nostrils. "I thought we proved that by smashing the Capitol."

"We would have. If our people had got away." Sturka moved his hand in an arc. "They're watching. If they see the bandwagon isn't moving anywhere they won't want to jump on it. You see?" Sturka's idiomatics were odd; he had spent a great deal of time among Americans, but most of it overseas.

"So what we're going to do is get our people out."

"With a skyhook." Peggy was expressionless.

"We've no room for your sarcasms," Sturka told her. "We pluck our people out—out of the country. Deliver them into asylum and watch the world jeer at Washington. That *is* the whole point. Prove how weak Washington is." Sturka's stabbing finger sought Peggy, Cesar, Alvin, Mario; his lips formed an accidental smile. "They will react the way high-octane reacts to a lit match."

Peggy's head turned back and forth rhythmically, disputing it. "What are we supposed to do? Buy television time, write 'Free the Washington Seven' on shithouse walls? Raid the jail when it's probably guarded by a whole regiment? I just don't see what you think we can——"

"Seven," Sturka said. "Seven?"

Cesar caught it an instant before Alvin did; Cesar explained: "They got Darleen."

Sturka absorbed it quickly and without visible reaction. "When?"

"It was on the radio when you was out. They had cops staked out at the place on Amsterdam."

"She should have known better than to go back there."

Cesar sat up. "The cops knew."

"Barbara," Sturka said absently. He was thinking.

"Maybe. But maybe they broke down those others."

"No. None of them knew about the Harlem place."

Cesar wasn't willing to let it go. "Linc knew."

"The hell," Alvin said, aroused finally. "Linc won't crack easy. They haven't had time to break him down."

"I didn't say they broke him down. Maybe Linc was a plant too —listen, they nailed all six of them practically on the Capitol steps," Cesar said. "Now that was just too easy."

"Not Linc," Alvin said. "I don't buy that."

Sturka turned the hawked stare toward him. His voice was very quiet. "Why? Because Linc is the same color as you?"

Alvin opened his mouth and closed it. Suddenly he felt defensive. Because Sturka was right.

Cesar said, "Barbara didn't know the time, she didn't even know the place. We never told her it was the Capitol. Add it up. Linc's the only one who knew the program and knew about the place on Amsterdam."

Peggy said, "Barbara knew about the Harlem place. She was there, remember?" Suddenly her head tipped back. She was facing Sturka. "You guys killed Barbara, didn't you."

"Sure." Cesar drawled the word slowly, pulling his head around toward Alvin. "Your soul sister finked on us."

Alvin played it very carefully. "All right."

Cesar shook his head. He had scored a point but he wasn't pressing it. Finally Alvin said, "I guess you had reason to believe that."

"She was a plant," Sturka said, as if that dismissed it.

Cesar was studying Alvin's face; Cesar gave way in the end. "She had this little toy camera in her bag and I caught her with a tin of talcum powder trying to lift Mario's prints off the bathroom glass. We left her dead for the cops to play with—we messed her up some. Maybe teach the pigs to use plants—maybe make the next one a little scared of what might happen."

All right, Alvin thought dismally. If she betrayed them then she had it coming. He had to keep his head.

Cesar was back on Sturka. "The point is somebody finked. They got our people."

"Barbara told them about the place on Amsterdam," Sturka said mildly. "Nobody told them about the bombs. Linc is straight."

Alvin felt gratitude; he almost smiled at Sturka but Sturka wasn't looking at him, Sturka was explaining to Cesar what all of them should have been able to figure out for themselves: "If Linc had given the pigs a tip in advance do you suppose the pigs would have stood around outside and waited for the bombs to explode? Don't you suppose they'd have evacuated the building and brought in the bomb squad? Our people must have tripped on their way out—someone made a revealing mistake at the wrong moment."

Cesar was frowning but he curbed his tongue; presently he nodded, recognizing that was the way it had to be. "But we have to figure Barbara made us for them. They know who we are."

"And that is why we're leaving the country tonight."

Peggy stubbed out her cigarette. She kept grinding it into the glass ashtray long after it was extinguished. "We're going to be on every post-office wall in the country by tomorrow, we're leaving the country on a slow boat to Lisbon, and you're talking about getting Linc and the rest of them out of hock. Sorry but I don't follow that."

"Discipline doesn't require that you follow it." Sturka opened Mario's canvas case and upended it over the bed and Mario's stock certificates cascaded into a disordered heap like bonfire kindling. "We'll trash them with these. It's fitting. Have you counted these?"

"Why?" Mario went toward the bed, suspicious.

"I have." Sturka touched one of the certificates. It was very large and imposing, the size of *Life* magazine, the color and style of a dollar bill, and it represented one thousand shares of common stock in Mezetti Industries. Mezetti common was selling in the neighborhood of thirty-eight dollars a share.

Mario's two hundred shares of NCI were worth about eight thousand dollars. His twelve hundred shares of Coast National Oil were worth just under sixty thousand. His four thousand shares of Whiteside Aviation were worth about eighteen thousand. And he had altogether thirty-five thousand shares of Mezetti Industries common. All inherited from the patriarchal grandfather who had used proletarian bodies for railroad ties. The canvas bag contained something over $1,200,000 in securities and they had been carrying it around on the streets for a month because Sturka had said they might need it fast when they needed it at all.

"It's time, then," Mario said.

Sturka began to stack the certificates neatly and slide them back into the case. "It's time."

Mario was dubious. "You can't just take this much stock into a bank or a broker and tell him to sell it. It would knock hell out of the market. They wouldn't do it."

"Don't sell them," Sturka said. "Hock them."

"For what?"

"What can you get? Half a million?"

"Probably."

"A cashier's check. Then you take the cashier's check to another bank and break it down into a number of smaller cashier's checks. Then you go to still other banks and cash some of them."

"How much cash?"

"At least half of it. The rest in internationally negotiable certified checks or cashier's checks."

Mario could become shrewd in the blink of an eye when it came to finance. He had been raised in a family of financiers and the wizardry had rubbed off on him.

He latched the case. "Large bills, I guess."

"Anything else would be too bulky. You'll have to buy money belts for us. The cheap canvas ones will do."

"It's pig money, isn't it?" Mario grinned. "We'll use it to smash the pigs."

"Spend an hour in a barbershop first," Sturka adjured. "Buy a good suit of clothes. You'll need to be presentable."

"Naturally."

"Peggy will go with you. You may take the car. Drive it into New York and leave it in a parking garage—tear up the ticket, leave it there. The police may have a description of it from Barbara." But the police wouldn't have the plate number; they had changed license plates on the car last night.

"Your chances of being arrested on the crowded streets are too negligible to worry about. You'll blend. But in the bank you'll have to give them a plausible reason for borrowing against the securities."

"Sure. Peggy and I are getting married, we want to buy a yacht for our honeymoon."

"No. That's frivolous."

Mario scowled; Sturka touched his arm with a fingertip. "It's a real estate deal. Very big. Be sly with the banker, take him into your confidence. You need the cash for an under-the-table bribe to persuade the land conglomerate to accept your bid. It's a short-term project and you'll be repaying the loan within three months."

Alvin stared at Sturka. The man had a command of the most unlikely things.

Mario nodded. "That'll work."

Cesar said mildly, "We'll have to clean *her* up."

"Jesus," Peggy muttered.

Sturka's finger stabbed toward her. "Your father is a college professor—you know how to comport yourself."

"My father's a phony liberal drunk. A fucking hypocrite."

"You're Mario's secretary. A very wealthy man's secretary—you'll behave as you would in polite society."

"Pig society."

"Peggy." Sturka's voice was very quiet, very mild, but it shut her up. "While Mario is in the barbershop you'll buy a demure dress and have your hair done."

When she made no rebuttal Sturka went back to Mario. "Impress on the banker that this is confidential. No one is to know about it, it might cause your deal to go sour."

"Sure. So no stocks change hands, no sale has to be registered with the SEC or the Exchange."

"And your family doesn't learn about it."

"Yeah."

Sturka went to Peggy. "When you've finished in the city take the Path Tube to Newark and go by taxi to the Washington Hotel. Time it to arrive between six-thirty and seven. Wait at the front entrance."

"Inside or outside?"

"Outside, we'll be watching. If I'm satisfied you haven't been followed we'll pick you up."

"What if we can't make contact there?"

"Use the usual method of leaving a message for me and we'll arrange something." Sturka employed a telephone answering service in the name of Charles Wernick; when you left a message for him you reversed the digits of the number: if you were calling from telephone 691-6243 you left word to call 342-6196.

Alvin yawned. Cesar said, "Wake up, okay?"

"I've been two days without sleep."

"You'll have a week to sleep on the boat." Cesar took the pillbox from his pocket. "Take one of these."

"Uppers?"

"Bennies. Just take one."

"I guess not." Alvin had come down off heroin in the Army and hadn't touched any kind of drugs since, medicinal or otherwise; he was terrified of them, he didn't want to get back into the spiral.

Sturka was shepherding Mario and Peggy to the door. Alvin

heard the car doors, heard the car start up and drive out of the motel.

Cesar was dragging out items from the theatrical makeup kit they had bought in New York a week ago. They made one another up: styrofoam pads inside the cheeks to change the shape of cheek and jaw; skullcaps and hairpieces to change hairlines; dye to hue eyebrows and hair.

A set of cheekpads and a cropped gray smudge of a moustache and a salt-and-pepper gray hairpiece in tight kink-curls added twenty years to Alvin. Cesar said, "Remember walk a little stooped over."

A skullcap receded Cesar's hairline and an application of makeup and eyeglasses changed him from swarthy brigand to middle-aged businessman. Sturka became an ascetic type in a wavy brown wig and neatly trimmed goatee.

"Let's go then."

Outside the air was heavy with a stink of heavy morning traffic grinding up Route 22 toward Newark Airport and the city. The parking court of the motel was busy with slamming car doors, people hustling luggage into car trunks, kids hollering, salesmen driving out into the heavy traffic. The sky was a murky brown—what passed for a clear day in the smog of northeast New Jersey.

WEDNESDAY, JANUARY 5

2:15 P.M. EST Lime left Satterthwaite's White House office in a dour mood and ambushed a taxi. "Police headquarters."

Lunch in the office of the President's sardonic chief security advisor had been dreary with takeout food and Satterthwaite's sonorous essay on political needs and realities. Lime spent the ride leaning his head far back against the cushion, eyes closed, unlit cigarette askew in his lips, thinking drowsy erotic thoughts about Bev Reuland.

"Hey man. We here."

He paid the cabbie and got out. Sunny today and not so damned cold. He threw his head back and searched for contrails, reflecting on his fantasies. Bev always managed to prove her point without waving banners: she was thirty-four, divorced, feminine, adminstrative assistant to Speaker of the House Milton Luke. He looked at his watch. Right now she would be dictating replies to Luke's constituents. Dear Mr. Smith, Thank you for your letter of January second. Regarding your request. . . . Efficient by day; languorous by night; she had compartmentalized herself crisply and Lime envied her.

The reporters knew him now. They laid siege in the corridor; its musty soot seemed to have settled in their clothes. Lime pushed at the air with his palms and when they subsided from baying to muttering he told them, "No comment—and you may quote me," and went past them through the cop-guarded doorway to the stairs.

Upstairs an FBI man had the interrogation; the subject was Sandra Walberg. The young lawyer from Harding's office sat in a corner, very bored. The kid looked like all Harding's disciples—shaggy, discontented, righteous. Harding had achieved his notoriety by inciting his clients to riot in court.

Lime crossed over and sat at the FBI man's right so that he wouldn't get the glare from the window when he looked at the girl. As he pulled the chair out and sat down the FBI man acknowledged him with a nod; the defense lawyer ignored him; Sandra glanced at him once. She was a small-boned girl with pinched features, full of sullen defiance.

The FBI man was young and vinegary, up to date in his field. His questions were compelling and logical. He spoke in a cautious tone, reserving malevolence. Of course none of it did any good: Sandra wasn't talking. None of them was talking. There had been a few remarks from the prisoners—particularly from Bob Walberg who was more nervous than the others. "A few alterations in the Capitol." And a grin and a clenched fist raised: "Right on!" But the young lawyer always cut in quickly, shutting them up: "Everything's cool, baby. Keep it."

Harding's clients were going to be executed and the state could not seriously pretend to offer clemency because Harding had to know such an offer would be in bad faith.

Harding was handling the case in the full knowledge that there was no way on earth for him to avoid losing his clients' lives to the executioner. The only advantage gained by anybody would be gained by Harding himself: by defending the bombers he would cement his position as mouthpiece for the radical left. Afterward he would be able to go to his people and say to them that he—the best of his kind—had tried, and had been beaten by the corrupt and unfeeling system: therefore choose violence, which I have advocated all along, because I have just proved to you that nothing else works. Lime despised the Hardings; they would fight to the very last drop of their followers' blood.

You had to go through this charade. It was all sham and nonsense; everybody, Harding included, knew it. But you brought the prisoners up separately and interrogated them politely all day long, always with a lawyer present, always with reminders that the prisoner didn't have to say a word.

In the evening you returned the prisoners to their solitary cells and the lawyers went home. Then after dinner you rousted the prisoners out again and took them secretly into interrogation cells and you worked them over *sans* lawyers and *sans* recitations of rights. You did this because the case demanded it: until you traced this thing to its roots you had no way of knowing how substantial the overall danger was. You had to find Sturka and you had to find out where Sturka would lead you in turn, and one way to find Sturka perhaps was to pry it out of these prisoners.

The normal pressures had been applied, and had proved minimally effective, so drugs had been introduced. Thus far the results had been poor but tonight might prove more satisfactory. In the meantime the prisoners each morning complained to their lawyers of the nightly roustings and the interrogators replied gravely that the prisoners were either dreaming or lying maliciously. The Establishment could produce a plethora of reliable witnesses to testify that the prisoners had lain undisturbed in their cells all night long; the Establishment could also produce doctors to testify that the prisoners had not been drugged. These radicals, Lime thought, had imagined a fascist police state and had created it.

In court it would be the Justice Department's job to goad the prisoners into confessing their guilt aloud. The issues were inflammatory and volatile and only public confession by the bombers would assuage public unease. Such a confession would be obtained.

It wasn't Lime's department to obtain it and he was thankful for that, but he recognized the Government's needs and knew that somehow the Government would find a lever to use against one or another of the prisoners.

He listened for ten minutes to the FBI agent's questions. Sandra Walberg said very little and none of it was in direct response to the questions. The kid lawyer in the corner yawned without bothering to cover his lips. Lime exchanged jaded glances with the FBI man and twisted past the table and went out.

In the lobby of the Executive Office Building he found his boss DeFord and Attorney General Ackert talking to reporters. Ackert was talking without saying much, with a politician's practice. He did it very well; his delivery was as impersonal as a print-out from a computer and he sounded like a cop testifying in court. It made him appear professional and competent; in fact he was both those things, but the act he was putting on at the moment was a conscious and deliberate role, therefore false. DeFord on the other hand was a fool but in public he had a way of giving the impression of informed crispness: he cloaked his incompetence in a fabric of secretiveness: *I know the answers of course but security prevents me from divulging them at this time.* He didn't exactly say it in so many words.

There was more questioning and Attorney General Ackert was saying tonelessly, "Naturally. They've been informed, in the presence of their attorneys, that they have every right to remain silent, that anything they say can and will be used against them, and that they have the right to counsel at all times during questioning."

Lime and DeFord broke away from the journalists and walked toward DeFord's sanctum.

DeFord, twisting the doorknob, said, "I'd like to see them hang that lawyer while they're at it."

They went inside and the woman at the desk gave them her equitably chilly smile. Lime followed on into DeFord's office.

DeFord sat down and tugged at the slack in his amply fleshed throat. "I, ah, had a telephone call from a gentleman named Walberg a few hours ago. The twins' father. He's just flown into Washington. I gather he's tried to see his children and nobody wants to talk to him."

Lime nodded. "He can't comprehend that his children could possibly have had anything to do with it. There must be some mistake—a misunderstanding or a frame-up. Or maybe under the influence of bad companions. But it can't be *their* fault."

"You already talked to him, then."

"No."

"Eh. Well. I'm sure that's the way I'd feel if I were in his place."

"I'm sure it is." Lime was thinking of Sandra Walberg. A determined up-yours resenter, that girl; how anyone could go on believing in her innocence——

"David, I'm sorry but I told the man you'd explain things to him."

"You did."

"He's, eh, waiting down in your office. I thought I ought to tell you. . . ." DeFord trailed off, turning an apologetic hand over, palm up.

"You damn fool." Lime's anger intensified the meaning of the drab words.

He walked out of the office and instead of slamming the door he pulled it shut with a quiet reproachful click.

Walberg had the lugubrious face of a professional mourner. His cheeks and hands were covered with freckles; his thin ginger hair was carefully combed across the baldness of his scalp. He appeared more doleful than indignant. Soft as a Number One pencil, Lime thought.

"Mr. Lime, I'm Chaim Walberg, I'm the fa——"

"I know who you are, Mr. Walberg."   •

"It's kind of you to see me."

"It wasn't my choice." Lime went around his desk, spun the chair, sat. "Specifically what do you want to ask me to do?"

Walberg inhaled deeply. If he'd had a hat he'd have been rotating it in his hands. "They won't let me see my children."

"I'm afraid they're the Government's children right now, Mr. Walberg. It's a security matter."

"Yes yes, I understand that. They don't want people leaking messages to or from the prisoners. They told me that. As if they think I'm in league with anarchists and assassins. In the name of God, Mr. Lime—I swear. . . ."

Walberg stopped to compose himself. Now he summoned dignity. "There has been an error, Mr. Lime. My children are not——"

"Mr. Walberg, I haven't the time to be your wailing wall."

It stung Walberg. "I was told you are a cold man but people think you a fair one. Evidently that was not correct."

Lime shook his head. "I'm only a faceless assistant to an assistant, Mr. Walberg. They shunted you onto me to get you out of their hair. There's nothing I can do for you. My job consists mainly of making out reports on the reports other people have made out. I'm not a cop, I'm not a prosecutor, I'm not a judge."

"You *are* the man who arrested my children, aren't you?"

"I'm responsible for the arrests, if that's what you wanted to hear."

"Then you can tell me why."

"You mean why I singled out your son and daughter?"

"Yes. What made you believe they were guilty of anything? Were they running? Because my children have had misunderstandings with officers, they're afraid of the police—you know how the young people are. But to run away from a uniform and a gun—is this proof that——?"

"You're jumping to conclusions, Mr. Walberg, but I'm not at liberty to divulge the Government's case. You'd have to see the Attorney General, but I doubt he'd tell you very much. I'm sorry."

"Are you old enough, Mr. Lime, to remember the days when you could tell good from evil?"

"I'm afraid I'm very busy, Mr. Walberg." Sorry, the number you have dialed is not a working number. Lime walked to the door and held it open.

Walberg stood. "I'm going to fight for them."

"Yes. I think you should."

"Where has morality gone, Mr. Lime?"

"We still eat meat, don't we."

"I don't understand you."

"I'm sorry, Mr. Walberg."

When Walberg was gone Lime emptied his In box. Intermittently for a half hour or so he thought of Walberg's stupefying naiveté: the twins had posted plenty of storm warnings, they hadn't rotted overnight, but the handwriting on the wall was always a message for someone else. Not *my* children.

Lime's son was eight years old this month, an Aquarius, and it was vaguely possible to hope Bill would be allowed to reach maturity alive and without finding it necessary to explode buildings and people. Until two years ago Lime had enjoyed fantasies about the things he would do with his son as he grew up; then there had been a point to it but now the boy lived in Denver with Anne and her new husband and Lime's visiting privileges were severely curtailed not only by court order but also by the distance to Denver.

He had been out just before Christmas. On the airplane he had dozed with his head against the window and at the airport the three of them had met him—Bill and Anne and the fool Dundee who hadn't known better than to tag along: a thin hearty Westerner who told the same jokes time and time again and manipulated fortunes in shale oil leases and evidently didn't trust Anne out of his sight with her ex. An awkward weekend, Anne forever smoothing down her skirt and avoiding everyone's eyes, Dundee bombastically fathering Bill and calling him "Shorty," both of them covertly eyeing Lime to make sure he was getting the point—that they had established a "real home here for the boy," that "He's much better now, David, with a full-time father."

Bill surrounded by ten thousand acres of grass and a herd of real cowponies had been singularly unimpressed by the toys Lime had bought at the last minute on his way to the airport. Last summer he had taken Bill camping and there had been rapport of a kind but this time in ankle-deep snow there was no place to take the boy except for an afternoon's ice skating and a Disney movie on East Colfax.

Sunday night at the airport he had pressed his cheek to the child's and rocked his head so that his whiskers scraped Bill; the boy had squirmed away and Anne's eyes had been filled with a glacial rebuke. She had presented her cheek for his ritual kiss with Dundee standing by, watching; she had smelled of cold cream and shampoo; and whispered savagely in his ear, "Keep it up, David, keep it up."

He was an unpleasant complication, she wanted him to stay away, but she wouldn't send the boy to him—Lime had to come to her if he wanted to see Bill. It was a way of keeping him on her leash. She was a possessive woman.

She had been a tall girl with cool hazel eyes and straight blonde hair, more comfortable than challenging; they had got married because there hadn't seemed any overpowering reason not to. But it had quickly got so each of them was bored with knowing what the other was going to say before he said it. In time that became the trouble with their marriage: they never talked about anything at all.

It became too much for both of them and finally she had walked out, walking heavily on her heels, leading the boy by the hand.

They had lived in one of those towns the existence of which was defined in terms of how many miles it was from Alexandria. He had kept the house six months and then moved to the city, a two-room walk-up.

Now the Executive Office Building was emptying and he did not want to return to the two-room walk-up. There was always Bev. But he went to the bar of the Army-Navy Club.

A vodka martini, very dry. Once, he had found comfort in bars, dim impersonal chambers where football and old movies provided conversational sustenance.

Lime had developed a passion for old movies: he could name character actors who had been dead for twenty years and all you needed was one fellow film buff to kill an evening with enjoyable trivia. "Eugene Pallette in *Mr. Deeds Goes to Town*." "No that was *Mr. Smith Goes to Washington*." "I thought that was Claude Rains." "It was. They were both in that one." Remember the beautiful cloaked melodrama of *Mask of Dimitrios*, Greenstreet and Lorre and was Claude Rains in that one too? He was in *Casablanca* with them but was he in *Dimitrios*? I don't know but it's running on one of the UHF late shows next week, I saw it in *TV Guide*. . . .

A slough of boredom. Halfhearted anger toward the rutting man and woman who had accidentally given him his ticket into the world. Too young, during the war, for anything but *Dave Dawson* novels and radio melodramas and sandlot baseball and junior rifleman badges. Too old, afterward, to join the concerned generation:

Lime had graduated from college without ever asking his room-mate's politics.

He had known too many bars. They had become too familiar. He left the club.

In the Fifties the Cold War had seemed real and he had enjoyed matching himself aganst the best the other side had to offer. *Are you old enough, Mr. Lime, to remember the days when you could tell good from evil?*

In those days American Intelligence was an infant modeled on the British system and things went on in a peculiarly arcane British fashion, as if nuclear superpowers could be treated in the same way as internecine Balkan intrigues of the Twenties. But gradually cyni-cism set in. Courage became suspect. It was fashionable to plead cowardice. If you chose to face danger for sheer thrill you were singled out as a case of masochistic guilt. No one was supposed to look for risks. Bravery became contemptible: if you did something dangerous you were expected to say you did it for the money or for a cause. Not because you *liked* it. To prove you were normal you had to boast you were chicken. They had effectively outlawed cour-age. Crime, and driving cars recklessly, had become just about the only outlets left.

Lime had an ungrammatical talent for picking up foreign tongues and they had used him in the field for fifteen years, mostly in North Africa but once for eighteen months in Finland. Gradually he had begun to detest dealing with his own kind—not only his opposite numbers on the other side but his allies as well. They were warped people playing a meaningless game and the computers had taken the thrill out of everything. What was the point of risking his life?

In the end Lime had used what little influence he had to post himself into an office where nothing was required of him, where sometimes he forgot what the business was all about.

He was a GS-11, he earned fourteen thousand dollars a year or at least collected it, he ran an office which investigated a thousand threats on the President's life every month and found all but three empty—an office in which lazy irresponsibility could masquerade as duty—and he had retirement to look forward to: a job as chief security officer for a corporation somewhere, with fate presiding over him like an expectant mortician.

It was all he deserved. When you reached the point where it was just a job you could switch off at five o'clock—when you no longer did it believing in it—you had been in it too long. You went through the old motions but it was like saying the same words over and over until they lost all meaning.

The evening gloom was chilly. He walked home, up the sooty row of turreted gingerbread Victorian houses, up the outside stair into his rooms. The steam radiators made a dense heat and the air was close—stale, as if it hadn't moved for a long time. The blown lamps had reduced the rooms to a grayish half-light and the demons of the place were on the prowl. Abruptly and uneasily he lifted the telephone and dialed.

"Hello?"

"Hi."

"*Caro mio*. How is it today?"

"Dreary," he said "Have you had dinner?"

"I'm afraid so."

Heavy silence clung to them. She said finally, "I tried to reach you but you didn't answer."

"I stopped in for a drink somewhere."

"You're not drunk."

"No."

"Well come over and I'll fix you something to eat."

"Not if you're feeling that way about it."

She said, "Don't be a fool David."

"I'm not the first and I won't be the last. I'm in good company."

"All right, you're a fool. But come over." Her voice underwent a thickening humid modulation that evoked his awareness of her sexuality: "Come on, David, I want you to."

Wondering which of them was the greater fool he went around to get his car. He wished he had thought better of calling her. He wanted to see her but last year there had been a tawdry affair with a banal woman from St. Louis and he didn't want to get embroiled that way again, not even with Bev; this time it was he who had nothing to offer.

But he drove out of the garage and let the avenue suck him into its flow. It took him north into the Palisades area—fashionable houses, pedigreed dogs, chic thin women and fat children.

Senators and Cabinet members lived around here and normally there would be two or three boiled-shirt dinner parties getting under way. Tonight there were none because of the bombing. But it would not be long before the parties resumed. Everyone would wear mourning black and armbands and everyone would be solemn

and judiciously angry, but the dinners would resume quickly because the Government still had to run and a great deal of its work
was done at these dinner gatherings.

He passed Dexter Ethridge's house. The windows were quietly
alight; the front window reflected the glow of a color TV within.
Lime was gratified to see the signs of normalcy—in a vague distant
way he had responsibility toward the Vice-President-elect, having
spoken the warning to him on the Capitol steps: it created a kinship,
an Oriental sense of obligation.

Bev's apartment building was an ultramodern tower of glass. She
made good money as the Speaker's adminstrative assistant; she
knew how to spend it tastefully. The front room was spacious—
off-white walls, Beri Rothschild sketches, solid furniture in solid
colors but uncluttered. Lime knocked, let himself in with his key,
threw his coat on a chair and called her name.

She didn't answer. He prowled the apartment; it was empty; he
went into the kitchen and mixed two drinks and was taking them
into the living room when Bev came in, dressed for the weather,
carrying a heavy brown grocery bag.

"Hi." She had a merry look. When he took the parcel she tipped
her face and he tasted her breath in his mouth.

He carried the groceries into the kitchen. Bev was pulling off her
gloves with little jerks, drawing her cloak off her shoulders, taking
off her scarf and shaking out her hair. It fell straight to her shoulders
and curled upward at the bottom.

She espied the drinks and took a long swallow before she came
into the kitchen, shoved him imperiously aside and started unload-
ing the paper bag. Lime rested his shoulder against the doorframe.
"Leftovers would have done."

"If I'd had any." She was on tiptoe putting something into the
refrigerator, the long calf muscles tensed, dress stretched tight
across ribs and breasts. When she turned and caught him watching
her like that she gave him a quick up-from-under look.

"Get out of here," she said, laughing at him, and he smacked her
rump and went back to the couch and picked up his drink.

She clicked and clanged furiously for several minutes; then she
appeared bearing place mats and silverware.

"I thought you ate."

"I'll have dessert. I'm in a sinful mood." She was setting the table.
"Wienerschnitzel with an egg on it—Holstein. All right?"

"Fine. Fine."

She came to the coffee table and bent down for him to light her cigarette: he looked down along the curve of her throat to the thrusting dusky separation of her breasts. She was watching him— smiling, eyes half closed, warm and lazy. She straightened up and blew smoke at the ceiling, took her drink to her mouth: ice clinked against her teeth. "Well then."

He closed his eyes slowly to slits and she took on a sort of surrealistic substance limned in red. When she moved toward the kitchen he closed his eyes and heard the click of the refrigerator door, the rattle of things.

"Come on, Rip Van Winkle."

He opened his eyes. The room was dim; she had extinguished the lights, she had two candles burning on the table. He grunted and heaved himself upright and she laughed at him with wild abandon; it disturbed him. She took his hand and guided him to the table. "It's Nineteen forty-seven Warner Brothers, but I just felt like it."

"The wine?"

"The setting, stupid. The wine's a Moreau."

"Chablis with veal?"

"Why not? I'm having sardines."

"Sardines for dessert."

"I told you I'm in a wild mood."

He tasted the veal. "Damn good."

"Of course. It has to be."

"You're dropping clues like size-twelve shoes. What am I supposed to be looking for?"

"Nothing, I'm just teasing you." She leaned forward with her wine in both hands. Soft warm glow against her eyes and skin. "What's happened to that wonderful *cojones* humor of yours? Remember when you filled out the GS transfer papers for DeFord —date of birth June 29, 1930; weight seven pounds two ounces; height twenty-one inches?"

"That was before I knew DeFord."

"What about those hundreds of introductory-subscription cards you filled out with DeFord's name and address? He must have started getting two hundred magazines and book-club books in the mail every week."

"I thought he needed to be better informed."

"You haven't done anything like that for a year."

"I suppose you get tired of it," he said.

"You're saying you outgrew it."

"I just got bored with it."

"You just got bored."

"All right." He pushed his plate away empty and reached for the wine to refill their glasses.

"At least you've got a good appetite." She lifted her glass in a gesture of toast that hadn't been used since Charles Boyer stopped playing romantic leads: eyes half-lidded, lips moist and parted. Suddenly she laughed. "I'm a little tight. Or high—I never got the distinction straight. I saw a movie on TV last night and I'll bet I can stump you. *The Great Sioux Uprising*. Do you know who wrote the screenplay?"

"For Christ's sake."

"It was a terrible movie. Whoever wrote it had the sense to use a pen name. The screenplay was written, it says in great big flaming red letters, by Fred C. Dobbs."

It took him two seconds and then he laughed. She looked hurt and petulant. Lime did a Humphrey Bogart snarl: "Liften, nobody putf nuffin over on Fred Fee Dobbf."

"I didn't think you'd get that one. I really didn't."

"Somebody really used Fred C. Dobbs for a pen name?"

"Scout's honor."

He laughed again. Dobbs was the Bogart character in *Treasure of the Sierra Madre*—the greedy one who would do *anything* for gold.

They took the dishes out to the sink. Lime trapped her against the counter. She gripped his tie and pulled his head down; her tongue was very hot. They left the candles burning, went into the bedroom; Lime sat down and began to unlace his shoes, watching her. Since she disdained underwear she was unclad before he was; she unbuttoned his shirt and pulled him by the hands to the bed. He made love to her slowly and knowingly.

They shared a cigarette. "*Ça va mieux?*"

"Abso-fucking-lutely."

"Say it with conviction, darling." She had a bright hard shiny-eyed look.

Lime inhaled the smoke fiercely; it made him dizzy. "Yeah," in a tone laced with anger.

"What's the matter now?"

"I don't know. It doesn't matter."

Her feet were tangled in the twisted sheets; she kicked free. "Just hang in there, man." She disappeared into the loo. Lime lay on his back, belly rising and falling with his breath, smoke hovering around him.

She came back and sat on the side of the bed and stroked his hair. He said, "I apologize."

"For what?"

"*Mein weltschmerz*, I guess. I don't mean to play Hamlet all the time."

"You're going through a bad patch, that's all. The bombing didn't help."

"You could say that. It didn't help anybody."

"Well what's the answer to it then?"

He shook his head back and forth on the pillow. "It's sheer innocence to believe there's an answer for every problem. There's no answer to this one short of eliminating all terrorists on suspicion."

"That's farfetched."

"Not really. It's standard procedure in most of the world. Here we still pretend totalitarian solutions are unacceptable, but we're learning." He smiled vaguely. "Revolution doesn't self-destruct automatically. You have to kill it."

"But you'd rather not have to."

"I committed something to memory a few years ago. A quote that's kind of revealing. Verbatim—'The earth is degenerating, there are signs that civilization is coming to an end. Bribery and corruption are rampant, violence is everywhere. Children no longer respect and obey their parents.'"

"A Russian bigwig?"

"Not even close. It's from an Assyrian tablet that's about five thousand years old."

She came into the bed and snuggled close with her fists together against his chest, one knee hooked over his waist. Her hip was mounded high, her hair spread on the pillow. "My darling Oblomov."

"All right."

"You're too cautious, David. You're a big tragic bear, but it's tragedy not from what you suffer but from what you don't feel."

"Then you shouldn't bother with me."

"You were born believing in things, but everything you were taught seems beside the point now."

"Yes Doctor," Lime murmured.

"Nothing really matters, is that right?"

"That does seem to be the problem, Doctor."

"That's my point," she said. "It matters to you that nothing matters. That's the point David—that's a beginning."

BOOK TWO

ABDUCTION

MONDAY,
JANUARY 10

10:15 A.M. Continental European Time The sky was weak lemon
in color and Perdido loomed above the hotel, powder snow blowing
off its peak in little gusty clouds. Eleven thousand feet of mountain
and nothing to do but ski. The lodge was huge with a heavy-handed
massiveness that failed to create the kind of rusticity it was evidently intended to provide. The Germans had built it just last year
—the Germans, who built everything in Spain. They had hacked a
road up the mountain and built Perdido Spa out of Krupp steel and
Hilton plastic, and endeavored to give it the quaint appearance of
logs. It was an abomination.

Liam McNeely stood outside the lodge on a wooden deck the size
of a football field, open to the sky. Ordinarily it would be crowded
with little tables occupied by lunching skiers but today there were
no tourists. Premier Perez-Blasco had shelled out of the Spanish
treasury enough to hire Perdido Spa for the duration of President-
elect Fairlie's skiing visit. The tables had been removed and Fairlie's Navy helicopter squatted there on its skids, motionless rotor
blades drooping.

Fairlie had originally planned to ski here but he had no interest
in skiing now—not after the bombing. Yet the Spanish plans were
not easily or quickly changeable. Fairlie was waiting here, resting,
en route.

Early this morning Torres, the Foreign Minister, had arrived
from Madrid in a black Seat limousine. As Fairlie's aide-de-camp
and chief factotum McNeely had met Torres's party at the car-park
steps and ushered them quickly into the banquet room which the
hotel had set aside for Fairlie's meetings.

Torres had with him his interpreter and two underlings and a squat brigand named Dominguez who turned out to be the director of the *Guardia Civil*. McNeely produced the aides and Meyer Rifkind, who was head of the Secret Service detail assigned to Fairlie, and they had all sat down in a little group near one side of the enormous empty room. Stiff and hesitant, as if they were the only people left from a crowded party that had broken up an hour ago.

But Torres was congenial and they had ironed out the schedule for Fairlie's visit to Madrid. Dominguez had done most of the groundwork; it remained mainly to coordinate Secret Service operations into the Spanish security arrangements.

These visits always required intricate and voluminous preparation. The precise time of arrival, the precise spot where the helicopter would land and be met by Perez-Blasco and the civil guardsmen, the motorcade route from helicopter to palace. Dominguez went over the maps for more than an hour with Meyer Rifkind. Here—a stubby finger jabbed the map—Perez-Blasco and Fairlie would make an "unscheduled" stop to pop out of the limousine and shake hands with members of the crowd. *Guardianos* were clearing the block in advance, screening every storefront and window and rooftop, posting themselves to enfilade the area.

Here, television cameras would be posted along the boulevard to cover the motorcade. There would be good camera shots of Fairlie and Perez-Blasco when they made a "spontaneous" stop to accept roasted chestnuts from a street vendor.

It was all contrivance, the game of personal diplomacy.

A *Guardiano* would drive the limousine and a United States Secret Service agent would sit beside him on the front seat. Two more, similarly paired, on the limousine's jump seats facing the dignitaries. *Guardianos* in their taut uniforms and hard tricorner hats would ride the running boards. Cars ahead and behind would carry security men.

At three-fifteen the motorcade would arrive at El Pardo palace; Fairlie and Perez-Blasco would dismount, the *Guardia* would form a flying wedge around them, they would enter the palace with Secret Service agents following in a fan.

There would be a midafternoon luncheon. Perez-Blasco and Fairlie would share the dais alone; was that acceptable to McNeely? Perez-Blasco would introduce the honored guest—here, a copy of the brief welcoming speech Perez-Blasco would deliver. Then Fairlie would make a brief address; was it possible for Torres to obtain a copy of that now? Then the dignitaries and reporters would be ushered elsewhere; Fairlie and the Spanish chief executive would retire with their aides for private discussions. . . .

On cue, Clifford Fairlie came down the wide stairs in his lounging jacket, the one with elbow patches, all smiles; shook hands warmly all around, sat down and chatted.

The protocols were observed and finally Torres was leaving. They all emerged from the hotel onto the deck and McNeely smiled vaguely at the chopper pilot when they walked past the helicopter toward the steps. The Secret Service men were scanning the corners, the shadows, the mountainside, even the sky; they were paid to do only one thing and they did it professionally.

Fairlie and Torres and the entourage descended to the pavement. The limousine drew up, *Guardianos* coming to attention. Later, trying to recall the exact sequence of events, McNeely had a great deal of difficulty sorting out the movements he had seen. The press car drove up behind Torres's limousine; the aides and guards got inside while Torres and Dominguez said goodbye—this after the usual nonstatements to the press pool: the discussions have been very useful, everything is going smoothly, we look forward to a frank exchange of views in Madrid. . . .

Several hotel employees had come along to the edge of the deck to watch. The chopper pilot and copilot were there, smoking cigarettes, looking at their watches, somewhat bored. Now Torres and his people were inside the stretched-out car. It was a vehicle designed for its times. Two-way radios, bulletproof glass, door locks that could be opened only from the inside. In the era of political kidnappings the technology of security was elaborate. A hard glass screen ascended from the top of the front seat and sealed itself shut with a click against the ceiling; Torres, leaning forward in his rear seat, waved and smiled and spoke through the open door before it chunked shut and the stately car slid quietly away down the mountain road.

The Navy pilots were wandering back to the chopper on the deck when McNeely and Fairlie reached the platform; McNeely later remembered that much. The pool of journalists was dispersing after unsuccessfully trying to pump the President-elect.

Fairlie was heading for the stairs inside the hotel, the Secret Service agents clustering around like sheepdogs. *No*, McNeely thought, *like barnacles*. That was going to try Fairlie's patience:

Fairlie liked room, he liked to spread out, he didn't like people being in his way. He was a man to whom occasions of solitude were important. *He's going to have to learn.*

McNeely stood on the deck near the helicopter. *What if,* he thought, and began to envisage a sniper with a high-powered rifle peering through a telescopic sight from one of the high timber patches. . . . Assassination was always so easy. If a man really intended to murder you there was only one way on earth to stop him: kill him first. And if you didn't know who he was, didn't even know of his existence—you had no chances at all.

Morbid thoughts. It was a place that gave rise to them: the mausoleum atmosphere of the huge empty hotel; the yellow-gray sky with sunlight hardly filtering through; the chill dry breeze, the immutable detachment of the mountain.

Later he wondered if he had been experiencing a premonition gone slightly awry: some sort of ESP, prescience, an unusual sensitivity to the portentousness of that day. He was never to give it very much credence; after all there was no sniper.

He turned toward the door, minding the chill, thinking about going into his room for an hour's work. But solitude was not McNeely's milieu; he worked best in the midst of noise and confusion. The great empty rooms would depress him and he would only fling himself outdoors again, and so he did not go inside at all.

Instead he engaged the two chopper pilots in small talk. They were Navy officers—easy to converse with; they had been chosen for their mannerliness and appearance as well as their aeronautical skill. McNeely himself had started building model airplanes at the age of nine and the fascination had never left him.

" . . . forty-five-foot rotor. Horsepower? Close to a thou, she'll cruise at one-thirty. We'll make Madrid easy this afternoon, hundred and thirty-five minutes, forty-five minutes' fuel to spare."

"Usually they use the Thirteen-Jay for this kind of thing, don't they?"

"Usually. But that's a smaller machine, it hasn't got the ceiling of this bird." Anderson spoke with proprietary pride.

The chopper was a Bell Iroquois, HU-1J, with VIP accommodations for six passengers in comfort; she had the Navy's blue paint job and stenciled Sixth Fleet markings. McNeely ignored the nibblings of his conscience while he killed nearly an hour chatting with Anderson and Cord about choppers and missions.

The two pilots were ten-year veterans whose seams and creases were not in their faces but in their worn leather flight jackets. They said "hep" for help and "thank" for think and they talked in a technological jargon that annihilated human communication; they had the kind of minds which McNeely despised in the collective sense—the Silent Sophomority, Muddle Americans—but they were good likable men and McNeely was not a man to let philosophical principle get in the way of human pleasures.

Guilt finally goaded him toward the papers in his room. He left the pilots on the deck drinking coffee out of thermoses.

He made the final cuts and changes in the speech Fairlie would deliver this afternoon and then he showered and changed into a gray Dunhill suit and walked along the mezzanine to Fairlie's room.

Fairlie was on the phone with Jeanette; he waved McNeely to a chair.

When Fairlie rang off McNeely said, "My God that's disgusting."

"What is?"

"All that billing and cooing at your age."

Fairlie just grinned. He was in the chair beside the phone in a Madras dressing gown; now, when he began to get out of his seat, he seemed to go on rising for an incredible length of time—a tall multijointed man unfolding himself hinge by hinge.

They talked while Fairlie dressed: about Perez-Blasco, about Brewster, about the Capitol bombing, about the U. S. Air Force bases at Torrejón and Saragossa and the Navy base at Rota.

Perez-Blasco was the Messiah, the Judas; the beloved savior of the people, the despot they were learning to despise; the liberal genius, the stupid tyrant; the incorruptible protector, the racketeering gangster; the Goddamned Commie, the Goddamned fascist. He might raise the nation's standard of living; he might spend everything on palaces and yachts and a numbered Swiss account. "You just don't know, do you. You just can't tell. I wish he'd been in office longer."

"He could say the same about you."

Fairlie laughed.

McNeely waited for him to knot his tie and then handed him the speech. "Nothing out of the ordinary. One of the standard variations on harmony and friendship."

"It'll do." Fairlie was looking it over carefully, committing blocks of it to memory so he wouldn't have to speak with downcast eyes glued to the page. He liked to eyeball his audiences. In this case it hardly mattered; the speech was short and it was in English and at least half the people in the room wouldn't understand one word in ten.

"Sometimes," McNeely said, "I wonder if we really need these damned bases at all. They're like sores on the earth, they keep festering."

"We're all developing a conscience, aren't we? This revulsion toward the idea of global power. We'd all like to return to simple times and unload these responsibilities."

"Maybe they're responsibilities only because we think they're responsibilities."

Fairlie shook his head. "I've been tempted that way but it doesn't hold water. It's an emotional isolationism—anti-militarism. We like to vilify our own military power but you know it's created a balance of sorts—not very satisfactory, I guess, but at least it's given us conditions where we've got some chance of success negotiating with the Chinese and the Russians. We're a stabilizing factor, we make our presence felt and I imagine it eases the crises a lot more often than it aggravates them."

McNeely replied with enough of a grunt to let Fairlie know he was listening, without interrupting Fairlie's train of thought.

"It's not the power that festers, I think. It's the inconsistency of its use. You can't be effective in foreign affairs without some philosophical direction—otherwise your actions are unpredictable and the other side is going to miscalculate all the time."

A knock: it was Rifkind at the door.

"Something wrong, Meyer?"

"A little trouble, sir. It looks like the helicopter broke down."

McNeely sat up. "What's wrong with it?"

"Cord explained it to me, sir, but I couldn't make much sense out of it."

McNeely poked an arm into his coat and strode out onto the deck. Cord and Anderson were on top of the fuselage poking into the engine. They had grease all over them.

"What's wrong?" McNeely was sharp; time was getting tight.

"Beats shit out of me," Anderson mumbled. Then he looked over his shoulder and recognized McNeely. "We started to warm her up, we were going to top up the tanks, and all of a sudden she starts letting go like a banshee. Man what a racket. Didn't you hear it?"

Fairlie's room was at the back; McNeely hadn't heard anything. He said, "What does it look like?"

"I ain't sure. Oil pressure checks out, but she's sounding like she got no oil in there. Everything scraping. Like sand in the works, you know?"

"You don't see anything?"

"No sir."

"How soon can we get another machine up here?"

The Sixth Fleet was off Barcelona—that was a little more than a hundred miles away. Anderson said, "About an hour, I expect."

"Get one."

He went back to the suite and reported to Fairlie. Rifkind trailed along and said, "Of course there's a possibility of sabotage, but right now we don't even know what's wrong with the machine."

"See what you can find out."

"Sir." Rifkind went.

Cord arrived to say they had radioed a request to the Fleet and a replacement chopper was on its way. Fairlie checked the time and said to Rifkind, "You'd better call Madrid."

"Yes sir. If they chug right along we oughtn't to be more than a half hour late."

Rifkind and Cord left; McNeely said, "It'll be good for a laugh in Madrid. Another case of marvelous American technology."

"Breakdowns happen. It doesn't matter." Fairlie slid the speech into his inside pocket.

The view through the window was spectacular: vast broken planes, an upheaval aglitter with snow, a craggy wilderness; Fairlie, McNeely thought, had a face that matched it.

Fairlie spoke abruptly. "Liam, you remember what Andy Bee said about a President running for a second term?"

"That it ties his hands? Yes, I remember. Why?" Andrew Bee, one-time Senator and now a Congressman from Los Angeles County, had been Fairlie's strongest opponent in the Republican presidential primaries and had only deferred to Fairlie at the last minute at Denver. A big lumberjack, Andrew Bee; and a thoughtful force in American politics.

Fairlie said, "I'm not going to run for a second term, Liam."

"What, tired of the job already?"

"Bee was right. It's got to hamstring a man. You can't be expected to be both President and politician."

"The hell. That's the object of the game."

"No. I'm going to announce it right up front. I want you to put it in the draft of the Inaugural Address."

"With all due respect I think you're nuts. Why commit yourself?"

"It frees my hand."

"To do what?"

Fairlie smiled a little with that unexpected self-deprecation that sometimes, out of context, warmed his face. As if reminding himself not to equate his person with the power of the office he was about to assume. "Andy Bee and I had some long talks. The man has some important ideas."

"I'm sure he does. Next time he runs for President maybe he'll get a chance to put them into practice."

"Why wait?"

"To do what?" McNeely asked again.

"Mainly to rip apart the committees."

"That's a pipe dream." McNeely knew all about that, it had been Andrew Bee's private crusade for years: the unraveling of the archaic committee system in Congress which governed not by majority but by seniority. The satrapies of Congress were tyrannies of old men, most of them rural, many of them corrupt, some of them stupid. No law could pass without the support of these old men, yet nothing in the Constitution required this shackling of Congress; for years the younger members, led by Andrew Bee, had called for reform.

"It's not a pipe dream, Liam."

"If you want to get legislation through, you've got to have committee support. If you attack the chairmen they'll eviscerate you."

"But if I'm not running for reelection what have I got left to lose?"

"All the rest of your programs."

"Not if I settle this one first," Fairlie said. "And don't forget those old boys have to be reelected too. I think they understand the sentiments of the times. Look at the kind of support Andy Bee has with the public. He's made his stand on the issue for years and the public's solidly behind him."

"You're the one they elected President. Not Andrew Bee."

Fairlie only smiled; he turned and reached for his coat. "Let's go outside, I want some air."

"Don't you realize how cold it is out there?"

"Oh come on, Liam."

McNeely went to the phone and summoned assistants to organize Fairlie's belongings and bring them along to the deck. When he put down the phone Fairlie was almost to the door. McNeely said, "You really want me to put that in the Inaugural Address?"

"Yes."

"Well what the hell. It won't do any harm. You can always change your mind later."

Fairlie laughed and went out. McNeely caught up on the mezzanine and joined the circle of Secret Service men moving along with him.

Cord was canted over the open engine compartment of the chopper; Anderson, on the deck, was rubbing his hands and exhaling steam. McNeely looked at his watch, buttoned his coat, turned the collar up around his ears. Fairlie was looking up the ski slope, squinting, smiling with visible wistfulness.

McNeely walked over to Anderson. "Find anything yet?"

"I sure can't figure it. Everything checks out good. But she's still screechin' ever time we start her up."

"Sounds like gasoline trouble. Did you check the fuel pump?"

"First thing." Anderson made a gesture of baffled disgust with his hands. "Anyhow they're flying a mechanic up passenger on the bird they sending in to replace this one. He'll figure it out."

McNeely nodded. A helicopter was not such a fragile mechanism as it appeared. True, it lacked the dubious visible stability of wings and for that reason a great many people distrusted it but the truth was a helicopter had a better glide chance than a jet plane: if a jet engine quit in midair the plane would hit the ground like a bomb; if a helicopter lost its engine in midair the rotors would freewheel and you could let yourself down dead-stick, and a chopper in distress required very little flat surface area to land on. McNeely respected the fluttery machines.

He patted the metal skin of the big chopper and turned away. Anderson was striding around the far corner of the hotel, possibly headed for one of the rear workshops to hunt up additional tools.

When the pilot went out of sight, McNeely drifted over to Fairlie's little circle, his mind going back to Fairlie's quietly explosive statement about not running for reelection. It was the kind of statement which, if made in heat, meant nothing; but made in deliberate calm, on the basis of obvious lengthy consideration, it meant everything. McNeely stood with the statement undigested, like a lump in his chest that wouldn't go up and wouldn't go down. Politics at the very top was the most fascinating game in the world and McNeely, a championship player, selfishly wanted it to go on: but Fairlie was dead right and intellectually McNeely could only accept that it was time to quit playing games.

A stray cool vesper brought the distant flut-flut-flut to his ears and he turned, searching the sky. Presently it appeared between the mountains, a dragonfly of a helicopter with its skinny tail in the air: a Bell Sioux 13R, the DC-3 of helicopters, the military workhorse since Korea.

McNeely hurried back to Cord, the copilot on the engine housing.

"Did you guys call for a Thirteen?" McNeely shouted to make himself heard.

Cord looked up. His head swiveled, he focused on the incoming chopper, he shook his head and cupped his hands around his mouth to shout down. "We only got two big ones aboard. Maybe the other one was out airborne someplace."

It could cause a problem. The Sioux was a reliable machine but it carried only three passengers. Two passengers if you insisted on having two pilots.

He threaded the cluster of Secret Service men and buttonholed Rifkind and moved him over next to Fairlie. "That's a three-passenger chopper," McNeely said.

The Navy helicopter descended slowly, expertly in the thin high-altitude air; it settled on its skids at the far end of the deck beyond the grounded Huey.

The group walked forward; Fairlie was saying, "It's all right, what the devil, I'll go along with Meyer and Liam. The rest of you can go down to Madrid by car."

Rifkind said, "No sir. You need more coverage than just me."

"Now come on, Meyer, there'll be an army of Spanish police to mother-hen me the minute we land."

"I'm sorry sir. You need at least two of us with you at all times. Preferably four."

"You're giving *me* orders, Meyer?"

"No sir. I've got my own orders, that's all."

They stopped just outside the circle of the slow circling rotors. The pilot was coming out to meet them, stooping low under the blades, a Negro lieutenant in Navy fatigues. He was fifteen pounds overweight, had a neat trimmed black-on-black moustache and slightly bulbous cheeks the roundness of which was accentuated by the wad of gum he was chewing. He emerged, stood up and rendered a crisp salute. "Mr. President-elect."

Cord had come over from the crippled chopper. "Where's the mechanic, Lieutenant?"

"Be along on the second machine," the black lieutenant said. He removed his fatigue cap to reveal a completely bald head; wiped his pate with his sleeve and replaced the cap.

McNeely turned. "What second machine?" He had the lieutenant's face on a bias toward the light and saw the ridge of a dark scar that ran along the jawline.

The lieutenant was chewing with the open-mouthed insouciance of the chronic gum addict. "Fleet didn't have a Huey to send, sir, so they ordered two Thirteens out. The other one will be along in a few minutes—they had to wait for the mechanic to get his gear. Captain said you'd probably want a second machine for the gentlemen from Secret Service."

Fairlie was nodding, reaching for his briefcase which was in one of the aides' hands. "That's fine then. Meyer, pick yourself a sideman and the three of us will ride this one. Liam, you come along in the second helicopter with two more of the boys. That soothe your feathers, Meyer?"

McNeely was swiveling on his heels. "Where's Anderson?"

Cord said, "He went to find a socket-wrench set."

"He's got a hell of a sense of timing."

Fairlie was moving toward the idling chopper. "Never mind, I'll ride with the lieutenant here."

"But Anderson knows the route—he knows the landing spot, the timing. . . ."

"Is he the only pilot alive? Good Lord, Liam, give the information to the lieutenant here and let's take off—we're more than half an hour late as it is."

Rifkind had turned toward the black lieutenant. "I'll have to look at some ID."

"Sure." The lieutenant took out his documentation and Rifkind flipped through it and handed it back. Rifkind was a man who stuck to the letter.

Cord had his two ratings over at the new chopper filling its fuel tanks from a gasoline cart. The lieutenant went over to the Huey with Cord and for a minute the two Navy officers stood plotting course on Cord's charts, after which the black lieutenant folded them and carried them forward, nodding briskly to Rifkind, popping a new stick of gum into his mouth.

They climbed aboard, Fairlie and Rifkind and Rifkind's number two, and the black lieutenant who strapped in and talked into a microphone and acknowledged responses from his earlappy headset. The ratings topped up and withdrew the gasoline hose and capped the tank, and Fairlie leaned forward to wave at McNeely.

McNeely gave him thumbs-up and the chopper lifted off a few feet, swung back and forth with a pendulant uncertainty, got its bite in the air and soared away. McNeely stood in the whipping downdraft and watched its graceful tilt and sway toward the mountain pass.

The chopper dwindled with distance. Haze absorbed it over the mountains.

Cord stood beside him, a scowl deepening, and with a sudden growl Cord turned and yelled at the ratings who were trundling the gasoline cart away across the ramp. "Hey. Go on back there and find out what the hell's holding up Lieutenant Anderson."

There was a brief discussion among the five remaining Secret Service agents as to which two would ride with McNeely. The reporters had already begun to scatter toward the parking lot and their hired cars.

Within a few minutes McNeely heard another helicopter and turned to watch it emerge from the haze, pushing between the peaks.

Cord was at McNeely's shoulder. "That's funny. I thought he said they couldn't get the other Huey."

And one of the ratings was running full tilt up the deck stairs, shouting. McNeely couldn't make out the words. The rating ran halfway forward across the deck and stopped, red-faced and out of breath, and made himself heard:

" . . . tenant Anderson back there—I think he's dead, sir!"

Certainty hit McNeely an abrupt physical blow. The Secret Service agents were running but McNeely grabbed Cord by the arm. "Never mind him. Get on your Goddamned radio and let me talk to Fleet. *Now!*"

1:43 P.M. Continental European Time   Fairlie had experienced it before but the sensation was always disturbing: the bubble canopy extended down to the level of your feet and it was as if there were nothing under you but air.

The chugging racket of the engine made conversation difficult; none of them spoke very much. The black lieutenant had a sure hand on the controls, one gloved fist on the cyclic stick and the other on a smaller lever at the left, both feet gently heel-and-toeing the pedals. The air was pungent with oil smoke and the spearmint aura of chewing gum.

He watched the jagged upheaval of the Pyrenees slide by beneath. Pamplona off somewhere to starboard—he thought of the running of the bulls; he had been there for it once, the Fiesta de San Fermin, summer of '64. His first and last bullfights: he had found he disliked them intensely. It wasn't the blood that angered him, it was the predestined formality of the slaughter. Spanish bullfighting and Spanish-style dancing had that in common: they had dehumanized these activities, shaped them into rote mannerisms—the bullfight and the flamenco dance had not changed in hundreds of years, they were static rituals, there wasn't a scintilla of creativity in them anymore. That worried him because it implied a key to the Spanish character which he did not comprehend. He was not altogether confident of his ability to persuade Perez-Blasco of anything at all, but he hoped the man was not a bullfight aficionado or a flamenco buff. Impossible to understand a nation of people who were satisfied with art forms that had ceased developing at the time of Velázquez and El Greco.

The helicopter swayed in gentle ballet through the valleys and passes of the mountains. A strange free feeling of dreamlike three-dimensional movement: he wondered if hallucinatory drugs had anything on this. He was a little frightened by the visual precariousness and that added something keen to his pleasure; he caught Rifkind's puzzled glance and realized he was grinning like a schoolboy.

A change in the engine's note; a tilt in the seat under him. He reached for a grip. The black lieutenant's expletive was loud and angry: "Oh Jesus."

Rifkind, straining forward, put his preternaturally white face over the lieutenant's shoulder. "What—what?"

"Not two in a row," the lieutenant growled.

"What is it?"

"Man we got trouble."

Fairlie's grip tightened on the handhold.

"Losing fuel. . . . She ain't pumping right." The lieutenant's gloved hands were all over the controls, his head shifting as his eyes whipped from point to point. "Man, I think we blew a hole in the gas line someplace."

Immediate childish anger exploded in Fairlie: what the devil was wrong with Navy's maintenance?

The black lieutenant was growling urgently into his radio micro-phone. Rifkind's eyes had gone round, the second agent was knead-ing his knuckles, Fairlie's fingers started to ache from squeezing the steel. The lieutenant flung the microphone down and jabbed at controls; the helicopter was changing its drumbeat, lurching a little now, and the lieutenant was talking to himself: "Oh man, oh man."

Rifkind let out an odd little sound—a cry, choked off; the lieuten-ant shot him a look. "Everybody take it easy now. Oh man, oh man. Listen, we ain't in no real danger, just take it easy. I got to find a place to set her down. Look for somewhere flat. Mr. President-elect, I do apologize sir, I do apologize."

"Just ease us down," Fairlie heard himself say in a voice filled with perjured calm.

Rifkind's eyes came around, grateful; Rifkind even essayed a smile. Fairlie found himself gripping Rifkind's shoulder in a gesture of reassurance.

Rifkind's number two was pointing past the lieutenant's shoulder. "That looks pretty flat."

The lieutenant glanced that way. "I don't know. You can't tell about those snowdrifts—sometimes nothing under them but air. . . . Wait now, look over there—that look like houses to you?"

Coils of thin mist hung in the passes; it was hard to make out detail; Rifkind said in a high-pitched tone, "It looks like a farm doesn't it?"

"Farm with a nice flat yard," the lieutenant said. "Aeah, we can make that easy." He sat back visibly relieved. The jaws resumed their rumination on the chewing gum. "All right, now you gentle-men snug up your seat belts real tight if you don't mind and sit back tight against your seats, hear? We'll set down like a fly on a soap bubble, I give you my promise. Everybody just take it easy. . . ." The lieutenant kept talking like a wrangler soothing an alarmed horse: after a while the words became repetitive and lost meaning but Fairlie found the steady sound of the lieutenant's voice had a good hypnotic effect and he thought, he's a good man.

It came up toward them slowly, three or four scrubby little build-ings in a flat white groin of the mountains. The helicopter's engine was sputtering noisily now but the black lieutenant did not act worried. The hands were steady on the controls; Fairlie felt the seat tip under him as the lieutenant put the chopper into a nose-high attitude and the descent slowed until Fairlie had no sensation of movement.

The farm had a look of disuse and long abandonment: paneless windows gaped, there were no livestock, the buildings looked ready to collapse. But as they closed slowly Fairlie began to see he had been mistaken. Smoke curled vaguely from the house chimney and the yard between house and barn had been chewed up by vehicles and foot tracks. Twin ribbons of tire tracks followed a thin corkscrew road away into the canyons below.

The lieutenant set the chopper down so gently Fairlie hardly felt the bump.

He heard a gusty exhalation and realized it had been Rifkind. Rifkind's number two was scanning the buildings and he had a gun in his fist and Fairlie said mildly, "Put that thing down out of sight, please."

The lieutenant was talking into his microphone, reading coordinates off his chart into the radio: "Fox zero-niner, about the middle of the northwest quadrant. It's a little old farm, you can see the buildings from quite a ways up, you ought to find us easy. Repeat, coordinates Fox zero-niner, center of northwest quadrant. Over. . . ."

Rifkind was scraping a palm down across his face and the number two was baleful: "They should've come out to have a look at us by now."

"Well maybe they think we're revenooers." The black lieutenant had an engaging grin.

"That's not all joke," Rifkind muttered. "Basque country—they do a lot of smuggling up here. Back and forth over the French frontier. These hills are full of Basque nationalists who fought Franco in the thirties and never got over it."

The rotors finally were coming to rest—whup-whup-whup. The lieutenant said, "Most likely nobody's home. But I'll have a look. Everybody sit tight."

The lieutenant pushed his door open and stepped down. Rifkind and his number two were watching the farmhouse with taut squints and Fairlie leaned forward for a better view.

The lieutenant was standing on the snow beside the open door. He had stripped his gloves off and was sizing up the farmhouse, in no hurry to move in; he used his hands to light a cigarette and then he turned a slow full circle to scrutinize the yard. Fairlie could not follow his glance beyond the periphery to the left; the helicopter was blind to the rear.

The lieutenant completed his turn. Then coolly as if there were nothing remarkable about it he snapped his cigarette into Meyer Rifkind's face.

Fairlie had no time to absorb it. Men appeared from the blind rear of the chopper—the door was opening on the right side, the lieutenant was jabbing the bunched rigid fingers of his hand into Rifkind's diaphragm; Rifkind folded up in his seat and sucked for breath, clawing for his service revolver; the abruptness of it electrified the skin of Fairlie's spine, he began to twist in his seat, and someone to his right fired a shot.

The number two's head snapped to one side: magically as if by stop-motion photography a dark disk appeared above his eyebrow, rimmed at the bottom by droplets of crimson froth. The lieutenant was hauling Rifkind out of the helicopter. A hand reached in past the number two, toward Fairlie; he saw it in the corner of his vision. There was another gunshot—Rifkind's hand went out to break the fall but by the time his body had fallen that far it was dead and the arm was crushed underneath.

Fairlie had just a glimpse of the gas pistol before he passed out.

10:20 A.M. EST   Bill Satterthwaite carried in his pocket the genuine symbol of status in Washington: a radio-activated beeper which uttered sounds when the White House wanted him.

It was mostly a source of sophisticated amusement. Washington hostesses joked about it ("My dear, when Bill's beeper goes off in the middle of my hors d'oeuvres I never know whether to continue the dinner or rush everyone into the basement in case it's World War Three"). The thing angered his wife, fascinated his sons, baffled the diplomats who came from countries where nothing ever required unseemly hurry.

Satterthwaite was one of the handful who hadn't been searched on entering the courtroom and that was a symbol too.

The courtroom was jammed. Reporters and sketch artists filled the seats. Satterthwaite sat near the side of the room, polishing his glasses, prepared to be bored.

This was only the arraignment. The Federal Grand Jury had taken a week to word its indictments because no one could afford loopholes.

It was the Government's serve. At precisely ten o'clock the District Judge had entered the courtroom and the defendants had refused to rise. Judge Irwin's lips had compressed; he had adjusted his robes and delivered an address from the bench on the subject of contempt of court, at the end of which he cautioned the defendants that if they attempted to disrupt the proceedings he would order them bound and gagged.

No one took it for overreaction. The trial of the Washington Seven gave every indication of turning into a spectacle. Philip Harding and his clients knew they had no hope of avoiding conviction; the only hope was to overturn it on appeal. If the court could be baited into losing its temper it might lay the basis for future appeals or the declaration of a mistrial. And since the defendants sought the overthrow of the system which the court represented they had no reason to obey its rules of decorum and etiquette; they meant to defy and provoke at every opportunity.

The Government's every ball had to clear the net and land inside the service court. There was not much doubt there would be basis for sufficient appeals to carry the case to the Supreme Court, but the Attorney General had to make certain the Supreme Court had no grounds to reverse the convictions.

The reading of the indictments was a rote formality; Ackert's presence was an indication of the President's personal involvement in the case, as was Satterthwaite's. Brewster had said, "Just show yourself. Let the reporters see you."

In the seats around him Satterthwaite counted four Senators and six Representatives—members of both parties, well-known figures. Congressman Molnar from California, who stood about four goose-steps to the right of Hitler; Congressman Jethro, the black socialist from Harlem; Senator Alan Forrester from Arizona, who stood plumb in the political center. The President's intent was to demonstrate the solidarity of the Government and it was interesting that the angriest of these spectators was the Leftist Jethro because in his estimation the bombers had set back his cause by ten years.

To Satterthwaite causes and ideologies were tiresome things. He saw history in terms of the theory of random games. The course of events was determined not by mass movements or ecopolitical struggles but by royal whims and feminine intrigues and the accidents of personalities and coincidences. Those in power had the responsibility for judging odds, estimating resources, placing the right bets on the right numbers; the long-term goal was to win more than you lost and the method was to study each turn of the wheel as an individual case. "Long-term policy" was a meaningless phrase because you could never predict when you might encounter an opponent's surprise gambit, a new Hitler, a new Gandhi. You did your best with what chips you had.

The Attorney General's voice droned on, the monotone of a man reading aloud from documents designed more to be printed than spoken. The defendants were skirting the boundaries of contempt: yawning, playing ticktacktoe, scratching themselves, laughing intermittently. Robert Walberg was flipping a coin continuously in an obvious effort to make a point about the trial and Establishment justice. Philip Harding with his thumbs hooked in the armholes of his vest grinned obscenely at Ackert throughout the reading of the indictments.

Ackert reached his summation and paused for breath and that was when Satterthwaite's electronic device began beeping.

The thing always alarmed him; this time it gave him a grateful sense of reprieve as well. He climbed across six knees and walked quickly up the aisle.

A guard held the door for him and Satterthwaite stopped to ask the location of the nearest telephone.

"Court clerk's office, sir."

He followed the direction of the pointing finger and entered an office occupied by several women behind desks. Satterthwaite spoke a few words; one of the women turned a telephone toward him.

The President's secretary was unusually crisp; she sounded distressed. "The President wants you immediately—we've sent a car for you."

So it was more than a trivial flap. He strode toward the street.

The EPS squadrol was just drawing in at the curb, the seven lights on its rooftop flashing red and amber. The driver had the back door open for Satterthwaite when he reached the foot of the steps, and as soon as he was inside the siren climbed painfully against his eardrums. The cruiser surged along the boulevards, slowing for the red lights, dodging lanes, and he felt the speed against his kidneys.

In the outer office the President's secretary told him, "They're in the Lincoln Sitting Room," and he went there, striding along on his short legs with a growing sense of urgency.

The President was on his feet pacing; he acknowledged Satterthwaite with a palm-out gesture that stopped Satterthwaite just inside the door. Satterthwaite quickly catalogued the half dozen men in the room: B. L. Hoyt, Director of the Secret Service; Treasury

Secretary Chaney; the directors of the FBI and the Central Intelligence Agency and the National Security Agency; and Secretary of State John Urquhart.

The President came forward speaking over his shoulder with his favorite executive mannerism, the disguised order in the form of a question: "Now shouldn't you boys get moving?" He came right by Satterthwaite and touched his elbow as he passed through the doorway; he took B. L. Hoyt in tow and the three of them tramped across the carpet. The President's cigar left a wake of ash and smoke through which the Secret Service agents traveled efficiently; one of them held the door and the three men passed into the President's office.

Brewster walked around behind the Lincoln desk and sat, a bit vague against the light that spilled in through the three windows behind him. Satterthwaite, making his guess from the selection of men who had been in conference with the President, said flatly, "Something's happened to Cliff Fairlie."

The President's twang was emotional and pained. "He's been kidnapped."

B. L. Hoyt had his finger on the large globe behind the flagstaff. "In the Pyrenees."

"For Christ's sake," Satterthwaite breathed. There followed the President's hard grunt. Satterthwaite's consciousness receded defensively: he could absorb only fragments of the President's story: ". . . on the way to Madrid to nail down the bases with Perez-Blasco. . . . was McNeely who tumbled to it first. . . . phony Navy helicopter . . . pilot's dead . . . a mountain called Perdido about seventy-five miles west of Andorra."

The President tapped his palm against the desk top gently and his ring clacked against the wood. Satterthwaite came to. "He was taken alive?"

"Apparently." That was B. L. Hoyt, very dry. "At least we have no evidence to the contrary."

"Do we know why?"

Howard Brewster said, "We don't know who and we don't know why." He removed the cigar from his mouth. He had nearly bitten it in two. "Goddamn it."

Satterthwaite had a little trouble with his knees; he found his way to a chair. "Sweet Jesus."

"We got word about two hours ago. I've put the machinery in motion, we're using every plane and helicopter and pair of eyes we've got in the Med. Madrid's cooperating, naturally."

. Satterthwaite plucked the handkerchief from his pocket, took off his glasses and wiped them. "I'm sorry, Mr. President. I feel stunned —it takes getting used to."

The President said, "I know," and spoke into a telephone: "Have you got McNeely yet? . . . Buzz me the minute he's on." He dropped the receiver on its cradle. "McNeely's all right. The minute he discovered what was going on he sealed off the exit road up there and restricted the telephone switchboard to official calls—he's got the reporters bottled up in there, he's giving it out that Fairlie's got a head cold, some temporary indisposition." Brewster smiled briefly. "McNeely's a country slicker just like me." He tapped the ash off the end of his cigar. "We want to keep it in the family for a few hours. Maybe we can get Fairlie back before it gets out."

"It doesn't sound too hopeful," Satterthwaite said.

"No, I reckon it doesn't."

Satterthwaite pulled his head around toward B. L. Hoyt. "On general principle I suppose you'd better intensify the guard on the Vice-President-elect."

"Already done. We've got a crowd around Ethridge a fly couldn't get through." Hoyt was a gaunt cadaver with a pulmonary pallor, the shrunken pattern of his skull clearly visible; but his china-blue eyes were bitter-bright.

Satterthwaite waited, attentive. He saw the President's eyebrows contract. "Bill, suppose they hide Fairlie somewhere. Suppose this thing drags out more than a few hours—suppose it turns into days, weeks."

"Don't we have to wait and see what it's all about, Mr. President?"

"Oh I expect we'll hear from them. Some sort of ransom demands. We'll deal with that when we come to it. But in the meantime we're obliged to hunt for them. Now that puts us in a mess, Bill. We're just not organized for this kind of operation. The jurisdictions aren't laid out, there's no chain of command, no real communications. Technically I suppose it's Madrid's ball but we're not about to let them carry it. State's in touch with Paris right now and if this lasts more than a few hours I guess we'll have to bring in some others—the Portuguese, Rome, maybe the North African countries. But in the meantime we've got Navy and CIA and NSA and Air Force falling all over each other, reporting each other's helicopters every ten minutes. All these Goddamn bureaucracies and no coordination at all."

"Then let's set up a center. Put somebody in charge."

"Uh-huh." The President removed the cigar from his mouth and blew smoke at its ash. "Hoyt here recommended you for that job."

"Me?" He glanced at Hoyt in surprise.

Hoyt's thin nostrils dilated. "Technically it's my bailiwick, protecting Fairlie. But overseas the Secret Service hasn't got a pot to piss in. We could turn it over to the Navy or one of the intelligence agencies, but it seems to me that would be inviting a lot of interservice bickering we haven't got time for. Put an admiral in charge and you'd have all the CIA types resenting it. Put the CIA in charge and the Navy would resist taking orders from them. We need somebody who's neutral—somebody up high enough to command respect."

The President said, "You're Cabinet rank, Bill, and you're neither military nor security-intelligence."

"But what qualifications have I got?"

"Brains," the President grunted, and sank the cigar in his mouth.

"It's not good politics," Satterthwaite said. "If anything goes wrong we'll all get roasted because we didn't have a professional in charge."

"The secret of administration," the President said, "is to know how to pick good men. You'll have your pick of every professional we've got."

Hoyt said, "You've already got a base of communications through the Security Council. We'll arrange to have all reports sent there. It'll be up to you to coordinate them. You'll get all the help you need."

"Don't argue the point," the President said, "we haven't got time."

"All right, Mr. President."

"Fine. Now when McNeely calls I want you on the extension. He's on top of things over there. In the meantime while we're waiting you can get some of the details from Hoyt." Brewster ashed his cigar in the glass tray, swiveled his chair to put a shoulder to them, and began to speak into a phone.

Hoyt came around the Presidential flag and took a stance in front of Satterthwaite on the seal of the United States that was woven into the carpet. He talked in a clipped monotone and he was good at it; Satterthwaite quickly began to form a picture of what had happened at Perdido.

It had been carefully timed and organized; they weren't amateurs. Someone at the hotel had sugared the helicopter's fuel tanks and poured finely ground glass into the engine lubricants. The same saboteur, it was assumed, had waited his opportunity to get Navy pilot Anderson alone and had killed him.

The sabotage had been committed at the last minute—probably while everyone's attention was distracted by the departure of the Spanish minister's car. The timing had been well planned, for it left insufficient time for Fairlie to travel to Madrid by car. So the Fairlie party had summoned a replacement helicopter from Sixth Fleet and the kidnappers had monitored those messages; the kidnappers had appeared ten minutes ahead of the real Sixth Fleet helicopter and in Anderson's absence the kidnappers' pilot had been employed. All of it obviously planned to every detail. There was only one clue of any significance. "The phony Navy chopper pilot was black, and he was either native American or a damned good imitation of one."

"That's something to start with, at any rate."

"We've already got Sixth Fleet checking. The FBI and the other agencies are running through their R & I files for black helicopter pilots."

The President was off the phone. "That probably brings you as up to date as any of us. Any ideas?"

"One, for a start. I'll need the best people I can get."

"Obviously."

He turned to Hoyt. "I'll want your man Lime."

"I'll see what I can do."

"Don't ask him. Order him."

Hoyt nodded. "I'd better get on my horse, then. Mr. President?"

Brewster waved him out.

When the door closed behind Hoyt the President said, "His head's going to roll of course. I guess he knows that."

"He's not stupid." The Secret Service had committed two grave blunders in a space of ten days and the public would demand a villain; Hoyt would be It and Hoyt would have to accept the blame publicly. In this room during the past twenty minutes Hoyt had known all that perfectly well but had shown no sign of it.

The President said, "We've got to get Fairlie back. I don't care how many feathers we have to ruffle on our good neighbors overseas. We're going to get him back if it takes the Marines." He was growling around a fresh cigar. "It's going to start a hell of a whipsaw in this country, Bill."

"Sir?"

"We'll be split right down the middle between the flag wavers and the libertarians."

"I suppose you're right. But we've hardly got time right now for theoretical arguments on the dilemma of protecting officials without limiting public access to them."

"At any rate we've got Fairlie to worry about first. I want you to ride them hard, Bill, make sure every agency in Warshington's on top of this thing. I want the rivalries dropped, I want absolute cooperation right down——"

The telephone buzzed.

"——the line. Yes Margaret? . . . Fine. About damn time. Put him on." The President glanced up at him. "It's McNeely. Get on that other phone, will you?"

5:10 P.M. Continental European Time   Fairlie was in some sort of vehicle. He could feel the crunch and jounce of its movement; there was the slight stench of gasoline exhaust.

He had come awake once before. Inside a room, the light very dim; someone had put a needle in his arm and he had gone out again.

He remembered it now: the helicopter, the shootings, the glimpse of the gas pistol.

His head was sluggish with drug. He blinked; there was no constriction on his eyelids but he could see nothing. A sense of blindness, and panic; he tried to move his hands but they were manacled or tied; tried to sit up and banged his forehead into something sickeningly soft. The world lurched crazily and tipped him half up on one shoulder but his head struck something soft again, and he was rolled onto his back again by a shift in the vehicle's attitude.

He tried to cry out but it was only a hoarse grunt against the wadding taped into his mouth.

Rising panic: he began to thrash in the darkness but all his limbs were tied and he began to drown, choking on the gag. When he understood that, he stopped straining: he made his muscles limp and focused on getting his breath. The wads in his mouth kept tickling the back of his tongue: he felt nauseous and wanted to cough but it was impossible to draw deep breath for a cough, the wadding strangled him; he had to force himself to breathe with shallow regularity, it was the only way to get air. In the blackness his eyes were wide and round.

The vehicle's gears gnashed. It lurched forward; he had a feeling it was going up a hill, rounding a sharp curve. Perhaps he was in the trunk of a car—but no; he was stretched out full length on his back and he knew of no car with a trunk that large. The floor of a station wagon perhaps? A truck?

He was contained within a very constricted space: something the size and proportion of his own body. He could define its limits with his elbows, his forehead, his toes. All of it was heavily padded with a soft cloth-covered substance. A padded cell, he thought, I always knew it would come to this. He was not ready to laugh but the thought eased his panic.

They had padded the enclosure to keep him from banging on it with his elbows and feet. They had removed every possibility of his making his presence known to anyone. Professionally done, he thought.

Now he asked a silent question and realized it was the question people were supposed to ask when they regained consciousness:

Where am I?

And what time was it? What day?

Questions to which there were no answers.

It was a land vehicle. Not a plane, not a boat; the motion was that of something on wheels, moving on bad roads, not at a very great rate of speed.

How long had he been moving? There was no way to know what country he was in—what continent.

The thought of time—the indefinite bubble of time in which he lay—made him sharply aware of hunger and thirst.

They would be looking for him. The whole world would be looking. He approached the thought with a certain detachment.

The blackness was absolute. He was totally enclosed. It made him acutely afraid: the lack of light suggested lack of air; the size of the enclosure was claustrophobic; how soon would he exhaust the oxygen? He breathed cautiously but the air did not seem preternaturally stale; there was only the faint stink of exhaust fumes.

Gently. Exhaust fumes: they weren't being generated inside his padded enclosure. They came in the air, from outside. There was an air vent somewhere.

The floor lurched over a bad bump, a chuckhole. Then there was the sensation of rumbling unevenness: a flat tire? But it kept moving, it didn't slow down. He was puzzled until the answer struck him: cobblestones.

He lay motionless, feeling cramped, his muscles knotting painfully even though he was stretched out full length. It was a physical manifestation of fear and he fought it by relaxing himself a muscle at a time.

The motion stopped.

His body tensed again, panic renewed: the vehicle had stopped, it was a new terror to reckon with.

His prison swayed under him and he thought it must be the weight of someone climbing into the vehicle. Then he felt himself in motion. Scraping, banging; he was rolled from side to side, there was one particularly sharp blow, and he felt the case around him sway unevenly.

They were carrying him somewhere. Clumsily, banging into things. He felt it when they set him down.

A squeak, and a quiet rhythmic scraping. For a moment he had a horrid gothic illusion of rats gnawing at his enclosure. Incredible what the mind could conjure in total darkness.

There was light. A thin ribbon at first, a crack that opened under the edge of the top of his enclosure. It was very faint but it made him blink. By its shadows he could see that the enclosure around him was lined with something glossy and quilted.

A coffin. They had him in a coffin.

The squeaking and scraping: they were unscrewing the lid.

Something out of a bad horror movie, he thought; it was unthinkable and it was silly. Laughter and fright chased each other through his veins. He felt the rapid heavy thudding of his pulsebeat.

Three of them lifted the lid away. He could make out their silhouettes, that was all; the light blinded him. He tried to sit up. A voice, curiously strained and muffled, spoke calmly: "Take it easy Fairlie."

Two of them lifted him to a sitting position. He went dizzy, felt his eyes roll up; he had to knot his stomach muscles and fight for consciousness. The same voice spoke again, but not to him: "Take the gag out, give him something to drink." Then it came closer: "Fairlie can you hear me? Nod your head."

He lifted his head and let it drop. The effort seemed to cost too much.

"All right, listen to me now. Where we are you could yell your head off and nobody but us would hear you. But I don't want any yelling. Understand? You don't speak unless you're spoken to. Otherwise we have to hurt you."

He squinted, trying to see. Shapes swam in the light, slowly becoming distinct, taking on form and color. A garage, he saw it was. Big enough for three or four cars. There were two: a small European coupe and a black hearse.

A hearse.

It was an old hearse, perhaps a Citroen; the tires looked bad. That was what they had transported him in. Steam rose from the hoods of both cars.

He saw the black lieutenant, in chauffeur's uniform now. Still chewing gum.

There were four others, he saw. All of them in Arab robes, their faces hidden behind Bedouin headgear, the wraparounds up to their noses. One of them came forward and began to peel the surgical tape from Fairlie's face. It stung like razor cuts as it ripped away.

The hands were small and deft: a woman, he saw, and it surprised him.

She did not speak. The black lieutenant brought a tin cup of water. "Small sips, man. Swallow easy." And tipped the cup to Fairlie's lips.

He sucked greedily. The water had a brassy taste, or perhaps that was only the fear on his tongue.

The other spoke, the one who had spoken the first time. A disguised voice, he could hear that immediately, but something Slavic about it. "Free his feet and sit him over here." He was beyond the light and Fairlie couldn't see him clearly.

The woman undid the wire around his ankles. "His hands too?"

"Not for the moment."

The woman and the black lieutenant lifted him to his feet. He was standing in the open coffin on the floor of the garage. They held him, each by one elbow. The blood rushed from his head and he almost passed out again; he fought it because it seemed essential to fight something.

It was as if his feet had gone to sleep. He had no muscular control of his ankles. The woman said, "Step over. Careful." She affected a Germanic sort of accent but it didn't sound real. Nonetheless, he thought, it served to disguise her real voice well enough. He could see nothing of her but her hands and eyes and cheekbones. She was perhaps eight inches shorter than Fairlie.

They walked him across the room slowly. He felt like a loosely strung puppet. His feet flapped uncontrollably at every step.

There was a workbench against the rear wall. Tools and scrap had been swept to the side. Packing crates were drawn up in the guise of chairs and the Slavic one said, "Sit."

His elbows were free but his hands were wired together; he sat forward with his elbows on the bench and his hands in front of his face, peering past his knuckles. It was very important to know where he was—vitally important, though he didn't think why. He tried to make out the license plates of the two cars but they had been smeared deliberately with mud.

The Slav said, "You can speak, can't you?"

He didn't know; he hadn't tried. He opened his mouth and uttered an unrecognizable croak.

"Come on now, you haven't been gagged that long."

"*How* long?" It came out better but it was still as if his tongue were shot full of novocaine.

"A few hours, that's all. It's only about sunset."

The same day, then. Monday, January the tenth.

A rusty work lamp on the workbench, the kind with a hook, and a cage over the bulb. The Slav picked it up, switched it on. "Abdul."

The black lieutenant: "Yeah?"

"Lights out."

Abdul, which clearly was not his name, went to a wall switch. The ceiling lights went out; only the work lamp in the Slav's fist burned. The Slav trained it on Fairlie.

"Do you know your name?"

"Don't be ridiculous."

"What's your name?"

"What is this?"

"What is your name please."

The light blinded him to the rest of the room. He closed his eyes, twisted his head, squinted into the dark corners.

"Name."

"Clifford Fairlie."

"Very good. You may call me Sélim."

Sélim and Abdul, then. It was very unconvincing; perhaps it was intended to be.

"Abdul. The recorder."

Footsteps on concrete. After a moment Sélim the Slav spoke at him again from the darkness. "Fairlie talk to me."

"What about?"

"You must have questions."

Names, Fairlie thought. Sélim and Abdul. They withheld their real names, they disguised their voices, they hid their faces from him. Conclusion: it was important he not discover who they were. Suddenly he felt a clawing surge of hope. They would not have gone to these lengths if they meant to kill him.

But he knew Abdul's black face.

But half a dozen people back at Perdido knew it too. They wouldn't kill Fairlie for that.

Uncertain all the same, he felt very cold.

Sélim said, "Perhaps you'd like to know what this is all about."

"I assume I've been kidnapped."

"Very good."

"For what purpose?"

"What purpose would you think?"

"I suppose I'm being held for ransom, is that it?"

"In a way."

"In what way?"

"I'm sure you recognize the facts of life, Fairlie. Political kidnapping is a highly effective weapon in the wars of liberation that are being waged against the forces of the imperialist regimes."

"I doubt it. This won't win your cause many friends." Fairlie rubbed his mouth against the back of his hand. "May I have something to eat?"

"Certainly. Lady."

Fairlie heard the girl moving around in the dimness.

"Are we still in Spain?"

"Does it matter?"

"I suppose it doesn't."

Abdul the black lieutenant inserted himself briefly between Fairlie and the light. He placed an object on the workbench at Sélim's hand. It was a small tape recorder.

Sélim did not touch it. Fairlie looked at the tape spools. They were not turning; the machine was not switched on.

Sélim said, "You were saying."

"What is it you want of me?"

"Only a little painless cooperation. It won't cost you anything."

"Speaking in whose terms?"

"Don't be alarmed. What do you think we want of you?"

The girl—she was a girl or a young woman by her hands and eyes

—brought him food on a scrap of cloth. A small crusty loaf split into a sandwich, chunks of cold boiled ham.

Sélim reached for Fairlie's hands. Fairlie drew back sharply; the Slav only clucked in his throat, reached out again and began to untwist the wires around Fairlie's wrists.

When his hands were free Fairlie rubbed his welted wrists vigorously. "Is this all of you? This little band?"

"We're everywhere, Fairlie. The united peoples of the world."

"I suppose to you self-styled revolutionaries your cause makes good sense. To me it's gibberish. But I'm sure you didn't drag me here just to engage in silly dialectics."

"Perhaps that's exactly what we have done."

"Nonsense."

"You refuse to listen to us unless we force you to."

"I listen to everyone. It doesn't oblige me to agree with everything I hear."

The bread and ham had no flavor; he ate mechanically.

Sélim said, "How long do you suppose we've been sitting here talking?"

"Why?"

"Humor me. Answer the question."

"Five minutes I suppose. Ten minutes. I don't know."

"I imagine it's long enough for you to have cleared your voice. It sounds natural enough to me." Sélim reached for the tape recorder, pushed it forward into the light. He did not switch it on yet. "Now we have a simple request. I have a short speech written out. You ought to find that familiar—you people always read speeches written for you by someone else, don't you."

Fairlie refused to be drawn; fear chugged in his stomach and he was not prepared to debate questions of that nature.

"We'd like you to deliver this little speech for us in your own voice. Into the tape recorder."

Fairlie only continued to eat.

Sélim was very patient, very mild. "You see we believe the greatest difficulty faced by the peoples of the world is that those in power simply do not listen—or at best, listen only to what they want to hear."

"You've got a captive audience," Fairlie said. "If it pleases you to bombard me with mindless invective I can't stop you. But I can't see how you expect it to do you any good."

"On the contrary. We expect you to help us re-educate the world."

"Thank you but I rarely send my brain out to be laundered."

"An admirable sense of humor. You're a brave man."

Sélim reached inside his robes, drew out a folded paper, pushed it into the light. Fairlie picked it up. It had been typewritten, single spaced.

"You'll read it exactly as written, with no editorial revisions and no imaginative asides."

Fairlie read it. His mouth pinched into tight compression; he breathed deep through his nose. "I see."

"Yes, quite."

"And after I've obeyed your instructions?"

"We don't intend to kill you."

"Is that a fact."

"Fairlie you're no use to us dead. I realize I can't prove this to you. It's true, however."

"You don't honestly think Washington will agree to these demands?"

"Why not? It's a very cheap price to pay for your safe return." Sélim leaned forward. "Put yourself in Brewster's position. You'd do it. So will he. Come now, Fairlie, you're wasting our time. You can readily understand that right now for us time is blood."

Fairlie glanced at the last line of the typewritten speech. " 'Instructions will follow.' What instructions? You can't bring this off, you know that."

"We've brought it off up to now, haven't we Fairlie." The voice was filled with quiet arrogance.

Fairlie tried to see him past the upheld hand lamp. Sélim's head, wrapped in linen, was only a vague suggestion. Fairlie's hand reached the table, gripped its edge; he put his fingertips on the document and pushed it away.

"You're refusing."

"Suppose I do?"

"Then we'll break one of your fingers and ask you again."

"I can't be brainwashed."

"Can't you? Suppose I leave it to your imagination. You have to decide what your own life is worth to you—I can't tell you that. How much pain can you bear?"

Fairlie lowered his face into his hands to shut out the blinding hard light.

He heard Sélim's quiet talk. "We're individually important to no one, not even ourselves. You on the other hand are important to a great many people. You have obligations to them as well as to yourself." Sélim's voice had dropped almost out of hearing.

Fairlie sat cramped and motionless facing the decision that would have to last his lifetime. Sophomoric questions of physical courage were beside the point; what mattered was position. If you stood for anything at all you must be seen to stand for it. You could not allow yourself to mouth words that mocked your beliefs. Not even when no one who heard you would believe for a moment that you had made the statement of your own free will.

He pulled the typewritten statement into the light and squinted against the glare. " 'They are to be released and given safe asylum.' Asylum where? No country in the world will touch them."

"Let that be our problem. Haven't you enough of your own?"

Sélim dipped the light a little, out of his eyes. Fairlie shook his head. " 'Fascist pigs,' 'white liberal swine,' 'racist imperialists.' Cheap propaganda slogans that don't mean a thing. This document would have to be deciphered like a broadside from Peking."

"I haven't asked you to interpret for us. Just read it."

Fairlie looked into the shadows beside the light. "The point is I have a position in the world, you see—alive or dead I still represent that position. The man in that position can't put his voice to words like these."

"Even if they're true?"

"They aren't true."

"Then you refuse."

He would have preferred to be able to meet Sélim's eyes but the light made it impossible.

"Given time we can force you to do it."

"Possibly. I think I'm reasonably tough."

"There are drugs."

"I doubt my voice would sound natural."

Sélim sat silent for a brooding interval. Fairlie felt cold, dismal. Possibly this refusal would cost him his life; he was not capable of facing that with equanimity.

Very soft: "What do you want, Fairlie?"

"What do *I* want?"

"Let's hear your side—perhaps we can strike a bargain. What is your price?"

"I cannot be bought, you know that. A man in my position hasn't the luxury of being able to afford being bought."

"I applaud your courage. But there must be some basis for discussion."

"Of course there is." He felt irresponsibly lightheaded. "Agree to turn me loose."

"And if I do?" Sélim shifted the light; it stabbed directly into his eyes. "You know what *we* want, isn't that right?"

"I've read your ransom demands."

"And?"

"I understand how from your point of view they may seem reasonable. They don't to me."

"Why not?"

"My freedom in exchange for the seven bombers we've got on trial? You don't really——"

"Now that's much better," Sélim murmured.

"What?" A sudden suspicion: he reached up, twisted the lamp in Sélim's hand.

Light fell across the tape recorder. But the spools were still motionless.

Sélim pulled the lamp out of his grip. "I'll switch it on when you're ready."

"I'll speak into that thing only on my terms."

"And what are your terms, Fairlie?"

"I speak my own words, free of restraint."

"We can hardly allow that."

"You're free to splice the tape. But I'll say no more than that I've been kidnapped and am alive and in good health. That should be evidence enough to serve your tactical purposes. It's all I'll give you."

"Of course you'd give us that much—it would suit your own purpose. You want them to know you're still alive. They'll search more strenuously, knowing you're alive."

"It's all I'll give you. Take it or leave it."

Sélim abruptly set the work lamp down on the bench. Fairlie reached out and turned it away so that it shone against the wall. Sélim did not stop him; the others, who probably had not heard most of the talk, watched from the dim corners like ghosts.

Sélim switched on the tape recorder, unreeled its microphone and spoke into it: *"Uno, dos, tres, cuatro. . . ."* He rewound the spools and switched it to playback and the machine said obediently, *"Uno, dos, tres, cuatro."*

Sélim rewound the few inches of tape so that the next recording would erase his test words. He pushed the microphone toward Fairlie. "Very well. We'll try it your way. Whenever you're ready."

Fairlie took the mike out of his hand, held it beneath his mouth. He nodded; Sélim's long-fingered hand pressed the start-record buttons.

"This is Clifford Fairlie speaking. I have been kidnapped, I'm being held in a place I can't identify by a group of people who have not shown their faces to me or otherwise identified themselves except by obvious pseudonyms. They have not harmed me physically and I believe they do not intend to kill me."

He lowered the microphone. "That's all."

"Say you expect to be released if your government agrees to our ransom demands."

He shook his head, standing mute; finally Sélim grunted and switched the recorder off. "Abdul."

The lights came on inside the garage; Sélim switched off the work lamp. "Abdul, tie him."

He watched, bleak, while Abdul came forward with wire and secured his hands. "The feet too?"

"Not yet." Sélim stood up, reached for the work lamp. He removed something from its cage—a disk, trailing fine wires. The wires ran down the lamp cord into the jumble around the socket. Sélim picked up the packing crate on which he had been sitting. Underneath it was a tape recorder identical to the one on the workbench. Sélim lifted it to the bench. "I think we have enough." He began to rewind the spools; he said conversationally to Fairlie, "A good editing job requires two tape decks, you know."

It was no good screaming oaths. Fairlie closed his eyes. He had allowed them to draw his words; they had duped him so easily. Everything he'd said in the past half hour was on that tape.

"You've been most cooperative," Sélim said. "We appreciate that. We really do." He placed the two machines side by side on the bench. "Ahmed, time for you to get to work."

One of the others came forward from the corner—stocky, this one, with dark brown hands. Possibly this one was a real Arab. Sélim relinquished the bench to him and Ahmed placed a set of earphones over his head and began to plug in wires that connected the two recorders together. His hands moved with professional adeptness.

Abdul removed a wad of chewing gum from his mouth and pressed it to the underside of the workbench; he turned and gripped Fairlie's arm. "Come on, Mr. President-elect. Time to get back in your box."

Sélim and Abdul walked him to the coffin. It was a simple box on the outside, its luxury limited to the quilted satin interior. The six handles were made of wood. A small hole had been bored through near the bottom at the head end, Fairlie saw; source of the fresh air for the occupant.

Sélim said, "Get in please. We're going to drug you. It's not toxic, it's an anesthetic which reduces respiration by a marked degree. You will be alive, but comatose. For a few hours, no more. During that time you'll give every appearance of being dead. Your skin will be very pale, your breathing will be too shallow for detection. But you'll be quite all right afterward, it wears off almost immediately. Lady?"

They pushed him down on his back; he did not struggle, there was no point to it with his hands wired. The woman approached with a syringe. Held it up, squeezed a droplet from the needle's tip. At least she appeared to know the drill—she wasn't a fool who'd kill him with an injected air bubble. Fairlie kept his eyes open, watched bitterly as the needle sank into the vein of his inner elbow.

Abdul loomed above the coffin and looked down at him and Abdul's jaws worked; Fairlie could smell the chewing gum. It, or the drug, made him vaguely nauseous. He heard Sélim talking to someone: "This Ortiz had better be what you make him."

"No sweat. You go looking to buy yourself an official, you'll find him sitting right on the counter."

Fairlie's head began to swirl. The sucking and clicking of Abdul's chewing gum became a very loud sound in the garage.

Sélim: "I have a meet in—twenty minutes."

Ahmed: "In Palamos?"

"Mm."

"Plenty of time then."

Fairlie's eyes slid shut.

"Kill the lights while I open the door."

Darkness. Fairlie fought. Very distantly he heard the scrape and thunder of the garage door: he tried to focus on it but he was falling in vertigo, a spiral without bearings. Slipping under, he was thinking toward the last that he was a fool and that was a shame because the world did not need a fool for a leader just now.

9:40 P.M. EST   The headache was a sharp burning blade against Dexter Ethridge's right eye. He tried to ignore it. President Brewster was saying, "It'd be a bad mistake to let this distract us completely from the Spanish thing. Nobody seems to realize how important those bases are."

"Well we're not going to be able to hang onto them forever," Ethridge said.

"You can't always think in terms of forever, Dex. First you've got to think of right now. Today, tomorrow, the next twelve months."

Ethridge recognized the philosophy: it was Bill Satterthwaite's and over the past few years more and more it had come to color the President's acts.

The President said, "Right now—and *right now* is the point—the Reds have got us outshipped and outgunned and altogether militarily outclassed in the Mediterranean. The only thing we've got to balance it is the Spanish bases."

"It's not as if we're on the brink of war though." Ethridge half-closed his right eyelid, trying to drive the pain away.

"Dex. We have been on the brink of war continuously since Nineteen and Forty-seven." The President was very tired; his voice had the quality of a rusty hinge in motion but Ethridge found it pleasantly abrasive, like a rough towel after a hot bath.

They sat in private conference in the Lincoln Sitting Room; they had been there more than two hours, uninterrupted except for a staff aide's intrusion with an item of news from Justice: an anonymous caller had warned Los Angeles police there was a plastic bomb concealed in the Federal Court Building, had said there would be an epidemic of bombs across the country if the Washington Seven were not released; the threat sounded as if it represented the voice of a vast nationwide conspiracy. But it turned out there was no bomb in the Federal Court Building; at any rate the Government had begun massive surveillance of known radicals a week ago and there was no sign of organized terrorist momentum. In fact the tragedy at the Capitol seemed to have brought quite a few hot-bloods to their senses; even the underground press was calling for a halt to violence.

Yet for nearly a half hour the President had digressed from the subject at hand—Fairlie's abduction—to talk a hard line, angry with the "sellouts who grovel at the feet of these radical punks." Ethridge had listened with dubious interest. When Brewster was warmed up his rhetoric improved but his marksmanship became erratic. Tonight the President was in an execrable temper. The air was poisoned by his cigar smoke.

The President had battled his demons with fervid passion: "We should have stomped the bastards right off. Back in the Sixties. But we're supposed to be tolerant and liberal. So we let them walk on us."

Brewster had been talking to his knees. He did not lift his head; he didn't stir, but his eyes shifted quickly toward Ethridge as if to pin him. "Their Goddamned dogmatic righteousness. It makes a man sick, Dex. They talk about 'liberate,' they mean blow somebody up. They talk about participatory democracy, they mean turning everything over to five delinquents with a can of gasoline. They've made us accept their dirty minds and their dirty language —when was the last time you were shocked when you heard the words 'fascist pigs'? They've radicalized all of us and it's time to stop it."

Ethridge's headache was a maddening distraction. He found it hard to summon the alertness Brewster's talk seemed to require. Brewster had harped on the subject of the radicals until a few minutes ago when he had shifted abruptly to the Spanish bases. It bothered Ethridge because he knew the President was not given to idle ramblings. There was a reason for Brewster's display of anger —it was a preamble to something specific and Ethridge kept trying to predict the President's next moves but the headache intervened and finally he said, "Do you think someone could get me a couple of aspirins?"

Brewster's head moved quickly; dark hair fell over his eye. "Don't you feel well?"

"Sinus headache, that's all."

"I'll ring for the doctor."

"No."

"Dex, you were bombed, you got hit on the head, now you've got a headache. I want you looked at."

"Really it's not necessary. I've had sinus trouble all my life—I get a headache every now and then. It always passes." Ethridge raised one hand a few inches to acknowledge the President's concern. "It's nothing, I promise you. The doctors gave me every test known to medical science. I'm quite all right. I only need a couple of aspirins."

The President reached for his chairside telephone. Ethridge heard him mutter into it; he caught the word "aspirin" and sat back in relief.

He didn't want another battery of them poking at him, rousting him from one diagnostic machine to another, subjecting him to an infernal variety of pains and peeping eyes and the prisonlike boredom of enforced isolation. There was nothing wrong with him; it was the weather, his perennial sinus. Earlier he had been troubled by lethargy, the great amounts of sleep he had seemed to require after the bomb explosions; he had awakened the morning after the blast with a splitting headache and a curious weakness in his right arm and leg. He had informed the doctors of these symptoms—he wasn't a prideful fool. There had been some somber talk about the possibility of a stroke or perhaps a "metabolic cerebral lesion." More skull X rays, another electroencephalogram. Dick Kermode, his doctor, had come into the hospital room beaming on the third morning: *Hell there's nothing wrong with you. A man gets hit on the head, he's got a right to a little headache. No lesions, no sign of a stroke. Headache gone today? Fine, then we'll turn you loose —we've exhausted all the tests, they're all negative. But if you have any trouble check back with me immediately, will you? Try a little Privine for that sinus.*

Howard Brewster cradled the telephone. "Promise me something, Dex. You'll call your doctor first thing in the morning and tell him about this headache."

"It's not worth——"

"Promise me this little thing, all right?"

He inclined his head. "Very well, then."

"You're important, Dex. We don't want any trouble with your health. If we don't get Cliff Fairlie back by Inauguration Day you're going to have to be healthy enough to step into these shoes."

"We'll have him back by then, Mr. President. I'm absolutely convinced of that."

"We've got to assume the worst," Brewster said around his cigar. "That's why you're here now. We haven't got a whole lot of time —you've got to be briefed on all the things I briefed Cliff on. My predecessor took six weeks showing me the ropes—I took just about that long with Cliff. Now you and I have got just nine days. You'll have to visit with Defense and State, you'll have to spend some time with my Cabinet people and the Security Council, but mainly there's only one boy who can guide you through this here wilderness and that's me. You're going to have to spend so much time at my right hand for the next nine days you'll get to hate the sight of me, if you don't already."

In point of fact Ethridge did not hate the sight of him. He rather liked Howard Brewster. But it had taken years for Ethridge to accrete his impression of the President because the political Brewster was very hard to pin down. Superficially he was the embodiment of American tradition: he had grown up in rural Oregon believing in hard work and patriotism, believing there was opportunity for everyone, believing God loved nothing so much as a good fighter. It was was as if Brewster's philosophers were Abraham Lincoln and Horatio Alger and Tom Mix. Brewster was an amalgam of liberal traditions and conservative mentality and the values of Main Street. And his weaknesses were typical: the transient piety, the chameleon sincerity, the flexible morality.

In Ethridge's estimation Howard Brewster was a respectable opposition President: he was not too terrible, considering that nobody could be good enough for the job.

"Long hours, Dex," the President adjured. "An awful lot to cram into your brain—top-secret stuff, in-progress stuff. That's why I want you healthy."

The President leaned forward for emphasis. His hand moved away from his face, carrying the cigar, swathed in smoke. "You can't afford headaches. You get me?"

Ethridge smiled. "All right, Mr. President."

A staff aide brought Ethridge's aspirin and a glass of ice water. Ethridge swallowed the tablets.

"My cigar bother you?"

"Not at all."

"That the truth or just politeness?"

"I enjoy an occasional cigar myself, you know that."

"Well, some people get a headache, they get sensitive to things." The aide withdrew and Brewster laid the cigar in the ashtray by his elbow. "You're a polite cuss, Dex. I recollect back toward the beginning of the campaign you kept showing up late for appearances and it turned out you kept getting slowed down holding doors open for people. Nobody else got to hold a door when you were around."

"They cured me of that after a while."

The President smiled, his eyes closed to slits. But his amusement seemed dispirited. "I wish I knew you better right now."

"Am I all that mysterious?"

"You're the Vice-President-elect, Dex. If we don't get Cliff back alive within nine days you're the next President of the United States. If I had my druthers I'd like to know you as well as I know m'own sons. It'd make me feel a whole lot easier."

"You're afraid of turning it over to me, aren't you. You don't know I'll be able to carry it."

"Well, I have every confidence in you, Dex."

"But you'd like reassurance. What do you want me to tell you, Mr. President?"

Brewster made no direct answer. He stood up, moved around the room curiously—as if he were a visitor seeing the room for the first time. Looking at the paintings, the furniture; finally coming back to his chair and standing in front of it, leaning over to pick up his cigar. "Governing the people of this country from the eminence of this White House," he said slowly, "is kind of like trying to swat a fly with a forty-foot pole. It's not a question of whether your heart's in the right place, Dex. I take it for granted your political beliefs aren't all that different from mine. Some, maybe, but not a whole lot. But you and I served together in that Senate what, twelve years? I never did get to know you very well."

"I was on the other side of the aisle."

"There were plenty of Democrats I didn't know nearly as well as some of the boys over to your side of the aisle."

"What you're saying is I've never been a member of the club."

"Not to be indelicate about it, yes. It's not that you were a maverick or one of those loudmouths nobody could ever talk to. Far from it. But you were an awful quiet Senator, Dex."

And the presidential eyes swiveled against him like twin gun muzzles. "An awful quiet Senator."

"Not my style to make much noise, Mr. President."

"Nine days from now if you step into this house you'll have to get noisy, Dex. Nobody listens if you don't make noise."

"I'll try to make the right noises then."

"Think you can?"

"I hope I won't have to. I hope Cliff Fairlie will be back. But if it comes to that—the answer's yes. I think I can, Mr. President."

"Good—good." Brewster settled into the chair, drawing the cigar to his mouth, crossing his legs. He wore a herringbone Harris tweed sport jacket; his tie was cinched up neatly, his trousers pressed, his shoes shined, but he always gave the impression of a baggy rumpled man.

"I get a feeling I haven't reassured you much."

"Dex, a lot of the boys over in my party are pretty worried about you. You've been in Washington twenty-four years and nobody's ever noticed you doing much except pushing legislation that would benefit your Big Three constituents back in Detroit. I'm being blunt now—I guess I have to be. You spent your last eight years in the Senate on the Judiciary and the Finance and the Commerce Committees—domestic seats every one of them. So far as I know you've never once stood up on the floor of the Senate to say a word about foreign affairs or defense. Your voting record on foreign affairs is fine, jim-dandy, but the boys on the Hill look to Pennsylvania Avenue for leadership, not voting records."

"I'm afraid I can't rewrite my record to suit the circumstances, Mr. President."

"I'm just warning you what you're up against. Your forty-foot pole is the Congress of the United States, Dex. If you want to swat your flies you've got to learn how to handle that pole." The cigar moved through a slow arc to the ashtray. "You got a lot of congressional barnacles to deal with. Certified anachronisms, a lot of them. I know Fairlie's got grandiose plans to ease them out to pasture but it ain't going to work, it's been tried before and it never works. You got to learn how to balance that forty-foot pole on one finger, Dex, it's the only way. You try to hold it up by one end and the thing'll slip right out of your hands. You're a Republican, boy, and that's a Democratic Congress out there."

Twelve hours earlier the possibility of becoming President of the United States had been vague and distant in Ethridge's mind. Ever since the election the realization had been there and he couldn't ignore it altogether but he regarded it much the way he might think about winning a lottery for which he held one ticket. It could happen but you didn't make plans.

Then Fairlie had been abducted and the Secret Service reinforcements had arrived. For the first time he had realized the significance of his place in the scheme of things. Long odds became short ones. He didn't dare stop and compute them; it would seem disloyal to Fairlie. But kidnappers often killed. Ethridge might find himself President of the United States for four years.

There had not been time to absorb it fully. The summons to the White House had been peremptory, the President's greeting filled with aggrieved concern and avuncular sympathy. But then had come the diatribe against radicals, the insistence on the importance of continuing the Spanish negotiations, now the emphasis on Ethridge's health and the blunt doubts about his fitness.

He turned, a heavy deliberation in the movement, toward Howard Brewster. "Mr. President, when I accepted the nomination at Denver I accepted the responsibility that went with it."

"You didn't campaign for that nomination very hard."

"No. I didn't. I was a dark horse, admitted."

"Have you ever campaigned for anything very hard, Dex?"

"I think I have." He smiled slowly. "Campaigned pretty hard against *you*, didn't we."

Brewster didn't bat an eye. "That was Fairlie's campaign."

"I think I had a hand in it. Am I flattering myself?"

"Not at all. You won him a lot of votes—you probably swung the election. But balancing that forty-foot pole takes a different kind of campaigning." The President's cigar had gone out. He found a new one in his pocket. "The hell with it. We'll have to do the best we can in nine days, that's all. At least you've been a long time on the Hill and you haven't made too many enemies. FDR came in, he was a state governor, the only people he knew were people who hated him, he didn't know the first thing about dealing with the club. It worked out—it always does."

Ethridge had the distinct feeling the President was talking mainly to convince himself—and that he wasn't succeeding. The pale eyes mirrored that. *You're not FDR, Dex. You'll never have his drive in a million years.*

Well, Ethridge thought, we'll see about that. And as he reached his decision a surge of exultation lifted him.

The President was on the telephone. "Bill? Update me." The big face nodding, the eyes brooding into space. He listened for several minutes with an actor's variety of expressions chasing one another across his face. His replies were mostly monosyllabic; he ended by saying, "Keep me posted," and rang off.

"Any news?"

"The Spanish police found the helicopter. Abandoned."

"Where?"

"A farm in the Pyrenees." Brewster had a deep suntan, the product of lamps, but in this light he looked very old. He had aged a great deal in two or three years. They always did, Ethridge observed, and the thought was tainted by an unwholesome personal regret; Ethridge knew his own vanity.

"They may be able to find some sort of fingerprints," the President was saying, not with great conviction. "Some sort of clues."

"There's no word from Fairlie?"

"No. Nor from the people who took him."

"It's an awful thing."

"It wouldn't have happened," Brewster intoned, "if I hadn't let him talk me out of cracking down on the bastards."

"I doubt you can say that. A crackdown wouldn't have netted these—they're in Europe."

The pale eyes flickered. "Dex, I want to get tough with these bastards. I need your help."

"You're asking me the same thing you asked him a week ago."

"The situation's got worse. Out of hand."

"We don't even know who these are yet, Mr. President."

"One of them's an American. A black. We know that."

"That hardly justifies a mass lynching."

"I don't want a lynching, Dex."

"A net would only catch thousands of innocent fish."

"It'll show them we won't back down." A gesture with the hand that ordinarily held the cigar. "That's important right now—a lot more important than people seem to think."

Ethridge knew the President wanted a crackdown not for any strategic purpose but to give the appearance that the Administration was doing something firm and functional. Right now the public needed that reassurance. Ethridge conceded the President had a point; but it was an equally valid point that an overt display of official violence could trigger the dissidents into rebellious mob riots which would force Washington into punitive reaction. It could only be military. And once you unleashed your military establishment against segments of your own populace you were admitting the whole democratic structure was a failure. Ethridge was not willing to risk that when, through Fairlie, the country's chances for reorganization and reform and ultimate stability were better than they had been in decades.

Pain stabbed his eyeball. He squinted. "Mr. President, I'm against taking any wholesale action right now. But I'm going to give this a lot of thought."

Brewster backed away with grace. "Do that, Dex." He looked at his watch. "Get a good night's sleep then; we'll start the briefings first thing in the morning. I imagine you'll——are you all right, Dex?"

"Headache, that's all." The spasm receded; he stood up to go. A slight weakness in his right leg but when he put his weight on it he had no trouble walking. In the morning he'd call Dick Kermode.

The President walked him to the door. "Mind your health, Dex." Partly in jest: "You know what happens if you bail out on us. Old Milt Luke's next in the line of succession."

It was a curiously bemusing thought. The old House Speaker

hadn't lost any marbles yet but he had reached the age where every point had to be illustrated by a long trudging ramble into reminiscence, an excursion into debilitating recall.

The President said, "I'm serious about that, Dex. Milt Luke's your backup man until you're inaugurated. Once you're sworn in you can nominate your own Vice-President and have him confirmed by Congress—have you picked anyone yet?"

"You're talking as if you don't expect we'll get Fairlie back."

"I hope we will. But things don't always come right in the end, Dex. We may not get him back in time, we may not get him back at all. You may have to swear in as President. Pick yourself a Vice-Prez—do it soon."

Agent Pickett and the protective squad picked him up in the corridor and convoyed him to his car. He had one of the presidential limousines now; he slid down in the seat and rested the back of his head against the cushion, closed his eyes, felt the headache begin to wane.

Sam March, he thought. March would make a good Vice-President. Level-headed, a good Senator, the right kind of Republican. . . .

Good God.

March was dead: killed in the bombing.

Ethridge sat up, winced, looked out the window. So many of them were dead. It was difficult to credit.

Silence inside the moving limousine. Thump of tires, the soft whoosh of the heat blowers. It was a cool steamy night, the windows fogging up, windshield wipers batting softly. The back of the driver's head was flat and complacent; the Secret Service guards always taciturn, were silent now.

Big black limousine: like a hearse, he thought. How many of them he had followed this week. The endless funerals. He couldn't get to them all. Most of them had been taken home to their native states but a few—those with war records who had indicated the preference—had been interred at Arlington. He had shuttled to and from them, reminded each time of the first state funeral he had witnessed. Raining, he remembered: hot and wet, and the cortege had marched from the Capitol all the way to Arlington on foot in the drenching rain. The caisson had rolled with stately grandeur and the Mall had been crowded with veterans and the honor guard behind Black Jack Pershing's casket had included Eisenhower and Hap Arnold and all those others who were dead now.

The overlap of generations was stunning: Ethridge had been a young congressman heading for the Seventies, perhaps the Eighties; Pershing had fought Indians on the frontier. . . .

The limousine drew up. The Secret Service had a van drawn up in the driveway—stakeout headquarters. Ethridge was ushered into his own house, an agent preceding him to check out the shadows. They were very tense now, these Secret Service men. They took their jobs seriously and there had been too many failures.

Judith had gone up to bed, he was told; he looked in surprise at the wall clock in the foyer: it was half past eleven.

A President keeps long hours. He hung his overcoat in the hall closet, put his hat on the shelf. Very weary. The headache had receded but he felt drained; it had been an unbearable week, an unbearable day.

He's right. Maybe I don't have the drive. Ambition for the Presidency was a pathological thing and he had never had it, not really.

He went into the study. The house man poured him a cognac according to habit and withdrew quietly from his presence. Ethridge sank into his chair, staring at the telephone by his elbow.

It was like the pre-wedding jitters. You never seriously thought of flight but there were moments of panic. The Presidency—of course he wanted it. Every politician wanted it.

He had to look up the number; he dialed, looked at his watch, made a slight face. At least the headache was gone.

"Congressman Bee's residence." It was Shirley Bee, trying to sound starched; he smiled.

"Hi Shirley, it's Dex Ethridge."

"Why Senator!" She sounded genuinely pleased.

"How you doing?"

"Why just fine, thank you." Her Birmingham drawl made it *jist fahn, thankye.*

"Andy around?"

"Why sure, I'll get him right away."

Noblesse oblige. Ethridge sat back, bemused by the petty exercise of power.

"Hello? Senator?"

"Andy. I'm sorry to disturb you this late at night."

"Not at all. I'm still up. Trying to write a letter to Senator March's widow—trying to think of the words."

That was like Bee. To write his own consolation letters. Ethridge felt the incision of guilt: he'd had his administrative aide take care of that.

He started to say *That's strange, I was just thinking about March,* but he held his tongue. "Andy, I need to talk with you."

"Right now?"

"Yes."

"Not on the phone, I gather."

"Better not."

"I'll be right along then. Save me a brandy."

Hanging up he saw how easily he was beginning to utilize the prerogatives of power. Until the convention he would have been the one to go to Bee's house—even though Bee was only a congressman. Bee had done two terms in the Senate himself, had been one of the most popular men ever to sit in that body. Then there had been that automobile accident four years ago just when he was up for re-election. There had been a wave of public sympathy but it hadn't been enough to overcome two things: Bee's hospitalization, which made it impossible for him to campaign, and the Brewster landslide which had swept Democrats into power everywhere. Even so, Bee had been nosed out by the slimmest vote margin.

Two years later after trying to work up an interest in private law practice Bee had run for office again. He had jumped into the congressional election in his home district in Los Angeles and had won by a majority that broke every California record. It was assumed Bee would use his House seat merely to keep himself warm —as a jumping-off place for the next senatorial election—but last summer he had chosen to make the big leap instead: he had campaigned for the Presidency.

It was unheard of, reaching for the Presidency from the House of Representatives: particularly when you were a member of the minority party. Ethridge had never been quite certain what Bee expected. Was he just making a trial run, getting the public used to the idea of Andrew Bee as presidential candidate? Would he go for the Senate two years from now and then make a serious bid for the Presidency two years after that? He would still be young enough; he was only forty-seven now.

It had been taken for granted Howard Brewster was unbeatable for re-election. But Bee had campaigned and had received surprising support. He'd won the New Hampshire primary and lost the Florida primary only narrowly to Fitzroy Grant. But then the Fairlie machine had got steam up and Fairlie had walked away with the primaries in Oregon and Texas and even Bee's home state of California; at the convention Bee had magnanimously thrown his support to Clifford Fairlie. To Ethridge's knowledge there had been no deals made but two of Fairlie's Cabinet designees were Bee campaigners.

Andrew Bee had spent two days stumping for Fairlie for every day he spent at home running for re-election in Congress—a race he had to make as an independent because he'd dropped out of the congressional primary to run for the presidential nomination— but Bee had been re-elected by a powerful plurality over both his party-line opponents and the victory had solidified him with the Republicans as an unbeatable vote-getter.

The fact was that even from his lowly House seat Andrew Bee was an important force in the Republican party and in American politics.

Ethridge went out front to alert the Secret Service men to Bee's arrival. "I forgot to give him the password but I'd appreciate it if you'd let him in anyway."

Agent Pickett, always an easy mark for Ethridge's quiet humor, smiled quickly. "We might strip him down and brainwash him a little but we'll let him through eventually, sir."

"Fine—fine." Ethridge withdrew to his study.

Bee arrived within twenty minutes, a tall burly man with deep-set blue eyes and a California tan and the stage presence of a leading actor. He had a slight limp from the automobile crash four years ago; it had taken some pieces of bone out of his legs. But he moved athletically enough; it hadn't crippled him. He had once been a logger in northern California and he still had the look of it.

"Very mysterious," Bee hinted as he accepted a globe of brandy.

Ethridge moved to his seat. "You've thought about the implications of Cliff Fairlie's kidnapping."

"Which implications did you have in mind?" Bee was being careful; it made Ethridge smile a little and Bee nodded in understanding. "You could be President—that implication."

"Andy, you had a lot of support at the convention. You might have made a hell of a fight of it."

"I had to defer to Cliff. His chances were better than mine."

"It was a big thing to do."

"Well I didn't do it expecting gratitude, Senator. Cliff and I were splitting the moderate-liberal support, and if we'd slugged it out to the finish Fitz Grant would likely have won the nomination. I don't think a conservative Republican could have beaten Brewster."

"You're saying you threw your support to Fairlie for the good of the party?"

"I didn't think of it like that."

It had been not so much for the good of the party as for the good, in Bee's estimation, of the country—the belief that Fairlie would make a far better Chief Executive than Brewster.

"You were Cliff's first choice for running mate."

"I know. But McNeely and the others counseled him against it. I'd have weighted the ticket too far to the left—he'd have lost too much conservative support."

"So they picked me instead of you. I'm supposed to be the conservative on the ticket."

"A lot of people made that assumption," Bee said. "I didn't. I know your voting record."

"You and I have always got along pretty well in the Senate. Can we still get along well, Andy?"

"I think I see what you're driving at."

"I've got to be blunt," Ethridge said. "There's a chance Cliff Fairlie won't be recovered alive—we have to face that. If I'm to take office as President my first act has to be to nominate someone to fill the vacancy in the Vice-Presidency."

"And you're asking my advice?"

"No. I'm asking you to be my Vice-President if Cliff doesn't come back."

A beat of silence: Bee's big lumberjack face dipping toward the brandy in thought. "It's mighty flattering, Dex."

"Frankly, I might have preferred Sam March but he's gone. But the important thing is you were Cliff's first choice. I feel obliged to honor his wishes—after all he's the one who was elected President."

"You *are* being blunt." The famous Bee grin.

"Next to March you'd be my own choice. That's the truth."

Bee lifted his head to sip from the globe. "Sam March was pretty good company to be in. I'm not offended."

"You and I might make a good team, don't you think?"

Bee uncrossed his legs and recrossed them in the other direction. "I guess you want my decision pretty fast."

"I'm afraid so."

The big Californian lifted to his feet. "Let me sleep on it."

"I'll call your office tomorrow."

"Fine."

They moved toward the door. Bee said, "It seems damned callous, doesn't it."

"It does. Like picking the pockets of a man who isn't quite dead yet."

"Sometimes I hate politics," Bee said. He gave Ethridge his quick firm handshake and went.

It was well past midnight. The headache was beginning to throb again. Ethridge thought of calling the doctor but decided to get a night's rest and see if the headache disappeared.

Feeling strangely guilty, thinking of the big desk in the White House, he went up to bed.

TUESDAY,
JANUARY 11

11:35 A.M. Greenwich Mean Time The signal came on a faint pulse
on the five hundred-kilocycle marine band. At Land's End the W/T
operator logged it in, time-of-origin 1135 hours. It was in Morse, an
awkward fist on the key. Written out it was brief: *Fairlie will broadcast this frequency 1200 GMT keep channel open.*

The W/T station got right through on the land line to Command-
er-in-Chief Portsmouth.

There was no time to think about the possibility of a hoax. C-in-C
sent immediate orders to all stations. By 11:48 every official wireless
set on the coasts of England and France was ready to receive.

At 11:50 a crackle of introductory static and then a voice transmission:

"This is Clifford Fairlie speaking. In . . . ten minutes . . . I will
speak . . . on this . . . band."

C-in-C Portsmouth had reached the Admiralty by telephone at
11:49. Word sped to 10 Downing Street.

Two lines to Washington were opened: the Prime Minister's hot
line to President Brewster and a satellite-relayed broadcast circuit
to convey the promised broadcast live.

At 11:55 another voice transmission on 500 KC: "This is Clifford
Fairlie speaking. In . . . five minutes . . . I will speak . . . on this
. . . band."

To a few monitors with good ears it was apparent the second
broadcast was the same voice recording as the first with the excep-
tion of the phrases "ten minutes" and "five minutes."

The PM heard it, live, by telephone from Admiralty; the PM
remarked the curious hesitations between words. It *sounded* like

Fairlie's voice. . . . The PM inquired of the First Lord of the Admiralty: "We are taping this of course?"

"Naturally."

"Very good, then. . . ."

"Whitehall is alerted?"

"Yes of course."

The PM went to the hot line telephone. "Mr. President?"

"Right here." The twanging Oregon drawl.

"We shall pipe this straight through to you."

"Let's hear what it has to say then."

8:50 A.M. EST   The National Security Agency had monster banks of computers designed to analyze ciphers and codes and electronic transmissions. The Fairlie tape had been punched into the IBM consoles and then had been put in again, this time as sound recordings on ultra-high-speed half-inch tapes designed to disclose every nuance of volume and frequency. NSA's electronic detection devices were the ultimate in Sherlockian analysis: an inaudible sound, an imperceptible fraction of time sufficed for clues.

Ames was the NSA official assigned to the Fairlie tapes and Lime had worked with him many times before. He had been Lime's supervisor during the years of foreign fieldwork.

"Voiceprints are all positive," Ames said. "We've matched it against his recorded speeches. It's not a phony—it's Fairlie's voice."

Satterthwaite was scowling through thick lenses at the turning tape reels. "Edited."

"Edited like mad," Lime muttered.

The place always put Lime in mind of space-flight mission control: the electronic consoles ran on relentlessly along great curved walls.

Lime held a computer print-out. It diagrammed the splices, showing where Fairlie's words had been cut and pasted together:

This is Clifford Fairlie speaking.

I've been kidnapped.

I'm being held for ransom

in a place I can't identify by a group of people who have not shown their faces to me or otherwise identified themselves.

They have not harmed me physically.

The

ransom demands
seem reasonable. I
think Washington will agree to these demands.
I understand how
you
may
suppose
I've been
brainwashed
but
I'm reasonably tough
and
I rarely send my brain out to be laundered.
They have not harmed me.
I speak my own words, free of restraint.
I cannot be bought.
A man in my position hasn't the luxury of being able to afford
being bought.
I
speak
only on my own terms.
The point is I have a position in the world—alive or dead I still
represent that position. The man in that position can't put his voice
to
words
that
aren't true.
The
revolutionaries
have a cause that makes good sense
to
them.
They
agree to turn me loose
in exchange for the seven bombers we've got on trial.
My freedom in exchange for the
bombers'.
They are to be released and given safe asylum.
Instructions will follow.
This is Clifford Fairlie.
Satterthwaite said, "Is this a professional editing job?"

Lime shook his head and Ames said, "A talented amateur, but not a pro. It sounds almost natural but I'd say they probably made their tapes by switching back and forth from one small portable stereo deck to another. There's a lot of background tape noise—the kind of thing you get from too much overdubbing. They had to do several tracks to wipe out the clicking sounds between splices—it shows up. At any rate it wasn't done in a well-equipped sound studio."

Satterthwaite had the expression of a man who has just tasted something foul. "He knew he was recording it. At least some of it. I mean, you don't say 'This is Clifford Fairlie speaking' unless somebody's holding a microphone in front of your nose. You'd think he'd have had more sense."

"With a gun pointed at his head?" Lime stuck a cigarette in his mouth, snicked his lighter open and flipped its wheel. It erupted into a bonfire.

The computer typing-recorders were spilling paper tapes on the floor; they writhed in Medusan agony. Satterthwaite said, "It's a nice propaganda coup for them."

They were killing time, really. Radio triangulation had narrowed the point of origin of the Fairlie broadcast to a Mediterranean coastal area north of Barcelona and international forces were combing it. There wasn't much left but to wait for whatever turned up.

3:15 P.M. Continental European Time   The boat smelled strongly of fish. In the confinement of the inboard cabin Fairlie watched the impassive face of Abdul, felt the restraining wire around his wrists and ankles, let himself move slackly with the roll and pitch of the vessel. Somewhere in the Med, he supposed. He had a dull headache, the hangover from the drugs they had administered last night.

"You want to talk, Abdul?"

"No."

"Too bad. I might talk some sense into you."

"Man, just don't tell me we'll never get away with it."

"Maybe you will. But you won't be able to live with it."

Pained disgust. "Come on, man."

"You know what they'll do to you when they catch you."

"They won't catch us. They're too stupid. Now you rest your mouth awhile."

He lay back. It was a narrow bunk; the wooden side jabbed his elbow and there wasn't room to shift over. He lifted his elbow over it and let it stick out.

The memory of last night was kaleidoscopic in his head. For an indeterminate time he had been asleep—unconscious, drugged into coma. He had come out of it slowly as if drunk. Aware at one point that he was still in the closed coffin and that it was moving with the quiet heave of a boat on open water. He wasn't sure of his recollection of sequences for it seemed they had removed the coffin from the boat: he had been awake when they had unscrewed the lid and it had been on dry land, but with the smell of the sea. Dark—a cloudy night, the cold wind whipping mist across the sands. Dead seaweed tangled around his feet. Someone talking—Sélim?—about driving the boat high up on the shoals so it wouldn't wash out on the tide. A quick movement, shadows rushing through the darkness; a grunt, the thump of a body falling onto the hard-packed sand. Sélim: "Abdul. Stick your knife in him. Hard." The black face motionless, hardly visible in the poor light. The jaws no longer chewing gum. "Go on, Abdul. It's discipline." Abdul moving slowly, disappearing. The distinct scraping-sliding thrust of knife into flesh and bone.

"Lady—now you."

"No—I. . . ."

"Do it." Very soft.

Remembering it now Fairlie thought he understood it: Sélim had faced reluctance among his troops and had achieved the solidarity he needed by committing the others to participation in his atrocity. Fairlie knew his Mao: cruelty was an instrument of policy.

It was dismal knowledge, it removed the last doubt of their inhumanity. They would kill him whenever it suited them. In that moment, or in this one, he gave up hope.

They had taken him up the dunes: Sélim the Slav, Abdul the black lieutenant, Lady and the one whose name he had not heard. He did not know whom they had murdered on the beach, or why.

He remembered now there had been a truck waiting, a small rusty van driven by Ahmed, the one who spoke English with a Spanish accent. In the van they had covered him with a blanket and injected a drug and he had gone out again.

He was not certain but he seemed to remember that they had been at sea, then on land, then at sea again, and perhaps yet again on land.

Now on the cabin bunk he felt the rise of a moderate sea beneath his spine and watched Abdul's unreadable features and wondered where God was.

10:10 A.M. EST   In a Boston hotel room with snowflakes drifting against the panes three men worked at revolution. Kavanagh and the Harrison youth molded their ten satchel charges while Raoul Riva worked over a map of Washington with a felt-tip pen and a District of Columbia federal directory.

The Establishment had been stung twice; it was alerted and that was supposed to make it difficult to move freely. But the Americans were suicidally and hysterically incompetent: they had no long-range plans for countering insurgency, they had a genius for preparing to meet the last attack rather than the next one.

Their Capitol had been bombed. Now it was surrounded by armed guards while workmen ripped out its damaged insides and prepared to rebuild. Federal buildings everywhere had been reinforced by sentries and checkpoints. The temporary House and Senate chambers that had been set up in the Cannon and Rayburn buildings were protected by platoons of soldiers. The Government in its stupidity had cordoned off federal office buildings in every major city and thrown guards around everything from post offices to city halls.

And in the meantime every Congressman and Senator went home each night to a serene unguarded house or apartment.

They were so stupid it was hardly worth picking a fight with them. Riva turned a directory page and ran his finger down the center column until he found the home address of Senator Wendell Hollander.

10:45 A.M. EST   Satterthwaite's war room had been set up in the NSC boardroom because communications were already laid into the building. The long table was a tangle of teletapes and phones and transceivers. A situation map covered one wall. Information was being fed into the pool of typists one floor below, where it was collated on update sheets and sent in to the analysis table in the war room. Senior executives of all the government security agencies sifted the data sheets, seeking not only information but inspiration.

They sat, winnowed, talked, in some cases complained. Satterthwaite had insisted on this bulky arrangement; he wanted instant liaison with all agencies and had insisted they assign men whose rank empowered them to make instant decisions and commit their agencies without needing to waste time in consultations outside this room.

The big chair at the center—ordinarily the President's seat—was Satterthwaite's now and he was in it when the Presidential summons came. He left the room without excusing himself and strode rapidly on his short legs to the eastern exit from the building.

The previous night's feathery snowfall had left a crisp crust. It was a clear cold morning and reporters in topcoats and overshoes were besieging both buildings in the largest concentration Satterthwaite had seen since the night of the presidential election. It took four EPS patrolmen and a Secret Service agent at point to elbow a path through the crush for Satterthwaite's passage.

Inside the White House even the press lobby was empty; the White House had been closed to reporters indefinitely. The President's announcements were delivered to the press by Perry Hearn on the mud of the trampled lawn.

On his way up to the President's office he found Halroyd, the Special Agent in charge of the White House Detail; Satterthwaite wheeled off his course to speak to him.

"Find David Lime, will you? Ask him to report to me in the NSC boardroom. He may still be at NSA—check there first."

"Yes sir."

Halroyd went, and Satterthwaite was admitted to the presidential presence.

The President had with him Dexter Ethridge and the press secretary. Hearn was on his way out. He nodded to Satterthwaite, picked up his briefcase and detoured past Satterthwaite toward the door. "They'll want more, I'm afraid," he said over his shoulder.

"It's all I'm giving them. Make them accept it, Perry—embellish it all you can, try to satisfy them."

Hearn had stopped at the door. "I'm afraid they're not going to be satisfied with anything less than hard news, Mr. President. 'We're doing all we can, we expect an early solution'—no matter how you word that it comes out sounding like something they've heard too often before."

"Damn it, I can't help it." The President was flushed; he looked very tired, his eyes were bloodshot.

Perry Hearn left quietly. Ethridge nodded to Satterthwaite without rising from his seat. Ethridge didn't look well. Drawn; loose bags under the eyes; the appearance of sickbed slackness. It was hardly surprising. He had been hit hard.

Satterthwaite was as tired as anyone; too tired for formalities. He spoke to the President with the acerbic intimacy he ordinarily withheld from public view: "I hope you didn't drag me over here for a progress report. When we've got something I'll let you know."

"Gentle down, Bill."

Mild shock in Ethridge's eyes; Satterthwaite grimaced and nodded to indicate his apology.

The President said, "I've got a policy decision to make."

"What to tell the press?"

"No. Nothing like that." The President put a cigar in his mouth but did not light it. It made his voice more gutteral. "It's that damn fool press conference they held last night."

"What press conference?"

"You didn't hear about it?"

"I've been up to here, Mr. President, you know that."

From his chair Dexter Ethridge spoke evenly. "Some congressional leaders held a joint press conference last night." He sounded very dry, disapproving. "Woody Guest, Fitz Grant, Wendy Hollander, a few others. Both houses and both parties were represented."

The President pushed a copy of the *New York Times* across his desk. "You'd better read it."

Satterthwaite had seen a copy of the *Times* earlier in the day but had not had time to read it. The headline at the top of the front page was probably the largest point type the *Times* used—FAIRLIE KIDNAPPED. Each of the two words ran the width of the page in high boldface.

It was near the bottom of the page under a two-column group photo of a dozen well-known faces.

CONGRESSIONAL LEADERS CALL FOR "GET TOUGH" POLICY—
INSIST GOV'T REJECT RANSOM DEMANDS

The President was talking while Satterthwaite read. "I've had calls from every one of them. And the telegrams are a mile high."

"How do the telegrams split?"

"About six to four."

"For or against the hard line?"

"For." The President spoke the word slowly and let it hang in the air. Finally he added, "The public sentiment seems to be let's not just sit around and bleed about it." He removed the cigar; his voice hardened. "I can hear the mob, Bill. They're gathering out there with picks and torches."

Satterthwaite, grunting to indicate he had heard, turned the page.

Dexter Ethridge said, "We decided this morning, Mr. President. We've already made the decision."

"I know that Dex. But we didn't make it public."

"You're saying we can still change our minds."

"We didn't anticipate the reaction would come down this hard on one side, did we?"

"Mr. President," Ethridge said. The tone made Satterthwaite look up at him. Ethridge stirred slowly in his chair. A deep breath, a reluctant voice: "You've never been the kind of man who makes his decisions on the basis of who talked to him last. You've never needed public consensus to confirm your judgment. I find it hard to believe you're going to let the unreasoning panic of a mob affect your——"

"The country could split apart on this issue." The President was harsh. "I'm not playing politics for God's sake. I'm trying to hold this country together!"

Ethridge was sitting up straight. It was the first time Satterthwaite could recall seeing him this angry. "You won't hold it together by giving in to the yahoos."

The President waved his cigar toward the newspaper in Satterthwaite's hands. "Some of those men are prominent public servants, Dex. Maybe some of them are yahoos too but you can't always judge a case by its advocate."

Satterthwaite set the newspaper aside. "I think the President's point is well taken. This morning we all listened to Fairlie's voice. We reacted straight out of our guts—we're civilized people, someone in our family is in trouble, we instantly concluded the ransom demands weren't impossible to meet so we decided to agree to the exchange. The paramount consideration was Fairlie's safety—we hadn't had time to study the ramifications."

Ethridge was watching him narrowly. The muscles and nerves twitched in his face.

President Brewster said, "If we give in it'll give every two-bit terrorist gang in the world a green light to try this kind of thing again and again. Turning these seven killers loose, sending them into asylum—assuming there's a country somewhere with the guts to grant them asylum—that would be kind of like telling every guerrilla in the world he's free to go ahead and blow up people and buildings with impunity."

Ethridge's skin was the hue of veal, he had unhealthy blisters under his eyes. He spread his hands in appeal: "Mr. President, I can only stick to what I said this morning. The kidnappers are offering an exchange and we all agreed that Cliff Fairlie's life is worth a great deal more than the lives of those seven ciphers. I don't see how that's changed."

Satterthwaite turned, catching the President's eye; he said to Ethridge, "If that were the real *quid pro quo* you'd get no argument. But it's not a choice between Fairlie's life and the lives of seven ciphers. It's whether we can afford to give carte blanche to the extremists."

Ethridge sat stubbornly upright, his silence disagreeing. He squeezed his eyes with thumb and forefinger and when he opened them it seemed to take him a long time to bring them into focus. "I think we have to face the fact that whatever we do isn't going to please everybody. We can't avoid a split. The theoretical arguments pretty well cancel each other out—look, I can give you a strong case against taking a tough stand. You can't simply refuse to turn the seven bombers loose, you'll have to follow up with a police operation against all the radical cells. You'll end up with a permanently enlarged security operation, and that means permanent curtailment of citizens' rights. It's the only way you'll keep the lid on, and it seems to me that's exactly what the militants want of us—a tough repression that will feed their anti-Establishment arguments."

Satterthwaite said, "You're maintaining we've already lost."

"We've lost this round. We have to accept that."

"I don't," the President snapped. "I don't at all." He pawed around the surface of his desk, his eyes not following his hand; he was watching Ethridge. His hand closed around the lighter; the wheel snicked and the President lit his cigar. "Dex, are you going to make a public fight of this? A public break with me?"

Ethridge didn't answer directly. "Mr. President, the most important thing—more important than this entire tragedy—is to establish a long-term system of policies that will rebuild the self-confidence and security of the people. If the society hasn't got enormous discontents to fuel the militant extremists, then the whole terrorist movement will wither away for lack of nourishment. Now it seems to me——"

"Long-term policies," Satterthwaite cut in, "are a luxury we haven't got time to debate right now."

"May I finish, please?"

"I'm sorry. Go ahead."

"I don't mean this as personal offense but I believe Cliff Fairlie is more likely to establish the kind of secure self-confident society we need than anybody else in government. His ideas are the first reform proposals I've ever seen that give us a real chance to build a more responsible and more responsive government in this country. And if we manage to recover Fairlie the wave of public sympathy will be so overpowering there's a good chance he'll be able to get congressional backing for a great many reform programs that could never be passed under any other circumstances."

Satterthwaite was rocked; he tried not to show it. The frail Vice-President-elect, with his sick eyes and his tall quixotic gauntness, was putting out a display of shrewd subtlety totally unexpected. Ethridge was crediting Fairlie with far more magic than Fairlie actually possessed; reforms had been proposed before, Satterthwaite saw nothing particularly new in any of Fairlie's, but there was one place where Ethridge had an undeniably powerful point: Fairlie, if recovered intact, would generate exactly the kind of public outpouring Ethridge foresaw. On the crest of that wave, with any political ability at all Fairlie indeed would be able to push all sorts of unheard-of reforms through Congress before the legislators regained their composure.

Satterthwaite's eyes went past Ethridge, past the hanging flag to President Brewster; and he saw in the President's lined face a surprise similar to his own—the awareness of the explosive significance of what Ethridge had just said.

12:25 P.M. EST In the war room Lime's patience was shredding. He had arrived almost an hour ago with his lunch in a paper bag stained dark around the bottom by coffee that had escaped from the

lidded takeout cup. The cheap food rumbled uneasily in his stomach.

He had pulled out an empty chair beside NSA's Fred Kaiser, who
was big and grizzled, a not unfriendly bear of a man; Lime knew
him, not well. Kaiser was keeping two phones busy, sitting with a
receiver propped between shoulder and one ear, a finger stuck in
the other.

Lime offhandedly sifted through typewritten reports, seeking
slivers and scraps, finding nothing worthwhile. The long table was
littered with growing piles of dog-eared papers—reports from the
typists downstairs, from the National Military Command Center in
the Pentagon, from stacks of Secret Service and NSA files that had
been brought out needing the dust blown off their covers. Down at
the end a woman with blue hair was typing up slotted index cards
and inserting them in their proper alphabetical places in a Wheel-
dex. The carriage of a teleprinter jerked back and forth, paper
popped up through the glass slot and a uniformed major general
ripped it off and stood reading it while the machine clicked beside
him.

The room was filled and busy. Mainly they were making lists and
then evaluating them. There were lists of known radical activists
and then there were other lists behind those: the lists of people who
weren't quite on the lists. Suspected but not known. Computer
banks plugged into the teleprinters were analyzing histories—
modus operandi, locale, the flimsy facts about the black American
chopper pilot and the tire tracks two vehicles had left in the snow
of the abandoned farm in the Pyrenees where the helicopter had
been found.

Over at the side of the room B. L. Hoyt had earphones strapped
over his head and was listening—probably to a copy of the Fairlie
tape—imbecilically calm with his chilled blue eyes raised toward
the ceiling. The end of the tape whipped through the heads and
spun around the takeup reel, flapping; Hoyt did not stir.

Fred Kaiser slammed down the phone and barked at Lime, "Jesus
H. Christ."

"Mm?"

"Nothing. Just rising to remark on the calamity."

"Mm." Lime's cigarette lay smoking at the rim of the table, growing a long ash, threatening to leave a burn on the wood. He rescued
it, dragged off the stub and crushed it in the ashtray.

"My wife thinks she's a psychiatrist," Kaiser said.

"Does she."

"I went home for breakfast, right? She spends half an hour analyzing the bastards. All I want's a quart of coffee and baconeggs, I get headshrinker guesses on why they snatched Fairlie."

"And why did they?" Lime pushed a typewritten sheet aside and overturned the next one.

"I didn't listen too much. She had it all doped out, their parents rejected them or something. It's all shit, you know. I can tell you what motivated them. Somebody put them up to it. Somebody recruited them, somebody trained them, somebody programmed them. Somebody took a bunch of damn fools and wound them up like walking toys and pointed them at Cliff Fairlie. Just like somebody pointed those seven assholes at the Capitol with fused bombs in their cases. Now we ought to find out who and why. You ask me we'd do worse than poke around Peking and Moscow."

"I don't know." Lime wasn't a subscriber to the conspiracy theory of history.

"Come off it. There used to be a day when we responded to this kind of crap with the Marines. This country used to be willing to go anyplace in the world with any cannon they needed to get back *any* lousy citizen of ours, let alone a President."

"Where would you send the Marines, Fred? Who would you shoot?" Lime kept most of the sarcasm out of his voice.

"Aagh." A phone rang: Kaiser turned with military abruptness, picked up the phone and talked and listened. Lime went back to his papers. Kaiser was a political infant but it didn't annoy him; people like Kaiser inhabited a masculine technical sphere, they didn't have to understand reality—only facts.

Kaiser rang off. "Why Fairlie?"

Lime glanced at him.

"I mean, I know he was handy and all. But the son of a bitch is a flaming liberal. You'd think they'd pick on somebody pure American. Somebody they really hate."

"They never do. The best scapegoat's the innocent one."

"Why?"

"I don't know. The Aztecs used to choose virgins for their human sacrifices."

"Sometimes you don't make a hundred per cent sense, you know that?"

"It's all right," Lime said. "Distribution limited on a need-to-know basis."

"What?"

"Nothing."

"You need a checkup, I swear to God."

Lime closed his eyes and nodded agreement. When he opened them they were aimed at the clock and as if by extrasensory signal Satterthwaite appeared.

Satterthwaite whirled into the room, topcoat flying, more cluttered and disordered than ever; stopped, swept the room with his magnified myopic stare, spoke while shouldering out of his coat: "Anybody got anything important to tell me? If it's not vital save it for later. Anybody?"

No response: like a classroom full of children too shy to volunteer the spelling of a test word. Satterthwaite scrutinized them all, very fast, stance shifting as he went from face to face. When he got to Lime he flung out his arm, leveled his index finger, overturned his hand and beckoned imperiously. "Let's go."

Without waiting acknowledgment Satterthwaite wheeled. Lime got to his feet, pushing the chair back with his knees, feeling curious eyes on him. Kaiser muttered, "Watch out for the son of a bitch's teeth."

Lime found Satterthwaite in the corridor unlocking one of the No Admittance offices. They passed inside. It was a small private conference room, windowless and bare, air fluttering from ventilator ducts. Heavy wooden armchairs for eight, a walnut conference table, a stenographer's desk in the corner. Lime closed the door behind him and located an ashtray and headed for it.

Satterthwaite said, "I understand you have a theory." Icily polite.

"Well theories are a dime a dozen, aren't they."

"Tell me about it."

"I didn't think we had time to waste trotting out every wild speculation that comes along."

"David when I ask you to give me details I think we can assume we're not wasting anyone's time."

Lime scowled furiously at him. "By what curious process did you arrive at the conclusion I had anything useful to contribute?"

"It's not a conclusion, it's a surmise, and it's not mine. It's Ackert's. He saw you staring at the map as if you'd discovered a message in secret ink. Come on David, I haven't time to drag it out of you word by word."

"If I had anything hard do you think I'd keep it to myself? What do you think I am?"

"I'm sure you don't really want an answer to that question. It's throwing raw meat on the floor."

"Look, I admit I had an idea. I played around with it but it shot itself full of holes. It turned out to have far too many ifs in it. It's not a theory any more, it's a pipe dream—acting on it would distract us from what we ought to be doing. We need more to go on."

Satterthwaite tucked his chin in toward his Adam's apple, showing his displeasure and his determination to carry on. "I think I know the direction your theory's taken. Are you afraid to risk getting thrown into the arena personally? David, we're talking about one of the most despicable crimes of the century. They've taken an innocent hostage—a man who's vitally important to the whole world. It's the kind of buck you just can't pass."

Lime grunted.

"David, we're talking about needs. Realities."

Lime looked down at his shoes as if he were at a high window looking down through smoke at a fireman's rescue net. "I guess we are," he said. "I do tend to hate an amateur who tries to tell a professional how to do his job."

"Get off it. Do you think I'm a patronage hack? I'm a dollar-a-year man, David, I'm not in this for glory. I do my job better than anyone else who's available."

"Modesty," Lime breathed, "is an overrated virtue."

Satterthwaite gave him a cold look. "You were born with an innate grasp of the subtleties of the hunt which most men will never learn from years of training. When it comes to operating in the western Mediterranean you're the only expert alive worthy of the name." And now Satterthwaite sank the knife, twisting it: "And when it comes to the Western Desert who else can you possibly pass the buck to, David?"

"I haven't been out there since Ben Bella."

"But I've hit it, haven't I."

"So?"

"You want Sturka for this one too, don't you. Why? Intuition?"

"I just don't believe in coincidences," Lime said. "Two well-organized capers, both on this scale, both with the same target. . . . But there are no facts. It was just an idea. You can't put it in the bank."

Satterthwaite jabbed his finger toward the chair. "Come back here and sit down. Are you ready to start working?"

"It's not my department."

"Whose job do you want? Hoyt's? He's due for the chop anyway."

"You can't fire civil servants."

"You can find shelves to put them on where they can't do any damage. Ackert's job? Would you settle for that? Name your price."

"There's no price for a fool's errand." He hadn't stirred toward the chair. A cigarette hung from the corner of his mouth, the smoke stinging his right eye.

"Come on, let's finish thrashing this out. You know I've got you over a barrel."

"I've got no facts to go on. Can't you understand that? *No facts!*" He took a step forward, filled with anger. "I've got no price—I'm not auditioning for your approval or anybody else's. I'm not lacking in conscience—if I knew I was better equipped to handle the field assignment than anybody else I'd take the job, you wouldn't need to degrade us both with stupid bribe offers."

Satterthwaite pushed his glasses up against his eyebrows. "You're not a superman, David, you're only the best chance we have among a variety of poor chances. You spent ten years of your life in that part of the world. You grew up in NSA before it rigidified into the kind of bureaucracy that became capable of fucking up the *Pueblo* affair—in your day imagination still counted for something. Do you think I don't know your secrets? I've sized you up, I know your talents, your choice of friends and entertainments, your record, how much you drink and when. You were the man who opened the channel between Ben Bella and De Gaulle. Christ if they'd only had the sense to send you into Indochina."

Lime shook his head. "It's no good, you know that." It wasn't altogether that he didn't want a crack at it. He had wanted this boredom; now he was eager to get away from it; *the old warhorse,* he thought, but he turned back before reaching the point of commitment. "Look, things have changed, it's a different world from the one I operated in. The quality of your mind doesn't count—only the quality of your marksmanship. I'm a lousy shot."

"That's a crock of shit and you know it."

"No. Nothing's decided by brains any more—in spite of that think tank of yours across the hall. There's no room left for chess players, you know that—it's all decided by assassination and counterassassination."

"All right. Assassinate them. But find them first. Find Fairlie and bust him out."

Lime laughed off key. "Use the local boys over there. Spanish cops, Bedouins, desert rats—hell it's their territory."

"I think it's important to have an American in charge."

"It's not Barbary pirates you know—these aren't gunboat days."

"Look, it's an American they've kidnapped and I suspect the kidnappers themselves are Americans. How would it look if a Spanish cop got too close to them and then bungled things? Do you have any idea what that would do to relations between Washington and Madrid? A little stupidity like that could slide Perez-Blasco right into Moscow's camp. At least if an American runs the show it's our success or our failure. If it's a success I think we'll climb quite a few notches in international esteem and we could use that right now, God knows."

"And if it's failure?"

"We've had them before, haven't we." Satterthwaite sounded abysmal. "It wouldn't be anything new. Don't you see that's why I don't want the CIA clumping about in their jackboots? They're such clumsy idiots—they're all hated over there, they'd never get the cooperation you'll get."

Satterthwaite stood up. He was too short to be imposing but he tried.

Lime shook his head—a gentle stubborn negative.

Satterthwaite said, "I don't give a shit what your motives are but you're dead wrong. You're the best we've got—for this particular job. I recognize what you're really afraid of is the responsibility—suppose you take the job and you fail, and they kill Fairlie. You don't want that on your conscience, do you. But how do you think *I'll* feel? What about all the rest of us? Do you think you'll be the only one who'll have to cover himself in sackcloth and ashes?"

Lime's silence was a continuing refusal.

But then Satterthwaite punctured him. "If we lose Fairlie because you refused to try—you'll be far more to blame."

There was a mad satanic beauty to it. Satterthwaite had been baiting the trap all along and had let Lime watch him do it.

"If you do the job," the little man breathed, "at least you won't have lost Fairlie for want of trying."

Neatly cornered. Lime's eyes drilled hatred into him.

Satterthwaite crossed half the distance between them and frowned a little behind his glasses; he lifted one hand in a vague gesture of truce. "Don't hate me too hard."

"Why shouldn't I?"

"Because I wouldn't want you messing this up just to spite me."

Lime saw how it could be. The little man was right again. A fiend —but you had to stand in awe of him.

"Now you'll go to Barcelona," Satterthwaite said, a down-to-business voice. "You're leaving Andrews Air Force Base at half past five —I've laid on a C-one-forty-one." A flap of wrist, glance at watch. "A little over four hours to pack your things and say your goodbyes. You'd better move along."

Lime, hooded, watched him in silence.

Satterthwaite said, "I won't give it to the press yet. You'll want a free hand. What do you need?"

A long ragged breath; the final surrender. "Give me Chad Hill from my office—he's green but he does what he's told."

"Done. What else?"

A shake of the head. "Carte blanche."

"That goes without saying."

Lime walked forward to pass him but Satterthwaite stopped him. "Your theory."

"I told you—it was too full of ifs."

"But I was right about it."

"I told you you were."

"Then my judgment's not that terrible after all. Is it."

Lime didn't answer the thin smile in kind.

Satterthwaite eeled past him through the door and Lime emerged, looked back into the room curiously—a crucible, but it looked ordinary enough. The door swung shut. No Admittance.

Satterthwaite was walking toward the war room. When he reached it he stopped. Over his shoulder: "Good hunting—I suppose I should say something like that." The grim little smile was glued on. "Get the son of a bitch out alive, David."

Having given himself the curtain line Satterthwaite disappeared into the war room.

Despising the man for his cheap theatricality Lime stood a moment burning his stare into the closed door before he shambled away, head bowed to light a cigarette.

WEDNESDAY, JANUARY 12

10:40 P.M. Continental European Time   Mario had grown up inculcated with a hatred of stinkpot powerboats. He had learned summer seamanship aboard the Mezetti ketch, a two-masted sixty-four-footer with the grace of a racing regatta champion. He knew nothing about engines—those were Alvin's job—but he had the wheel and the responsibility of navigation by binnacle and charts. The boat was American built, a thirty-nine-foot Matthews powered by a single big diesel. She was probably at least twenty-five years old although the diesel was newer, a French engine. A stubby wooden craft with belowdecks cabins both fore and aft and only a tiny fishing deck between the rear-cabin ladder and the transom, she had been built with customary Matthews shipyard economy and there was not quite enough headroom for a six-foot man in the wheelhouse. Mario was stocky enough to have no trouble but both Alvin and Sturka had to stoop when they came inside.

There was no chart table as such; the paper image of the western Mediterranean was spread across the wooden dash to one side of the binnacle where Mario could read it while standing with one hand on a wheel spoke. He was using compass and chart to dead-reckon from lighthouse to lighthouse. The sea had lifted, an hour before sunset, to a nine-foot chop and had not become any calmer in the hours since; the chunky round-bottomed hull made heavy going of it and Mario had to tack at five-minute intervals against a sea that was running quarter to his course—Southwest by Cabo de Gata, then west around the headlands toward Almería. The weather was running in from the Straits, slanting against the shore. A rough night for seafaring—there were very few boats out, the only lamps were buoys.

It was Cesar who had proved the worst sailor and Mario felt remotely vindicated by that: he knew they all held him in contempt but Cesar was the most arrogant of any and it was satisfying to see him green with *mal de mer*. The malaise had infected Peggy to a lesser extent; she and Cesar were glued to their bunks in the after cabin. Alvin and Sturka were forward, below with Clifford Fairlie, probably trying to indoctrinate him by the dialectic exchange. A stupid pursuit—you couldn't change their minds once they'd gone over the hill. Mario had learned that at home. Mezetti Industries destroyed the environment from day to day with the willful malice of a Genghis Khan and you pointed this out to your father and he came back with engineers' lies contrived to prove it was all Communist propaganda.

Mario knew the others held him in low esteem because he wasn't terribly smart and his Maoism was more doctrinaire than practical. None of them really liked him, Sturka especially, but it didn't matter. Mario was useful; it was important to be useful. Not just the money he could provide but other things as well—like the seamanship they demanded of him now. An ignorant sailor would have swamped the boat in cross-seas a dozen times by now, or run aground on coastal shoals.

The thing that mattered was the liberation of the human race and if you contributed anything at all, regardless how small, your existence was justified. One tiny chink in the endless battering that would destroy the walls of Amerika. One effort to fuck the robber barons whose institutional violence perpetuated the power of the few.

He saw a distant beacon off the starboard bow and he timed the intervals between its flashes. "Right on," he said aloud, pleased with his navigation. He judged the sea and found it safe to drop the retaining loop over the wheelspoke; with the rudder locked he put on his Halloween mask, went down the five-step ladder to the door of the forward cabin and banged with his knuckles.

Sturka pulled the narrow door open, stooping with his thin face close against the ceiling deck. The light was poor, a single low-watt bulb somewhere behind Sturka.

Mario said, "Almería."

Sturka checked the time. "We're behind."

"In this weather you don't keep tight schedules."

"We wanted to make Málaga before dawn."

"You'll never make that. It's a hundred miles."

Sturka registered no emotion. "Well stop wasting time. Take us in."

Behind Sturka he had a glimpse of Alvin—the neo-Alvin, fuzz-wigged, belly and cheeks rounded by stuffing, makeup that made him non-Alvin, jaws riding up and down with the chewing gum he had never used before. Fairlie wasn't supposed to be able to identify any of them. Sturka said it was security—suppose Fairlie got loose? —but it was possible Sturka actually meant to turn him loose and Mario hated the thought.

Sturka was shrouded in a burnous, his face almost invisible; Fairlie behind him sat pale on the pitching bunk gripping its edge. He looked scared and that gave Mario a savage joy.

Hot behind the silly mask Mario went up to the wheelhouse and stripped it off; unlocked the wheel and turned a few points to port. The slight correction increased the roll underfoot and he gripped the red rich walnut spokes of the three-foot wheel.

The red buoy passed astarboard and Sturka came up into the wheelhouse stripping off his Arab headgear and robe; in Levi's and T-shirt Sturka sat down in the canvas chair abaft the locker trunk. "Recite for me Mario."

He was obedient. "Sure. I bury the raft, and walk in, and call the Mezetti office in Gibraltar and tell them to send a car to Almería for me. I take the recorder and the radio into Gibraltar with me. Tomorrow I spend the day making sure things are set up—the Citation and the pilot, refueling stops at Tunis and Bengasi. Friday morning I set up the radio and the recorder with the timer. Then I go over to——"

"What time do you set it for?"

"Eight o'clock Friday night. Right?"

"Go on."

"Friday morning I set the timer and then I go to the bank. I cash the cashier's checks."

"How much do you cash?"

"A hundred thousand dollars." He had been watching the sea—the lights of Almería moving up ahead, the headland sliding up to port. Now he slid a glance at Sturka. "What do we need that much for?"

"Grease."

"What?"

"To persuade some people to keep quiet about us."

"Who?"

"Some people in Lyon and Hamburg. And where we're going, in Lahti." Sturka pronounced it with the hard guttural Finnish "h."

Mario indicated his understanding. The Cessna Citation was a seven-place executive jet with a range of twelve hundred miles; they would have to set down twice for refueling and someone had to provide the landing areas and the fuel at Lyon and Hamburg.

The harbor lights moved off the starboard quarter and Mario kept them there, aiming for the dark beach west of Almería. Depth markings on the chart showed it to be an easy beach; the surf would not be strenuous behind the headland and he would be able to drive the raft right up on the sand. He would have to walk a couple of miles but that didn't bother him.

"Continue your recitation."

"We take off at eleven Friday morning. When we're in the air and out of the traffic pattern I switch the radio off the way Alvin told me and I put my gun on the pilot. I tell him to land at the place you've picked here." He gestured through the salt-crusted windows; the field was fourteen miles inland from Almería, a pocket in the foothills. "If the pilot gives me trouble I shoot him in the leg and tell him to land us fast so we can give him medical attention before he bleeds to death. If he still tries to turn around and get back to Gibraltar or land in Almería I shoot him in the other leg. Then I tell him I'll kill him and take my chances landing it myself."

"Do you think you can?"

"If I have to, I guess. Alvin's coached me a lot."

After the landing they would kill the pilot and bury him. Get everyone aboard and head out into the Med, flying up the channel between Ibiza and Majorca; across the coastline east of Marseille and hedgehopping to avoid the coastal radars. But that leg and the rest would be Alvin's responsibility; all Mario had to do was get the plane from Gibraltar to Almería.

He kept the throttle up, triangulating with his eyes to judge the shore; he would see the combers in time and he had to keep the screw turning in the strong following sea. "I can do it. Don't worry about me."

"I'm not," Sturka said. "But you have the telephone number in Almería. Did you forget that?"

"No. I phone you every two hours. I let it ring exactly four times and hang up." Sturka would be within earshot of that telephone and would be waiting for its ring at even-numbered hours. If it did not ring he would have to assume Mario had been discovered. There was no reason to suspect they would discover him. As far as Mezetti Industries was concerned Mario was traveling on the continent on company business. While the rest of them—Sturka, Alvin, Peggy, Cesar—had journeyed clandestinely to Lisbon aboard a tramp freighter Mario had spent four days at home in New York and then had flown quite openly to Marseille aboard a scheduled Air France flight out of Kennedy Airport. It had been a test and Mario had been willing to undergo it: his passport had not been questioned at the airport, no one had detained him, and therefore he was not a suspect.

It had been a necessary risk because Mario was the one who had to continue operating in the open and they had to be sure the pigs weren't onto him. Maybe he wasn't bright but he understood these things and realized why he had to take the chance. He was glad he had taken it; it had made him more sure of himself, and it had succeeded, and it was necessary to the cause that it succeed.

He began to see the dim phosphor crests of breaking whitecaps on the sea ahead. A mile, perhaps; then it would be time to throttle down. "I don't like putting all that money in greedy hands. We ought to find a better use for it."

"It will further the cause—what more do you need?"

"Why not treat them the same as we treated the greedy pig with the helicopter?" The helicopter hadn't cost them anything.

"Because they're people we may need again." Sturka got to his feet, swayed with the lurch and lunge of the deck, bowed his head under the low overhead decking and moved forward to stand just off Mario's shoulder, watching Mario con the boat into the surf. The boat was crashing hard on the crests; there was still a half mile but the bottom was a shallow shelf that beat up the waves. Everything shuddered, Mario heard brightwork rattling. His plimsolled feet were sure on the deck planks.

He spun the wheel a half turn to starboard but it was a fraction late and a crest broached the windward scuppers; foam rolled across the deck and sprayed him when it caromed through the overhead hatchway. "You sure you can get across there in this?"

"We'll make it," Sturka said.

"I'd better not go in any farther. You want to drop the anchor?"

Sturka went up through the door forward. Spray hosed into the cockpit and wind slammed the door shut. Mario watched him move catfooted to the anchor windlass. He waited until Sturka had a good grip on the railing and then he watched for a wide trough. When the boat pitched into one he spun her fast, rudder hard over, wanting to bring her into the wind before the next crest hit; but she was a little slow and the crest caught her awkwardly and rolled her hard over. There was a great deal of rolling foam and he peered through it anxiously. The lather cascaded away and Sturka was still there, rooted, drenched but relaxed. Mario held the bow straight into the wind and throttled back only a little, needing steerageway; Sturka was pitching the anchor over, letting the chain run through the ratchet.

A big one lifted her ten or twelve feet and she slid down the backside of it nose first. The bow dug into the following comber and Sturka again was buried in black marbled water but when the bow wallowed out of it he was still there with water rolling off him like oil. The chain slacked a little at trough-bottom and Sturka set the ratchet and began to make his way aft, hand over hand along the railing. Mario idled the screw down and waited with his hand on the throttle to see if the anchor had taken hold. The chain drew up taut and he had a feeling, nothing more than an intuitive sensation, of a brief distant scraping before the arrowpoint of the anchor took a grip and the boat hung, cork-bobbing like a buoy, from its straining chain, stern toward shore.

Sturka swung himself into the wheelhouse acrobatically, his clothes pasted to his bony skin. Alvin was coming up from the forward cabin and Mario gave him the wheel and followed Sturka aft to inflate the rubber raft.

He slid the folded raft out from under Peggy's bunk. Peggy gave him a bloodshot look and rolled over; Mario said, "Won't be long now," in an effort to be encouraging but she only grunted. Cesar on the opposite bunk was in bleary agony and the cabin reeked of vomit; Mario was glad to hurry topside, dragging the raft, Sturka pushing it up from below. Sturka came out into the little fishing deck to help him hold the raft down while they inflated it from its canister of compressed air. It was tricky work with the deck pitching eight feet in the air and slamming down; he was soaked through within seconds.

Sturka put his mouth close to Mario's ear to make himself heard over the roar of the sea. "If they catch you."

"They're not going to."

"If they do."

"I don't say a word."

"They'll pry you apart in time. You'll have to talk—everyone does."

"I hold out." Shouted gasps in the roiling night. "As long as I can. Then I give them the thing we made up."

"Recite."

"Now? Here?"

"Recite Mario."

"You're in Tangier waiting for me to pick you up in the plane."

"Go on." Sturka's voice very thin against the roar.

"Jesus. I promise you I haven't forgotten anything."

After a moment Sturka pulled the raft toward the stern rail by its gunwale rope. "All right Mario."

They got it overboard and Sturka held it against the transom while Mario climbed over the rail and braced himself in the raft. The bottom was already awash; he would be in water up to his navel in instants but the raft would hold. The oars were plastic, bolted into their locks; he fixed his grip on them and shouted and Sturka cast him off. He pulled hard; the boat loomed momentarily and then a wave took him; for a bit he was under water with the taste of salt. When it cascaded off him the boat had disappeared and he was alone in the raft—lost, for a bit, until the next breaker picked him up and he had time for a quick glance over his left shoulder to locate the lights of Almería. They gave him bearings and he began to row toward the black silent beach.

BOOK THREE

PURSUIT

THURSDAY,
JANUARY 13

8:00 A.M. Continental European Time Lime paced the garage floor with apathetic weariness. He had slept on the plane but that had been more than twenty-four hours ago and things had moved maddeningly slowly in the day and night since.

The place was cluttered with scientists and their equipment; they were analyzing everything—grease spots on the floor, a wad of chewing gum stuck to the underside of the tool bench, the 500 KC marine transmitter and the Wollensak tape recorder that was plugged into it.

Triangulation by Sixth Fleet and Spanish shore stations had located the point of origin of the Fairlie broadcast—somewhere in the town of Palamos. But Sixth Fleet's radio plot had been faulty by some decimal fraction and the location was an area, not a pinpoint; it had taken nine hours of house-to-house searching to find the transmitter in this place.

The garage sat in solitary squalor along the side of a country road half a kilometer outside Palamos. Its owner was on vacation—visiting a sister in Capetown; he had been away since the ninth of January, which happened to be the day before the Fairlie kidnapping. The garage owner's name was Elías; the South African Government was seeking him for questioning but he hadn't turned up yet.

When they did find Elías he wouldn't be able to tell them anything useful; Lime knew how these things worked. Some faceless intermediary would have offered Elías a hundred thousand pestas to disappear for a week; the intermediary would be described by Elías, and another John Doe would be added to the list of individuals sought for questioning. It would consume far more time than was available; it was the kind of lead Lime never bothered with. You left that sort of thing to the minions of organization. If they turned up something useful they passed it on to you; otherwise you ignored it.

Yesterday at dawn Lime had landed at Barcelona in an Air Force jet with Chad Hill and a team of agents and technicians sent along by Satterthwaite. At the airport they had been collected by a delegation of American and Spanish types and it had been tedious; Lime disliked the boredom of establishing credentials.

The Spanish *Fuerza Aérea* had flown them up to Perdido and Lime had talked with Liam McNeely, who had told him President Brewster had announced that European governments were cooperating with Washington in a vastly expanded program of "protective surveillance" on suspected revolutionaries throughout the Western world. From Perdido Lime had reached Bill Satterthwaite by telephone: he had not tried to conceal his anger. "You're only driving them deeper into their holes. How do you expect me to make contacts if they've all gone to ground?"

"Contacts?" Satterthwaite had sounded confused. Lime had explained it tersely—you had to hope there were scraps of information floating around the Maoist underground; you had to look for pigeons willing to tell you things. One revolutionary could lead you to another—but not if he'd been scared into hiding.

"I'm sorry." Satterthwaite had been cool. "It was a matter of policy—hoping to forestall any further violence from the left. We can hardly rescind it now. You'll have to do the best you can, that's all."

Before ending the transatlantic dialogue Lime had said, "Find out Fairlie's blood type for me, will you?"

"You haven't found blood."

"No. But we might."

"All right. I'll check—where can I get back to you?"

"I'll get back to you." And he had rung off.

There had been an insider at Perdido obviously but he had got away, possibly in the confusion of departures that had attended the end of the Spanish ministers' visit an hour or two before the kidnapping. At any rate no one had kept tabs on the parking lot or the exit road until after the kidnapping and by that time the insider was gone. Careful interrogations by Spanish *Guardianos* had produced the likely possibility the insider had been a handyman who'd been hired on the day before the kidnapping—a Spanish-speaking mestizo with a Venezuelan passport who had paid the chief grounds-keeper fifty thousand pesetas to give him the job, saying he had to prove he had employment or the Spanish government would deport him at the expiration of his alien labor registration. Evidently the Venezuelan had been very persuasive and had triggered the groundskeeper's sympathies—either that or the groundskeeper's price was cynically low. Now the groundskeeper was filled with contrition; he was being held by the *Guardia*, he had been fired by the spa, he probably would be subjected to brutal interrogations for weeks. That would keep a small army of bureaucrats occupied for a while but would produce no useful results.

Lime had gone over the ground at the mountain farm where the kidnappers had abandoned the phony Navy helicopter. The serial numbers had been filed off and acid-eaten but a team of Spanish detectives had etched them out with alcohol and hydrochloric; the helicopter belonged to the Pamplona branch of a German rental concern used by wealthy skiers seeking untouched slopes in the high areas inaccessible by road. The manager of the office had been found dead Monday morning in his bed in Pamplona—at first glance from a heart attack, but autopsy showed he had been murdered with a long thin needle jabbed between the upper ribs into the heart. Only a tiny scab on the skin gave clue. Perhaps he had seen the kidnappers' faces too clearly, or had found out something he shouldn't have—or perhaps he had refused to rent the helicopter to them. At any rate that chain of investigation was broken by the manager's death.

The helicopter had been painted Navy colors and the ID numbers proved to have been splashed on by means of hand-cut stencils. From more than a few feet away they looked perfect and of course at the time no one had had reason to inspect them closely.

The helicopter had been left inside the barn; its rotor blades had been removed crudely by the use of hand tools. The bodies of two Secret Service Agents were in the barn with the chopper, shot by 9mm slugs fired from two different handguns, neither of which had been found.

The helicopter abounded with fingerprints of Fairlie and the two Secret Service men; those were the only identifiable prints found anywhere except for a variety of small partials in and around the house; they were being checked out but were probably the prints of children and wanderers who had stopped by the deserted farm last summer.

The farm did offer one clue: a pair of black leather gloves a *Guardiano* had discovered while sifting through the powder snow piled up by the helicopter's movements. The descending chopper had swept a barnyard area free of snow; this was the clue that had attracted the searchers' attention from the air and had brought investigators here late on the afternoon of the kidnapping. Half buried in one of the loose drifts the gloves had gone unseen until the following morning; a Spanish inspector was studying them when Lime arrived. Handling them gingerly with tweezers.

Lime had told Chad Hill, "Send them to London."

"Why London?"

"Scotland Yard. They've worked out a glove-print identification scheme. They can get glove prints off the helicopter controls," he had explained. "If they match these gloves then we know these were worn by the pilot. About half the time London's been able to pick up latent fingerprints—enough for an ID—from the inside surfaces of the gloves. These are plain leather, they're not lined— I think we've got a pretty good chance."

So the gloves had been flown to London aboard a United States Navy Phantom Jet, along with the dismantled control stick of the helicopter, and Lime and Chad Hill had proceeded to Palamos.

Now in the garage he sat on an upturned packing box wearing a rumpled tweed suit the color of cigarette ashes and a five-o'clock shadow. He felt customarily benumbed, subject to dull pains of resentment—Dominguez, the top man in the *Guardia*, had wasted hours of his time during the night by insisting that Lime address himself personally to the variety of woebegone witnesses the Spaniards had rounded up. There was nothing for it but to comply; not so much because of the demands of international courtesy but because it was indeed possible one of them had something to offer by way of information.

It had consumed most of the night. An old woman who claimed to have seen a hearse drive in and out of the garage. (An old hearse *was* found near the waterfront; whether it was a clue was indeterminate since it had been wiped clean of fingerprints.) A young man who claimed to have seen several Arabs in the vicinity of the garage. (Immigration was checking; questions were being asked in Palamos. No results yet.) A bus driver who had passed the hearse Monday night and seen its driver—a black man in chauffeur's uniform. (The phony helicopter pilot? Possibly; but what did it add?)

There was also a Basque fisherman with a strange tale about

several Arabs and a coffin and a fishing boat. The story was unclear. The fisherman had been taken before Dominguez and Lime had watched as Dominguez infuriated the fisherman to the point of stubborn silence. Dominguez had fired his questions arrogantly and impatiently; Dominguez's accent was Castilian, the fisherman was a Basque. Lime had fumed silently: surely the *Guardia* had a Basque member who could do this interrogation more successfully? But Dominguez wasn't the sort to whom that kind of suggestion would be welcome. Dominguez thought he had a natural gift for intimidating people; with the Basque it produced only defiance but Dominguez couldn't see that.

On his way out Lime had dropped a word to an R.N. subaltern: "See if you can bring that fisherman around to see me when he's through with him, will you? I'll be at the garage."

Three hours ago. Now he sat on the packing box still awaiting the Basque because there was nowhere in particular to go.

Chad Hill kept trotting back and forth bringing items of useless news to him from the various knots of technicians. "It's American gum—spearmint. No fingerprint on it—he must've pressed it with a rag. The alarm clock's a Benrus."

"A Benrus." Lime had learned how to repeat the last word or two whether he was listening or not. It made people go on talking. It was even possible Hill might eventually tell him something he could use.

The 500 KC transmitter was a fishing-boat model. The Wollensak recorder was an old model but a common brand. The mylar tape was also German, available anywhere on the continent; the alarm clock had been used to trigger the broadcast. The tape was reeled onto five-inch spools, Hill explained. It ran at one and seven-eighths inches per second. It was long enough to play about an hour. All three of Fairlie's speeches were on it, separated by five-minute intervals of blank tape.

It was a simple robot device. The ordinary alarm clock was evidence the kidnappers had set the transmitter not more than twelve hours before the broadcast; but that was meaningless—you could travel forever in twelve hours, and by the time Fairlie's voice had been aired at 12:30 P.M. local time last Tuesday the kidnappers could have been anywhere. And by now they had a lead of fifty-six hours on Lime. . . .

They've moved, Lime thought. They didn't stay around here, they'd have known the search would be too intense. They went out: how? Not by public transport; Fairlie was too recogniz-able. Not by car. Helicopter, airplane or boat—it had to be one of those.

Boat, he thought. Because Palamos was a sea-front town, and because the Basque fisherman had seen Arabs on a boat. There had been Arabs around the garage; too much coincidence unless they were the same Arabs. All right then. Boat. What next?

A commotion in the corner: Chad Hill bouncing on his feet, wheeling, loping across with his loud voice preceding him:

"A fingerprint!"

Hill was very excited and Lime stared bleakly. When Hill came to an awkward stop above him he threw his head back. "Chad it could be anybody's fingerprint. Maybe the owner of the place."

"Well of course. But I mean they seem to have wiped the whole place clean before they left—but they missed this one."

"Where is it?" So many people were crowded into the corner he couldn't see.

"On the panel where the light switch is."

It was a possibility to be conceded. He got to his feet with an effort. Their last act would have been to switch off the lights before driving out. They'd have done that after having wiped the place. Yes; a possibility. He went across.

One of the Spanish technicians looked up. He smiled but his eyes were ready to show fear. "She look like they ef-forgot thees wan." He was very proud of his English.

These Spaniards were all James Bonds, trying to decode every laundry list they found in somebody's trash basket. But you couldn't tell; you had to check everything out. *Give us this day our daily break.*

"Put it on the wire."

"Ahjess."

It would be cabled out to Madrid and London and Washington. In a few hours they would have an answer.

7:30 A.M. **North African Time**   The two engines made a racket in the plane like the thunder of a Second World War bomber, Fairlie thought. The fuselage vibrated a great deal. Some loose piece of metal in the cabin kept chattering.

Fingers closed on his wrist: Lady's hand, checking his pulse again.

She seemed to do it quite frequently. Perhaps they were worried about the effects of the drugs they had given him earlier on.

He wasn't drugged now. Blindfolded, his mouth gagged with tape, his hands bound with wire. They didn't want him throwing tantrums. They weren't sure of him yet, they weren't sure he wasn't about to go berserk.

He wasn't sure of it himself.

Lady had warned him not to struggle because he might make himself sick; vomit could make him choke to death. They had taken him ashore in a dinghy and from snatches of talk he pieced it together that they were sinking the boat. A stranger's voice then—an unfamiliar tongue, but the voice had a husky gravel quality, a high-pitched wheezing sort of voice, as if its owner had a bad case of catarrh.

Back into the dinghy again. They'd rowed him out into a fierce chop. He had tried to keep relaxed: he wasn't ordinarily susceptible to seasickness but the young woman's cool warning about vomit had fixed his mind on the subject and it was almost impossible to ignore. He remembered one of McNeely's jokes: *All right, you can do anything in the world as long as you don't think of a white hippopotamus.* Then the McNeely grin: *Ever tried to not think of a white hippopotamus before?*

McNeely. That was in some other world.

They had lifted him, with some strugglings and mouthings of oaths, into a cramped cabin of some kind; helped him feel his way into a seat and settled him into it. Then they had wired his ankles together.

The gravel-voiced wheeze taking its leave; Fairlie had heard oarlocks squeak—evidently the wheezer rowing back to shore alone.

He had thought he was aboard a boat—the same boat or a new one—until he'd heard the engine choke and sputter and begin to roar; he realized immediately it was an airplane.

A seaplane, then.

The second engine had whined into life and there was a great deal of gunning before he felt it begin to move. Taking off seemed to be touch and go: the sea had a wicked slap to it, the cabin lurched and pitched. The epithets of Abdul the black pilot were intense. Fairlie remembered Abdul's cool handling of the helicopter when Abdul had somehow killed the engine while pretending something had gone wrong with it; Abdul's anger now terrified Fairlie but finally they were airborne and he felt the seat tip under him as the plane climbed steeply.

There was no accurate way to estimate the length of time they had been in the air or which way they were heading or even where they had started from, but there was enough talk for Fairlie to identify the various voices and realize there were at least four of them in the plane with him: Abdul, flying it; Sélim, the leader who spoke with a Slavic accent; Lady, who attended him with a professional detachment; Ahmed, who had a Spanish sort of accent and tended to talk in dogmatic clichés.

It was very hard to concentrate. He thought there must be plans he ought to be making. Spotty recollections of all those Second World War memoirs by British aviators who had spent five years organizing incredibly elaborate schemes to escape from Nazi POW camps. *We have a duty to escape.*

There was no *we*, there was only Fairlie, and escape was beyond question; his duty appeared clear enough for the moment—to maintain sanity. He could demand nothing more of himself, not now.

8:10 A.M. Continental European Time   Lime was still on his packing crate. One of the Spanish uniformed cops came into the garage and beckoned: there was a radiophone call from Fleet. Lime took it in the *Guardia* jeep.

The Admiral. "I thought you'd better know—the rival firms are moving in."

Lime went back inside, somewhat depressed. It was not to be avoided that agents for the other side would come into the case. The Russians, the Chinese, an indeterminate number of others. Suppose an Albanian hard-line field agent got in ahead of you, rescued Fairlie—suppose the Albanians decided to keep Fairlie? Far-fetched, but it was a risk; you didn't want to exchange one set of kidnappers for another. What it amounted to was that you had to try and prevent the rival firms from finding out what you had found out. It wasn't easy, not with communications tapped routinely and areas of the world where members of the opposing teams sat on the corners of one another's desks. It meant Lime had to tighten his communications, use safe lines whenever possible, code his transmissions—another time-consuming chore.

More likely the rival firms were eager to help out. For a Russian or a Chinese team to rescue Fairlie would be a propaganda victory unprecedented in decades—a triumph of public relations if nothing else. But you still couldn't afford to work with them. Once you admitted them to partnership you would be delayed at every junction place; your partners would be required to check back with superiors and clear every decision through layers of bureaucracy.

You could expect a certain amount of help—technical stuff, manpower, communications—from the allies; but these were equally hamstrung by tiers of authority and in the end you had to keep your hand free. So you used everyone and gave nothing to anyone. In a very short time all of them would begin to resent Lime and he would find resistance when he sought further assistance.

The CIA had a hundred thousand employees of whom twenty thousand were field agents; of these a thousand or more were strung through the Mediterranean area, on call if and when Lime needed them. At the moment they merely had orders to check whatever contacts they had, find out what sort of rumors were floating through the underground.

The English sailor arrived at half past eight with the Basque fisherman in tow. The fisherman's name was Mendes; his smile looked slack-muscled, as if he had been posing too long for a slow photographer. His eyes were a faded blue and his drooping pinched mouth suggested a discontented lifetime of anxieties and disappointments. He smelled faintly of fish and the sea. He spoke no English and minimal Spanish. Lime had summoned a Basque-speaking *Guardiano* two hours ago; now he brought the *Guardiano* into the circle and began the session.

It was very kind of Señor Mendes to make the time to assist. The *commandante's* unfortunate manner was regrettable; it was to be hoped Señor Mendes had not been too offended—everyone was under great strain, perhaps the *commandante's* abruptness was understandable? Would Señor Mendes care for an American cigarette?

Lime made sure he had Mendes on the hook before he began to tug the line—gently at first: a day's fishing was being lost by Señor Mendes's detention, the American government assuredly wished to compensate him for his loss of time—would a thousand pesetas be sufficient? But very gently always because you couldn't afford to offend; when Mendes took the money it was with the proud agreement he was not being bribed but rather being paid a suitable wage for his time and labor as a detective assisting in the search for the abducted American President-elect.

It took time to undo the damage Dominguez had inflicted but in the end the Basque's story came out. He had not seen any faces, only the Arab robes of three figures; a fourth man in some sort of uniform. Arriving on the coast in a hearse. Mendes had been a few hundred yards up the beach, walking from the boat basin to his home which was above the dunes not far from the breakwater where the hearse had drawn up. It had come without headlights; it was met by a dinghy from a boat lying close to shore.

The three Arabs and the man in uniform had carried a coffin from the hearse to the dinghy. Someone—a fifth one, unseen by Mendes —had driven the hearse away. The others had gone aboard the boat with the coffin and the boat had set out to sea.

Plainly it was not all Mendes had to say. Lime waited him out, not prompting; the man's agreeability was fragile, the wrong question might close him up.

Finally it came in a blurted rush: Mendes had recognized the boat.

He had agonized; it troubled him deeply; the boat belonged to a friend, a colleague, and in Spain a Basque did not inform on a fellow Basque—yet it had to do with the kidnapping of the *presidente. . . .*

"We understand," Lime breathed sympathetically.

The friend was Lopez, his boat the *Maria Linda* after Lopez's wife. An old boat, somewhat the worse for age, but you would recognize her easily by the smokestack—she had this raked stack, *comprende?* Like a miniature ocean liner. You couldn't miss her, there wasn't another like her on the Costa Brava.

Maria Linda had not returned to Palamos since that night, Mendes said sadly. Assuredly it was a long voyage, wherever she was bound.

Lime turned, raised his eyebrows at Chad Hill. After a moment Hill came to; bounced away in belated obedience to start the machinery in motion for the wholesale search for *Maria Linda.*

Lime kept at Mendes, his question-hammers wrapped in courteous padding. Details emerged; no further startling developments. He kept it up for an hour and sent Mendes away with his thanks, having learned a few things of possible interest: chief among them an address and Lime sent a runner immediately to locate Lopez's wife.

At quarter past ten she appeared, Maria Lopez, a tired woman gone to stoutness, the vestiges of beauty remaining in black eyes and long-fingered hands. Lime was straightforward with her: he told her of the seriousness of her husband's predicament, he offered her money—ten thousand pesetas—and he asked his question: what did she know of the Arabs her husband had taken off the beach on Monday night?

He had given her ten thousand; he held twenty thousand more in his hand. The woman spoke without moving her eyes away from the money. Lime listened coolly to the interpreter. They had approached Lopez Sunday after church, three Arab men and an Arab woman with a veil. They said they were from Morocco. Their brother had died in Barcelona but they could not get official permission to remove the body from the country. They said it was important to Bedouins to have their dead buried in family ground. They admitted it was a smuggling thing, against the law, but they appealed to Lopez's sympathies and they offered a great deal of money. Lopez knew what it meant to be buried in consecrated ground of course. Mrs. Lopez was not sure how much money was involved but it was possibly fifty thousand pesetas or more, plus fuel and expenses.

Had she seen the Arabs up close? No she had not seen them at all; Lopez had described them as four Arabs—three men and a woman. She spread her hands toward Lime: it was winter, a fisherman's life was thankless. They had known nothing of any kidnapping.

Chad Hill intercepted him at the garage door: "For Christ's sake," Hill complained.

"What?"

"They've had it twenty-four hours."

"Had what?"

"The boat. The *Maria Linda.*"

It was a fifty-minute helicopter ride from Palamos up the coast to the beach where Spanish coastguardsmen had found *Maria Linda* Wednesday morning impaled on a shoal in the lee of a breakwater. She hung at a vertiginous angle, anchor-chain taut. It looked as though she had sought shelter in a storm and been smashed aground. But there had been no storm Tuesday night and the weather since then had been blowy but not monstrous.

By the time Lime's chopper set him down a captain of *Guardia* had arrived to meet him with everything the Spanish police had collected on the case. Ordinarily it would have taken much longer but ordinarily no one was holding a blowtorch to the *Guardia*'s backside.

The body had been removed to the police morgue in Barcelona. Lopez had been found dead on the beach within sight of the grounded boat, hidden by dunes from the coast highway which ran close along the Med at this point: they were north of Cape Creus, the French frontier was only seven kilometers away.

Lopez had been stabbed several times, with more than one knife. The weapons had not been found. The murder case was being investigated but until now there had been no connection with the Fairlie kidnapping and therefore it hadn't been brought to Lime's attention.

A few latent fingerprints had been found on the polished wood surfaces of the boat's interior; photos were included in the folder just delivered to Lime. The prints were being processed in Madrid; as soon as Hill's call had alerted the *Guardia*, copies of the prints had been forwarded to Interpol and Washington. It was assumed most of the prints were Lopez's but everything was being checked: fingerprints were being lifted off the corpse for purposes of comparison and elimination.

The *Guardiano* was a captain by rank, a precise cop with a professional voice. It droned on, filling Lime in, while a cool gray wind ruffled the sea and blew sand in Lime's face. Tire tracks had been found between the highway and the beach, indicating that a vehicle had pulled off the road and driven up onto the small promontory overlooking the beach. It had parked there, pointed toward the sea, possibly to flash its headlights out to sea in signal. High tide had come and gone between the murder and the discovery; the only footprints found were high up, near the body and the tire tracks. The vehicle had been considerably heavier when it left than it had been when it arrived, and the departure tracks merged with the highway in a southerly direction, indicating the vehicle had arrived from the south and departed toward the south, retracing its course. Unfortunately the sand was too soft to reveal a tread pattern. The width between tires indicated a standard wheelbase for medium-sized automobile or small van.

As for the reason for the abandonment of the boat, it appeared the engine-oil line had rusted through; the oil had leaked out and the engine had seized up.

To Lime there was only one clue in all this that wasn't ambiguous; it was a straightforward indication of the kidnappers' intent. The Lopez boat had cracked up *north* of its point of departure. Assumption: they had been heading for France, or Italy.

It was there in plain sight and because the kidnappers weren't careless men it had to be assumed they meant it to be seen: they could have sunk the boat easily enough and left no traces. That was the thing. They had put it on display, they hadn't concealed it. Lopez's body, the boat. These had been meant to be found.

He had to read something into that. They told him they were heading north. Now it was a question whether they wanted him to hunt north or, conversely, whether they wanted him to think that far ahead and hunt south.

There were many layers of bluff. First level: if a clue appears it should be believed. Second level: if it is an obvious clue it must be a red herring designed to waste time and resources; it is so obvious it had better be dismissed. Third level: if it is so obviously an invitation to dismiss it and do the opposite then perhaps it ought to be obeyed after all because the kidnappers made it blatantly obvious just to confuse. Fourth level: the kidnappers, anticipating this dilemma in his mind, want him to think it through all the way to the end and then go ahead and investigate the clue exhaustively because, all other things being equal, a clue is a clue and even if it is a deliberate plant it may give away something it wasn't intended to reveal.

It came down to a question of the order of subtlety of the bluff and he knew once he became trapped analyzing levels of possibility he could burn his brain out trying to guess the truth.

The one thing that stood out was that the kidnappers were professionals. Or at least they were led by a professional. A professional was a man who didn't leave clues unless he intended to. This entire operation had been set up not by any amateur revolutionary but by a pro who had planned every step and timed every movement. The snatch caper at Perdido had been a model of economical efficiency. The mountain farm had been selected with exact precision for its proximity to the Mediterranean coast and its flying distance from Perdido because the kidnappers knew they had to get the chopper under cover before the authorities got a search operation under way. The kidnappers knew just how much time they had for each step of their operation and obviously they hadn't rushed anything. They had taken Fairlie, concealed the chopper, driven openly by car from the farm to the garage outside Palamos—all this during the period of time when the authorities were still organizing for a search, still absorbing the impact of the incredibly simple crime that had been committed. But once under cover in that Palamos garage the kidnappers had stayed put, not allowing panic to push them into movement again until after dark. By that time they had to assume the police and security of a dozen nations were searching for them but they acted with aplomb, delivering Fairlie by hearse to the waterfront, getting aboard Lopez's boat and heading out to sea.

They hadn't left things to chance at any other step and there was no reason to assume the abandonment of Lopez's boat had been an accident. If the engine had frozen up it was probably because the kidnappers had poked a hole through the rusty oil pipe to make it look like an accidental failure.

They might have left one inadvertent clue: the fingerprint on the light switch in the Palamos garage—if in fact the print belonged to one of the kidnappers and not the owner of the garage or one of its customers.

It was the fingerprint that gave him the impression the kidnappers were amateurs led by a professional. A professional developed habit patterns, he never left fingerprints on anything and never had to think about it. By reflex he always went back and wiped things off.

The light switch was the last thing they had touched on their way out and someone had forgotten to wipe it.

If the print turned out to be Fairlie's then Lime would believe it had been left on purpose to attest to the fact that Fairlie was alive. But he doubted it was Fairlie's fingerprint; they wouldn't have allowed Fairlie near a light switch. If the print belonged to any of the kidnappers then it hadn't been left there deliberately; leaving misleading clues was part of the game but giving away the identity of your own man was not.

Barcelona in winter was a distressing gray city of industrial blight and waterfront rot.

The Spaniards had provided an office in an overflow annex a block from the government admin building; it was a quarter of bleak narrow streets—cobblestones and soot-black walls. From the aircraft carrier a whaleboat had brought ashore a Navy UHF scrambler transceiver; it had been manhandled into the office.

The crew had arrived ahead of him and the office crawled with personnel but what took Lime by surprise was the presence of William T. Satterthwaite—rumpled, tired, his curly black hair awry.

There was a small private room set aside for Lime's use but Lime took a quick look at it and declined. "Have you got a car outside?"

"Yes. Why?" Satterthwaite pushed his glasses up.

"Let's sit in the car and talk."

In the car Satterthwaite said, "Do you honestly think they'd have the nerve to bug that office?"

"It's what I'd do. You don't want foreigners running king-size security operations on your turf without finding out what they're up to."

Satterthwaite was capable of dismissing the problem instantly: "All right. What about this coffin they carried Fairlie in? Do you think he's dead?"

"I doubt it. You don't kill your ace in the hole until you have to —or until you've run out of a use for it. There's a better question than that, though—how do we know it was Fairlie? It may have been a hundred fifty pounds of bricks."

"You mean you're not buying the Lopez boat thing at all?"

"Suppose they had accomplices who took Lopez's boat to make it look as if they took Fairlie that way?" Lime hunted around the dashboard for the ashtray. "The only thing definite is they've given us two pieces we were meant to see."

"The Arab costumes and the boat headed north. One suggesting North Africa and the other suggesting western Europe. Do you think they could both be phonies? Maybe they're going for the Balkans?"

"It's all guesswork right now. We're chasing our tails."

"Don't get so damned defeatist, David. There are hundreds of thousands of people working on this. Someone's bound to come up with something."

"Why? We're not dealing with wild-eyed freaks."

Satterthwaite's eyes burned behind the high magnification of the lenses. "Who *are* we dealing with?"

"A pro and a cell of well-trained amateurs. Not a government job, not a people's liberation-movement thing. We won't find an organization working the caper, although we may find one paying the bills."

"Why not?"

"Because you haven't told me anything to the contrary."

"I don't follow that."

Lime tapped ash, missed the ashtray, brushed ashes off his trouser leg. "If any establishment was behind it your hundreds of thousands of agents would have had a hint by now. It's not the kind of operation a power bloc would try. The only political effect it can have is to solidify the existing powers. The Communists will help *us*, they won't help the kidnappers; they'd expect reciprocal treatment if somebody snatched one of theirs, they can't afford to open this kind of can of beans. It would start a free-for-all of assassinations and abductions. You can't conduct international relations on that level and everybody since Clausewitz has known that—look what happened after Saravejo."

Lime snubbed the butt out in the ashtray and pushed it shut. "Look, what's their motive? You've heard the ransom demands. All they seem to want is the seven bombers. It's the Marighella technique—nothing unusual about it. They arrest yours, you kidnap theirs and make a swap."

"Then we all know who's running this show, don't we," Satterthwaite said. His eyes rested complacently against Lime.

"Probably," Lime replied, quite evenly. "But we've had the search out for Sturka and his people for more than a week. He may have gone to ground—this may be an entirely different bunch."

"You're grabbing at straws," Satterthwaite growled; he leaned even farther forward and his voice was an angry hiss: "Why in the hell do you think we had to force you onto this job?"

"Because you assumed I knew it was Sturka."

"And Sturka is your boy, David. You know him better than anybody else—you've proved you know the way he thinks. You've covered the same ground he's covered."

"I've never laid eyes on the man."

"But you *know* him."

"Maybe it is Sturka's caper. But I'm not putting all my eggs in that basket. Logic points to Sturka but logic is a test of consistency, not truth. If it's not Sturka, and I try to play as if it is, then we'll end up farther behind than we started. I've got to work with facts, don't you see that?"

"Assume it's Sturka, David. What then?"

Lime shook his head. "We've made too many wrong assumptions already. Give me a fact and then I'll go to work." He found another cigarette in the crumpled pack. "Now you didn't fly over here just to tell me I thought it was Sturka. You knew that already. Or are you just shuttling back and forth across the Atlantic to keep tabs on me?"

"Don't be an idiot."

"I just wanted it cleared up. That being the case I assume you've got orders for me—something you couldn't even trust to a scrambler."

"All right. Knowing that much let's see if you can guess what they are."

"Well you want him back before Inauguration Day, for openers."

"Yes, but you knew that. It gives you a little over six days."

"It's not likely."

"Make it likely."

"Don't be an ass."

"I know. All right. Suppose I tell you I've brought an A-team from Langley with me."

"Then I'd say you're a damn fool. I suppose you've got them running around loose in the Spanish countryside sighting in their scopes on sheep and peasants."

"Hardly. They're aboard the *Essex*. When you need them you ask Sixth Fleet for the Early Birds and they'll be at your disposal by helicopter."

Too little sleep, too many cigarettes; he had a headache, his mouth tasted brassy. It was absurd to think about it. Langley was CIA's sprawling Virginia headquarters, a place which was top secret —*Time* said so. "An A-team from Langley" was a euphemism for a killer squad.

"These are the best professionals in the Agency. Twenty-eight men. Three helicopters."

"And carrying as many guns as a heavy cruiser I'm sure."

"It's a direct Presidential order, David."

"Face up on the table, will you? It was your crackbrained notion, you took it to Brewster and he okayed it."

"Not really. I only provided the methodology."

"It guarantees you won't get Fairlie back alive."

"On the contrary. You don't use them until you've got Fairlie out. Fairlie and the kidnappers. *Then* you use them."

Lime understood it up to a point; it was all based on a flimsy assumption regarding the kidnappers' whereabouts. The premise behind Satterthwaite's idea was that the kidnappers were holed up on territory belonging to a regime that wouldn't assist in capturing them and wouldn't agree to extraditing them to the United States even if it did capture them. So you had to go in, get them, take them out, and leave no clues behind to indicate you had ever been there. It was very Wild Bill Donovan in concept and Lime found it tiresome.

"David, if we put them on trial we have to admit how and where we took them. It could be embarrassing."

"Embarrassing. For Christ's sake." Lime shook his head. "At any rate you're still jumping to that conclusion."

"And you're wasting time in Spain when you should be down there."

"Not yet. I still want a fact. Suppose they're halfway to Albania?"

"You're dragging your heels. Everything points to it—you know that."

"You've already got plenty of gumshoes prowling around down there, I'm sure."

"Damn few of them with your knowledge of the territory. And none of them with your knowledge of Sturka."

"That's two assumptions—the place and the identity—and I'm not buying either one of them yet."

"Why?"

"Because of the Arab robes."

"So it's a bluff," Satterthwaite said. "You've seen bluffs before."

"The boat headed north. Is that the same kind of bluff?"

"Obviously a different kind of bluff."

Filled with simmering anger Lime said, "You've got to understand this. I can't do it by myself. I've got to have a fact, and then I can start taking advantage of their mistakes. I need their help."

"Fat chance of getting it."

"I don't know. I only need to help plan their mistakes."

Satterthwaite was silent for a bit; finally he said, "I'm going to let you alone from here on. But I want it clear that you're under orders to use the A-team if and when you've extracted the kidnappers."

"It's so fucking cheap."

"It's politics. You don't ask favors when you don't have to—it only leaves you owing somebody a favor. With that crowd we can't afford to be obliged to them for anything at all."

"Then use an intermediary. The Russians?"

"It would have to be the Chinese and we don't want to be owing them any favors either." Satterthwaite sat back, reached for the door handle but didn't open it. "Oh. You asked for Fairlie's blood type—a wise question. Unfortunately it's AB negative. I've left in-

structions to have a case on the ready helicopter aboard *Essex.*
Good enough?"

"For the moment."

An hour later Satterthwaite was on his way back to Washington and Lime was running a battery shaver over his chin in the rancid loo of the annex building. He wanted a shower and a good meal and twelve hours' sleep; he settled for a quick wash and a desk-corner lunch of bread and cheese and jug sangría from a nearby café.

He locked himself in the tiny office cubicle and stretched out on the floor with his hands interlaced under the back of his head; stared at the ceiling and tried to fit things together in his mind. The way to do this was to let the mind go. His upper thoughts immediately swayed toward Bev Reuland but he made no effort to correct the drift.

Two days ago on his way to Andrews AFB he had made time to see her: called Speaker Luke's office and arranged to meet her in the Rayburn cafeteria. He had stopped at a claustrophobically narrow shop to get a dozen pink roses and had arrived in the cafeteria carrying them. Bev, in a harlequin skiing jacket of some green-and-white synthetic fiber that glistened like plastic, her hair tied in a horsetail with a small ribbon, had watched his approach with suspicion, a shadow crossing her eyes.

"What's this for?"

"A little grace if you please."

"Those are break-it-to-her-gently roses." She unwrapped enough of the green-wrapped package to see the buds. "They *are* lovely," she conceded.

It was the middle of the afternoon and the place was nearly empty; conversations were faint distant mutters across the room. He said, "It's nothing much. I'll be gone a little while."

No reply. She got up and went to the counter and he watched her go through the railed route to the coffee urn, a stop at the cashier, her high-hipped stride as she returned bearing two cups of coffee. She sat down on the edge of her chair as if she expected at any moment it would explode beneath her. "How long?"

"Open-ended."

"They've sent you after Fairlie." A flat statement, but she was very tense with eyes hungry for information.

"I remember Bev Reuland. The girl who only goes with people if they're fun."

"Oh shut up David, you're not funny."

Things had changed far more than he had wanted. It had always been no-questions-asked between them. She was a girl with a slow carnal smile and a healthy set of appetites and they liked each other. Now she was a different girl because if something happened to Lime a little piece of Bev would go with him. The cup and saucer rattled in her hand; she put them down. "Well. What are we supposed to say to each other?"

"Nothing. I'll be back—you can think about what you want to say, and tell me then."

"You weren't going out in the field anymore."

"I know."

"I suppose they turned your head. It must be very flattering to be told you're the best they've got—the only one who can do the job." Her lips quivered before she drew them in between her teeth.

"I'm not dead yet," he said very gently. The roses lay across the table between them; he pushed the roses away and covered her hand with his palm but she drew it away in pique and Lime laughed at her.

"It's not funny."

"You said that before."

"Now I'm sure you're listening," she said. "God damn it they've got millions of people. It doesn't have to be you. If you don't find the kidnappers you'll be blamed for it for the rest of your life—and if you do find them they'll probably kill you."

"I like your overwhelming confidence in me."

"Oh I know, you're the master spy, you're the best in the world —I've heard all that drivel from your fawning admirers. I'm not impressed. Shit, David, they're setting you up for a fall guy."

"I know they are."

"Then why in the hell did you agree to it?" She sat snapping her thumbnail against her front teeth. "When you were making up your mind," she said, "you didn't think of me at all."

"That's right."

"That's pretty shitty."

"I know."

"I'm beginning to wish you loved me a little."

"I do."

Now she smiled but it was crooked. "Well I suppose loving is more important than being loved. But really I don't like this—we're starting to sound like two characters in an Ingrid Bergman movie. You're even beginning to look a little like Paul Henreid."

She was trying to play at his own game and it pleased him, ludicrously; he pushed his chair back and stood. She opened her handbag, fished for a lipstick, spread it on her mouth and squeezed her lips together to distribute it and inspected the result in her compact mirror. She was the closest to an unselfish human being he had ever known; he waited, keeping the jet waiting at Andrews, and heard the small crisp snap of her handbag and watched her get up and come around the table. She coiled her fingers around his arm. "All right. I'll wait dutifully. Is that what you wanted to hear?"

"Yes."

"One of these days you may learn to express your feelings. At least I've got you admitting you *have* feelings."

That was true, and it was why he loved her.

Now his hands remembered the feel of her hard tight little ass and he opened his eyes to look at the ceiling and wondered how long he had dozed. The noise that had awakened him was repeated: urgent loud knuckles against the door. He climbed to his feet and unlocked it to Chad Hill.

"We've got a make." Hill had a teleprinter decode in his hand. Lime took it.

FROM: SHANKLAND
TO: LIME
REF: LATENT FINGERPRINT PALAMOS
SUBJECT IDENTIFIED AS MARIO P. MEZETTI X WHITE
MALE AMERICAN X AGE 24 X HT 5–10 X WT 170 X
HR BLK X EYS BRN X NO IMS X WIREPHOTOS ENROUTE
X TRACER IN PROGRESS X SHANKLAND

Lime read it twice. "Never heard of him."

"Not one of the people you identified with Sturka last week?"

"No." Lime's eyes whipped up from the decode to Hill. "Corby. Renaldo. Peggy Astin. One John Doe."

"Mezetti could be the John Doe."

"So could the man in the moon."

"Alvin Corby's black. Haven't you had him in mind for the chopper pilot from the beginning?"

"Offhand how many black revolutionaries would fit the description? The helicopter pilot was twenty pounds heavier than Corby. McNeely's seen the mug shots of Corby and said it wasn't the same man."

He walked out into the bullpen and turned toward the UHF table where technicians were feeding incoming signals into the tape printers. There ought to be more coming in now; with a positive make at last there would be data from all over.

It came in bits and pieces during the next half hour. Mezetti was the son of an important industrialist. Five years ago he had been associated with one of the SDS wings and had been arrested, fingerprinted, questioned and released. No other criminal record. No FBI file; Mezetti was on the list of people not on the list.

Two CIA items: Mezetti had turned up in Singapore two and a half months ago ostensibly as a tourist, had been frisked by Singapore Customs because he looked freaky but had not been found to be carrying drugs of any kind; routine CIA coverage with crossreferences to Passport Bureau records showed Mezetti had made fourteen trips from UCLA to Acapulco in ten months two years ago: he had been tossed seven times out of the ten but no drugs had been found on him. Narco Bureau had a note in a dead file that Mezetti had been suspected as a courier but had been found clean; whatever the purpose of his trips to Acapulco, it hadn't been narcotics. Subsequent notation from CIA's Acapulco stringer revealed Mezetti's mother and sister had spent the winter in question in Acapulco. Lime made a face.

SEC records by way of FBI showed Mezetti listed as owner-ofrecord of thirty-five thousand shares of Mezetti Industries Common. An IRS note appended: he was also listed as an officer of the corporation—probably a tax dodge, a funnel through which his father could pour funds into his son's account without facing inheritance taxes later on.

FBI was commencing washes of subject's known hangouts. Routine telephone checks established he was not at home; no one knew where he was; his mother thought he had gone to Europe on company business; his father knew nothing of any such thing.

Then a signal from FBI over Shankland's signature: Mezetti had flown by Air France from New York to Marseille on Saturday, January eighth.

That was thirty-six hours before Fairlie had been kidnapped.

"Christ," Hill said. "Walking around right out in bare-ass open."

"Well they must have done it to find out if he was clean."

"So he's their outside contact—they need to know he's still free to move around."

"Using a cover—his mother said he told her he was over here on company business." He considered it. "All right. Items. He was clean Saturday night, they can't know about the fingerprint, so they've got to assume he's still free to move in the open. They'll keep using him." His face changed abruptly: "Mezetti Industries. That's pretty big stuff. Then the kid's their bankroll."

It made it a notch more likely the operation was fully independent—not a hire-contract job paid for by an organization. That made Lime's job harder; it meant the kidnappers were working alone without a network. You couldn't infiltrate a network that didn't exist.

Hill spoke slowly. "Now the question is do we keep it in the family or let the rival firms in?"

The rival firms would come into it in time even without invitation —KGB's immense machinery in Moscow would find out within twenty-four hours that the hunt was on for one Mario P. Mezetti. Peking would be close on the Russians' heels.

Lime made his decision in the time it took to formulate the words. "If we haven't found something by midnight we'd better bring Bizenkev into it."

"Do we let it drop as if it's an accident or do we print him a formal invitation?"

"As formal as it can get." If their help was solicited openly and with the knowledge of the world press, the Soviets would have less room for double crosses.

"And the same with the Chinese, I imagine," Hill said.

Lime nodded. "Midnight. After that we can put out an APB on Mezetti."

"What about between now and then?"

"Find out who deals with Mezetti Industries over here. They may even have offices of their own on this side. See if he's made contact with anybody. Put out an APB in the family but try to keep it confidential. The *Guardia* will have to know who to look for."

"Tangier?"

"Not yet. Their mouths flap too much."

"You're banking on them being on a boat, aren't you." The question wasn't as astute as it seemed; Hill could make his deductions from a simple understanding of the timetable. If the kidnappers

were using a boat they wouldn't have had time to reach Tangier yet.
Hill said, "What about SDECE?"

"They'd better be in on it."

"I know. But it makes it a fair bet the Russians will have it before
midnight. If the French don't leak it the *Guardia* will."

Which was being very polite to the CIA, Lime thought, but he let
it go.

At half past four Madrid reported that Mezetti had checked
through the French-Spanish border on Saturday, January eighth,
driving a hired Renault four-door. The car hadn't turned up yet. Its
description and plate number had been broadcast to all Spanish
police.

It placed Mezetti in the Barcelona area shortly before the kidnapping; it added little to what Lime had already assumed but it was
confirmation and that never hurt.

At five-ten the break came.

Hill took the call and hanging up turned to Lime: "Agency
stringer in Gibraltar. He's just left the Mezetti Industries office. The
kid's in a hotel there."

Lime exhaled deeply.

Hill still had his hand on the cradled telephone receiver. "Pick
him up?"

"No. I want a tail on him."

"We could pull him apart, make him talk."

"Tail him."

"Jesus I wouldn't. He loses the tail, our heads roll."

"And Fairlie's. Don't you think I know that? Button him up tight
—but don't touch him." Lime turned toward the door. "Hustle me
up an airplane, will you? I'm going down there."

3:30 P.M. EST   Riva was acting the part of a Puerto Rican tourist.
He had papers to prove it, if anyone should care to ask; no one had.
His only concession to the need for a precautionary disguise was a
hairpiece which filled in his widow's peak, gave him a head of
salt-and-pepper hair and a lower forehead. Nothing more was
needed; Riva was amorphous, people had to meet him eight or ten
times before they could recall what he looked like.

He had come down from New York on the Metroliner and found

a taxi driver at Union Station willing to take him around Washington on a sightseeing tour. Riva told the driver he particularly wanted to see the homes of Congressmen and Senators and Cabinet members.

He and Sturka had gone over the same route several times a month ago to check out locations and security arrangements; the tour today was designed mainly to discern what added security precautions had been taken. If any. Riva was unimpressed by the Americans' notions of security.

There was a house trailer in the driveway of Senator Ethridge's place; he had expected that much. The trailer would contain a Secret Service crew. That was all right; they could afford to bypass Ethridge. The cab drove on.

Milton Luke had an apartment in a high-rise building on Wisconsin Avenue. The cab cruised past and Riva saw no armed men on the curb or in the visible sector of the lobby. But that didn't mean much; later he would have to reconnoiter the building on foot.

On Massachusetts Avenue just above Sheridan Circle was a massive apartment building that housed among others Congressmen Wood and Jethro, Secretary of the Treasury Jonathan Chaney, Senator Fitzroy Grant, and syndicated political columnist J. R. Ilfeld. The concentration of targets made the building important in Riva's calculations and he studied it with care as they drove past. Again there was no indication of protection or surveillance.

Senator Wendell Hollander had a house in the same district, not three blocks from the apartment tower; the house was an elephantine structure of Georgian tastelessness surrounded by heavy trees whose branches were seasonally bare. Hollander, President pro tempore of the Senate, was third in line for the Presidency after Ethridge and Milton Luke; surely there would be a Secret Service mobile home in his drive.

But there was no trailer. Riva smiled a little and the cab proceeded toward Senator Forrester's house on Arizona Terrace.

FRIDAY, JANUARY 14

4:10 A.M. EST   Dexter Ethridge lay awake with a mild headache reviewing his cram course in the Presidency. It was all flavored by Brewster's noxious cigars. Cabinet members and generals had been delegated to brief Ethridge on the endless list of facts and questions; but President Howard Brewster was the dominant figure, always looming. Ethridge was learning how easily his appraisal of the frailties of a man like Brewster could obscure the overriding presence the man projected.

Everyone knew the folksy mispronunciations were the smoke-screen of a politician incarnate. The consummate shrewdness showed through; nobody was fooled. But Ethridge was learning that Brewster's ways were even more misleading than he had always assumed.

When Brewster said, "I'm gon' be interested to know what you think, Dex," it came out with a sincerity that almost persuaded him that what he thought was of paramount importance to Howard Brewster. Brewster did crave public attention like an addict, but that was what misled. It concealed the enormous self-confidence of the man. When Brewster asked an opinion he wanted support; but the support he required was merely political, never intellectual. Once Howard Brewster made up his own mind he *knew* he was right and he didn't need the agreement or consensus of any group. It was a throbbing vital rectitude: an awesome and monumental self-assurance.

It frightened Ethridge because each day's White House consultation added to his conviction that Brewster's larger-than-life stance of power and authority was a basic requisite for the job. A President needed to have that Sophoclean tragic-hero quality—and it was a quality Ethridge knew he didn't possess.

They said you grew into it. It came with the territory, look how Harry Truman grew. But Ethridge wasn't satisfied with that. He thought himself an open-minded man, willing to hear out all sides of a question before making up his mind; it had always been a virtue but now it became a handicap and he was beginning to regard himself as an indecisive man. In the President's chair that was no good: often you couldn't wait for all the results to come in—often you had to make a spot decision.

It was something Ethridge wasn't sure he could learn to do. He wasn't unaware of his own lackluster record in Congress and looking back he believed a good part of it was due to his overdeveloped willingness to sympathize with all sides—something that led to compromise rather than decision. Compromise was the basic weapon in any official's political arsenal but there were times when it should not be employed. Would Ethridge recognize those times? Would he be prepared to act accordingly?

The worry had kept him awake on rumpled sheets. He tried to take solace from his observations of others who had changed, grown, toughened. He remembered Bill Satterthwaite landing by helicopter late yesterday afternoon on the White House lawn after his exhausting trip to Spain. Satterthwaite had come striding into the Oval Office on his frail short legs and reported on his meeting with David Lime with all the assured authority of a born administrator. Cynicism had enlarged Satterthwaite, in Ethridge's estimation; it had instilled political savvy in the little thinker.

He remembered Satterthwaite from the old days—Satterthwaite's early arrival in Washington, two cabinets ago. A young intellectual, donnishly provincial—fiery, loud, positive, insensitive. Satterthwaite had carried an intellectual chip—a contempt for the unsophisticated, a preposterously belligerent liberalism. Nine years ago they had been pushing a bill to unload a few hundred square miles of Kentucky swampland, formerly a Federal CBW testing range, onto the state as a wilderness preserve. The key to the bill's passage had been the cooperation of Kentucky's crusty Senator Wendell Hollander and the President had wooed Hollander energetically and it was clear Hollander was coming around despite the administrative expense the park would load on Kentucky. Then at a dinner party thrown by the wife of the Secretary of the Interior —Ethridge recalled it vividly—Satterthwaite had buttonholed Senator Hollander with an oblivious diatribe about elitist white neocolonialism in the South. Hollander had been astonished, then insulted. Satterthwaite kept grinding relentlessly away until he reached his climax, shouted in triumph and stalked away filled with righteous vindication—and Senator Hollander had said his chilly good-nights, the Kentucky wilderness bill dead as the League of Nations.

Satterthwaite had outgrown that. He was still capable of arrogance but he had learned where to tread softly.

It was Wendy Hollander who hadn't outgrown it. Hollander's seniority had increased his power but his mind remained fixated in the nineteen forties. He survived on the Hill like a hardy troglodyte, literal and opinionated, hating in plurals: Commies, Negroes, the beneficiaries of the give-everything-to-the-poor programs. A cantankerous patriotic yahoo with a rheumy old-timer's thoroughly prejudiced view of his fellow man.

One of the prospects of the Presidency that horrified Ethridge was that every time he turned around in office he was going to have to deal with the chairman of Senate Appropriations. How did you deal at all with a man who was still capable of phrases like "crypto-pinkos" and "the international Commie conspiracy"? Hollander was a rigid fundamentalist conservative, albeit a Democrat; he saw the world's conflicts as a cut-and-dried dispute on the level of a cowboys-and-Indians game and anyone who denied this simple truth was a Commie trying to lull the Good People into a feeling of false security.

Hollander chastised his farm constituents who received enormous government subsidies but he himself clung to the huge income from crops he didn't grow on his Kentucky farm. Larcenous, almost senile, he had pared his political philosophy down to simpleminded slogans: exterminate the Commie enemy; let the poor dig out of poverty with their bare hands if they've got the gumption; restore the Constitution to virginity; return to law and order.

The seniority system was rotten with Hollanders. It was what Cliff Fairlie was pledged to reform. Without Fairlie the impetus for reformation would dwindle because Ethridge couldn't carry it: he knew that and it filled him with depression.

Yet in six days' time he might be taking the oath of office.

An ordinary man forced by circumstances to meet an extraordinary challenge. That was how Ethridge had described himself in yesterday's off-the-record background briefing to the press; it was in fact what he believed.

He had spoken with quiet candor. He liked reporters as a group —that was inevitable; a man who enjoyed talking always liked those whose job was to listen. For an hour he had chatted with the White House press corps. And at the end of it, saving it for last because he wanted it to have appropriate impact, he had said with slow and carefully chosen words, "Now this is on the record—for immediate release. As you know, governments all over the world are working together to do everything possible to secure Clifford Fairlie's immediate release. But we must all face the possibility that the President-elect will not be recovered in time for his inauguration. In that case of course I will be sworn in as interim President until such time as Clifford Fairlie returns. At that time I will be required to take certain steps in order to comply with the Constitution. Section Two of the Twenty-fifth Amendment to the Constitution specifies that the President must nominate someone to fill any vacancy that may exist in the office of the Vice-Presidency. The nomination must then be confirmed by both houses of Congress."

He had their attention; they saw what was coming. He let the silence hang a moment before he went on.

"We all hope this won't be necessary—we all hope Clifford Fairlie will be installed as President at the appointed time. But if our hopes aren't realized, I've asked a fine American to accept the Vice-Presidential nomination. He has agreed, and I will ask the Congress to confirm this nomination as its first matter of business following my inauguration. The nominee, as I'm sure most of you already know, is Congressman Andrew Bee of California."

It wasn't news to the reporters but it was official confirmation. Ethridge had already informed the leaders of both houses; inevitably the word had begun to circulate but Ethridge's public announcement would forestall any opposition claims that he was trying to railroad the nomination through in secret, behind closed doors.

The key was the support of the majority leaders in both houses. Both were Democrats; Ethridge and Bee were Republicans. But no one could expect a Republican President to pick a Democratic Vice-President. Still, if Ethridge took office with an opposition Congress he had to start off on the right foot. He was playing the Bee nomination strictly by the rules.

The public might resent it: the announcement, with its appearance of prematurity, appeared to imply disrespect for Cliff Fairlie. But Congress needed time to consider the proposed nomination—and, more important, Congress could not afford the appearance of having been bulldozed into compliance by the hasty arrogance of a last-minute President-designate.

When Bee agreed to accept, Ethridge's first move had been to consult with President Brewster. It was more than courtesy; if Brewster approved the nomination he would grease it. Speaker of the House Milton Luke was in Brewster's pocket; the majority leaders were Democrats; they could be expected to follow the Brewster lead. And Brewster seemed willing to support Ethridge's choice.

Ethridge's announcement last night had received ample coverage but it hadn't stirred up any wave of public response; the public was preoccupied with Fairlie's kidnapping as it should be. The telegrams that poured into Washington were the most numerous in history and they were divided starkly on the question whether the United States should accede to the kidnappers' demands. The left wanted Fairlie back safe; the right wanted a once-and-for-all extermination of radical terrorists.

Fitzroy Grant, leader of the Senate Republicans, had proclaimed that the nation could never allow itself to give in to extortion and the threat of terrorist violence. Grant implored the Administration to make the kidnappers understand that all the vast resources of the world's most powerful police and military establishment would be used to track the kidnappers down—therefore the kidnappers should release Fairlie immediately and unconditionally as the only means of mitigating their guilt, forestalling execution, and preventing the world from discrediting leftist movements totally.

Wendy Hollander, a Democrat but representing the yahoo wing on the far right, had been making an almost continuous series of inflammatory appeals: Washington should round up every suspected revolutionary-radical in the country and start executing them daily by platoons until Fairlie was released.

The Hollander proposals had a simpleminded practicality which appealed to the Birchite fringe: Orange County was solidly behind Hollander, but his native Kentucky was not.

Andrew Bee and the moderate-liberal alliances within both parties were publicly alarmed by the saber rattling of the Hollander wing. The Hollander proposals brought to mind the specter of Nazi reprisals. Even responsible conservatives like Fitz Grant were disavowing Hollander's bloodthirsty cries for action, but Hollander had a frightening amount of support from men like House Armed Services Chairman Webb Breckenyear and FBI Director Clyde Shankland, who had been a Hoover protégé.

Bee and the liberals had reminded the public that the office of the Presidency was more important than considerations of revenge or reprisal. The life of the President-elect was the issue. When all factors were weighed the balance had to come down in favor of saving Clifford Fairlie's life; what happened afterward—to the seven fanatics on trial in Washington, and to the kidnappers, and to the radical revolutionary movement as a whole—was a matter for later decision.

Both the left and the right employed the powers of reason and logic to support emotional conclusions. Compassion was the guiding factor for the liberals and rage was the guiding factor for the rightists. As usual Ethridge saw both sides: he had the compassion and the anger together in his own guts. In the end what decided him was the same vision that had guided him earlier: the feeling that if Fairlie could be recovered alive it would give Washington an unprecedented chance to institute reforms that could restore a stable democracy and discourage this kind of thing from happening again.

But the hard-line opposition made it tough. The voice of reprisal was loud; it was forcing Howard Brewster to listen. The Pentagon, most of the members of the National Security Council, the law enforcement chiefs and the entire right wing were calling for a preemptive crackdown on all radical activists. The national uproar was tumultuous. Not many supported Hollander's call for reprisive executions but millions wanted the radicals jailed.

It made a kind of sense; that was why it got right to the nerve ends. But once you began that kind of crackdown it would lead inevitably to a full-scale conflict—a kill-or-be-killed war between the Establishment and the radicals. Militants at both extremes wanted just that. The fragile center held them at arm's length—and at sword's point.

One man had been kidnapped: and it could ignite the world.

His head throbbed, the pain fluctuating from moment to moment, stabbing behind his right eye. It didn't worry him but it was an annoyance. The painkillers Dick Kermode had prescribed were brain-dullers as well and Ethridge hadn't used them. He had already undergone endless examinations in Kermode's office and at Walter Reed—an agonizing spinal fluid tap for fluid analysis, skull X rays, electroencephalograms; penetrating eye examinations; tests of plantar responses and flexion, half a dozen others he could hardly remember. All negative. He'd known they wouldn't find anything wrong. It was tension: what could you expect? Everybody had some reaction to pressure. People got ulcers, heart trouble, asthma, even gout; with Ethridge it was sinus headaches.

He glanced at the green glow of the bedside alarm. Nearly five o'clock.

Crossing the carpet in his bare feet toward the bathroom door he felt disoriented, light-headed; he braced his hand against the door and stood still to gather strength. Perhaps he had got up too quickly, the blood rushing from his head.

He glanced back toward the beds. A faint street-lamp illumination filtered in through the lace curtains and fell across the twin beds; Judith remained sound asleep.

He stepped into the bathroom and pushed the door shut before he reached for the light switch; he didn't want the light to wake her. His hand fumbled for the switch but suddenly there was no feeling in his fingers.

He tried the left hand. The light clicked on.

It was too bright against his eyes. He stood before the sink sweating lightly, staring down at his right hand. He tried to flex the fingers; his hand responded sluggishly, as if at a great distance.

He took it badly. His hair rose, he dragged his uneasy left hand down across his face and began to shake.

When he looked into the mirror his face was drawn with pain—unnaturally decayed, ravaged by a surreal gray putrefaction.

An abrupt red explosion: the blinding stab of pain in his head.

The mild eyes mirrored panic before they rolled up into the sockets.

Faintly he heard the thrashing clatter his limbs made as he fell across the bathtub.

10:30 A.M. Continental European Time   David Lime sat behind the wheel of a blue Cortina watching the face of the bank across the street, waiting for Mario Mezetti to appear.

Shadowing him seemed the best option. Today was the fourteenth of January and Fairlie was due to be inaugurated on the twentieth; there were six days, less whatever time it took to transport Fairlie to Washington from wherever he might be found: latitude enough to spend a few hours tailing Mezetti—or even as much as a day or two. If it failed at the end of that time Lime would reconsider.

Leaving Mezetti to his own devices had already produced an impressive amount of raw information. Mezetti had booked a room at the Queen's Hotel on Grand Parade but he evidently intended to check out today because he hadn't renewed the booking and he had arranged with Mezetti Industries for a plane and pilot to take him to Cairo today. Surveillance teams had been alerted in Cairo and all intermediate stops where the plane might set down to refuel; and Lime had a Lear jet with British civilian markings on tap at Gibraltar to shadow Mezetti directly in the air in case Mezetti failed to keep to his flight plan.

In the meantime Mezetti had been making telephone calls every two hours at even-numbered hours. Because the calls were international—Gibraltar to Spain—it was easy enough to ascertain the number of the telephone receiving his calls; the phone was in Almería. Every call since eight o'clock the previous evening had been monitored by British and American agents but the eavesdropping hadn't contributed much because Mezetti's telephone calls were never answered. Mezetti would let it ring four times and hang up.

A continuation signal, Lime guessed. Someone within earshot of the recipient telephone was supposed to be listening at even-numbered hours. If the phone did not ring it would indicate Mezetti had been detained. But Lime had ordered a stakeout on the house in Almería. It had gone into effect before ten o'clock last night; since then Mezetti had made seven calls to that number but no one was there. *Guardianos* had combed the house and found it vacant. Neighboring houses had been evacuated, their residents taken into custody, but it didn't look as if any of the arrested people had any connection with the kidnapping. The line had been traced from the receiving phone to Almería Central in order to find out if the kidnappers had a tap on it but none had been discovered. Even the long-distance telephone operators were being interrogated.

It was a puzzle and it nudged various suspicions in the back of Lime's mind. But if it was a red herring it could operate either of two ways and there wasn't time to analyze it to death. Mezetti was a warm body, Lime had a rope on him, and he intended to keep hold of its end until he saw where it was going to drag him.

So Lime in the Cortina awaited the emergence of a Mario Mezetti he had never laid eyes on. He had a collection of photographs and the information that Mario had been reported this morning wearing a belted brown leather coat, brown slacks and suede desert boots. He'd be difficult to miss; at any rate a gray Rolls with his luggage aboard awaited him in front of the bank and Lime's men had all the exits covered.

Lime had taken charge last night but had left the routine surveillance to his armies. If Mezetti saw him too often he would begin to recognize Lime's face. It was always better to let the minions handle shadow jobs with frequent changes of relays—always fresh faces.

Mezetti's Cessna Citation had a cruising speed of four hundred mph and a range of twelve hundred miles. Lime had inscribed a circle of that radius on a map and arranged for close-interval air cover within it. Sixth Fleet had jets airborne waiting to shadow the Citation and Lime had organized a second-string team of commandeered civilian planes because the Navy Phantoms, easily recognizable, would have to keep their distance and tail mainly by radar to avoid alerting Mezetti. If Mezetti decided to fly at treetop altitudes where ground contours would absorb his radar image, he would lose Navy Air; it was better to keep visual contact. The CIA had set up a complex of ground spotter stations and Lime had a dozen planes ready to pick up the baton depending which direction Mezetti flew —Spanish jets now orbiting Málaga and Seville and Cape St. Vincent, a Moroccan oil-company plane over Cape Negro, Portuguese civil-air over Lisbon and Madeira, a pair of seaplanes at Majorca and Mers-el-Kebir.

At ten forty-three the young man for whom the police and security forces of fourteen nations had been searching emerged from the main entrance of the bank carrying a heavy suitcase and entered the rear passenger compartment of the big elderly Rolls.

Lime stirred the Cortina's transmission and squirted the little car into the northbound street ahead of the Rolls. Another car would be closing in behind it. Lime drove unhurriedly past the old Moorish castle and out past the open crossgates which were closed across the highway whenever an airplane was making use of the GibAir runway. Lime turned into the car park by the terminal, glancing in the rearview mirror and seeing the Rolls draw up at the passenger door.

Lime went through private doors, had a brief conference with Chad Hill in the airport manager's office, passed the customs line without a check and had ensconced himself beside the Navy pilot in the Lear jet before Mario Mezetti came along the runway in a courtesy car and was decanted beside the Citation, which stood warming up about fifty yards down-runway from the Lear.

When Lime's plane swung around into position to make its takeoff run Lime twisted his head and through the plexiglass saw the Citation begin to roll.

Lime was off the ground, pressed back into his seat by the G-force of takeoff, three minutes ahead of the Citation. The Navy pilot put the Lear out over the Straits and orbited off Tangier until the Citation climbed steeply into sight and banked around toward the northeast.

"That's enough of a lead," Lime said. "Let's go."

The Navy pilot pulled the Lear around and held a position directly behind, and slightly below, the Citation. It was the Citation's blind spot: Mezetti's pilot would not be able to see the Lear in his rearview mirror unless he made a sudden turn or backflip.

The Citation steadied on a course east by northeast. It didn't climb above three thousand feet. Lime, a few miles behind and five hundred feet lower, studied the millionth-scale map on his lap and reached for the copilot's headset. "Is this thing locked in?"

"Clear channel," the pilot said, and reached for a dial.

Lime settled the earphones over his head. "Is there a send button?"

"No. It's an open two-way. You just talk and listen."

That simplified things, eliminated the need for an "over" at the end of each transmission. Lime spoke into the mike that hovered before his mouth:

"Hill, this is Lime."

"Hill right here." The voice was metallic but clear in the headset.

"Have you got their course?"

"Yes sir. I've alerted Majorca."

"It looks like a change in flight plan."

"Yes sir. We're ready for it."

The Citation flew straight and level for fifteen minutes and then the pilot jogged Lime's knee. "He's got his wheels down."

Lime looked up from the map in time to see the Citation start a slow left turn, the nose going down into an easy glide. The sea was beneath the Lear's starboard wing, the Spanish coastline immediately below and the foothills rising to his left; the peaks of the Sierras loomed several thousand feet above the airplane, some miles north.

It began to appear the Citation was descending straight toward the mountains.

"Hill, this is Lime."

"Yes sir. We've still got him on radar—hold it, he just disappeared."

"I've still got him. He's put his gear down."

The airplane ahead was still turning slowly. Lime nodded to the pilot and the Lear followed in the Cessna's wake.

"You want our gear down, Mr. Lime?"

"No." There were no commercial airfields in the area toward which the Citation was descending. If Mezetti was about to set down in a pasture it would hardly do to land right behind him. "Keep some altitude," Lime said. "Swing a little wide—if he lands we want to see the place but we'll shoot past."

"All right sir."

Hill on the headset: "Sir, he picked up the consignment as ordered."

"Thank you." Mezetti had telephoned the bank yesterday and requested they have one hundred thousand dollars in cash on hand for him. This was confirmation he had collected it. Clearly then he was doing courier duty and it could be assumed he was now headed for a rendezvous with the others in order to turn over the money.

It all looked a little too easy; but Lime reminded himself they wouldn't have been shadowing Mezetti at all if it hadn't been for the single fortuitous fingerprint on the garage light switch in Palamos.

The Cessna was quite low along the foothills, banking back and forth, obviously searching for something. Lime said, "Keep going—make it look as if we're on a regular flight to Majorca. Don't slow down and don't circle."

Into the microphone he said, "Chad?"

"Yes sir."

"He's going down in map sector Jay-Niner, the northwest quadrant."

"Jay-Niner northwest, yes sir. I'll alert the nearest ground team."

"We're going by. We'll want a crisscross."

"Yes sir."

The Spanish plane from Málaga would overfly the sector within four minutes to confirm the Citation had actually landed. Lime, looking back with his cheek to the plexiglass window, had a last glimpse of the little jet descending toward a field encircled by foothills. There were two or three small peasant-farm buildings on the edge of the field and a ribbony road that headed south toward Almería.

"Swing out over the Med and take us back to Gibraltar."

The Lear touched down neatly and braked the length of the runway and made a slow turn at the end of the strip to taxi back to the terminal.

Chad Hill came loping out to meet him. The young man seemed unable to contain himself. "They've got another tape!"

Lime said, "What tape?"

"He left one of those tapes on the roof of the hotel. You know, with a transmitter. Like last time."

"Fairlie's voice again?"

"No sir, it's in Morse."

He was out of cigarettes. "Anybody got a cigarette?" One of the technicians obliged. It was a Gauloise and when Lime lit up, rancid fumes instantly filled the little room.

The police station was crowded; the CIA people were working on the apparatus Mezetti had left on the hotel roof. It had a timer set to start the tape playback at eight o'clock tonight.

It was just short of noon. Lime said, "Put it together and take it back where you found it."

Chad Hill's mouth dropped open.

Lime said in a mild voice that didn't betray his exasperation, "If that thing doesn't broadcast on time they'll know something went wrong."

Chad Hill swallowed visibly. Lime said, "You've made copies by now."

"Yes sir. Sent it to Washington by scrambler transmission."

"Any prints on that equipment?"

"No."

"All right then, take them up on the hotel roof and watch them set it up. When they're finished, bring them back to this room and post a man on the door. Nobody goes in or out of this room until eight tonight—and no phone calls except to me. Right?"

"Yes sir."

"You understand this, do you?"

"Yes sir. It'll give us a jump on the rest of the spooks—no leaks. I understand."

"Good." Obviously Chad thought the measure was extreme but

he knew how to follow orders and that was why Lime had picked him. "When you're done here find me—I'll have more chores for you."

"Yes sir." Chad swung away.

Lime reread the transcription in his fist. The Morse decode was brief:

> ATTENTION WORLD X FAIRLIE IS ALIVE X
> FLY WASHINGTON SEVEN TO GENEVA BEFORE
> MIDNIGHT 17 JANUARY X MOVEMENT MUST BE
> PUBLIC WITH RADIO & LIVE TV COVERAGE X
> AWAIT FURTHER INSTRUCTIONS GENEVA X

At twelve-fifty there was a flash from Chad Hill: "He's taking off again."

"You sure Mezetti's still in the plane?"

"Yes sir. They've had field glasses on him for half an hour."

"What's he been doing?"

"Nothing. Poking around the place as if he lost something. Hooker says he looks confused and kind of pissed off—as if he expected somebody to meet him there and they didn't show up."

"Did he spend any time inside the farm buildings?"

"Long enough to poke around. He came right out again."

"What about the suitcase?"

"He never took it off the plane."

"All right. Track the plane and send Hooker down to look through those buildings."

"He's already down there sir. That's where he's calling from. I've got him on the other phone—you want me to ask him anything?"

"Well I assume he found nothing?" Lime was a little wry.

"That's right sir. No sign anyone's been there in weeks. Except Mezetti of course."

"How about the basement?"

"No sir. He looked."

"All right. Call me back."

He hung up and lit another cigarette and tried to get his brain in working order. Somewhere in all this there ought to be a pattern but it wasn't emerging. Perhaps he was missing it: he was running on his batteries, he'd had less than four hours' sleep last night and it hadn't been enough to make up for the previous two days without.

The phone rang. Chad Hill again. "For Christ's sake. He's coming back to Gibraltar. The pilot just radioed for landing instructions."

"All right. Put an eight-man tail on Mezetti. As soon as he's separated from the pilot bring the pilot in."

"Yes sir."

Lime cradled it but within seconds it rang again. "Sir, it's Mr. Satterthwaite on the scrambler. You want to come over here?"

Satterthwaite's high-pitched voice was shrill with unreasoning anger: he was getting rattled, things were piling up against him. "What have you got out there, David? And don't tell me you've drawn a blank."

"We're moving. Not far and not fast, but we're moving. You saw the message we're supposed to get tonight?"

"A lot of good that is," Satterthwaite said. "Listen, they've taken Dexter Ethridge to Walter Reed in an ambulance."

It made Lime sit bolt upright. "Bad?"

"Nobody knows yet. He seems to be out cold."

"You mean somebody tried to assassinate him?"

"No. Nothing like that. Natural causes, whatever it is—he was home in bed, or in the bathroom. Listen, you know what happens if Ethridge packs up. We've got to have Fairlie back by the twentieth."

"Well you've still got a line of succession."

"Milt Luke?" Satterthwaite snorted. "Get him back, David."

As usual Satterthwaite was trying to sound like Walter Pidgeon in *Command Decision* and as usual his voice was wrong for it. Lime ignored the heroics. "What's the decision on the exchange?"

"We're divided. It's still, ah, hotly contested, as it were."

"It's up to the President, though. Isn't it."

"We live in a democracy," Satterthwaite said, quite dry. "It's up to the people."

"Sure it is."

"David whether you like it or not it's a political decision. The consequences could be catastrophic if we do the wrong thing."

"I've got a piece of news for you. The consequences will probably be catastrophic whatever you do. You'd better shit or get off the pot."

"Funny—Dexter Ethridge said the same thing. In somewhat more genteel language of course."

"Which makes Ethridge a little brighter than the rest of you," Lime said. He glanced across the communications room. A dozen men were busy at phones and teleprinters; a few of them wore headsets. Chad Hill was handing a telephone receiver back to the man seated at the table beside him. Hill started to gesture in Lime's direction—something had developed that required Lime's attention. Lime waved an acknowledgment and said to the scrambler, "Look, we're glued onto Mezetti. Right now he's leading us in circles but I think he's going to take us to them if we give him a little time. I can't have——"

"How much time?"

"I'm not an oracle. Ask Mezetti."

"That's what *you* ought to be doing, David."

"Are you ordering me to pick him up?"

Static on the line while Satterthwaite paused to consider it. Lime was dropping the ball in his lap. "David, when I talked you into this it was with the understanding that the best way to get a job done is to pick the best people and give them their heads. I'm not going to start telling you how to do your job—if I were capable of that I'd be doing the job instead of you."

"All right. But Mezetti may lead us right into the hive, and it could happen any time. I need to know how much latitude I've got if I have to start talking deals with them."

"You're asking blood from a stone."

"Damn it I have to know if you're going to agree to the exchange. Any negotiator has to know his bargaining points. You're tying my hands."

"What do you want me to tell you? The decision hasn't been made yet. The instant it's made I'll let you know."

It was all he was going to get. He stopped pressing it. "All right. Look, something's come up. I'll get back to you."

"Do it soon."

"Aeah. See you."

He broke the connection and crossed the room and Chad Hill bundled him outside. In the Government House corridor Chad said, "He's changed course on us."

"He's not landing in Gib?"

"The plane turned north."

Lime felt relieved and showed it with a tight smile. "Now we're getting somewhere. Who's on him?"

"Two planes at the moment. Another one coming across from Lisbon to pick him up farther north."

"All right then. Just let's don't lose the son of a bitch."

The worst part was doing nothing, knowing things were happening out there but sitting still waiting for news. Lime sent a man out to buy him half a dozen packs of American cigarettes and if possible a large order of coffee. He retreated to his monk's cell and tried to put his head together.

His sense of time had been blurred: fatigue gave him a sunless sense of unreality, everything took place at a distance as if seen through a camera. He had to rest. Once again he stretched out on the floor and closed his eyes.

He pictured Bev but the image drifted and he was thinking of Julius Sturka, the vague face in the grainy photograph.

He didn't want it to turn out to be Sturka. He'd tried to get Sturka before and he'd failed. Failed in 1961 and failed again in the past fortnight.

In the old days he had wasted a lot of time learning nonfacts about Sturka—the sort of rumors that were always available to fill the holes between facts. Maybe it was true he was a Yugoslav who had watched the *fascisti* torture his parents to death in Trieste, or a Ukrainian Jew who had fought Nazis at Sevastopol, but Lime long ago had begun to distrust all the simplistic Freudian guesses about Sturka. There wasn't any doubt Sturka had a romanticized picture of himself but it wasn't the messianic sort that had characterized Ché Guevara. The nearest Lime could come to a definition was to think of Sturka as a sort of ideological mercenary. He couldn't fathom what motivated Sturka but it seemed clear enough that Sturka was preoccupied more with means than with ends. He had an unrealistic view of political strategy but his tactics were impeccable. He was a methodologist, not a philosopher. At least from a distance he resembled the master criminal who was more concerned with the mechanical complexity of his crime than with its reward. Sometimes it tempted Lime to think of him as an adolescent prankster doing something outrageous just to prove he could get away with it on a dare. Sturka had the traits of a game player, he took delight in moves and countermoves. At what he did, he was superb; he was a professional.

A professional. Lime understood that; it was the highest accolade in his lexicon.

Two professionals. Was Sturka the better?

What is Fairlie to me that maybe I'll have to die for him? But the adrenaline was pumping and Bev had been right: he had sought peace but boredom had become a kind of death and he was joyous with this job. He was at his best when he risked the most.

Needing sleep, his nerve-ends raw, his belly afire from caffeine and nicotine, he was alive. The malaise of David Lime: I have pain, therefore I am.

Five days to spring Fairlie. Well anyhow that was the spring Satterthwaite was trying to wind. If you didn't get Fairlie back there was always Ethridge and if Ethridge turned out to be dying of something there was always Milton Luke. A senile cipher, Luke, but they'd survived Coolidge and Harding and Ike in his last years. The deadline was real but if it passed the world might hang together in spite of Lime's failure. . . .

Thinking in circles now.

Was it really Sturka at the other end of the test line? Well it did have the earmarks, didn't it. The little cell of operatives striking straight to the system's nervous center. The knife straight into the vitals. The exquisite timing.

But if you assumed that much you still couldn't jump to conclusions about Sturka's base of operations. The fact that Sturka had once operated out of the *djebel* did not place him there now. Algeria was the logical place to look because Algeria was Sturka's old stamping grounds and because Algeria had one of the few governments in the world that wouldn't actively cooperate in the hunt for Fairlie; but the assumption it *was* Sturka was what militated most powerfully against the Algerian answer. Algeria was so obvious it was the one place Sturka would avoid.

And he had the signs they had blazed for him. The Arab robes, the boat turning north, now Mezetti flying north across Spain toward the Pyrenees with one hundred thousand dollars in his satchel. All of them deliberate misleaders, with the Arab robes a double bluff? Sturka was clever but was he that subtle?

Geneva, he thought, and that farm outside Almería where Mezetti had landed expecting to meet someone.

There was too much missing. In the field there was nothing to do but follow the facts and hope Mezetti would produce.

Sturka, he thought reluctantly. I suppose it must be. He dozed.

1:45 P.M. EST Satterthwaite sat tense with one shoulder raised, dry-washing his clasped hands. Images crowded his mind: the operating-room glances between doctors, eyes bleak over the tops of white surgical masks; the obscene pulsing of a respirometer bag; rhythmic green curves darting across a cardiograph screen with eyes watching it fearfully hoping the curve would not become a steady green dot sliding straight across from left to right.

Out at Walter Reed the neurosurgeons were drilling holes toward Dexter Ethridge's brain. Cutting biparietal burr holes. At last report blood pressure was down to eighty over forty; a clot was suspected.

Satterthwaite looked at the man behind the big desk. Worry pulled at President Brewster's mouth. Neither man spoke.

David Lime was in an airplane somewhere between Gibraltar and Geneva—an airborne jet transport with his big communications crew aboard. All of them following the track of the Mezetti Cessna. Maybe it would lead them to something. But if it didn't?

The telephone.

The President looked up but only his eyes moved; he didn't stir.

Satterthwaite reached out, plucked at the telephone.

It was Kermode. Dexter Ethridge's doctor. He sounded aggrieved as if by some petty annoyance. "Ten minutes ago. It was a subdural hematoma."

Satterthwaite covered the mouthpiece with his palm. "He's dead."

The President blinked. "Dead."

Kermode was still talking. Satterthwaite got phrases: "Medicine's not an exact science, is it. I mean in half these cases the diagnosis isn't made until it's too late—in a third of them it isn't even considered. It's my bloody fault."

"Take it easy. You're not a neurologist."

"We've had them on the case since the bombing. Nobody spotted it. I mean it's not a common problem. We found out by arteriography, but it was too late to evacuate the thing."

"Take it easy, Doctor."

"Take it easy. Sure. I mean I've just murdered the next President of the United States."

"Nuts."

Brewster stirred—reaching for a cigar—but he didn't speak. Satterthwaite listened to the telephone voice: "It was an injury caused by the bomb blast when that desk hit him on the head. What happens, the cerebral hemispheres get displaced downward and you get a compression against the brain. It's a hemorrhage but it's not the usual run of cerebral hemorrhage. It's between the layers —you can't spot it with the usual diagnostic tools. These things take weeks to show up—sometimes months. Then it's usually too late."

Satterthwaite wasn't willing to go on listening to Kermode's *mea culpa*. "What about Judith Ethridge?"

"She's here in the hospital. Of course she knows."

"The President will call her."

"Yeah."

"Goodbye," Satterthwaite said, and removed the muttering phone from his ear and hung it up.

The President glared at him.

"Shit." Brewster spoke the word as if it had been chipped out of hard steel.

8:00 P.M. EST   The snow had quit falling. Raoul Riva let the venetian blind slat down and left the room in hat and overcoat, walked to the elevator and pressed the concave plastic square until it lit up. He rode down to the lobby and stood just inside the front door ignoring the doorman's inquiring glance; stood there for a few moments as if judging the weather, then strolled outside with the air of a man in no hurry who had no particular destination in mind.

The phone booth was a few streets away and he approached it at a leisurely pace, timing his arrival for eight-twenty. The call wasn't due until half past but he wanted to make sure no one else used the phone at that time. He stepped into the booth and pretended to be looking up a number in the directory.

The call was three minutes late. "I have an overseas call for Mr. Felix Martin."

"Speaking."

"Thank you. . . . Your call is ready sir. Go ahead."

"Hello Felix?" Sturka's voice was a bit distant; it wasn't the best connection.

"Hello Stewart. How's the weather over your way?"

"Very mild. How's yours?"

"A little snow but it's let up. I wish I were over there in all that sunshine. You must be having a ball."

"Well you know, business, always business." Sturka's voice became more matter-of-fact. "How's the market doing?"

"Not too great I'm afraid. A bad thing, Dexter Ethridge dying like that—you heard?"

"No. You say Ethridge died?"

"Yes. Some sort of hemorrhage—after effect of those bombs that blew up the Capitol. The news sent the market down another four points."

"Well what about our holdings?"

"They're slipping. Like all the rest."

"I suppose things will recover. They always do. We'll just have to hold on and wait for our price."

Riva said, "Well the way things are going I wouldn't be surprised if the SEC slapped some tougher controls on."

"Yes. I suppose we'll have to expect that."

"These radicals are really pretty stupid, aren't they. If they don't turn Cliff Fairlie loose there's going to be all kinds of hell breaking loose."

"Well I don't know, Felix. I get a feeling they've got some pretty brutal plans. I wouldn't be surprised if they killed Fairlie and assassinated the Speaker of the House at the same time. Then they'd be guaranteeing that old Senator Hollander'd get the Presidency, and maybe that's exactly what these clowns want—a right-wing fool like that in the White House would do more for the cause of the revolutionaries than anybody since Fulgencio Batista. You think maybe that's what they've got in mind?"

"That sounds pretty fanciful if you ask me. I mean the Speaker must be ten feet deep in Secret Service protection. I can't see how they'd be able to pull that off."

"Well I'm sure they'd find a way. They always seem to, don't they. Anyhow this call's costing a bloody fortune, let's not spend hours talking politics. Now look, from what you say about the market I'd think it might be a good time to get out of our blue chips, unload them first thing Monday morning. What do you say?"

"I think it might be better to hold off a few days, see which way things go."

"You may be right. I'll let you be the judge of that. But I do think it's a damn good thing we unloaded that block of Mezetti Industries stock—we got out right under the wire."

"You got out of it entirely?" Riva asked.

"Yes, we just took payment for the last block."

"Then that *was* a good break."

"Well you know me, Felix, always willing to cut my losses. I'm not one to hang onto something once it's started to lose steam."

"On the other hand," Riva said, "I'd hang onto those blue chips a while longer before I unloaded them, if I were you. It's too early to think about dumping them."

"Well we'll give it a few days then. I'll talk to you again Monday night, all right?"

"Okay, fine. Have a good weekend."

"You too."

"Give my best to Marjorie."

"I'll do that. So long."

"Bye."

Riva left the booth and glanced toward the sky. The city's glow reflected back from the underbellies of heavy rolling clouds. He turned the coat collar up against his throat and walked back toward the hotel.

SATURDAY, JANUARY 15

7:00 A.M. North African Time It was Fairlie's second morning in the gray room.

There were no windows. The iron legs of the cot were sealed into the concrete of the floor. The mattress was a flaccid tick.

No pillow or sheets. The light was a low-watt bulb recessed into the stucco ceiling with a steel grille imbedded flush with the ceiling to prevent the prisoner's fingers from reaching up and unscrewing the light. It was never switched off.

Evidently it had been built to house prisoners. Possibly a relic of the Second World War. It had been designed to contain the kind of people whose first reaction to imprisonment was to escape. There was nothing he could tear apart to make a tool or weapon: the cot was a single welded frame with a plywood bed. And even so there were no window bars to pry open. The door was iron and fitted flush into its metal frame. It had no handle or keyhole on the inside. The crack beneath it was barely sufficient to admit air, which circulated up and exhausted, apparently, through ducts above the ceiling light. Up there a fan hummed constantly.

They had been feeding him twice a day since they'd captured him. It was his only way of reckoning time; he had to assume they were still keeping to the same schedule of meals.

An hour ago they had brought him coffee and a hard loaf of bread and a bar of soap. He took it to be breakfast; they usually fed him an adequate evening meal. So it was morning again.

He had no way of telling where he was. He had last seen the sky the other night aboard the pitching boat before they had blind-folded him. Then the ride in the amphibious airplane. The flight had seemed interminable but eventually the plane had come down

—on land; the surface on which it landed was rough, no regular airport runway.

They had carried him a short distance and seated him in another vehicle. He had heard the airplane take off again and fly away, the sound of the engines diminishing as the car in which he sat began to move slowly across bumpy terrain: an ungraded dirt road, if it was a road at all.

The mask with which they had blinded him was opaque and they had taped it so tightly there was no way for light to reach his eyelids. But he had felt heat against his left cheek and shoulder during the ride and it made him certain the sun was up. If it was morning he was traveling south.

The car stopped once and evidently Ahmed got out; there was a rattling of metal, perhaps jerrycans. Lady was testing the pulse in Fairlie's wrists. They had given him a shot shortly before the airplane had landed and from the vague euphoria it produced he assumed they were keeping him doped up on mild tranquilizers to maintain his docility. It did more than that; it kept his mind afloat, he couldn't concentrate on anything long enough to think anything out.

It had been another journey too long to be timed subjectively. It might have been forty-five minutes, it might have been three hours. The car stopped; they lifted him out and walked him across some gravel. Into a building, through a number of turns—hallways? Down a flight of hard steps which seemed to be half buried in rubble; he had to feel his way carefully, kicking things off the steps. Finally they had turned him through a door into this cell where they had removed the mask and the gag and the wires that bound his hands.

It had taken a little while for his eyes to get used to the light and by the time he was able to see they had locked him inside alone, having stripped him of everything except the rudiments of his clothing.

That first evening Lady had brought him a good-sized helping of lamb stew on a military metal plate and an unlabeled bottle of raw primitive wine. Ahmed stood in the doorway, shoulder tilted, arms folded, showing the hard black oily gleam of a revolver. Watching him eat. "Just don' make trouble. You don' want your wife marching to slow organ music."

They still hadn't shown him their faces—none but Abdul, the

black pilot; and Abdul apparently was not here. Fairlie had to assume Abdul had flown the airplane back to its source, or at least away from this area.

For hours after Lady and Ahmed left him he sat like a stone, brooding, offended by his own sour body smell and the heavy stink of cheap disinfectant in the cell.

Drugs had sealed him in a protective shell within which he had become a passive observer, defending himself against outbursts of terror by the basic expedient of withdrawal. Emotionally dulled and mentally numbed, he had observed without reacting; he had absorbed without thinking.

The solitary incarceration allowed him to begin to emerge.

He sat on the cot with his back against the wall and his knees drawn up against his chest, arms wrapped around his legs, chin on knees, eyes fixed without focus on the water faucet opposite him. At first his brain stirred with sluggish reluctance. In time his muscles became cramped and he stretched out face down on the cot, chin on laced hands. It got the light out of his eyes and he tried to sleep but now his mind was awakening from its long recession and he began to reason.

Up to now he had accepted that he would be killed or he would be released: alternatives over which he had no control and therefore against which he should not struggle. He had prepared himself atavistically to wait in this limbo, however long it might take, until it ended with freedom or death.

There were further considerations but he began to recognize them only now.

The first was the idea of escape. A variety of fanciful schemes presented themselves and he entertained them all but in the end dismissed them, all for the same reasons: he was no storybook adventurer, he knew virtually nothing of physical combat or the methods of stealth, and he had no knowledge of what lay beyond the door of this cell.

They were feeding him, enough to sustain life; they had not assaulted him physically. They had gone to a great amount of evident trouble to spirit him away intact. They were using him as a bargaining tool; they needed him alive.

They wouldn't have gone to all this trouble if they meant to kill him in the end. They had never showed their faces; he clung to that.

He spent the entire night reasoning it out. At times he was convinced they were going to let him go. At times he felt they would use him up and toss him away like a squeezed lemon, as dead as yesterday. At these times the chilly sweat of fear streamed down his ribs.

For hours too he though of Jeanette and their unborn child. The effect all this would have on her. On them.

That was what finally stirred his anger: Jeanette and the children.

Until now it had all had an odd impersonality for him. In a way his abduction seemed an extension of politics: a military sort of thing. Abominable, inexcusable, terrifying—yet in its way rational.

But now it became personal. They had no right, he thought. There was no possible justification. To put an expectant mother and two adolescent children through this agony of unknowing. . . .

That made it personal and when it became personal it became hate.

He had been afraid of them; now he hated them.

He began to wonder why it had taken so incredibly long for him to think of Jeanette and the children. It was the first thought he had given to them in—how long? Three days? Four?

He had taken the coward's refuge in mindless despair. Dulled his mind, curled up in a tight defensive little ball around *himself*—a total selfishness of reaction which appalled him. . . .

He had to get to know these animals. He had to penetrate the burnouses and the phony voices. He had to watch for every clue, no matter how trivial.

By the time they released him he had to know them: he had to be able to identify them for the world.

He dozed finally and came awake when they brought food: Abdul and Sélim. So Abdul had returned from wherever he had left the airplane.

He tried to draw them out but they both refused to speak. They took his plates away and the lock latched over with a heavy clank.

The rest of that day he had struggled with the problems he had set for himself. No simple resolutions offered themselves. He slept awhile and awoke dreaming of Jeanette.

A second dinner of stew, a second endless lamplit night, and now his second morning in the cell.

Sélim came in: a cold figure in his disguising robes, hard and poisonous—something sleek and cruel about him. No movement in the hooded eyes. Eyes that had seen everything. So cold. A man with whom he could make no real contact. Sélim seemed to possess a superb self-control but Fairlie sensed in him a wild animal unpredictability: an underlying mercurial spectrum of moods and tempers that could be triggered at any time. What was most frightening was that there would be no way to predict what might turn out to be the trigger.

Fairlie studied him, tried to form an estimate: five feet eleven, a hundred and seventy pounds. But he couldn't tell much about what was concealed under the Arab garb.

"I could use a change of clothes."

"I'm sorry." Sélim's sardonicisms were perfunctory: "We're roughing it."

Abdul came through the door and stood beside Sélim. Chewing spearmint gum as always. Fairlie studied him too: the broad dark face, the brooding inward expression. Five-ten, a hundred and ninety, possibly late thirties. The hair was shot with gray but that might be fake. The olive chauffeur's uniform was powdered with the same fine dust Fairlie had found on his own clothes, on his skin, in his hair. Sand particles.

Sélim's hands: hard, scarred, yet graceful with long deft fingers. The feet? Encased in boots, overflowed by robes. No help there, no help in the eyes which were set deep in secretive recesses, always half shuttered, their color indeterminate.

"It won't be very long," Sélim said. "A few days." Fairlie had the feeling Sélim was giving him a close curious scrutiny. Appraising the appraiser. *Sizing me up. Why?*

"You're not afraid, are you."

"I wouldn't say that."

"You're a little angry. That's understandable."

"My wife is expecting a child."

"How nice for her."

"You're guaranteeing your own extermination," Fairlie said. "I hope I have a hand in it."

It made Abdul smile. With Sélim as always there was no gauging the reaction. Sélim said, "Well with us it doesn't matter. There are always others to take our places. You can't exterminate us all."

"By now you've encouraged quite a few people to try. Is that what you want?"

"In a way." Sélim stirred. "Fairlie, if we'd been Jews and that Capitol of yours had been a beer hall in Berlin with Hitler and his storm troopers inside, you'd have congratulated us. And it would have encouraged a lot of Germans to follow our example."

The argument was as simpleminded as a John Birch Society leaflet and it was amazing a man as sophisticated as Sélim could believe in it. Fairlie said, "There's one difference, isn't there. The people aren't on your side. They don't share your ideas—the fact is they're more likely to support repression than revolution. I quote one of your own heroes—'Guerrilla warfare must fail if its political objectives don't coincide with the aspirations of the people.' That's Chairman Mao."

Quite clearly it had taken Sélim by surprise, even more so than Abdul. Sélim almost snapped back at him. "You presume to quote Mao to me. I'll give you Mao—'The first law of warfare is to protect ourselves and destroy the enemy. Political power grows out of the barrel of a gun. Guerrillas must educate the people in the meaning of guerrilla warfare. It is our task to intensify guerrilla terrorism until the enemy is forced to become increasingly severe and oppressive.' "

"The world's not a clinic for your experiments in stupidity. Your brand of star-chamber justice stinks of murder. Why don't you go ahead and kill me? It's what you really want, isn't it?"

"I'd like to," Sélim said in his emotionless monotone. "But I'm afraid we won't get the chance. You see we've been listening to the radio. Your friend Brewster has agreed to the exchange."

He tried to conceal his feelings. "It might be better if he hadn't."

"Not for you. If he'd decided to call our bluff we'd have given him your dead body."

"I'm sure you would have."

Abdul said, "You got balls."

When they left Fairlie sagged back on the cot. They had diseased minds, these self-appointed revolutionaries. They lived in moral twilight with their sterile dogmas that were limited to what could be daubed on a placard. Their frenzied attachment to the apocalypse was terrifying: like the Vietnam generals they didn't care if they had to blow up the world to save it.

Most of them were congenitally naive; they saw things in a fool's terms—what wasn't totally acceptable was totally unacceptable; if you didn't like something you destroyed it utterly.

But Sélim didn't ignore things; he took everything into account. Assuredly he was a psychopath but you couldn't merely label a man and then dismiss him; a good number of the world's leaders had been psychopaths and it was a bad mistake to call them madmen and let it go at that. Sélim's mind might function without inhibition but that didn't mean it functioned without ambition.

Sélim didn't fit into any concept of the quixotic rebel. He had none of the earmarks of the zealous reformer or the tantrum-throwing resenter. Some of his troops were that kind: Lady for one. ("Get your ass moving before I put my boot up it," and a little while later, as they had got out of the car, "Do what you're told. If you hear a loud noise it'll be you dying.") But Sélim didn't play at that game. Sélim had something else in mind.

Fairlie thought he saw what it was. Sélim did not so much want to improve the world as he wanted to improve his position in it.

10:30 A.M. EST Bill Satterthwaite accepted his wife's unimpassioned kiss and left the house. Backed the car out of the garage and headed down New Hampshire Avenue toward the center of things. The Saturday morning traffic was moderate and he had good luck with the lights.

It was the first time he had been home since the kidnapping and it had proved unnecessary; if Leila had noticed his absence there was no sign of it. She had cooked breakfast for him. The boys were both well, and doing well, at Andover; the man was coming Monday to lay the new carpet in the upstairs hall and on the stairs; the nice pregnant young couple across the street had had a miscarriage; the new Updike novel was not up to his usual standard; how much of a contribution should we make this year to the Arena Theater?

He had called her at least once every day and she knew he was involved in the search for Clifford Fairlie; she knew better than to ask and he knew better than to volunteer anything.

They had married when they were both university instructors but he had learned that the intellectual gamesmanship at which she was adept was a strain for her; when they had come to Washington she had settled instantly and with evident relief into the less challenging *hausfrau* role and it suited Satterthwaite well enough. His home, now that the boys were away most of the year, was an unabrasive resort. Leila didn't complain when he shut himself in his study all evening, week after week, jotting in his crabbed hand and reading endless reports.

The three hours with Leila had relieved the pressure but when he set foot in The Salt Mine it hit him with renewed force.

Its symbols were trite: the big white electric clock on the wall, ticking toward inaugural noon; the teleprinters banging, hunched figures at the long table, the disordered mounds of documents. Some of these men had hardly left the room in the past sixty or seventy hours.

He spent nearly an hour with Attorney General Ackert and an Assistant Secretary of State discussing the details of the movement of the seven accused mass murderers to Geneva. Because of the Swiss Government's rigid neutrality regulations they would not use an Air Force plane; a commercial 707 would have to be chartered. Security would be maintained by FBI and Secret Service agents aboard the plane; Swiss police would reinforce the coverage once the plane landed. Permissions had to be arranged for international television and radio coverage at Geneva. Brewster had decided to follow the kidnappers' instructions to the letter—at least on the visible level.

Satterthwaite had lunch with FBI Director Clyde Shankland and an Assistant CIA Director. They reviewed the items that had been pinned down in the past twenty-four hours. Mario Mezetti had obtained at least six hundred thousand dollars in negotiables within the past few weeks, but what was being done with that much money was hard to tell.

Bob Walberg had opened up in last night's interrogation; the questioners had persuaded him they had obtained a confession from one of the other prisoners and Walberg had come apart under the influence of scopolamine. The confession and evidence weren't admissible in court but they were mildly useful. Walberg seemed to think Sturka had a partner, someone outside the immediate cell. Riva? The search was intensified. At the same time Perry Hearn had leaked Walberg's confession to the press, unofficially and without naming Walberg. The leak was designed to dispell the growing rumors of an enormous international conspiracy at work. It might be an international conspiracy but it was not enormous, at least in numbers. The public needed to know that.

The doubles were being coached, Shankland assured him. They would be ready in time.

The *Guardia Civil* had found the leak in the Gibraltar-Almería telephone operation—Mezetti's bi-hourly calls. It was a telephone operator in Almería. She had been paid an enormous sum of money by her reckoning: fifteen thousand pesetas. She had been supplied with a small radio transmitter, set to broadcast on an aviation-band wavelength, and she had been paid to tap the electronic pickup circuit of the transmitter into the switchboard line that fed the telephone to which Mezetti's calls had been dialed.

The gadget had been locked in an open-transmission position. It meant anyone within broadcast range—a hundred miles or so depending on altitude and interference—would be able to hear everything that took place on that particular telephone line.

The limited range of the transmitter meant nothing; someone might have been posted anywhere within a hundred-mile radius for the express purpose of listening for the telephone bell and relaying an alarum to another recipient if the Almería phone failed to ring.

There was one more item. Scotland Yard had used several chemical processes on the pair of gloves found by the abandoned helicopter in the Pyrenees; the experiments had lifted a vague partial thumbprint and it had been run through the FBI's computers. It was not conclusive but the circumstantial web was too tight to dismiss: the print fitted several thumbs but one of them was that of Alvin Corby.

Corby had been tied to Sturka nearly two weeks ago. The helicopter pilot had been black, an American. It fit. Satterthwaite had sent the word on, not without petty satisfaction, to David Lime who was in Finland glued to Mario Mezetti's eccentric movements.

They had a growing accumulation of clues but still there was only one solid contact and Lime was sticking with Mezetti.

The Russians had the inside track in Algeria, if that was where Sturka had gone after all. The KGB had a far better network in North Africa than the CIA. At the moment there was no reason to believe the Russians knew Sturka was the quarry—but there was no proof they didn't. The KGB was dogging Lime's heels in Finland, and undoubtedly knew Mezetti was the subject under surveillance but they were hanging back, letting Lime carry the ball—perhaps out of political courtesy and perhaps for other reasons. When the trail had led as far as Finland the Russians had instituted a massive but very quiet search operation within the Soviet Union; it could prove acutely embarrassing to find the American President-elect was being held prisoner inside Russia somewhere.

Everybody in the world had a piece of this, Satterthwaite thought. The magnitude of it awed him even though he usually wasn't susceptible to reverence. This was the largest manhunt in human history.

At two o'clock he reported to the White House. Brewster was bloodshot from sleeplessness and expectably irascible. "I've just had a very rough phone conversation with Jeanette Fairlie."

"I imagine it must have been."

"She wants to know why we haven't got him back yet."

"Understandable."

Brewster was striding back and forth. "We haven't even got five full days left. Ethridge picked a hell of a time to die, didn't he." He stopped and yanked the cigar out of his mouth and stared belligerently at Satterthwaite. "You're convinced you know the identity of this man who's got Fairlie?"

"Sturka? We're morally certain."

"Do you think he'll keep his word?"

"Only if he thinks it'll profit him."

"Otherwise he'd kill Fairlie. Whether or not we turn the seven loose. Is that what you're saying?"

"I can't read Sturka's mind, Mr. President. I don't know what his plans are. He'd kill without hesitation if he thought he had reason to."

The President circled his desk and slumped into the big chair. "Then let's not give him an excuse."

"You want to recall the doubles?"

"I think we'd better."

"We can still send them along to Geneva. Keep them out of sight, use them if things look right for it."

"Only if you can be damn sure nobody ever sees them."

"We can do that," Satterthwaite said. "Easy enough. If they go in singly nobody will give them a second glance anyway."

"Play it tight, will you?" Brewster made a face at his cigar and put it down in the ashtray. "Milt Luke might survive a few days as interim President but God knows we couldn't afford him for four years."

SUNDAY,
JANUARY 16

9:00 A.M. Continental European Time   Lime pressed the field glasses into his eye sockets and made a square search pattern until he found the window he wanted. It was across the town common a good hundred yards away but the high-resolution lenses brought it up to arm's length. It was a Mark Systems gyroscopic binocular that had cost the Government something over four thousand dollars.

His breath poured from his nostrils like steam. He hadn't thought to pack clothes for the subartic; Chad Hill had scraped up scarf and gloves and tweed overcoat at Stockmann in Helsinki and Lime had borrowed an earflap cap from a local cop. The gloves were too small but the coat was a reasonable fit.

The Englishman said, "Well?"

"He's reading the *Herald Tribune*."

"How frightfully unsporting of him."

Mezetti hadn't drawn his drapes. He sat in the hotel room beside the telephone reading yesterday's Paris edition.

"Fat lot of good." The Englishman drew his collar away from his jowls. They had the window wide open because it steamed up if they closed it. Mezetti's room evidently had double-pane windows. They were frosty in the corners but clear enough to see through.

The Englishman was fairly high up in MI-5. He was spherical and bland and appeared boneless; he wore a sandy officer's moustache and a striped regimental tie.

CIA kept a stringer in Lahti but like most of his kind he was so well known Lime didn't want to use him. All competent authorities, both Finnish and otherwise, would be expected to have dossiers on him and there was no point taking the chance of frightening Mezetti's contact away.

If there was a contact.

It stood to reason, if only because Mezetti had finally come to rest after leading them erratically across the length of Europe. He had checked into the hotel yesterday and taken all his meals in his room. He seemed to be waiting for the telephone to ring. Lime had a tap on it.

The Englishman said, "Have a look down there."

Cars were parked haphazardly along the curbs; an East German Wartburg was slipping into a space.

"Ridiculous. Getting like a bloody business convention down there."

"You know him?"

"He's with the Vopos. Plainclothes."

The driver wasn't getting out of the car. The passenger had walked into the hotel lobby. After a moment he came out again, got back into the car and sat there. The car didn't move.

"Does he wear Moscow's collar?"

"I shouldn't think so. Not any more."

There was a Renault containing a spook from the French SDECE and a four-door Volkswagen containing four large members of Bonn's BND. Lime swept the square with the 20x binoculars and spotted occupants in five other cars. He recognized one of them—a Spanish agent he'd met in Barcelona three days ago.

It was a comic-opera medley. The Englishman was right; it was ridiculous.

Lime reached for the phone. "Chad?"

"Go ahead."

"The square's crawling with spooks. Let's get them out of the way."

"I'll try."

"Use muscle."

"They won't like it."

"I'll apologize later."

"Okay. I'll see what I can do."

Lime went back to the window, preternaturally drained. Sleeplessness glazed his eyes; his lids blinked slowly with a grit-grainy sort of pain.

The Englishman sat by the window like a Buddha. Lime said, "It bothers me, the Russians not being down there. Everybody else is."

"Perhaps you've got a point."

"This is still Yaskov's area, isn't it?"

"You know him?"

"I've been here before. A while ago."

"Yes, it's still his bailiwick."

Yaskov was around here somewhere, Lime thought. Not as bru-tally obvious as these others, but around somewhere. Watching, biding.

He resumed his seat at the window beside the Englishman. Had a quick look through the glasses—Mezetti hadn't stirred; he was turning a page and Lime could read the headlines effortlessly through the gyros.

He set them aside and leaned forward to look down over the sill. A Volvo had entered the square, unobtrusive and quiet; it pulled over to the curb and four uniformed Finns got out and began to saunter along the storefronts. They approached the Volkswagen and Lime saw one of them stoop to talk to the occupants. The three remaining Finns continued up the walk; one of them approached the parked Wartburg and made a cranking motion with his hand to indicate he wanted the passenger to roll down his window.

Evidently there was some acrimony at the Volkswagen but in the end the Finn stood up and saluted stiffly and the VW's starter gnashed. It pulled out and rolled across the square, moving very slowly like a child dragging his heels; it disappeared into the south-bound high road and the Wartburg left soon after.

The Finns continued on their rounds and presently seven cars had left the square. The Finns went back to their Volvo and drove away.

"Quite neat," the Englishman applauded.

"We'll catch hell for it."

"Well one could hardly have them falling all over themselves, could one."

It would mark the end of whatever international cooperation there had been. But Lime had known that at the outset. Henceforth the cooperation would take the form of lip service. Nobody liked being insulted.

The Englishman was smug. By openly volunteering his services he had forestalled similar eviction. That was all right; Lime needed to keep a few friends.

He rubbed his eyes. Yaskov's not showing himself wasn't very surprising. Yaskov wasn't fool enough to crowd in with the pack.

He's around here somewhere.

Forget it, he thought. Other fish to fry. Where's Mezetti's contact? What do you suppose the bastard's waiting for?

There were other leads and they weren't altogether standing still. The "Venezuelan handyman" who'd been hired by the chief groundskeeper at Perdido—the one who'd evidently sabotaged Fairlie's original helicopter and killed the Navy pilot—had been identified by the groundskeeper from mug shots: Cesar Renaldo.

Together with the Corby fingerprint in the glove it banished any possibility this was anyone's caper but Julius Sturka's.

But still everything was flimsy. Hundreds of thousands of people were working on it, looking for Sturka and the rest, looking for Raoul Riva. Nothing. There was only one physical lead: Mezetti.

Mezetti sat in a chair reading a newspaper.

The wind came in through the open window. It came right down from Lapland, picking up chill moisture over the frozen Finnish lakes. The sun was a low thin rime in the south, weak pink through haze; it had risen late and would set within three hours.

"I say," the Englishman muttered. Lime jerked awake.

Across the way there was movement. He snapped the glasses to his eyes and made the rapid search until he found Mezetti's window. Locked onto it and watched.

Mezetti had put the newspaper down and was at the wardrobe, shouldering into a coat, reaching for a hat.

Lime handed the glasses to the Englishman and wheeled to the telephone. "He's moving. Coat and hat."

"Right."

He got into the Mercedes. Chad Hill at the wheel craned his head around inquiringly.

"Don't get your hopes up," Lime told him wearily. "He's probably headed for a drugstore to buy a toothbrush."

They watched the face of the hotel. Lime plucked the two-way's mike from its dashboard hook. "Just checking the communications."

"Loud and clear."

After two or three minutes Mezetti appeared on the step. He looked around the square with a great deal of care before he walked the half-block distance to the Saab he'd hired in Helsinki yesterday.

Lime had planted a bleeper under the Saab's bumper. It gave off an intermittent radio pulse. Two vans were equipped to receive the signals and follow by radio triangulation but Lime still preferred line-of-sight tailing; you never knew when the car might trade drivers and then just keep moving with your radio eavesdroppers none the wiser.

Mezetti was having a little trouble getting the car started. Probably the damp cold in the carburetor. Lime flicked the microphone switch. "I'm on him but we'll want two other cars."

"All set."

Finally smoke puffed from the Saab's pipe and it moved away from the curb.

"Here we go. . . .Heading into the middle of town."

"Two vans and three cars on him."

Lime latched the microphone and spoke to Chad Hill. "Hang back. Don't tailgate him."

The Mercedes threaded the narrow streets. Mezetti had turned on his foglights and the red taillights were easy to follow.

A sharp turn into a narrow passage. "Don't follow him in there," Lime said. "We'll go around the block." And into the mike: "He's turned into an alley. Maybe checking his tail—I'm letting him go. You're on the parallel streets?"

"Alcorn's picked him up. Going west on Alpgatan."

Lime looked at his map. It was the next boulevard over, running parallel. He spoke terse directions and Chad Hill took the Mercedes around a corner. Lime said, "Slow down. We'll let the others ride him for a while."

From the radio: "He appears to be driving around a block now."

"Not looking for a parking place?"

"No. Trying to make sure he hasn't got a tail. It's all right, we're swapping relays every other corner. He won't spot us."

"What's he doing now?"

"North on the main drag."

Lime pointed and Hill turned the Mercedes into the main street. The radio: "He's going around another block."

"Sure?"

"It looks that way—okay, he's made the third turn. One more and he's gone around the block. Where are you?"

"Near the north edge of town."

"Keep going. He'll probably catch up—right, he's behind you."

Lime said to Chad Hill, "Can you see him in the mirror?"

Hill had presence of mind enough to move his eyes to the mirror without moving his head. "Not yet."

"Keep going."

Things were thinning out; the Finnish pines crowded down toward the road, the paving got narrower, there was ice on the shoulders and snow under the trees.

"There he comes."

"Keep it down. Let him pass us if he wants to."

"I don't think he—oh shit." And Hill was standing on his brakes. Lime screwed around in the seat to look back.

Nothing.

"What happened?"

"He turned off back there. Side road."

"All right. Take it easy, don't fly apart."

Hill jockeyed the Mercedes back and forth across the narrow paving, scared to risk the ice shoulders. Finally they made the U-turn and Hill put his foot to the floor.

The acceleration jammed Lime back in his seat. "Slow down damn it."

The sun flickered through the pines like a moving signal lamp. A car was coming toward them from Lahti; Lime squinted into the sun haze. He made it out to be a green Volvo, the old model two-door. Probably Alcorn.

Hill made the turnoff sedately enough. Lime looked over his shoulder and Alcorn was right behind them.

Ahead the road one-laned into the timber, snow banked close along both sides. The trees shut out the sun. Lime spoke into the microphone, reporting the turn. Afterward he consulted the map.

The road on the map ended at a T-junction with a secondary road that went northwest from Lahti to a string of villages farther north. There were no turnings between here and the T-junction.

"Step it up a little. Let's see if we can get him in sight."

An S-curve that made the Mercedes sway on its springs, and then the Saab was there, its taillights just disappearing around a farther bend. "All right, let's stick to his pace."

At the T-junction the Saab turned left and Chad Hill spoke a sour oath.

Lime reported: "He's headed back into town."

"Son of a bitch. He's still shaking shadows."

"He'll recognize this Mercedes if he sees it again. Tell Alcorn to pull past us. Get me a fresh car at this end of town. You've got about fifteen minutes."

Mezetti drove straight through Lahti without going around any blocks. Alcorn relayed the Saab over to another shadow at the near side of town and at the far edge, going south on the main highway to Helsinki, a new tail picked him up. Lime swapped his Mercedes for a waiting Volvo and went on through along Mezetti's track. By the time they were out in the pine country Lime had caught up to the other tail; there was some radio chatter and then Lime took over the tail's position while the tail overtook the Saab and went on ahead, bracketing Mezetti.

They rode him fifteen or twenty kilometers that way. It was getting on for two o'clock—close to sunset in these latitudes. Scandinavians kept their roads cleared in weather far worse than this but there wasn't much traffic. Pines hugged the road, endless forests of them. Here and there the pavement skirted the edge of a lake and passed a cabin snug with its lights glowing through frost-framed windows: half the residents of Helsinki and Lahti had vacation places on the lakes.

Mezetti seemed oblivious to his company. After dark it would be harder because he would be more acutely aware of headlights if they rode constantly in his mirror.

A Porsche closed from behind, rode a few curves on the Volvo's bumper and then pulled out to go by. Lime tried to get a glimpse of the driver's face but the side curtain was steamed up. The Porsche pulled ahead and they were glad to have it between them and Mezetti for a while. Mezetti was doing a fair clip but the Porsche got impatient after a mile or two, put on a burst of speed and slithered past.

Time to switch on the lights. The road hit a quick series of sharp bends, slithering along the shores of linked lakes; occasionally the Saab's lights winked through the trees.

Mezetti's performance was amateurish. He'd obviously been coached on blowing a single tail but his maneuverings weren't the kind that would disclose a multiple shadow, or shake it.

If his people were listening in on the shadowers' radio chatter they would know he was bracketed but Lime's organization was not using the standard police-car band; Mezetti's people would have to know what frequency to monitor and that was unlikely. At any rate they had no way of knowing about the sneak bleeper affixed to Mezetti's car. It hadn't been mentioned on the air and it wouldn't be.

They, he thought. Sturka. Was Sturka somewhere within a few miles, squirreled away in the pines with Clifford Fairlie?

"Speed it up a little. I can't see his lights."

Chad Hill fed gas and the Volvo started to lean on the turns. The headlights swept across thick stands of timber, the forest shadows mysterious in the farther depths.

The road squirmed through three sharp turns; Hill had to use his brakes. They weren't doing more than thirty kilometers an hour when they came out of the last bend and the headlights stabbed a car standing crosswise in the road.

Line's hand whipped to the dashboard and gripped its edge. The tires skidded on ice crystals imbedded in the road surface but the treads held and the Volvo slewed to a stop, just nudging the bole of a pine.

Lime dropped his hand and put his bleak stare on the car that stoppered the road.

It was the Porsche that had whipped past them ten kilometers back.

No keys in it; and no papers. "Find out who it's registered to," he said to Chad Hill. They were pushing it off the road.

It crunched and bounced down into the trees and Chad Hill was jogging back to the Volvo to call in. Lime got into the driver's seat. Chad Hill stood outside the open right-hand window with the mike in his hand, talking. Lime said, "Get in," and turned the starter.

The car rocked with Hill's weight. The door slammed and Lime backed onto the pavement and put the Volvo in gear and jammed his foot to the floor.

They clipped forward at ninety and a hundred kilometers per hour where the road permitted. But there were no taillights out ahead. "Ask him where those damned vans are."

Hill into the mike: "Where are the vans?"

"Coming right along," said the speaker. "We haven't dropped the ball yet."

But they had. Fifteen minutes later the signal stopped moving and at half past three they found the Saab on a private road parked at the edge of the trees. Mezetti had got away.

It was a summer cottage. A pencil lake perhaps a mile long, a modern cabin large for its kind, a wooden dock with a gasoline pump. There was ice around the edge of the lake but it hadn't frozen over yet. Lime stood scowling at the Saab. One of the vans was parked behind it and they had headlamps and spotlights switched on; the place was lit up like an arena. A crew of technicians crawled around the car but what was the point?

The voice crackled on the car radio. "What about footprints in the snow?"

"Plenty of them. Mostly from the driveway down to the dock. Have you got a registration on that Porsche yet?"

"Rental outfit. We're trying to find out who they rented to. It's taking a little time—it's a small outfit, they're closed Sundays. We're looking for the manager."

"He won't know anything." Lime let the microphone hang slack in his fist and glared at the Saab.

One of the technicians was talking to Chad Hill down by the dock, making gestures toward the gasoline pump.

From the mike: "Maybe we ought to put out an all-points on him. Throw a blanket net, his picture on TV, the whole thing. What have we got to lose?"

"Forget it." The manhunt until now had been massive but private. If it went public it might increase Fairlie's jeopardy.

Chad Hill came loping up from the dock. "Something here, sir. That's aviation gasoline in that pump."

Lime growled in his throat and put the mike to his lips. "He may be in a seaplane. There's a lake here, a pier. An aviation gas pump on the dock."

"I'll get coastal radar right on it."

Headlights swung around the approaching bend and Lime squinted at the advancing car. Nobody would have any business here in wintertime.

The car stopped behind the van and one of the Finnish cops went over to talk to the driver. A moment's uncertainty and then the wave of an arm—the Finn was beckoning and Lime walked across the drive.

The newcomer was a fat man with a cropped gray head and a roll of flesh at the back of his neck. When he got out of the car Lime recognized the clothes right away—the heavy shoes and the Moscow serge suit.

"You are David Lime."

"Yes."

"Viktor Menshikov. An honor." His little formal bow was anachronistic, it needed a clicking of heels to complete it. "I understand you are attempting to locate Mezetti."

Menshikov strolled off toward the trees at the fringe of the van's splash of illumination. The studied casualness was too much; it was something out of a Stalinist movie, heavy-handed and full of melo-drama, not the suave cleverness it was intended to provide.

Lime followed him to the trees. They were out of earshot of the others. Lime only stood and waited with a cigarette pasted to his lip.

Menshikov's face glowed in the chill wind. "It is possible we may be able to help."

"Is that a fact."

Menshikov tugged at his earlobe. It was one of Mikhail Yaskov's gestures and obviously that was where this one had picked it up. Yaskov was the kind of man who inspired imitation by his people. This fat goon with his clumsy efforts at elegance was poor fodder —a fifth-rate agent pretending to be a second-rate one, filled with conspiratorial mannerisms. A bureaucrat; but then everybody had the same problem with personnel these days.

"I am instructed to give you an address and a time."

Lime waited patiently.

"Riihimäkikatu Seventeen. At sixteen hours and forty-five min-utes."

"All right."

"Alone of course."

"Of course."

Menshikov smiled briefly, trying to look villainous. Bowed his head, inserted his heavy rump into his car and drove off.

The wind rubbed itself against Lime. He took the cigarette from his mouth and dropped it into the snow at his feet. Menshikov's red taillights receded, turned the bend and disappeared. Lime walked over to the Volvo.

He settled wearily into the car, put a cigarette in his mouth, jerked at his tie and opened his collar button and said to Hill, "Yaskov wants a private meet with me at four forty-five."

That was an hour hence. Chad Hill started the car. "Do you think they've got Mezetti?"

"It's one theory. I'm willing to take an option on it but I'm not buying it yet. I was hoping we wouldn't get stuck in this kind of flypaper. We haven't got time. I hope I can sell that to Yaskov—he's reasonable."

"He is, maybe. Sometimes his bosses aren't."

"Sometimes our bosses aren't."

"Uh-huh. You don't think they're going to want anything big in trade, do you?"

"They're careful. That wouldn't be like them. The price won't be out of line. It's all a game, isn't it." Lime didn't care; he was too tired. "At least we haven't lost him. We thought we had. Better the familiar enemy. . . ."

He dry-scrubbed his face violently, fighting the red wash of fatigue that kept sliding down across his eyes.

He got out of the car a block up from Number Seventeen. He had a *pointilliste* view of the street through the slowly drifting mist; moisture gleamed on the pavement like precious gems. He felt the weight of the stubby hammerless .38 that was snugged into the clamshell under his arm. At least Yaskov was a professional. There was a bit of comfort knowing he wasn't going to get killed accidentally by a trigger-happy amateur.

He turned up his collar and put his hands in his pockets and walked down the black sidewalk, avoiding puddles, his heels echoing on the wet concrete. Lights sparkled along the street and he saw a few blocks away the high lamps that outlined the town's landmark, the high restaurant built on top of the tall phallic water tower.

The emptiness of the street hardened his gut. He fought down the sour spirals coming up from his stomach and lifted his shoulders defensively.

Just as he went by Number Twenty-one a man came out its door and stood there. It could have been coincidence. The man gave Lime the quick distracted smile of a polite stranger. Threw his head back and drew in a loud breath.

Lime went on a dozen paces and looked back at the steps of Number Twenty-one. The man was still there.

A sentry, and a warning to Lime. The man was posted there to watch the street and give the alarm if reinforcements appeared.

Seventeen was a two-story structure, elderly, colorless. It looked as if it probably contained eight or ten flats. Here and there lights burned behind drawn shades. Lime uneasily pictured guns aimed at him from the shadows.

The door admitted him to a corridor at the foot of a flight of wooden stairs. Menshikov came forward from the hallway beside the staircase; smiled and swept his arm toward the stair. It was all dreary and tedious. Lime went up the stairs and Menshikov remained at the front door like a cheap gangster in a Bogart movie.

The stairs creaked when he put his weight on them. At the top there was a landing and a corridor that ran the length of the building front to back. Toward the front a door stood open and General Mikhail Yaskov stood there smiling amiably in comfortable English slacks and a gray turtleneck sweater.

"Hallo David."

Lime crossed the distance between them and glanced into the room behind Yaskov. It was a dismal flat, the kind that rented furnished. "They must have cut your budget again."

"It was available. Housing shortage you know."

Mikhail Yaskov spoke English with a London accent. His smile revealed a chrome-hued tooth; there was humor in the steady gray eyes. He was a tall easygoing man, but the aristocratic face was deeply and prematurely lined.

At one time Lime had felt affection and respect for Mikhail. He had learned better; every face was a mask.

"Well then David. You look God-awful."

"I haven't been sleeping well."

"Pity." There was a bottle of *akvavit;* Mikhail tipped it toward a glass, handed the glass to Lime and poured another for himself. "Cheers."

"I haven't got time to play Oriental games."

"Yes. I realize there's a shortage of time. You're rather rigid about having your leaders keep their appointments."

"Have you got Mezetti?"

The Russian settled into the armchair and waved him toward the sofa. The room was poorly heated and Lime kept his coat on. Mikhail said, "Let's say I might be able to help you find him."

"I'm not carrying a microphone."

"Well if you were you'd find anything it picked up had been jammed to gibberish." Mikhail touched a device on the end table by his chair. It looked like a transistor radio; it was an electronic jammer.

"No time for scavenger hunts. Have you got him or haven't you?"

"I have an idea where you might find him."

"All right. And the price?"

Mikhail grinned. "How quickly you come to my point." He sipped the liqueur and watched Lime over the rim of the glass. "The Organs had a signal the other day from Washington." The

Organs was KGB in Moscow. "We've been instructed to cooperate with you. It was all very correct you know—everyone being polite to one another in cool voices."

"Where is he, Mikhail?"

"Abominable weather we're having isn't it." Mikhail set the glass down, steepled his fingers and squinted. "Let me tell you a bit of local history, David. Your man Mezetti drove to that lake cottage with the evident expectation of meeting his friends there. Or perhaps I should say the hope, if not the expectation. If he'd been certain of it he'd have brought the money with him, wouldn't he? I mean, for a tourist with a definite itinerary he was a trifle short on luggage." The quick smile, a fast remark: "No, let me finish please. It's one hundred thousand dollars, isn't it? Yes. Well then, Mezetti comes to the lake cottage empty-handed. Why?"

"To find out if his friends are there."

"One must assume his friends were supposed to make contact with him at the hotel before a certain hour. When the deadline passed he drove out to the meeting place to find out what had gone wrong. Correct?"

"Did he tell you all this or are you just trying it on for size?"

Mikhail tugged his earlobe. "There was another car you know. Mezetti switched cars at the lake cottage."

Lime became attentive. "Then you didn't put the snatch on him?"

"I had no orders to detain the man, David. He's probably still unaware he's under surveillance."

"Where did he go?"

Another sip of *akvavit*. "He arrived at the lake, he poked around. He looked at his watch several times and sat in his car watching the dock as if he were waiting for something. An airplane to collect him? We don't know that, do we? The point is no one came. There was no airplane. After a while Mezetti went over and looked inside the other car. He found a note fixed to the steering wheel. He then drove away in this second car."

"Make and model?"

"A Volkswagen," Mikhail said drily. "A rather old one I should judge."

Lime was beginning to see now. It was Mezetti who had been sent out on a snipe hunt. The scavenger hunt was once-removed. They had played it cleverly and it had bought Sturka at least four days.

It reduced Mezetti's importance markedly but this still had to be played through to the finish. "What's the price then?"

"Mezetti evidently thought someone would be there to meet him." Mikhail leaned forward and peered. "Who, David?"

".Vhoever left the note in the Volkswagen, I imagine."

A thin smile, and Mikhail got to his feet and went to the window to peer past the blind.

The entire performance was sad. Mikhail was imprisoned in this dingy room because the Finns hated the Soviets and officially Mikhail—a known KGB operative—was *persona non grata*; officially, no doubt, he wasn't in Finland at all. So he had to play at these back-street games: secret meetings, sleazy hideouts, second-string underlings to do his legwork for him. Yet in spite of all those handicaps he had got a jump on everyone else. He had isolated Mezetti from his shadowers without alerting Mezetti and was now the only man alive who could put Lime back on Mezetti's trail.

And naturally there was a price.

"Of course you know who they are, Mezetti's people."

"If we knew who they were would we be bothering with Mezetti?"

"You don't know *where* they are," Mikhail said smoothly. He smiled to show he *knew*; he wasn't just guessing. Well it was understandable. The Soviets would have had little trouble piecing together the fact that the Americans knew the identity of the quarry. It surprised Lime a little that they hadn't already picked up the name as well. But then he realized Sturka's name hadn't been mentioned at all except in scrambled transmissions and those were virtually impossible to tap. The Russians would know Sturka was being sought for the Capitol bombing but they wouldn't have reason to tie him into the Fairlie case too.

"We'd like a name or two," Mikhail said, returning to his chair.

"Why?"

"In the interests of peaceful coexistence. Open cooperation between allies, so to speak." The smile this time was to show the falsehood of it.

"Look Mikhail, you've thrown a little roadblock at us but I don't think it entitles you to voting stock in the corporation. Suppose I publicize the fact that the Russians are being obstructive?"

"We'll deny it of course. And how are you going to prove it?"

"Let's put it this way. I can see what your people are worried about. Some of the satellites have come loose of their moorings and

Moscow wants to make sure none of the troops are being bad boys. It would give you a black eye if it turned out Romania or Czechoslovakia was involved in this. All right, I'll give you this much. We have no reason to believe any government's behind the kidnapping. No government, and as far as we know there's no national liberation movement behind it either. Is that enough for you?"

"I'm afraid not."

"I'm playing fairly loose as it is."

"I know you are." Mikhail's mouth became small and mean until he no longer seemed to have lips. It was anger not so much against Lime as against his own superiors. "One has one's orders." It was almost an epithet.

You could picture them in the Kremlin, uniforms buttoned to the choke collars, refusing to take compromise for an answer. They held the ace and they knew it, and if Mikhail didn't take the trick they'd throw him in the Lubianka.

Lime really had no option. "Julius Sturka. He's got a little crew of amateurs. Raoul Riva may be in on it, maybe not."

"Sturka." The Russian's thin nostrils flared. "That one. We should have taken him out years ago. He's an anarchist. But he calls himself a Communist. You know he's probably done more harm to us than to you, over the years."

"I know. He doesn't exactly contribute to your good name."

"And you have no idea where to look for him?"

"No."

"That's a pity." Mikhail drained his glass. "Mezetti has taken lodgings in the railway hotel in Heinola. We have three cars covering him. Two or three men in the lobby at the moment. They're expecting you—they won't interfere."

"Tell them to pull out when I arrive."

"Of course."

"I don't suppose you people have a decent photo of Sturka in your files."

"I doubt it."

Lime had one—the snapshot Barbara Norris had taken with her Minolta. But it was a 16mm negative, grainy and not in sharp focus.

When they parted they didn't shake hands; they never did.

Snow came up onto the windshield in lumps of gray slush and the wipers flicked it away. It was falling hard on a slant, lashing the windows. Chad Hill leaned forward over the wheel trying to see;

they were crawling. It was a convoy, four cars and a police van.

Lime had watched the teletype operator word his message before they got in the cars and set out for Heinola.

> FROM: LIME
>
> TO: SATTERTHWAITE
>
> IGNORE PREVIOUS SIGNALS X HAVE
>
> CORNERED MM IN DEAD END X IN VIEW
>
> OF TIME FACTOR AM TAKING MM INTO
>
> CUSTODY FOR INTERROGATION X

It would be an open transmission for part of the way so he hadn't said anything about the Russians.

Only six o'clock but the world seemed adrift in the formless subartic night. The darkness had the viscosity of syrup.

Chad Hill drew in at the curb; the lights of the railway hotel flickered in the falling snow.

A man in knee boots and fur hat was shoveling snow clear of the exhaust pipe of his Volkswagen; another man was scraping frost off its windshield. Lime walked over and spoke to the man at the windshield.

"*Tovarich?*"

"Lime?"

"*Da.*"

The Russian nodded. Turned, tipped his head back until snow-flakes hit his face, pointed to a window on the second floor. Light shone through the drawn drapes.

Chad Hill came up from the car. Lime said, "You know the drill now."

"Yes sir."

Lime was making vague arm signals to the procession of vehicles that had drawn up; men got out of them without slamming the doors and fanned out to cover every side of the hotel.

The ice sheet on the porch splintered under Lime's heels like eggshells. He tucked his face toward his shoulder against the frozen wind and peered inside through the misty windows. A few indistinct shapes in the lobby. It wasn't a setup, they weren't posted for it. Anyhow there would have been no reason for it; it was just that he always suspected the worst.

He went along to the door with Chad Hill in tow; batted inside with matted hair and ruined shoes.

Three of the men in the lobby got up and converged on the

door. Lime and Chad Hill stood aside until they were gone.

It left two old men in chairs reading magazines. The clerk behind the desk watched Lime with fascination but made no protest when Lime headed directly for the stair.

Chad Hill stuck close. Lime said, "Got the tools?"

"Yes sir."

"Keep it quiet," he adjured. They climbed the stairs with the predatory silence of prowlers. Lime made a quick scrutiny of the hallway and went toward the front of the building.

A ceiling light burned above the door of the front room. He reached up and unscrewed the bulb until it went out. He didn't want the light behind him; no one knew whether Mezetti was armed.

He considered the door. Got down on one knee and looked into the keyhole. It was blocked by the key inside.

Chad Hill held the lock-pick case open and Lime selected a slim pair of needlenose pliers.

Behind them four men came up to the head of the stairs and deployed themselves along the corridor.

It would have been easiest to knock, use some ruse or other. But they couldn't tell how nervous Mezetti might be; why risk alerting him? Lime pictured bullets chugging through the door panels. . . .

It was an old lock with a sloppy big keyhole and there was room for the pliers. He got a grip on the stub of the key and with his right hand dragged the .38 out of its armpit rig.

Chad Hill was biting his lip. His knuckles were white on his revolver.

Lime nodded. Squeezed the pliers and turned.

Nothing; he'd turned it the wrong way. You always did, somehow. He turned it the other way and when the lock clacked over with a rusty scrape he twisted the knob and burst into the room.

Mezetti had no time to register alarm.

"Turn around and hit the wall."

The six of them crowded around Mezetti. Lime frisked him, felt the heavy padding around his torso and made a face. "He's had the money on him all the time. Strip his shirt off."

He put his gun away and did a quick wash of the apartment. In the bathroom a faucet dripped relentlessly; there was an old-

fashioned bathtub standing on clawed feet. Trust Mezetti—
it was probably the only room with private bath in the entire
hotel. Revolutions were fine as long as you could conduct them in
luxury.

The agents had the money piled up on the floor and Mezetti was
blinking rapidly, trying to watch everybody at once. Lime waved
them all back and stood close in front of Mezetti. "Who's supposed
to meet you?"

"Nobody."

"Where's the note they left for you in the car?"

Mezetti was startled and showed it. Lime said over his shoulder,
"A couple of you look for it. He won't have thrown it away."

Mezetti stood in his drawers trembling, not from the chill. Lime
went to the little desk and pulled the chair out. It had one wobbly
leg, or perhaps the floor was out of kilter. He lit a cigarette. "Stand
still."

"What the fuck do you pigs think you're doing? Do you know who
I——"

"Shut up. You'll speak only when spoken to."

"That money belongs to Mezetti Industries. If you think you can
steal——"

"*Shut up.*"

Lime sat and smoked and stared at Mezetti.

One of the agents had been going through Mezetti's coat pockets
in the wardrobe. "Here it is." Chad Hill took it from him and carried
it across the room to Lime.

Lime glanced at it. *Mario, Wait for us at the railway hotel in
Heinola.* Hill had it in tweezers and Lime nodded; Hill put it in an
envelope.

"Come over here."

Mezetti didn't move until one of the agents gave him a brutal
shove.

Lime made hand signals and the agents brought the straight
wooden chair over from the window. They set it by the desk and
Lime said, "Sit down."

Mezetti moved cautiously into the chair.

Lime reached across the desk, put his hand on top of Mezetti's
head and shoved his face down onto the desk top. Mezetti's teeth
clicked, his jaw sagged, his eyes rolled up.

Lime sat back and watched. Mezetti gathered himself sluggishly,
showing his distress. He worked his jaw back and forth experimen-
tally.

Lime waited.

"You fascist filth," Mezetti breathed.

Lime allowed no reaction to show; he puffed on his cigarette. After a moment he slammed the rim of his shoe into Mezetti's shin.

Mezetti doubled up holding his leg against his chest and Lime stiff-armed him in the face. It tipped Mezetti backward, the chair went over and Mezetti rolled on the floor.

The agents picked up Mezetti and the chair and positioned him where he had been before. Mezetti was about to snarl when Lime took the needlenose pliers out of his pocket and used them on the top of Mezetti's right ear. Squeezed. Pulled upward, and Mezetti strained to come along but the agents held him down on the chair.

Lime let the ear go and prodded the points of the pliers up into the hollow under Mezetti's chin. Mezetti's head strained back like a dental patient's.

Chad Hill was watching it all with alarm and disapproval.

Lime kept digging with the pliers until Mezetti began to bleed small droplets under the jaw. When Lime withdrew the pliers Mezetti felt his chin and saw the blood on his fingers. The last of the bravado drained out of him as if a plug had been pulled.

"All right. Which one was supposed to meet you here? Sturka? Alvin Corby? Cesar Renaldo?"

Mezetti licked his lips.

Lime said, "Put it this way. You can tell me or you can try to hold out. You'll get pretty bloody and the pain will be a lot more than you can stand, but you can try. But even if you don't tell me anything I'll let them understand that you did tell me. On the other hand if you're realistic we'll keep your name out of it until we've nailed them all."

Abruptly he japped the pliers into the back of Mezetti's hand. Blood started to flow freely; Mezetti clutched his hand.

Lime turned to Chad Hill. "It might be a good idea to let word out that he's cooperating anyway. It may force Sturka to move."

It was strictly for Mezetti's benefit; Lime was certain Mezetti didn't know where Sturka was. Of course Sturka knew that too; a news release wouldn't force Sturka's hand.

"I don't know where they are. That's the truth." Mezetti's voice was a defeated monotone. He was looking at the desk, keeping his eyes down.

Lime said, "I want you to be very, very careful of your answer to this question. How many of them are there?"

It was a calculated way of putting it. It didn't sound like a fishing expedition; it sounded as if he already knew the right answer. He drummed the pliers against the desk.

It came out slow, reluctantly. "Four of them. The ones you named and Peggy Astin."

"It's a bad idea lying to me," Lime said. He lifted the plier points against the pit of Mezetti's chest and began to twist and grind.

"That's the truth for God's sake."

Lime kept grinding.

"Look if you—Christ get that fucking thing off me!" Mezetti was trying to squirm away from the pliers but the two agents held him pinned in the chair. He began to reek with the sweat of fear.

Abruptly Lime withdrew the pliers. "Now."

"If you know so much you know I'm telling the truth. Shit."

"But there's outside help isn't there?"

"Well Sturka knows people all over the place. He's got contacts you know."

"Name them."

"I don't——"

"Raoul Riva," Lime said, and watched.

It puzzled Mario. Lime dropped it. "When you left that boat on the shoals you killed the skipper. Then what did you do?"

He made it sound like another test. Mezetti said, "It wasn't me. I didn't kill him."

"You're as guilty as the rest, you know that."

"For God's sake I didn't kill anybody."

"You threatened to kill the pilot who flew you up here from Gibraltar."

"That was just to get him to cooperate. I didn't kill him, did I?"

"What did you do after you killed the boat owner?"

Lime was toying with the pliers and Mezetti slumped in the chair. "We had another boat waiting."

"You still had Fairlie in the coffin?"

Mezetti's eyes grew round. He swallowed visibly. "Off and on. We didn't keep him in it when we were out at sea."

"Where did you go from there?"

"Down the coast."

"To Almería."

"Well that was the other boat," Mezetti said. "I mean we did a couple of hundred miles in a truck about half way down the coast. We didn't have time to do the whole thing in boats—it was too far."

"All right, you used a truck. Who set it up?"

"Sturka did."

"No. Sturka arranged for it but Sturka wasn't the one who put the truck there for you. Who delivered it?"

"I never saw the guy."

"It was Riva wasn't it?"

"I never heard of any Riva."

"Hold him," Lime said. He stood up and posted himself beside Mezetti and gently pushed the points of the pliers into Mezetti's earhole. When he felt it strike the eardrum he put slow pressure on it; he held Mezetti's head against the pressure with his left hand. "Now who was it Mario?"

Mezetti started to cry.

Lime reduced the pressure but kept the pliers in Mezetti's ear and after a little while Mezetti hawked and snorted and spoke. "Look I never even met the guy."

"But you've seen him."

". . . Yeah."

"What's his name?"

"Sturka called him Binyoosef a couple of times."

Chad Hill said, "Binyoosef?"

"Benyoussef," Lime said absently, scowling on it. He withdrew the pliers. "A fat man with a bit of a limp."

"Yeah," Mezetti said dismally. "That's him."

Lime sat down facing him across the desk. "Let's go back to that garage at Palamos where you made the tape recordings."

"Jesus. You don't miss much."

"Now you were packing things up. You had Fairlie in the coffin. The coffin went in the hearse. Corby drove the hearse. The rest of you cleaned up the place—wiped it for fingerprints, gathered up everything you'd brought with you. Now everybody gets into the hearse.

"But somebody had to switch off the light and close the garage door. You did that."

"Yeah. Christ did you have the whole thing on television?"

"Sturka told you to go over and switch off the light."

"Yeah."

"Then you walked out and pulled the garage door shut. You wiped your fingerprints off the door and got in the hearse."

"Yeah yeah." Mezetti was nodding.

"Sturka watched you switch off the light didn't he."

Mezetti frowned. "I guess he did, yeah."

"Then maybe when you came to close the garage door he handed you a rag to wipe it with."

"Yeah. Jesus Christ."

Lime sat back brooding. It was what he'd had to know.

After a moment he changed the subject. "You went ashore at Almería. Did everybody go ashore?"

"Just me. I rowed in on the raft."

"The rest of them stayed on the boat? What was the plan?"

Mezetti was looking at the pliers. "Jesus Christ. You're going to kill me anyway, aren't you?"

"We're going to take you back to Washington. You'll get killed but not by me."

"Pig justice. A fascist gas chamber."

"A gas chamber has no politics," Lime said mildly. "Your friend Sturka gassed a whole village once."

The mistake he'd made was stopping to think. It had given Mezetti time to reflect on the hopelessness of his position. It was going to be harder to get more out of him now; the pliers would open his mouth but he'd start trying lies. An extended interrogation would fix that; put pressure on and keep it up until they got the same answer every time.

But Lime didn't have that sort of time. He stood up and handed the pliers to one of the agents. "Take him down to Lahti."

It was about nine o'clock. Chad Hill trailed him into the police office. Lime's coat was heavy and steamy with moisture; he got it off and threw it across the chair.

"I think Benyoussef Ben Krim is around here somewhere. We'd better have a net. Photo and description to the airports particularly —he's probably on his way out if he hasn't left already."

Chad Hill said, "I thought Benyoussef was the guy who supplied the boat."

"He was."

"But that was in Spain. What makes you think he's up here?"

"Somebody left the car and the note for Mezetti."

"Why Benyoussef?"

"He used to be Sturka's errand boy. It looks as if he still is."

Chad Hill was still puzzled and Lime explained it. "Mezetti's fingerprint in the garage was deliberate—Sturka's idea. Sturka watched him switch off the light but didn't tell him to wipe it."

"So?"

"We were supposed to identify Mezetti," Lime said. He struggled to his feet; sitting in the chair was too dangerous. He couldn't afford to fall asleep just yet.

Eighty-seven hours to inauguration. He arched his back, bracing his fists against his kidneys; heard the ligatures crackle. "Have we got that Concorde?"

"It's in Helsinki," Hill said.

"Good. We'd better get to it."

"You need sleep. You look like a corpse."

"I'll sleep on the plane."

"Where to?"

"Algiers," Lime said. "That's the place to start." It was the place he should have started in the first place. Satterthwaite had been right. Sturka was a pro; a pro was somebody who didn't make stupid mistakes. The fingerprint in the garage—you'd have to practice to get that stupid. Except that it wasn't a mistake.

So the red herring had drawn them off all the way to Finland and in the meantime Sturka was down in the Western Desert all the time. Benyoussef was the evidence that supported that. If Sturka was using the members of his old Algerian cell then that was where he had to be.

The old stamping grounds. The place where Sturka had outwitted Lime every time.

MONDAY,
JANUARY 17

3:20 A.M. EST The preparations had been completed and tonight Riva's part of the plan went operational.

Riva had watched the weather forecasts and timed the action to coincide with the arrival of the low-pressure front over Washington.

The temperature was 34 degrees and that made it a wet snowfall, the flakes congealing in lumps and splashing where they struck. The thick flurries made bad visibility and that was what Riva wanted.

They were working in two cars, Kavanagh and Harrison in a Chevrolet and Riva in the Dodge. They had ten of the molded satchel charges in the Chevrolet. Riva had fitted together a hose-pipe bomb and had put it on the seat beside him under a folded newspaper.

The attack on Milton Luke was the key to the rest; it had to work; yet of them all it was by far the most difficult since none of the others would be half so well guarded.

Luke lived in a top-floor apartment in a high-rise on Wisconsin Avenue. It was virtually impossible to penetrate into the apartment itself; Secret Service had people everywhere in the building.

So they'd ruled that out. It was always senseless attacking the enemy at his most strongly guarded points. Luke was the key target but there were satellite targets and the thing to do was to hit some of them first because they would help act as diversions.

So they hit Senator Hollander's house first. The idea was to shake up the old fascist but not hurt him. Riva drove by first. The big Georgian house was set well back from the street; its porch lights flickered through the snowfall and he could make out the heavy outline of the Secret Service van in the driveway. It looked like the same van they used to post at Dexter Ethridge's house before Ethridge died.

He drove straight past at a steady twenty-five and picked up the walkie-talkie when he had gone by. Spoke one word: "Copasetik."

He drove the Dodge on, heading for Massachusetts Avenue, listening for the walkie-talkie to reply. It would take a few minutes. The Chevrolet would drift past Hollander's house and Kavanagh would toss the satchel into the shadows. They had picked the spot for it earlier. It wouldn't do too much damage—perhaps uproot some shrubs and clang bits and pieces of shrapnel against the house and the Secret Service van—but it would wake everybody up and it would bring a great many cops up this way.

The satchel had a half-hour time fuse and that would give them plenty of leeway.

"Copasetik."

He glanced at the walkie-talkie on the seat. It resumed its silence. He turned three blocks up the avenue from the massive apartment building that housed a Senator and two Congressmen and the Secretary of the Treasury. Parked and turned the interior dome-light switch to the off position before he opened the car door and stepped out into the falling snow.

It was a corner building and had two entrances, one on either face. There was also a service ramp that gave access to the basement in the rear. All three entrances were guarded: the Executive Protection Service had a man on each door and the two main entrances had armed doormen as well.

Riva went softly into the service drive, a muffled figure moving without sound. He lifted the gun—a .32 caliber revolver with a perforated silencer screwed to the barrel. He cocked the hammer and then held the weapon down at his side where it was covered by the flapping skirt of his coat.

The cop saw him approaching. Straightened up and stepped out under the light with his hand on his gun. "Hi there." Friendly but cautious.

"Hi," Riva said and shot twice.

The shots made little puffs of sound and the cop sagged back against the brick wall and slid down to the pavement. He left a glossy smear on the wall.

Riva dragged the cop into the shadows and put the cop's cap on his own head. From a distance it would do. He took up a post by the door with the cop's key ring in his pocket.

Americans had such childish ideas about security.

A car turned in at the far end of the service drive. It flicked its lights. Riva lifted his left hand high over his head. The Chevrolet backed out of the driveway onto the street, pulled forward along the curb, backed into the driveway and came all the way to the service ramp in reverse.

The lights went out and the car doors opened.

"Everything okay?"

"Everything's fine."

It might have been one cop talking to another—his relief.

Riva used the cop's key to open the service door. "Easy now."

"Sure—sure." Kavanagh and Harrison went inside lugging the five satchel charges.

Riva checked the door to make sure it could be opened from inside without a key. All they had to do was push the crossbar down. He tossed the key ring on top of the dead cop and walked up the service drive past the Chevrolet. Its engine was pinging with the sound of cooling contraction. He wiped a droplet of snow off his nose and walked unhurriedly out to the street, around the corner, across the street and down the block to the Dodge.

He sat in the car for thirty-five minutes—the length of time they had judged it would take. There was no reason to expect any trouble. There were no hallway guards in the apartment house and the various dignitaries didn't have sentries posted at their doors. Americans couldn't stand living that way. So all you had to do was get into the building; from there on you would be undisturbed.

The bombs probably wouldn't waste them all. Senator Grant's bedrooom was in an outside corner of the building on the top floor and the nearest hallway was one room removed from the bed. The bomb would make a shambles of Grant's kitchen and it would make him good and angry. That was just as good. With any luck the Treasury Secretary would get buried under a good deal of heavy debris. The satchel charges in the trash chutes next to the bedrooms of Congressmen Wood and Jethro would almost certainly kill both Representatives and their wives. As for columnist J. R. Ilfeld he would lose the priceless art works in his sybaritic parlor and that would serve to inflame his rage beyond reason.

Riva heard the distant cry of sirens. The bomb on Hollander's lawn, he thought. Before the night was over they'd be running in panic-stricken circles—chasing their tails. A pack of prize fools, the American security forces.

"Copasetik."

He turned the key and waited with the engine idling until the Chevrolet drove past; he switched on the lights and pulled out to follow at a leisurely distance, heading for Wisconsin Avenue.

4:05 A.M. EST They had floodlights all over Senator Hollander's lawn and the bomb squad was examining the pieces of shrapnel they had found imbedded in the siding.

"A hell of a lot of force in that thing," the sergeant said. "Christ look at that tree it knocked down." It had been a giant of an old maple.

Senator Hollander and Mrs. Hollander were stomping around the snowy lawn in slippers and robes, bellowing at everybody in sight. Lieutenant Ainsworth spoke into the radio: "It looks like a professionally made bomb. You'd better try and get in touch with Mr. Satterthwaite."

4:08 A.M. EST Riva drove slowly along Wisconsin Avenue and parked a block short of Milton Luke's apartment building. The snow was still fluttering down in heavy wet streamers. It was beginning to accumulate on the sidewalks and lawns; the temperature had probably dropped a degree or two.

A garage would have made it easier but there wasn't any. It had been the last apartment building raised in Washington before the zoning laws forbade throwing up high-rises without built-in garages. So everybody had to scramble for parking spaces in the street —everybody except the VIPs. The limousine assigned to Speaker Luke, now President-designate Luke, had its own cordoned-off parking space immediately in front of the building. The chauffeur was a Secret Service agent and was always with the car. Two more Secret Service men were on the apartment house door. There were dozens of them inside the building, in the corridors, at the other entrances. You couldn't get at Luke inside; you had to do it out here.

Riva lifted the walkie-talkie. "All set?"

"Copasetik."

"Synchronize. Three minutes from . . . now."

He was studying the crystal of his watch; now he slipped the hosepipe bomb out from under the newspaper, got most of it inside his coat pocket and the rest up his left sleeve, and stepped out of the car with his left hand in his pocket. The bomb was only an inch and a half in diameter but the charge inside was a German explosive gel that had the destructive equivalent of a six-inch naval shell. One end of the hosepipe was capped with aluminum, the other with a heat-sensitive detonating device, and powerful magnets were fixed to both caps and a ring around the center of the pipe. The magnets would hold the bomb snug against any piece of steel.

The detonator was a tin-copper electrical device that relied on an increase in temperature to affect the expansion differential of the two metals: any temperature above 100 degrees Fahrenheit would cause contact and thereby detonate the bomb.

He walked down the street on the sidewalk opposite the apartment building and glanced casually in its direction. The Secret Service agents were watching him as they would watch any pedestrian abroad at ten past four in the morning.

Ahead of him a car was sliding among the lights of the intersection two blocks distant. Riva timed his turn to coincide with the bleat of the car's horn as it came into the block.

The horn attracted the Secret Service agents' attention. The chauffeur was standing under the awning watching the limousine but his head also turned toward the advancing Chevrolet. Riva stepped off the curb between two parked cars and stood there waiting for the Chevrolet to go past him so he could walk across the street. He made it look as if he were walking toward the building beyond the apartment house.

He heard the pneumatic hiss of the car as it grew closer and he took a step back to avoid the splash of snow. The car went by, doing about twenty-five; the agents' heads swiveled, indicating their steady interest in it. Riva stepped out into the avenue, looked both ways and began to cross. His path was designed to take him past the back of the limousine toward the next building down.

The agents were dividing their attention between Riva and the receding Chevrolet when Harrison in the back seat of the Chevrolet began to shoot. He was shooting at the windows of Milton Luke's apartment. His shots were not expected to do any damage; it was a very high angle. But they accomplished their purpose; the Secret Service agents got behind pillars and cars and began to blaze away at the Chevrolet.

Riva did what anybody would do. You're a pedestrian in the middle of the open and suddenly guns start going off: you dive for cover.

The cover he chose was the shadow of the VIP limousine and as he rolled past its rear bumper his left arm snaked up underneath the rear of the car. It took only a second or two to locate an exhaust pipe. He snapped the magnetized bomb on top of the pipe, immediately beneath the gasoline tank, and kept right on rolling over against the curb. Now he was a few feet behind the limousine, not within reach of it, and the Secret Service agents could see him if they chose to look.

The Chevrolet was just disappearing around the corner with a wail of tires and the agents stopped shooting. Riva got to his feet and when the nearest agent swung to glare at him Riva said, "Jesus Christ Almighty. What in hell was that all about?"

4:20 A.M. EST   Satterthwaite scraped a hand down across his chin. The stubble stung his palm.

Bleary faces along the length of the big table in The Salt Mine. Voices barking into telephones. Satterthwaite had FBI Director Clyde Shankland on the line. "It looks like a maximum effort they're putting up. First Hollander's lawn, then five Goddamned bombs in that one building, then a sniper shooting at Luke's windows. God knows where else they'll hit. Look, I want every man you've got. We've got to provide immediate protection for every VIP in Washington."

Kaiser was tugging at his sleeve. Kaiser had a telephone cupped in his hand. "It's for you. The President."

Satterthwaite said to Shankland, "Get on it, Clyde," and slammed down the phone and grabbed the other one from Kaiser. "Yes, Mr. President."

4:23 A.M. EST   The city was amok with crying sirens. Riva circled the block and got back into his car and reached for the walkie-talkie. "Copasetik?"

"Copasetik."

"They're on their toes. Let's do the alternate."

"Copasetik."

The central area was getting too hot; they would skip the other targets and head for the outskirts.

The Secret Service men had questioned him for several minutes but Riva's identification was in order and his story was plausible and they had bigger things to worry about than him.

He put the car in gear and headed up toward Senator Forrester's house.

4:28 A.M. EST   Special Agent Pickett slid into the front seat of the limousine to use the radio. His hand brushed the manila folder on the seat and when he pushed it aside the ID sheet came ajar and he was looking straight into the face of the man they had questioned less than ten minutes ago.

He picked up the ID sheet and stared at the photo and blurted into the microphone.

"This is Pickett. I've just seen your man Riva."

4:31 A.M. EST   DeFord and B. L. Hoyt marched into the war room and Hoyt said to Satterthwaite, "Listen, they may be pulling something in that apartment house. Those rifle shots could have been a diversion to distract our people's attention while someone slipped into the building. We'd better get Milton Luke out of there."

"And put him where?"

"The White House. It's the best guarded place we've got."

DeFord said, "I'll arrange for a heavy escort. We'll want motorcycles and squadrols." He reached for a phone.

4:33 A.M. EST   The two FBI agents reached Arizona Terrace and parked at the curb.

"That's the Senator's house."

"All right. No point waking him up. Look, I'll post myself in that open garage across the street. You stick here in the car. Anybody shows up, we'll have them crossfired."

"Okay."

4:37 A.M. EST   Riva parked at the mouth of Arizona Terrace and within moments the Chevrolet drew up alongside. Kavanagh at the wheel.

"Everything okay?"

"So far," Riva said.

"You want to do this hit and run?"

"He's got that plate-glass picture window in front. Just throw it in through the window."

"I don't know. It's a cul-de-sac, this street."

"I'll sweep it first," Riva said. "Give me two minutes." He pulled out into the street and headed up the hill in low.

Forrester's house was at the bottleneck of the street just before it widened into a circular turnaround. Riva drove slowly into the turnaround. Was that a shadow in the parked car? He looked again. Nothing.

Getting nervous. He chastised himself. It would take them a lot longer than this to get men out this far. Forrester was only a junior senator from an unimportant state.

He cruised around the loop and headed out again. Glanced into the shadows of an open garage; nothing there. The snowfall had let up, the flakes were drifting down singly. He drove back over the crest and down to the mouth of the drive.

"All clear."

4:41 A.M. EST   The FBI agent spoke low into the microphone of his car radio. "Somebody's just cased Forrester's house. You better get another car or two up here."

4:42 A.M. EST   Harrison put the satchel charge in his lap while the car climbed the hill. He set the timer for two minutes.

Kavanagh drove past the parked Plymouth and pulled in across the front of the Senator's driveway. "Go."

Harrison shoved the door open and stepped out. Started to walk up the driveway toward the front of the house.

"Hold it right there. FBI."

Harrison turned slowly on his heels, twisting his head to look over his shoulder.

The FBI man stood beside the Plymouth, aiming the pistol casually at the middle of Harrison's coat and making it clear he felt it was an easy shot.

The timing device was ticking. Harrison dropped the bomb and dived for cover but the FBI man switched his headlights on and caught Harrison blindingly in the beams.

Kavanagh was coming out of the Chevrolet with his gun but there was a wink of orange flame and a roar from the dark open garage across the street and Kavanagh pitched onto his face.

Harrison got up to run—he couldn't stay there, the bomb had thirty seconds at most. . . .

He felt the bullets thud into him but before he went under he heard the earsplitting thunder of the satchel bomb. Something whacked agony against the back of his neck.

4:43 A.M. EST   The shots alerted Riva and he reached for the walkie-talkie. "Copasetik?"

When they didn't answer right away he switched on his lights and drove for the mouth of the street.

A pair of cars came swerving into it. Saw him approaching and slewed across the pavement to block his exit. Riva turned the wheel and floored the pedal, ramming the Dodge up onto the sidewalk, heading for the open boulevard beyond them. But he had their headlights straight in his eyes and it was hard to see.

He heard the bomb go off. Something starred the windshield in front of his face. His wheels banged up across the concrete and the car was slithering on wet snow, the rear wheels shrieking. He spun the wheel to go with the skid and crashed into one of the cars.

He dived across the seat and got out the far door, rolling, bringing the silencer-pistol up. But his eyes were still blinded from the headlights and he couldn't find a target and then three or four of them were shooting him from behind the lights.

5:10 A.M. EST   Four Secret Service cars formed a convoy escort around the limousine and there were pairs of motorcycles fore and aft. Speaker of the House Milton Luke and his wife were surrounded by a flying wedge of security agents from the door of their apartment to the elevator, down to the ground floor, across the lobby, through the doors and across the sidewalk to the waiting limousine. The Lukes settled in the back seat looking aged and half asleep and showing the signs of having dressed hurriedly. Men were emerging from the building with the Lukes' two overnight bags; more clothing would follow later.

The sirens climbed to a shriek and the limousine pulled out into Wisconsin Avenue.

The burst of engine power sent a hot stream of waste gases through the limousine's exhaust pipes and the heat ignited the detonator of the hosepipe bomb. When it exploded it ruptured the gasoline tank and the fuel exploded.

The rear section of the limousine was blown to fragments and the passengers with it. The noise was audible thirty blocks away.

8:40 A.M. EST   In the clamor of the war room Satterthwaite couldn't hear the President's voice. He went out and across into the private conference room and picked up the phone. "Yes Mr. President."

The President's voice was thin against the sound of trucks and helicopters and sirens that penetrated the frosty window. The Army was grinding its way through Washington.

"Bill, I want you to get over here as soon as you can."

"Of course sir."

"We've got a problem here by the name of Wendy Hollander."

"I wish that were the only problem we had."

"No you don't," the President said, and rage trembled in his voice. "I'd settle for every other problem we've got in preference to Wendy Hollander."

"I don't follow that, sir."

"You think about it and you will. Listen, he's over here camping in the Lincoln Sitting Room. I want you to try and get him off my back for a few hours until I've had time to get my head in working order."

"How am I supposed to do that?"

"Hell, I don't care. Put him in command of a battalion of shock troops, he ought to love that."

The President was showing his strain. After a moment Satterthwaite said, "You intend to keep pouring these troops into the city, sir?"

"I do."

"I don't think it's necessary."

"Well then you're wrong," Brewster snapped.

"The FBI nailed them all. There aren't any of them left, we know that."

"We've been told that. We don't necessarily know it. And we've got to make a show of force."

"Yes sir. But we'd better keep a tight lid on them."

"Let's worry more about keeping a tight lid on the crazies, Bill."
And the President hung up.

The net hadn't yet been thrown; the roundup was not underway
but nothing would stop the pressure for it this time. Milton Luke
and Representatives Jethro and Wood and all their wives were
dead.

Satterthwaite listened to the wail of sirens and the clatter of Army
trucks moving through the streets and when he moved to the window he saw an armored limousine moving up Pennsylvania Avenue
surrounded by jeeps in which soldiers were standing up with rifles
and submachine guns leveled at sidewalks and windows; they
looked ready to fire at anyone who moved.

He didn't know who was inside the limousine; it could have been
anyone, those who moved at all moved like colonial administrators
traveling through revolution-torn jungle provinces.

The city was not under siege but it thought it was and perhaps
that amounted to the same thing. The Army was reacting with the
vexation of a laboratory rat presented with a no-exit maze: all am-
munitioned up and no one to shoot.

Anguish blazed in Satterthwaite's eyes. He turned away from the
window but a new siren went by, perhaps no louder than the others,
and he reacted as he would have to a fingernail's scrape across a
blackboard: with an involuntary shudder. He went back into the
hallway and entered the war room, found Clyde Shankland and
made himself heard over the din:

"I've got to go to the White House. Have you got anything more
for me?"

The FBI Director had a telephone at his ear. "Tell him to wait.
Put him on Hold." He put the receiver down and looked at Satterthwaite. In his left hand Shankland held a pencil upright, bouncing
its point on the table as if to drill a hole in the surface. "We've traced
Raoul Riva back to the Cairo Hotel. Of course he wasn't using that
name. But it was him. He only had two visitors—the same two guys
several times during the past few days."

"The two that were with him last night?"

"Yeah. Harrison and the dead guy, Kavanagh."

"Well that's what Harrison said, isn't it."

"I'm not ready to believe the son of a bitch yet."

"But everything confirms it. Doesn't it?" He put it to Shankland as a challenge but Shankland only shrugged. Satterthwaite said angrily, "You're not listening to the rumors are you? Of all people you ought to know better."

"What rumors?"

"About the enormous conspiracy."

Shankland said in his flat prim nasal voice, "Mr. Satterthwaite, we thought we had them all the first time and it turned out we were wrong."

"You still think there's an endless supply of them coming out of the woodwork?"

"I'll only repeat what I said to the Security Council an hour ago. Until we've got dependable airtight information to confirm what Harrison says, I have to go on record as recommending a full-scale crackdown."

That was the way Shankland always talked. He was straight out of the Hoover mold.

Satterthwaite said, "What else have you got for the President?"

"Well they still had three bombs left. Unexploded ones, in the back seat of that Chevrolet."

"Any idea who they were meant for?"

"Harrison says it was flexible. They figured to hit whoever was available—they'd figured out ways to hit eight or nine VIPs on the outskirts of Washington."

"Harrison," Satterthwaite said. "Is he going to pull through?"

"He wouldn't if I had my preferences."

"Goddamn it we need him alive. If he dies we'll never have any way of proving it ends here."

"Who's going to believe him anyway? If he pulls through alive you'll just have to hold off a lynch mob on top of everything else. I'd as soon he kicked off right now."

"The point is he's willing to talk."

"Talk? He's willing to *boast*. He knows he has no chance to squirm out of it; he's a dead man, he just hasn't been executed yet. He seems to think the more cooperative he acts the longer we'll keep him alive, if only to keep pumping him. Or maybe he wants everyone to know how clever they all were. Maybe he's looking for a place in the history books."

"I still want to know what his chances are."

"I guess they'll patch him up. He took a couple of thirty-eights in his guts."

On his way out of the room Satterthwaite felt a rising sense of alarm. If the rumors could get into this room they could go any-where. Hard facts were in short supply, the events were beyond everyday understanding, and nothing terrified men more than am-biguous uncertainties that directly affected their lives.

The rumors were to the effect that there was a giant international movement bent on toppling the American government. It was based in Cuba or Peking or Moscow; it was the brainchild of an evil genius—Castro, Chou En-lai, Kosygin; it was Communist-inspired or Communist-led or both; it was, in short, the opening skirmish of World War Three.

"How long's he intend to keep me waiting like a Goddamn office boy?" Wendell Hollander demanded with biting scorn.

Satterthwaite's nostrils flared. "The President's up to here with troubles, Senator. You can see that."

"His troubles," Hollander snapped, "are gon to last exactly seven-ty-five hours by my timepiece. My troubles might well last the next four years." His eyebrows narrowed shrewdly. "If the country lasts that long, that is." Even when he was using his confidential tone of voice Hollander tended to yell; he was somewhat deaf.

And if you last that long. Hollander for the past decade or more had had the rheumy appearance of a terminal patient. But like most unhealthy men he took extremely good care of himself; it was not impossible he would live to be ninety and if that was the case he still had thirteen dyspeptic years to go.

"With all due respect," Hollander shouted, "I would like to sug-gest you remind that yellow-bellied coward down the hall that I'm waiting here to see him." His face bulged thick with blood and anger.

"Senator, the President will see you as soon as he can."

Hollander's indignation reached its peak. For a moment he stood gathering himself—drawing himself up, pumping air into his caved-in chest. In an effort to be reasonable Satterthwaite said quickly, "These are terrible times for us all."

He had never been any good at personal diplomacy; he wished the President had assigned someone else to this chore. But protocol required it be someone at least of Cabinet rank.

"That son of a bitch," Hollander growled, and abruptly shot his eyes toward the ceiling corners, darting from one to another. "And I hope he's listening to me. You think I don't know these rooms are bugged?"

Why he's senile, Satterthwaite thought in awe. Senile and para-noid and probably the next President of the United States.

Satterthwaite ran his fingers through his wild thick crop of hair. "Senator, I can't force the President to see you right this instant. You know that as well as I do. Now if there's anything you'd like me to do for you. . . ."

"There is. You can tell me just what's being done about this war they've started on us. What's being *done*, boy? Or is it that all you mangy neurotic intellectuals are still just sitting around arguing the fine points?" Hollander's moist pale eyes flicked causally across Sat-terthwaite's face. The gnarled fingers produced a curved and pol-ished pipe. Packed it with care and lifted it to the wizened mouth. It took Hollander three matches to get the pipe lighted to his satis-faction. He was still on his feet, too agitated to sit. On his head the vanishing gray wisps of hair were carefully combed across the pate; he was as old-fashioned in dress and bearing as a badly tended antique.

It had been a bad mistake, Brewster sending Satterthwaite on this chore. It couldn't help but antagonize the old man. Hollander, neither thoughtful nor subtle himself, believed these qualities in others were superficial and untrustworthy. No one thought himself a poor judge of human nature; Hollander, seeing before him an arrogant and myopic little fighter and remembering Satterthwaite from years ago when Satterthwaite hadn't known better than to offend him unforgivably, could only assume Brewster had flung Satterthwaite in his face as a calculated affront.

It was something Satterthwaite supposed the President simply hadn't had time to think of. But he should have thought of it himself and declined to meet Hollander here.

Hollander was building his jaws on the stem of his pipe. "The Army's been sent out, I've seen that much with my own eyes. But I'd like to know what their orders are."

"Their orders are to protect public officials."

"Nobody ever won a war by confining his tactics to defensive operations."

"Senator, if you want to call this a war we're in, then the first rule of strategy is never to let the enemy stampede you into doing what he wants you to do." He leaned forward. "The Communists aren't behind this, Senator. At least no recognized Communist parties. In a way you can look at this whole sequence of disasters as a terrible accident—a catastrophe as arbitrary as a hurricane. It's not——"

"Young man, I've been reasoned with by the most devious men on the face of this earth. You don't hold a candle to some of them, so there's very little point in your trying. All I see when I look at your stripe of animal is cowardice. Cowardice and vacillation. I don't even see tears in your eyes for the wonderful and distinguished Americans who've been sacrificed to your endless cries for appeasement."

"Yes I have tears, Senator, but I don't let them blur my vision."

Suddenly unable to stand any more of this Satterthwaite shot to his feet and made for the door. "I'll find out if the President can see you."

"You do that boy."

The silence was such that he could hear the President's pen scrape across the pad.

Brewster's heavy features had gone pale and begun to sag so that the bones showed through the flesh. He gave a gloomy sigh and dropped the pencil; his hands came together in a prayer clasp. "I don't suppose he's calmed down any."

"All I scored was a few debating points. He's hard of hearing, remember?"

"If that were all it was. . . ." The President reached for a cigar and stood up. He came around the desk and stood rocking heel-to-toe. "He still inveighing about mass reprisals?"

"It amounts to that."

"Put him in this office for forty-eight hours," Brewster murmured, "and he'll have us at war."

"War or martial law."

"Or both. He's a platitudinous medieval fossil." The cigar was jammed into the pugnacious mouth and the President made a sudden gesture with the blade of his hand, like a sharp karate chop. "We can't have it, Bill. That's all there is to it. We just can't have it."

"He's the top man on the line of succession."

"We've got to get Cliff Fairlie back."

"That may be impossible."

"You think there's no chance at all?"

"I think there's a fair chance. But we can't count on it. There's no guarantee. Don't we have to proceed on the assumption we *won't* get him back?"

When the President made no audible reply Satterthwaite shoved his hands in his pockets and spoke with slow care, using his cautious voice, not committing himself: "Mr. President, he's unfit to serve. We know that. We've got to remove him."

"I'd welcome suggestions."

"The Twenty-fifth Amendment. . . ."

"That wouldn't work. He's politically undesirable but that doesn't make him unfit. We'd have to prove it to the satisfaction of the Congress. Three days? We'd never make it. I don't think you could prove he was legally insane. And you can't disqualify a President just because you disagree with his political philosophy."

"He's seventy-seven years old."

"So were De Gaulle and Adenauer when they were in office." The President finally got around to lighting his cigar. "We can't start wasting time with ideas that aren't going to work. Hell, I've been up one side of it and down the other for the past hour."

"Maybe he could be forced to resign."

"*Wendy?* After he's had this whiff of the Presidency?"

"There must be something in his past. Everybody knows he's a crook."

"Well, that's his insulation, isn't it? If everybody already knows, it won't be much of a shock if you give them proof. Besides it would take weeks to put together that kind of evidence and afterward he'd probably make political capital of it—he'd say we were trying to blackmail him. Everybody hates a blackmailer."

"You should have been his campaign manager," Satterthwaite growled.

"I've already covered all this ground in my own head. I just don't see the answer to it—except for one thing. Recover Fairlie."

"We're trying, damn it."

"I know you are." The President was too abrasive to be soothing but that was his intent and Satterthwaite nodded to show he understood. "Well Bill?"

He searched for an answer. Finally he threw up his hands. "There's only one way. You know what it is."

"I do?"

"Kill him."

A long time seemed to go by, during which the President returned to his seat behind the desk and gnashed on his cigar. Finally Satterthwaite broke the ugly silence: "Make it look like one more revolutionary atrocity."

A slow bleak shake of the head. "God knows I'm no Boy Scout. But I couldn't do that."

"Nobody's asking you to do it personally."

"I'll put it another way then. I won't accept it. I won't stand for it. I won't have it." The big head lifted with great weary effort. "Bill, if we did anything like that—what difference would be left between us and them?"

Satterthwaite began to breathe again. "I know. I couldn't do it either. But it's there. It's an answer, you know. And if it's the choice between assassination and the kind of Armageddon he'd bring down on us. . . ."

"I still won't do it."

It came down to ancient basics: did the end justify the means? Satterthwaite turned to the chair and sank into it. Chagrined and elated at the same time by Brewster's righteousness.

Then the President punctured it. "There's a point you're missing."

"Yes?"

"Have a look."

The President pushed the pad across the desk. Satterthwaite had to get up to reach for it.

Brewster's fitful handwriting:

> LINE OF SUCCESSION
> ? *President*
> X *Vice-President*
> X *Speaker of House*
> *President pro tem of Senate*
> *Secretary of State*
> *Sec of Treasury*
> *Sec of Defense*
> *Atty General. . . .*

"You see the point, Bill? Cross out Wendy and who's next? Secretary of State? Hell, John Urquhart's no better qualified for this job than Willie Mays. He's a pencil pusher. You've been doing his job for the past four years. I'd have dumped him a long time ago if you hadn't been here."

Of course that was old-fashioned politics; Urquhart was a fool but he'd helped elect Brewster to the Presidency and he had his job through patronage, just like Treasury's Chaney and several of the others. It was one of the weapons the Republicans had used in the presidential campaign: Fairlie had roasted Brewster for his Cabinet appointments and the people seemed to have heeded him.

A year ago Brewster had toyed with the idea of replacing Urquhart—had tentatively offered the post to Satterthwaite; but then the Republicans had started sniping and Brewster had to vindicate himself so he had not only kept Urquhart in the job, he had vowed loudly his undying support for the Secretary of State. That was the way the game was played.

"I'll tell you, Bill, Wendy might go charging right into a war with his eyes closed tight, but John Urquhart would likely go blundering into one just as fast with his eyes wide open. Fairlie was dead right, damn him. I shouldn't have been such a prideful fool."

"We all shared in that decision. It was a party decision. We couldn't afford to retreat under fire. I still think it was the right decision at the time."

"Let's not waste words on hindsight," the President said. He opened the desk drawer against his belly and lifted out a pamphlet-sized copy of the United States Constitution. "You read this thing lately Bill?"

"Why?"

"I keep thinking there's an answer in here but I'm damned if I can find it." He opened the covers and began to paw through. "Here. Article Twenty, Section Three. '. . . the Congress may by law provide for the case wherein neither a President-elect nor a Vice-President shall have qualified, declaring who shall then act as President, or the manner in which one who is to act shall be selected, and such person shall act accordingly until a President or Vice-President shall have qualified.'"

"That's clear enough, isn't it? Congress was authorized to decide who succeeds to the office. They did so—that's what the Act of Succession is."

"Seems to me you can't read the Constitution the way a brimstone fundamentalist reads the Bible, Bill. It's not a literal document."

"You'd have to take that up with the Supreme Court, Mr. President."

"The Final Resort of Exalted Conjecture," the President muttered. It was one of his time-honored phrases; he used it whenever the Court voted him down.

"I still don't see what you're getting at."

"Well neither do I to tell you the truth. But it just seems to me there's got to be some way to use this Constitution to help us prove the Government wasn't set up for the express purpose of installing the oldest and most senile member of the Senate as President of the United States."

"The Constitution doesn't say anything about that. All it says is the Congress may provide for filling the office when there's a vacancy. The Constitution doesn't spell out *how* they're supposed to do it."

The President gnawed thoughtfully on his cigar and Satterthwaite scowled at him. In the end Brewster began to smile. "That's it, ain't it Bill."

"Sir?"

"You put your finger on it. The Constitution doesn't specify how they're supposed to fill the vacancy."

"Yes but that's immaterial isn't it? I mean they've already complied with the Constitution. They've provided for a line of succession. It's a *fait accompli.*"

"Is it now."

"I guess I'm not following you. But I'm no expert on constitutional law. Maybe you ought to be talking to the Attorney General."

"I'm talking to the right man. Every time I rub brains with you it strikes sparks. That's what you're here for." The President tossed the pamphlet back in the drawer and slid it shut. "The Act of Succession is an Act of Congress, right?"

"It's the law of the land, as they say."

"Uh-huh. You got any idea how many Acts of Congress get passed every year, Bill?"

"Not exactly. A fair number."

"Aeah. And how many get amended every year?"

Satterthwaite shot bolt upright in the chair. The President waved his cigar; suddenly he was looking almost smug. "Now I'm not a hundred per cent positive, mind you, but it's becoming my horseback opinion that this here Act of Succession is not exactly carved into stone tablets. I seem to recall it's been amended four or five times in the years I've been in Washington. Back in Nineteen and sixty-six, and I believe again in Nineteen and seventy. And a couple-three times before that too."

Satterthwaite was still absorbing the impact of it. Brewster reached for the intercom buzzer. "Margaret, see if you can scare me up a copy of the Act of Succession, will you?" He released the button and examined his cigar. "Yes sir, that may be just the ticket out of this hole."

"You're talking about ramming a new Act of Succession through Congress in the next three days?"

"Not a new Act. An amendment to the old one, that's all."

"Designed to take Hollander off the list?"

The President squinted at him. "They'd never stand still for that, Bill."

"Then I still don't see the option."

"What we do, Bill, we ask the Congress to insert one name on that list between the Speaker of the House and the President pro tempore of the Senate."

"What name?"

"The man best qualified to act as interim President until the rightfully qualified President-elect is recovered."

It dawned on Satterthwaite a split instant before Brewster voiced it: "The most recently retired former President of the United States, Bill."

And the President added in a very quiet voice: "Me."

5:20 P.M. North African Time   The CIA chief in Algiers went by the name of Samuel Gilliams. He was one of those Americans who thought the United States owned the mortgage on the whole world and could foreclose any time it pleased. It was the standard CIA philosophy and it was one of the things that had driven Lime out of the intelligence service. Gilliams was almost the archetype; Lime detested him on sight.

Years ago Algeria had broken off diplomatic relations with the United States; Gilliams had a cubicle in the *chargé d'affairs'* office in what was called the American Affairs Section of the Swiss Embassy. Behind his desk Gilliams was self-important and miffed. "We've been on it for five days now. I don't know what-all you expect to accomplish that we haven't already covered."

"We have reason to think they've got Fairlie down here."

"Because this fellow Sturka used to operate in the *bled* ten-fifteen years ago?"

It was so damned tedious. "Mostly because we've identified Benyoussef Ben Krim as one of the cell."

"Yeah I heard that, I heard that. Well we've had a net out after Ben Krim ever since we got your signal from Helsinki. He ain't turned up and he ain't lakly to."

Lime wondered if they had filled Gilliams in on him. Did Gilliams know it had been Lime who had set up the secret negotiations between De Gaulle and Ben Bella back in the ALN days?

Lime said, "Information's highly marketable here. It always has been. If Sturka's here there are people who'll know about it. I need to arrange a meet with Houari Djelil."

He saw by the surprise in Gilliams' face that he had scored a hit. It was evidence enough: nobody had bothered to tell Gilliams Lime was not just another tenderfoot.

"Well——"

"Djelil is still alive isn't he?"

"Yeah sure. But he ain't always inclined to cooperate. You know these Melons, I gather."

Melon was what the *pieds-noirs,* the Algerian-born French, called the Arabs; the only equivalent was *nigger.* Lime only said, "I know Djelil."

"Well I'll see what I can fix up." Gilliams picked up a phone—a direct line, Lime noticed, because Gilliams didn't dial—and spoke into it.

In the inferior regions of the city—the Casbah, named after the sixteenth-century fortress which surrounded the height overlooking the old quarter—Lime stood at the corner of a brasserie and viewed the street's squalid colors and scented the alleys' smell of urine and waited for the signal. He heard the long slow wail of a muezzin calling for evening Islamic prayers.

In the old days Djelil would sooner have been tortured to death than betray Sturka but in those days Sturka had been fighting for the Algerians.

But now there were arguments that might sway Djelil. If nothing else he was a practical man.

The present rulers of Algeria had functioned underground for so many years they had got into the habit and hadn't been able to break it. They still went under their revolutionary aliases and not many people knew their real names. The regime tended to support every self-styled national liberation movement that came along anywhere in the world: the State was socialist but the enemy was "imperialism" whatever its ideology. For these reasons the ruling party was often willing to assist murderous movements anywhere whose objectives claimed to be the overthrow of imperialism.

The only American mission recognized in Algeria was the Black Panthers. The Canadians were represented by the Quebec Liberation Front which had abducted and murdered various Canadian and British officials. FRELIMO, the Mozambique liberation movement, had training camps in the Algerian *bled*, and the desert was being used by training cadres of Al Fatah, the Palestine Liberation Movement. Altogether the ruling NLF accredited fifteen or sixteen liberation movements and granted them varying degrees of assistance in their attempts to overthrow established governments.

The Europeans closed their official eyes to what was going on because everyone wanted a piece of the thirty million metric tons of oil that Algeria produced every year.

Clandestine intrigue was standard procedure in Algeria and the whole structure was supported by the continuing existence of profiteers like Houari Djelil who carried out functions which the government could not fulfill officially. Most arms manufacturers were located in countries which Algeria's friends were trying to overthrow; Algiers could hardly approach them formally and so it was up to men like Djelil to provide the vehicles, ammunition, matériel and Kalashnikov AK-47 automatic rifles with which the NLF equipped the revolutionaries who trained in the Western Desert.

It meant Djelil was a man whose movements were of frequent concern to various bashful agencies. If you wanted to meet with him you had to go to elaborate lengths. And so Lime stood on a street corner in the Casbah and waited to be informed it was proper to move on.

Finally the signal. A rickety old Renault 4CV came clattering through the narrow defile with its sun visors lowered.

He walked through the streets following it: every block or two it stopped and waited for him. Through the winding streets of the *medina*, the old maze of intricately woven alleys and dead ends. Urchins and beggars caromed toward him—"Hey Mister you want hash? You don't like, I get you grass?" Black market money and leather goods and taxis and their sisters: they sold everything, the Arab kids. An old Berber in yellow slippers and a flowing robe accosted him with an arm strapped solid with wristwatches from palm to shoulder: "You want to buy cheap?"

He followed the Renault through a swarm of Arabs listening to a storefront blare of loud twangy music. A woman in gray stared at him from behind her veil, and a block beyond that an Arab passed him in the crowd and spoke distinctly in his ear:

"Ask for Houari in the next bar on your right, Monsieur." In French.

When Lime turned to look the Arab had been absorbed by the throng.

It was a rancid little room, dim and crowded, filled with the smell of the stale sweat of habitual garlic eaters. The bar was tended by a big man in a fez; his neck bulged with folds of fat. Lime pushed to the bar using his elbows and the bartender spoke in Arabic: "Lime *effendi?*"

"Yes. I was told to ask for Houari."

"Through the back door please."

"Thank you." He made his way through the heavy mob and squeezed into a passage no wider than his shoulders; it was open to the sky and gave him the feeling he was at the bottom of a fissure created by some ancient earthquake.

At the end of the passage a car was drawn up in the Rue Khelifa Boukhalfa. A black Citroen, the old four-door model with the square hood. The Arab at the wheel watched Lime come forward and reached across the back of the seat to push the rear door open.

Lime got in and pulled the door shut. The Arab put the car in motion without speaking and Lime settled back to enjoy the ride.

The St. George was the state-owned deluxe hotel high on a hillside with a magnificent overview of the city. The Citroen drew up at a service door and the Arab pointed toward it; Lime got out of the car and went inside.

The corridor was heavy with kitchen smells. He walked toward a small man in a business suit who watched him approach without changing expression and spoke when Lime stopped in front of him: "Mr. Lime?"

"Yes." He saw the bulge under the man's coat; Djelil certainly surrounded himself with protection.

"The stairs to your right please? Go to the second floor, you'll find Room Two Fourteen."

"Thank you."

Djelil's door was opened by a heavy woman with a well-developed moustache who stepped aside and admitted him.

Djelil stood in front of an armchair from which he had just risen. He salaamed Lime and smiled a little. "I thought they had retired you, yes?"

"They should have," Lime said. Djelil made a discreet gesture and the woman withdrew from the room, shutting the hall door after her.

Obviously it was not Djelil's residence. There were no personal possessions. The decor was plastic-Hilton and the window looked out against a hillside.

"*Ça va*, David?"

"Poorly," he said, doing a quick wash with his eyes. If the room was bugged it didn't show; if they had company it would have to be under the bed or in the wardrobe.

"There's no one," Djelil said. "You asked we meet alone, yes?"

Djelil was swarthy and narrow; he looked less like an Arab than a Corsican hoodlum but his face had authority—the strength of a consciousness that had seen many things and not been changed by them. It was his weakness as well as his strength; he had been fundamentally untouched by his lifetime of experiences.

Djelil smiled lazily and lifted a canvas satchel onto the chair. From it he produced bottles. "Cinzano or rum?"

"Cinzano I think." He needed a clear head.

"There should be glasses in the lavatory."

Lime found a pair of heavy chipped tumblers and realized as he collected them that Djelil had sent him after them to reassure him there was no one in the bathroom.

He carried the glasses inside and glanced at the greenish turban that lay on the bed. "I see you've earned the mark of a *Haj* to Mecca."

"Yes, I went six years ago."

Remarkable, Lime thought.

Djelil handed him the drink and he waved his thanks with the glass.

"At any rate it's better than the *pinard* we used to drink, yes?"

Lime sat on the edge of the bed; hotel rooms were not made for conversations. "And how's Sylvie?"

Djelil beamed. "Oh she is very grown up, yes? She is to be married in a month's time. To a government minister's son."

She had been four years old when Lime had last seen her. It was not a thought worth dwelling on. "I'm very glad to hear that."

"It pleases me you remember, David. It's kind."

"She was a lovely child."

"Yes. She is a lovely woman too. Do you know she is acting in the cinema? She has a small part in a film. The French are shooting it here now. Something about the war, the Rommel days." Djelil smiled broadly: "I was able to supply the producers with a great many things. Practically an entire Panzer battalion."

"That must be rather profitable."

"Well ordinarily, yes? But persuading them to use one's daughter as an actress was more important this time. I've allowed them to hire the tanks for a beggar's price. She can't act of course. But she has the beauty for the camera."

Djelil's glistening black hair was combed carefully back over the small ears; he looked prosperous and content. Lime said, "Julius Sturka has our new President out there somewhere. Probably in the *djebel.*" Like Lazarus, he thought, just lying in an open grave waiting for a savior to come.

Djelil's smile coagulated. Lime proceeded with caution. "My government can be generous in times like these."

"Well that is most interesting, yes? But I am not sure I can help." Djelil's face had closed up, with guilt or with innocent curiosity; from his expression it was impossible to guess but from experience Lime knew.

"For information that led to the safe recovery of Clifford Fairlie we could pay out as much as half a million dollars." He spoke in Arabic because he wanted Djelil to reply in Arabic: when a man spoke a language other than his own you couldn't be certain of the subtleties of his meaning—his inflections might be caused by his accent rather than his intent.

"I'm quite sure you can help," he added gently.

"What made you come to me, David?"

"What made you freeze when I mentioned Sturka?"

Impenetrably discreet, Djelil only smiled. In Arabic Lime said, "Your ears have access to many tongues, *effendi*. We both appreciate that."

"It is difficult. I haven't seen Sturka since the days of the ALN, you know."

"But you may have heard a few things?"

"I am not sure."

"Sturka needed a hideout. He needed transportation and supplies. He needed access to the ministries in charge of government patrols out in the *djebel*—to make sure the FLN keeps clear of his hideout."

"Well I suppose that must be true, if as you say they are hiding in the *djebel*. But what makes you think so?"

"We've identified Benyoussef Ben Krim."

"Surely you have more than that?"

Lime only nodded gently; he had given away all he was going to give, it was no good adding that through Mezetti they had traced Sturka's movements as far as the south coast of Spain and had concluded that Sturka must have made the crossing to North Africa.

Djelil stood up and paced to the door, turned, paced to the window, turned. Lime lit a cigarette and looked around for an ashtray. There was no hurrying Djelil; he had to think about the money a while. Then he would start to bargain. Djelil was a past master at horsetrading; he had learned his art as a slave auctioneer.

At the door Djelil turned, stopped, scowled at the wall, tapped his foot a few times and grunted. He walked slowly to the window and stood in front of it looking out. Lime studied his back.

Abruptly Djelil turned to face him. Djelil's features were obscured; the twilit sky silhouetted him. "Do you recall the village of El Djamila?"

"A few kilometers up the coast—that one?"

"Yes."

"They're not holding him there?"

"No, no. Of course not. I have no idea where they might be. But there is a man in El Djamila, a *pied-noir* who was a spy in the French camp for Ben Bella. For various reasons I think he may be able to help you in your search. . . ."

Lime had not heard the movement behind him because Djelil's voice had his attention but when he turned his head slightly he caught a tail-of-the-eye impression imperfectly—the door swinging soundlessly open—and his scalp contracted. With the speed of long-forgotten habit he rolled off the bed and dropped to the floor, hearing the crack of the silencer-pistol and the thud of its bullet into the wall above his head; he dragged the .38 out of the armpit clamshell as he rolled.

His shoulder blade struck the wall. He saw the squat zigzagging shape across the room and fired the .38 three times very rapidly, recognizing the intruder slowly as he fired.

It was the woman with the moustache. She died with a kind of low-comedy surprise on her face and Lime spun toward Djelil as she was collapsing.

Djelil had a curved knife. His arm was swinging up toward Lime.

Lime parried with the revolver. It cracked against Djelil's wrist. Djelil didn't lose the knife but his hand had been numbed and Lime dropped the revolver, snapped a grip on Djelil's arm at wrist and elbow and broke the arm across his knee.

He shoved Djelil back out of the way; Djelil fell against the wall and Lime scooped up his revolver and crossed the distance to the woman with four long strides. She didn't look as if there were any trouble left in her but he stopped to pick up the silencer pistol before he went on to the door, feeling like somebody in a Randolph Scott western with guns in both hands.

There wasn't anyone in the corridor. The hotel had thick walls and any guests who might have heard the racket wouldn't do anything about it; a tourist alerted by sharp noises in strange places would be confused and uncertain, not eager to look for trouble.

If Djelil had more guards in the hotel they must have been beyond earshot. The one downstairs in the corridor wouldn't have heard anything.

He locked the door from the inside and glanced at Djelil. The Arab sat on the floor with his back to the wall, cradling his broken arm.

Lime squatted by the woman and put one of the pistols in his pocket; plucked a bit of fuzz from his tweed jacket and placed it on the woman's nostrils and held her lips shut.

The fluff didn't stir. She was dead.

Djelil started to mouth a litany of sibilant invective. Lime swatted him hard across the side of the head with his open hand. Djelil tipped over with a cry of bursting pain, the agony of broken bones grating when his ruined arm hit the floor under him.

Lime knew the telephone went through the hotel switchboard but he had to risk it. He gave the operator Gilliams' number.

"It's David Lime. I'm at the St. George, Room Two Fourteen. Send a clean-up squad, will you? One DOA and one busted wing, we'll want a medic. But let's not be ostentatious about it."

The use of the American slang might confuse anyone who had an ear to the line. Lime added, "And put out a pick-up order on Houari Djelil's daughter Sylvie. She's acting in a movie the French are shooting somewhere around town."

"You sound rattled. Are you all right?"

"Barely. Make it over here yesterday, will you?" He hung up and collapsed in the chair.

Djelil was struggling to a sitting position, gathering his shattered arm against him. Lime waited for him to get his breath. Anguish distorted Djelil's face but Lime knew he had been listening to all of it.

Finally Lime said, "Now tell me again about that *pied-noir* in El Djamila."

Defiance: "I'm getting to be an old man, David. I haven't that much to lose by remaining silent."

"You've got as much to lose as anybody. The rest of your life."

"Such as it is." Djelil was a realist.

Djelil had been telling the truth about the *pied-noir* in El Djamila because he wouldn't have had any reason to lie; he had thought he was talking to a dead man. The monologue had had the ring of truth; it had been designed to hold Lime's attention while the woman took him out from behind.

Lime tried another tack. "There are thousands of us on this you know. Hundreds of thousands. What difference would killing me have made?"

"Of them all I suppose you were the one most likely to find them."

"How much did Sturka pay you?"

"Don't be an ass."

"I've told them to collect Sylvie."

"I heard that."

"I just wanted to make sure you had."

"Your people won't harm her. I know you."

"Think about the stakes and then convince yourself of that again."

Djelil's face twisted with agony and then relaxed as the spasm passed. Lime reloaded the spent chambers of his revolver, thrust it into the clamshell and then had a look at the silencer pistol. It was a 7.62mm Luger. He removed the magazine and popped the cartridge out of the breech, put the ammunition in his pocket and the pistol on the bed. "Who was she, your mother?"

Djelil grunted: *That's not funny.* Lime looked again at the dead features. The face had gone gray, ruddy at the underside from postmortem lividity. She must have been about fifty. European, or of European stock; possibly one of the *pieds-noirs*.

"All right, you've had time to think about it. Now give me a name."

Djelil lifted his shoulders and poked his head forward with the Arab gesture known as *ma'alesh*—the nothing-can-be-done shrug. What controlled Djelil now was the kind of hyper-awareness of masculinity the Arabs called *rujuliyah:* a mystical thing that steeled your courage. It was always a hard defense to break.

Lime said, "You realize we're very short for time. We won't play with you. We'll let you watch us work on Sylvie and we're going to be Goddamned hard on her."

Djelil sat on the floor with his pains. It was getting through to him; he was thinking about it and that meant Lime had won. In the end Djelil summoned the bravado to smile. "Well then how do you say it, one has to live."

"No." Lime's reply was soft. "You don't have to live, Houari."

It was damp in El Djamila.

They made the trip in two cars. Chad Hill drove Lime in a Simca and there followed an old station wagon—the kind made of real wood—containing a six-man team. In the back of the station wagon was a UHF scrambler transmitter. Its range was limited but all communications were being funneled through the U. S. Naval Station at Kénitra in Morocco.

Last night's sleep on the jet hadn't revived Lime. He felt logy and glazed. Gilliams' anger still buzzed in his ears; Gilliams had been very upset by the killing and the roust of Djelil and Sylvie and the two guards Djelil had downstairs in the hotel. Gilliams was one of those bureaucrats who pictured a fine balance in things and couldn't stand having it upset.

They had to move fast because Djelil's disappearance would be noticed soon. The thing was to find his contacts before they could go to ground.

"Turn right and go slow on the coast road. I think I'll recognize the place."

El Djamila was a beach resort where visitors enjoyed uncrowded cheap rates and the natives lived briefly and wretchedly. The moon was up, glinting off the Mediterranean whitecaps.

Djelil had given him a name: Henri Binaud. A *pied-noir* who had betrayed his own kind to spy for the FLN; now he ran a charter outfit—three boats and an amphibious plane—and was one of Djelil's chief carriers.

Lime was a bit weak with delayed shock from the episode of the woman with the Luger. He suspected that Sturka had got a message to Djelil saying if any investigators got as far along the trail as Djelil it would be appreciated if Djelil got rid of them; appreciated in terms of substantial money. Lime wondered if Sturka knew the identity of his tracker. Not that it really mattered.

Nearly nine o'clock. Three in the afternoon in Washington. They had about sixty-nine hours.

A bar. Cinzano signs, an old rusty car up on blocks, its tires gone. Sandy vacant lots on either side of the square little stucco building. The charter pier across the road from it: several boats tied up, a twin-engine amphibious plane tied to a buoy and bobbing on the swell.

The bar was empty except for two men who sat at a table that was hardly big enough for their dinner plates and glasses and elbows. They were eating *rouget,* the local fish. Both of them looked up but kept eating. Chad Hill hung back and Lime spoke in French: "Monsieur Binaud? We understand the Catalina is for hire?"

One of them wiped the back of a hand across his mouth and reached for the wine to wash down his mouthful. "I am Binaud. Who sent you to me?"

"Houari Djelil."

Binaud studied him suspiciously. He was bullnecked and florid. Cropped gray hair, a hard little potbelly. "And you wish to hire my aircraft."

"Perhaps we could discuss it outside," Lime suggested smoothly.

It was the kind of thing Binaud understood. He muttered something to his companion and stood up and made a gesture. Lime and Chad Hill turned, went outside and waited for Binaud; he came out right behind them and Lime showed his gun.

Binaud grunted; his eyelids slid down to a half-shuttered secretiveness and he flashed his teeth in an accidental smile. "What's this then?"

"Come along."

They shepherded Binaud around to the side of the building. The others were standing by the station wagon. Three of them pulled revolvers and they put Binaud in frisk position with his hands on top of the car while they went over him with care.

The search produced a pocket revolver and two knives. After they had disarmed him Lime said, "It's a little public here. Let's take him on board one of the boats."

They walked him out onto the pier and prodded him down the ladder into the forward compartment of a cabin cruiser. The boat rode gently up and down against the old tires that hung on the pier as fenders. One of the men lit the lantern.

Lime said to Binaud, "Sit down."

Binaud backed up slowly until the backs of his knees struck the edge of a bunk. Sat and watched them all, his eyes flicking from face to face.

"We're looking for Sturka," Lime said.

"I don't know that name." Binaud had a high wheezing husky voice. Gravelly; it made Lime think of "Rochester" Anderson's voice.

"They came to you a few days ago—it was probably Wednesday night. They'd have wanted you to take them somewhere, by boat or by plane."

"A great many people hire my boats and my plane. It's my business."

"These had a prisoner."

Binaud shrugged and Lime turned to Chad Hill. "He thinks anything we could do to make him talk would be nothing compared to what Sturka and Djelil would do to him if he did talk."

"Offer him money," Chad said in English.

Binaud understood that; his eyes became crafty.

Lime said in French, "Two hundred thousand dinar, Binaud. The price of a good airplane."

He had the man's attention at any rate. He added, "You've nothing to fear from Djelil—he's the one who sent us to you. As for Sturka he can't come out of this alive. You know who his prisoner is."

"No. I do not."

"You mean they kept his face hidden."

Binaud said nothing. Lime sat down on the bunk facing him. They were crowded into the small cabin; Binaud showed his distress. Lime said, "Two hundred and fifty thousand dinar. Call it twenty-five thousand pounds. In gold sovereigns."

"I do not see any money in front of me."

Lime spoke in English without looking up. "Get it."

One of the men left, going up the ladder; the boat swayed when the man stepped onto the pier. Lime said, "We have it with us. There wouldn't have been time to do it another way. You can understand that."

"Can I?"

"The prisoner is Clifford Fairlie. If you didn't know that already."

No indication of surprise. Binaud sat silent until the agent returned. The leather case was very heavy. They opened it on the deck and two of the agents started counting out the big gold coins, making neat stacks.

Lime said, "Now what about Sturka?"

"I know no one by that name."

"Call him any name you like then. Don't you want the money, Binaud?" Lime leaned forward and tapped the man's knee. "You realize the alternative. We'll squeeze it all out of you. When it's finished there won't be much left of you."

"That's what I don't understand," Binaud told him, and met his eyes. "Why don't you do that anyway? It would save you the money."

"We haven't time. We'll do it if you force it, but we'd rather do it fast."

"How do I know you won't kill me and take the money back?"

"You don't," Lime said, "but what have you got to lose?"

The coins were counted out to the sum of twenty-five thousand pounds and the rest went back into the case. Binaud watched every movement until the case was shut; finally he said, "My information probably is not worth that much money you know."

"If it helps at all, the money is yours."

"And if it doesn't?"

"We'll see."

"I didn't know their names. I didn't know the man was who you say he was. The prisoner."

"Where did you take them?"

"I didn't. They had their own pilot."

Lime felt a sour taste. "Describe him."

"A Negro. Large, heavy, always chewing on something."

"When was this arranged?"

"Ten days ago perhaps."

"Who arranged it with you? Djelil?"

"No. It was a man named Ben Krim."

"Benyoussef Ben Krim," Lime breathed. "Again. What story did he give you?"

"None, Monsieur. He reserved my airplane for the night of the twelfth. It was to be filled with fuel. He said he would provide his own pilot. I only had to row them out to the plane."

"Was Ben Krim with them when they came?"

"No."

"How many were there?"

"Four," Binaud said, and frowned. "No, five. The prisoner and four others. One was a woman, one was the Negro. The other two were dressed in burnouses, I did not see their faces."

"What condition was the prisoner in?"

"He appeared unharmed. I recall his face was masked."

"Masked?"

"You know. White tape and plasters." Binaud made gestures across his eyes and mouth.

"Did they explain him?"

"Not really. They said something about the OAS. I thought perhaps he was an OAS they had captured. The Berbers still hold grudges you know."

It was very glib and it was probably a lie. But it really didn't matter. Lime said, "Now I see you have recovered the airplane. How?"

"I had to go down to a wadi to pick it up. Beyond the mountains."

"Where?"

"Have you a map?"

Chad Hill provided one from his pocket and they unfolded it on the bunk beside Binaud. Binaud inserted his lower lip between his teeth and leaned over the map. Presently his index finger stabbed a point. "Here."

It was south-southeast of Algiers perhaps four hundred miles. Beyond the Atlas Mountains and the Tell—out in the arid plateaus of the *bled,* on the fringe of the Sahara. Binaud explained, "A friend drove me down."

"Now think carefully. How much fuel had been used?"

"The Catalina? I do not recall."

"The tanks weren't full though."

Binaud was thinking hard. "No. There was enough to get me back here—more than enough. If there had been any question I'd have worried and I'd remember that. There's no petrol at that wadi."

"A landing strip?"

"No. Just the plain. No trouble landing and taking off on it, though."

"You came straight back here from the wadi?"

"Yes of course."

"And then I imagine you filled the tanks when you got here."

"Yes I did."

"How much fuel did she accept?"

"Ah. I see—yes." Binaud put his mind on it. "One hundred and forty liters, I believe it was. Yes, I'm quite sure of it." It was the kind of thing a man like Binaud would remember. He added, "And the distance from the wadi to here was perhaps five hundred and fifty kilometers. But then one has to clear the Atlas Mountains and that takes added fuel. I should say it required forty or fifty liters, the flight home."

"Then they put enough miles on her to consume a hundred liters or so," Lime said. "They had to cross the mountains the same as you. So we'll figure the same rate of consumption." He was talking mainly to himself.

"They probably covered about five hundred miles altogether. Approximately eight hundred kilometers."

Some of that mileage would be the distance between Sturka's lair and the wadi of course. But how much? Ten miles or two hundred?

More likely it was a fair distance. It left a depressing amount of earth to cover. Draw a half circle around El Djamila with a radius of four hundred and fifty miles or so. . . . Even if you narrowed it to a wedge with the wadi at the center of its base you had forty or fifty thousand square miles.

It wasn't quite a dead end but it was tough. Lime stood up and took Hill aside. "We'll have to get people into all the villages out there. Find out if they heard that plane go over Wednesday night. Try and find out where it landed."

"That'll take a lot of time."

"I know it. But what else is there?"

"I'll get on it," Hill said, and went up the ladder.

Lime went back to Binaud. There was one more avenue to explore. "You say Ben Krim was not with them Wednesday night."

"No."

"Have you seen him since then?"

"No. . . ." Binaud seemed to hesitate. He hadn't lied but he had just thought of something.

Lime waited. Binaud said nothing. Lime sat down opposite him. "What is it?"

"*Rien.*"

"It's Ben Krim isn't it. Something about Ben Krim."

"*Alors. . . .*"

"Yes?" Suddenly Lime had it. "You're expecting him to come here, aren't you."

Binaud's eyes wandered away. Drifted down toward the stacked sovereigns. In the end the fatalistic shrug. "Yes."

"He's coming here?"

"Yes."

"When? Tonight?"

"No, not tonight. He said it was not certain. I was to expect him Tuesday—that's tomorrow—or Tuesday night."

"Exactly where does he ordinarily meet you?"

"On the pier here."

"Not in the bar."

"No. He likes privacy, Benyoussef."

Lime nodded. "I'm afraid we'll have to intrude on it."

10:15 P.M. North African Time Peggy lit a cigarette and gagged on the smoke. These foreign brands must be made out of cow shit. She remembered the head nurse's furious lectures on the suicidal toxicity of cigarette smoke and the thought made her crush the Gauloise out unsmoked. Then it occurred to her how ridiculous that was and she emitted a little laugh like a hiccup.

Sturka glanced at her coolly from the far side of the room and Cesar said, "What's funny?"

"I had a training nurse who used to lecture us on the evils of smoking. I was thinking about it and I got so upset I put my cigarette out."

"That's funny?"

"Look we're all likely to get killed in a matter of days and here I'm worrying about getting cancer when I'm forty-two. You don't think that's funny?"

Cesar picked his way across the rubble-strewn floor and squatted in front of her. The weak illumination of the kerosene lamps made him look jaundiced. There was a generator that provided power to the underground cells but the upper part of the building had been smashed thirty years ago by Italian bombs and nobody had bothered to repair the damage. Evidently some of Sturka's old comrades in the Algerian liberation movement had fixed up the underground part with electricity and spartan accommodations but they'd never touched the aboveground wreckage. Probably because that would have given them away to the French.

Cesar said, "Nobody's going to get killed, Peggy. Everything's worked fine so far. Why are you so down?"

"They got Riva's guys in Washington, didn't they?" They had shortwave and they had been listening to all the news.

"They did their job before they died. That's what matters in the people's struggle, Peggy. Your life don' count—it's that you got to accomplish something before you die. Listen if we all died right now this minute we'd of accomplished something."

"I guess."

"You don' sound very convinced. Look this is a hell of a time to get cold feet Peggy."

"I haven't got cold feet. Did anybody say I wanted to back out of this? All I said was I thought it was funny about the cigarettes." Cesar had her angry now and she picked up the mashed cigarette and smoothed it out and lit it again.

Sturka broke loose of his thoughtful stance and came striding across to them. "Has the drug had time to work on him?"

"What time is it?" she asked.

"Twenty past. You gave him the shot half an hour ago."

"It should've had time to work."

"Then let's go down." Sturka beckoned to Alvin.

Peggy reached for the veil and the Arab robes and by the time she was costumed she saw Cesar and Sturka had engulfed themselves in their rough burnouses. Alvin had put a stick of gum in his mouth and they went down the dim broken stone stairs into the dungeons.

She put her thumb on the vein in Fairlie's wrist. He gave her an incurious look; he didn't even lift his head. His eyes weren't tracking very well. She said over her shoulder, "Maybe we made the dose a little too big."

"We gave him a smaller one last time and it didn't work," Cesar said.

She tapped Fairlie's cheek. "Can you hear us? Say something."

"I hear you." His voice had a mausoleum tone, like a phonograph record being played at too slow a speed.

"Sit up. Come on, I'll help you." She got her arm under his shoulders and he obeyed, levering himself upright with sluggish concentration. She pushed at his chest and he slumped back against the wall, sitting on the cot sideways with his knees straight, looking like a small boy. His face was bloodless and his eyes were pouched and unrevealing.

She glanced at the others. Alvin stood guard in the doorway and Sturka was preparing the tape recorder; Cesar sat on the cot beside Fairlie and said in a reasonable tone, "Talk for a while, mister pig. Talk to us. Tell us about all the good people you've persecuted. Tell us about the fascist system back home."

The hollow eyes settled painfully on Cesar.

Sturka was clicking controls on the tape recorder. Cesar said, "Can you read, pig?"

". . . Of course I can read."

"I mean aloud. Read to us, pig." Cesar held up the speech they had written for Fairlie.

Fairlie's eyes tried to focus on it but his head went back against the wall and his mouth slacked open. "Tired," he muttered. "Can't see very well."

Too much, Peggy thought. They'd dosed him too much. She turned in anger toward Sturka. "He's out of it, can't you see that?"

"Then bring him around. Give him a shot of adrenaline or something."

"I haven't got any. What do you think I've got in that little kit, a whole drugstore?"

Sturka's head lifted a little. She couldn't see his face under the hood but she knew those awful eyes were burning into her. "Lady, your concern for the pig isn't touching, it's out of place. You're forgetting who he is—what he is."

She blanched. "He's no use to us like this. That's all I'm saying. I let you talk me into it but you can see he can't handle the dose. We'll just have to wait for it to wear off."

"How long will that be?"

"I don't know. It has a cumulative effect—he's got an awful lot of it in his system. It may take three or four days for the whole thing to wear off. Maybe by morning he'll be able to talk for you."

She knew the trouble; it would cut things awfully fine. *But it's your own stupid fault. You just had to shoot the poor bastard full of stuff because he had the guts to stand up to you.*

Cesar said, "Maybe he's acting. Maybe he's a lot wider awake than he looks." He slapped Fairlie's cheek and the handsome face rolled limply to the side; Fairlie blinked slowly and painfully.

"He's not acting," Peggy said. "Christ he's had enough junk poured into him to knock an elephant on his ass. *Acting?* He hasn't got any inhibitions left to play games with. Look at him, will you?"

There were flecks of white saliva in the corners of Fairlie's slack mouth.

Sturka switched off the recorder and picked it up. "All right. Morning."

They left Fairlie on the cot and went outside and closed the cell door. Peggy said, "I'll try to get him to eat something later. A lot of coffee might help."

"Just don't bring him too wide-awake. We can't have him resisting this time."

"A few more cc's of that junk and he'd be dead. He wouldn't resist at all then. Is that what you want?"

"Talk to her," Sturka said mildly to Cesar, and went ahead of them up the stairs.

"You're getting to sound like a deviationist," Cesar said. Alvin squeezed past them to go up the stairs; a blank look at Peggy and he was gone.

She slumped against the wall and listened with half her attention to Cesar's voice. She made the proper responses mechanically and it seemed to satisfy Cesar. But under it all she knew they were right about her. She was sliding. She was worried about Fairlie—she was a nurse and Fairlie was her patient.

Fairlie had been extraordinarily gentle with her. It didn't make her trust him. But it made him very hard to hate.

4:45 P.M. EST   The Secret Service men were numerous: silently present, indifferent but not inconspicuous. They watched Andrew Bee enter the President's office.

Brewster's face had a gray haggard look. "Thanks for coming over, Andy." It was meaningless courtesy: you didn't ignore a presidential summons. Bee nodded and muttered a "Mr. President" and took the indicated chair.

Brewster's head tipped sideways toward the side door. "Winston Dierks just left. We've been having a string of conferences here all afternoon. I reckon it'll go on half the night, so you'll have to forgive me if what I say to you comes out sounding like a set-piece speech." The big lined face poked forward; Brewster's lips pulled back slowly in a smile. "I guess I could have asked for a joint session and talked to everybody at once, but it just ain't the kind of thing you can do that way."

Bee waited patiently. His grief-stung eyes lay against the President's face; he felt at once reproachful and sympathetic.

The President glanced at the television set in the corner. Bee didn't remember having seen a television set in this office since the departure of Lyndon Johnson; it must have been brought in today. The sound was off and the picture was a still shot of a bathroom product. Brewster said, "The seven prisoners will be landing in Geneva in the next hour or so. I thought I'd watch."

"It hurts you to have to do that, doesn't it Mr. President?"

"If it'll get Cliff Fairlie back I'm all for it." The President halved his smile. "It's what happens if we *don't* get him back that I'd like to talk to you about, Andy."

Bee nodded without surprise and the President said, "I suppose you've been giving it some thought too."

"Everybody has. I doubt there's another subject of conversation anywhere in the country today."

"I'd like your views."

"Well they're probably not the same as yours, Mr. President." Bee grinned a bit. "They rarely are."

"I do value your advice, Andy. And I reckon the differences between you and me get to looking pretty small when you compare them with some others."

"Like Senator Hollander?"

"Like Senator Hollander."

The President looked unhappy as a soaked cat, Bee thought.

Brewster was waiting for him to speak. With an effort Bee summoned his thoughts. "Mr. President, I don't have a great deal to offer right now. I do think we're between a rock and a hard place. If you think of yourself as any kind of liberal at all, you just don't have any place left to stand. I've watched the troops move in all day. I gather every city in the country's the same way—like a state of siege. I understand they're arresting anybody who looks cross-eyed."

"That's kind of an exaggeration."

"It may not fit the facts but it suits the mood of things. I think people in this country feel as if they're in occupied territory. A lot of people are being arrested, or at least watched to the point where they've got no privacy left."

"And you'd like to defend their rights?"

"There was a time when I would have. I'm not so sure now. I think to defend their rights would be to hasten their destruction, the way the country's temper is right now. Frankly I think most of the radicals are showing admirable restraint."

"Sensible, maybe. They know they'd get massacred if they tried to resist."

"That's just it. It seems to me when we deny them their rights we're hastening another kind of destruction. The destruction of everybody's liberties."

"There haven't been any mass arrests, Andy, whatever you may have heard."

"There've been enough arrests to cause a great deal of alarm."

"Fifteen or twenty known radical leaders, that's about the size of it. I might point out there've been enough bombings and kidnappings to cause a great deal of alarm too."

"I can hardly dispute that, can I." Absently Bee massaged the right knee that had been shattered four years ago and mended with steel and bone grafts. It still gave him arthritic stabs of pain. "Mr. President, I'd like to say I think your administration has showed admirable restraint too. I know what it must be like for you, with Hollander and that bunch keeping the pressure up all the time for lunatic reprisals."

"Well thank you Andy. I reckon that brings us around to the speech I've got to make to you. About Wendy Hollander. I'm sure you must have been giving that some thought too?"

Bee shook his head, not in denial but in morose agreement.

The President lit a cigar; the pale eyes peered at Bee. "I've talked to a dozen, fifteen leaders from both houses this afternoon. I've sworn every one of them to secrecy and they've agreed. Can I ask the same promise of you, Andy?"

"I think that has to depend on what secret I'm supposed to keep."

"Have you heard any rumors? No matter how wild they may have seemed."

"I've heard nothing but rumors, Mr. President. That the bombings are a Russian plot, that the White House is gearing up for war, that the Army's only pretending to move into the cities to protect public officials—the rumor says the real purpose is to get the troops in position to strike simultaneously all across the country, grab every known or suspected radical and herd them all into concentration camps. I've heard rumors about Clifford Fairlie and rumors about the Japanese and rumors about——"

"Not that." The President cut him off smoothly. "Have you met up with any rumors about a stop-Hollander campaign?"

"I've heard a lot of wishful thinking along those lines."

"It was actually suggested to me in this office that we ought to have him assassinated and blame it on the radicals," Brewster said. "What do you think of that?"

"I'd rather not think of that, Mr. President."

"Andy, I don't need to tell you the kind of hell this country's going to be plunged into if Wendy Hollander occupies this seat Thursday."

"No. I can picture it vividly enough for myself."

"There's a way to prevent that happening," the President said, and squinted through the smoke of his cigar to see how Bee would take it. "I mean ruling out assassination of course."

Bee's jaw rode from side to side with his speculative frown. "Declare him incompetent, you mean? I'd thought of that—I suppose a lot of us have."

"I doubt we could make that work."

"So do I. But you say you've discovered a way?"

"I need your assurance it stays inside this room until I take the wraps off, Andy. God knows it's a genuine matter of national security—if anything ever had to be kept top secret this does. May I have your absolute promise?"

"Mr. President, if it's a scheme that you're sure will work, why does it need to be kept secret?"

"Because if Hollander gets wind of it too soon he might find ways to head it off. If we can spring it on him by surprise it'll have a better chance of working."

"But I gather it requires the cooperation of the Congress."

"Yes. I'll give you a list of names of the men I've already spoken to. They'll be the only ones you'll be allowed to discuss it with. Tomorrow morning I'm going to call a private caucus of leaders from both houses and we'll discuss it in a general meeting then, but in the meantime I wanted to talk to each of you personally."

"On that basis I don't see any reason why I shouldn't go along, Mr. President."

"I have your word on it then?"

"You have my word on it." A bit of a smile: "For whatever a politician's word is worth."

"Yours has always been worth quite a bit, Andy. You've fought me pretty damn hard on a lot of things and you've done as much backroom logrolling as I have, but I've never known you to back out on a commitment."

There was a kind of do-or-die melodrama to the President's manner; for all his deserved reputation as a wheeler-dealer he was curiously old-fashioned in his beliefs. His concepts of honor and gallantry were those of the Victorians. Brewster was a gentleman and that was odd in a world that regarded those values as pointless and often suspect.

The President leaned back in the big chair. "Here it is, then. I don't need to give you my ten-minute number on why we don't want Wendy Hollander coming up the White House doorstep Thursday afternoon with all his suitcases. We're agreed on that, aren't we?"

"Completely."

"Now I might mention also that there's no time left to brief a new man on the complexities of running this here office. I had my hands full trying to fill Dexter Ethridge in. Dex is gone now and we're stuck with Wendy Hollander. Andy, you've been on the Hill a few years, do you remember the debate over the Succession Bill back in Nineteen and Sixty-six?"

"Vaguely."

"There was talk about how maybe we ought to specify that if there was a national emergency that wiped out the whole line of succession—say a full-scale military attack that destroyed Warshington completely—that we ought to make some provision for the military to take over the Government on a temporary basis in order to meet the emergency. You remember that?"

"Yes. The proposal was turned down because nobody was willing to pass any law that could authorize the generals to take over."

"Yes exactly. Congress was scared to put that in writing no matter how it was worded. Rightly so, too, I believe. The argument that tabled it was that if we ever had an emergency of that magnitude the generals would just naturally step in and take over without needing any paper authorization. That satisfied everybody and the idea was dropped.

"But the thinking behind it did make a kind of sense, Andy. Any time you lose both your President and your Vice-President you've got a kind of emergency, because the rest of the people on the line of succession aren't really qualified for the office in the sense of being briefed on all the administration's inside operations and foreign negotiations and whatnot. Let me put it to you this way. Suppose a vacancy occurs in the office, and the office is filled by somebody like Wendy Hollander—forget his politics for a minute—and suppose five hours later, say, Egypt decides to take advantage of the confusion by jumping all over Israel. Now Hollander not only doesn't know what kind of secret meetings may have been going on between us and the Middle East, he doesn't even know how to operate the machinery of diplomacy and military countermoves. You see what I'm getting at?"

"Yes sir. But that would apply to anybody in the line of succession."

"Except for somebody who's held the office of the Presidency before," Brewster said. "Somebody who already knows all the means and methods."

Bee listened, intent and rapt.

"The most recently retired former President—that's the way I've been putting it. Of course it refers to me since I retire at noon Thursday. It wouldn't conflict with the Constitutional two-term limit on the Presidency, since I've only served one term in office. I have to grant it's a special-interest proposal caused specifically by the threat Wendy Hollander presents, but I maintain it makes a good deal of generic sense too—it could apply as a general rule, although I'm not ruling out the likelihood Congress will want to change it back after we've shunted Wendy aside."

The room was sealed against the winter cold and the smell of Brewster's cigars was heavy. The President had the balls of a brass gorilla, Andrew Bee thought, but he continued to listen, uncommitted.

"I'm asking Congress to amend the Act of Succession in a way that'll allow me to continue as interim President until Cliff Fairlie is recovered. The alternative, I have to keep repeating, is Wendell Hollander—and to the bottom of my soul I don't believe the country can survive that."

"Do you honestly think you can persuade Congress to go for this, Mr. President?"

"I've talked to leaders on both sides of both aisles and the majority appears to be with me. I remind you virtually every Congressman and every Senator stands at least slightly to Wendy's left. And most of them stand *far* to his left."

"I'd be interested to know who refused to go along with you—and what reasons they gave."

"I'll give you their names. All of them, the ones who agreed and the ones who didn't. Before you leave the office this afternoon. But I've got too much to do spending an hour with you running down the roll call. You can understand that, Andy."

Suspicion nibbled at a corner of his mind—that the President would make the same statement whether or not it was true. Like a cop telling a suspect his partner had confessed. It was one of the things he wouldn't put past Howard Brewster.

"Mr. President, suppose Congress supports you. Suppose you don't get shot down by the Supreme Court, suppose everybody goes along with it—everybody except Wendy Hollander and the other yahoos, naturally. Then what happens? What do you propose to do?"

"Conduct this office as I've been conducting it for the past four years."

"That's not what I mean and I think you know it, Mr. President."

"You mean what do I intend to do about these radicals. The polarization in the country."

"Yes."

"I don't have a quick answer for you, Andy. It's something we're all going to have to get together and thrash out. I can guarantee you one thing—I won't do what Hollander would do."

"Just what do you think he *would* do, when it came right down to it?"

"You're suggesting maybe the weight of responsibility would gentle him down, are you?"

"I don't know. It's happened."

"Andy, if you could put that in writing with Wendy's signature under it I might buy it. Otherwise how can we take the chance?"

The cigar had grown two inches of ash. The President tipped it off carefully into the ashtray, using his little fingernail. "Don't let me down, Andy. You're crucial."

"I'm only a Congressman, Mr. President."

"You're probably the most widely respected Representative in the House. I want you to be the Republican floor leader in this fight. I want you to steer our supporters, get the best speakers to fight down the opposition, keep track of the votes."

"You intend to make an open floor fight of it?"

"Once it comes out in the open we've got to. I may be a rigid old mossyhorn but I do recognize it when times change. The House don't tolerate the kind of backroom juggling there used to be. Things have got to be out in the open nowadays—I've heard a lot of them talking about letting it all hang out. Well, when it comes to that kind of fighting you're the best scrapper I know, Andy. Will you do this?"

Bee looked at his watch. Just past five-thirty. Clearly the circumstances, if not the President, demanded an immediate decision: it wasn't possible to go away and think about it.

"It's very bad odds, Mr. President. We've only got two days. If Hollander starts a filibuster it's dead."

"I need you to corral enough votes for a cloture. I think we've got to assume he'll filibuster."

"You really believe we can get two-thirds behind this in two days?"

"I believe we've got to."

"And you're not taking the wraps off until tomorrow morning."

"At nine we'll caucus in the Executive Office Building. I'd like you to get up and make a little speech supporting me. The meeting will be attended only by those who've agreed to support me, so you won't be debated, but I want everybody in that room to recognize everybody else—I want them to see how broad the support really is. It's the best way to convince them it can work. I'm hoping you can get it onto the floor by the middle of the afternoon. There'll have to be an extraordinary session—it'll have to run right through tomorrow night. Hopefully we can bring it to a vote by then, or by early Wednesday morning at the latest. By that time you should have been able to get together with Philip Krayle and Winston Dierks and drawn up companion bills for both houses so we don't have to waste time in House-Senate conferences afterwards.

"As soon as you've got things moving I'll have Perry Hearn call a background press conference for an off-the-record briefing. But we'll want the announcement held up until Congress has voted—otherwise it'll give the right-wing *hoi polloi* time to break out their Goddamned arsenals, and we don't want that. It's going to hit the people like cold water but it can't be helped. I think if we take the press into our confidence a few hours in advance it'll soften the blow."

Bee sat weak; he felt debilitated. "Mr. President, I've got no choice but to agree with you in principle. But what happens if we try this and it fails? The cost could be a divided country—far more divided than it is now."

"What difference is there between that and what'll happen if we don't try? A Pyrrhic victory for last-ditch defenders of the Constitution?"

"But we're going to have to fight the most powerful vested interest of all—inertia."

"I'm glad you said 'we,' Andy."

"And what about the Supreme Court? Suppose they strike it down?"

"On what grounds? Congress has every right to amend its own laws."

"But the Constitution goes to considerable lengths to put rigid limits on the term of office of a President. Essentially you're asking the Congress to allow you to perpetuate yourself in office beyond your elected term. The Court would have to look at it that way."

"I don't think so. I'm only asking to be held over as interim executive until the elected President shows up to qualify. The judges on the Court understand reality when they see it."

"There's another reality, Mr. President. Suppose we never get Cliff back. Suppose he's killed."

"Then I expect I'd have another four years in office, Andy. I think that's clear to everybody I've talked to. Naturally you've got to weigh that. But it's still a choice between that and Hollander. Everything comes right back down to that."

The President sat forward and put both elbows on the desk. "I wouldn't worry about the Court if I were you. I've already consulted with the Chief Justice. I know that's considered bad form but I had to cover that flank. The legal position the Court will probably take is simple enough. Congress has the power to provide for a vacancy in the Presidency by any method it chooses, so long as the candidate qualifies according to Constitutional basics—age, place of birth, that kind of thing. If Congress wanted to it could appoint the third assistant postmaster of Bend, Oregon to head up the line of succession. I can see how there might be a constitutional argument if I'd completed two terms in office, but I haven't. And I'm not proposing that my present term of office be extended. The new law won't take effect until one minute past noon on the twentieth day of January, and at that time I'll have retired. It'll be a new administration. I'll simply be walking out the back door and back in through the front door, but it satisfies the legal requirements."

"Will it satisfy the people's requirements, Mr. President? Will the people accept it?"

"I hope they will if it's explained to them by men like you, Andy."

A beat of silence, and Bee dragged himself out of his fatigue. "I'd like to be very blunt for a minute."

"Please do."

"If the law can be changed to allow anybody to become the next President, why does it have to be you?"

"Because I expect I'm the only one who can rally enough support. Do you think if you went to the Congress and asked them to elect *you* to the Presidency they'd do it in forty-eight hours?"

"No," Bee admitted. "I'm sure they wouldn't. It would be far too raw. But it's pretty raw to do it your way too."

"But my way is the only way that has a chance of succeeding. I'm the only man alive who's got the power to lead this fight—to swing the support of both parties in both houses. And the only one who knows what's going on in the Executive branch. Now I'm being just as blunt with you. It's a question of practicalities, Andy. You can't afford to give consideration to my ambitions or your misgivings. The only thing you can do is decide whether you'd rather have me or Wendy Hollander sitting in this chair come Thursday afternoon."

11:40 P.M. North African Time Lime went through to the after cabin. Chad Hill sat by a portable radio. Binaud was somewhere up on the dock or in the bar across the road, being watched from the shadows by three agents; Binaud understood that if Ben Krim tipped to anything Binaud's head would roll. The gold sovereigns were the carrot on Binaud's stick; he probably would go along with it. If he didn't Lime would lose another round. All he could do was hope.

Chad Hill was listening to an announcer describe the arrival of the Washington Seven at Geneva Airport. Lime pictured a scene crawling with armed police and agents—like the arrival of the war-crimes prisoners at Nuremberg before the trials. The Seven had breached United States security to blow up hundreds of people; now the same security forces had to protect them against ambushes and lynch mobs. Those cops were less than happy about it and the announcer conveyed the flavor of their sentiments.

"Oh Christ," Lime said abruptly. He stared at Hill. "Ben Krim's bound to be there isn't he. And there's still a pickup order out on him from Finland. We've got to cancel it or they'll grab him in Geneva."

Hill said mildly, "I already took care of that."

It was a good thing somebody around here was using his head. Wordlessly Chad Hill handed a paper-wrapped sandwich to Lime. He sat down and ate it, getting crumbs on his knees, listening to the radio.

". . . prisoners will be sequestered under heavy guard at an unspecified hotel until further instructions are received from the kidnappers of Clifford Fairlie. . . ."

Of course they would have Ben Krim on the scene. To have a look firsthand. He probably had phony press credentials; Sturka had what seemed to be an endless supply of expertly forged documents for all occasions.

"Anything from down south yet?"

"No. And we're not likely to get much. Too many oil company planes going back and forth all the time out there. Who's going to remember whether or not they heard Binaud's PBY go overhead four nights ago?"

But it had to be tried. If they lost Ben Krim it was the only lead they would have left.

There was coffee from Binaud's galley. Lime drank two cups greedily. He drank it too hot and burned his tongue. "If we assume Ben Krim's in Geneva now it'll take him at least five hours to get here. Probably eight or ten—I don't know of any direct connections from Geneva to Algiers."

He glanced at Chad Hill. The young man's fingernails were chewed down to the quick.

"I need air." Lime left the cabin and made his way abovedecks and stood on the fishing deck by the transom looking at the gloomy lights of the tavern and the quiet wave crests and the plentiful stars. The Med was calm tonight and it was quite warm. Not hot but pleasant.

He checked the time. It was past midnight. A new day: Tuesday. In Washington it was still Monday evening. It brought up a fine point of interest. Suppose they recovered Fairlie. Suppose they recovered him at eleven o'clock in the morning Algerian time. Thursday. Suppose they rushed him to the American Embassy in Madrid or Tangier and the Ambassador administered the oath of office on the stroke of noon. By then it would be only six in the morning Washington time. Who would be President then? Fairlie or Brewster?

Here I am counting angels on pinheads.

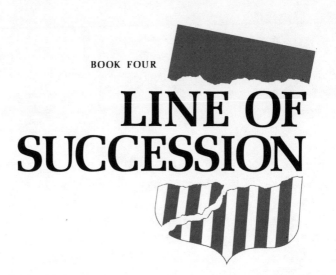

BOOK FOUR

LINE OF
SUCCESSION

TUESDAY, JANUARY 18

6:30 A.M. North African Time Someone was shaking Peggy by the shoulder. "Go down and get him ready."

She sat up. Squeezed her eyes tight shut and popped them open. "God I'm tired."

"Pot of coffee over there. Take it down with you—he might need some." As she struggled to her feet Sturka was adding, "He must talk this time, Peggy."

"If he's not dead." The anger was returning.

"He's not dead," Sturka said with a kind of disgusted patience. "Alvin has been sitting up with him."

She took the coffee down to the cell. Alvin nodded to her. Fairlie was on his back, flat out on the cot, asprawl and asleep, his chest rising and falling very slowly.

"Wake up please." Her professional nurse voice. She touched his cheek—gray and cool, an unhealthy pallor. Respiration still low, she noted clinically. The pulse was slow but not terribly weak.

His eyes fluttered, opened. She gave him a few moments to absorb his surroundings. "Can you sit up?"

He sat up without help. She studied his face. "How do you feel this morning?" Echoes of the tutor in nursing school: *And how do we feel this morning?* An infuriating chirp.

"Logy," Fairlie was mumbling. He was making strange faces, popping his eyes, rolling them around, grimacing—trying to clear his head.

Cesar appeared in his robes carrying a plate of food. She spent twenty minutes forcing Fairlie to eat and pouring coffee down him. He consumed everything obediently but without appetite and he chewed very slowly and sometimes seemed to forget to swallow.

At seven o'clock Sturka entered with the tape recorder. "All ready now?"

But Fairlie hadn't even glanced to see who had entered. He's still out of it, she thought. Too far out of it to put on the performance Sturka wanted?

She waited in growing fear: she didn't know what Sturka would do if it didn't work. To Fairlie, or to her. The past few days Sturka had let his anger show through. She had never seen that before; he had always been emotionless; now the strain was showing and Sturka had begun to slip. She caught the edge of his feelings once in a while and the intense force was alarming. It was a chill that came off him like death.

Sturka switched on the machine. Cesar sat on the corner of the bunk holding the microphone where it would pick up Fairlie's voice. This time there wouldn't be any editing; they wanted the pigs to know it was no trick this time, that Fairlie was talking without revisions.

They had spent a long time working out the wording. There had to be topical references to prove the tape had been made recently.

It was a fairly long speech because it contained detailed instructions for the release of the Washington Seven. Fairlie would have to read the whole thing cohesively. If his voice sounded weary and low that was all right but he couldn't stumble over every other word.

Sturka put his hand under Fairlie's chin and lifted his head sharply. "Listen to me. We've got something for you to read aloud. Another speech like last time. You remember last time?"

". . . Yes."

"Then just do it. When you've done it you can go back to sleep. You'd like that wouldn't you—to go back to sleep?"

Fairlie blinked rapidly; it was as much of an affirmative as anyone needed. Sturka became harsh: "But if you don't read this for us we'll keep you awake until you do. You've heard of what happens to the minds of men who are prevented from sleeping for too long? They go completely insane. You know that?"

". . . I know. I've heard that."

His voice did sound better than it had last night. Peggy walked in relief to the front corner, out of the way.

Sturka held the paper out to Fairlie—a long yellow ruled sheet from a legal pad.

"Read this aloud. That's all you have to do. Then you can sleep."

Fairlie held it in his lap and frowned at it as if trying to focus his eyes on the hand lettering. A finger came down on the sheet. "What's this? El Dzamiba?"

"El Djamila. It's the name of a place."

Fairlie tried to sit up but it seemed to require too much effort. He sagged back against the wall and held the speech up, squinting at it. Cesar moved the microphone closer.

"When should I start?"

"Whenever you're ready."

Fairlie's eyes wandered over the sheet. "What's this about Dexter Ethridge—and this about Milton Luke?"

"It's all true. They're dead."

"My God," Fairlie whispered.

The shock of that seemed to bring him around. He sat up again and maintained the position this time. "They're dead? How?"

"Ethridge seems to have died of natural causes," Sturka lied. "Luke was killed by a bomb which blew up his limousine. Please don't ask me who did it. I don't know. As you can see it was none of us—we're here, we're not in Washington."

"My God," Fairlie muttered again. "Has it started then?"

"The revolution? If it hasn't it's about to."

"What time is it? What day?"

"Tuesday. The eighteenth of January. It's early morning. Who knows, if you cooperate promptly enough you may be home in time to be inaugurated. Or perhaps you'd rather just sleep a while. But you have to read this first."

Fairlie was trying to grapple with it but he was too far under, too drowned by the resistance-destroying weight of the drugs. He picked up the yellow sheet and began to read in a listless monotone, eyelids drooping, voice wandering into whispers every once in a while:

"This—this is Clifford Fairlie speaking. I am very tired and under the influence of mild tranquilizers, which have been administered to me to insure that I don't do any reckless things that might—uh —jeopardize my physical safety. That will explain the . . . sleepy sound of my voice. But I am in good health.

"Uh—I have been informed of . . . deaths of Vice-President-elect Dexter Ethridge and Speaker Luke, for which I am allowed to express . . . deepest personal anguish.

"The seven . . . political prisoners from Washington have been delivered to Geneva as instructed, and my captors have asked me

to announce their further instructions now. The seven . . . prisoners
are to be transported by air to Algiers. They are then to be transported to the town of El Dzam—El Djamila, where an automobile
is to be provided for their use. They are to be told to drive south
along the highway toward El Goléa until they are contacted.

"If any surveillance—surveillance is detected, I am told I will not
be released. Neither the Algerian Government nor any other government is to follow the prisoners or make any other effort to
determine their whereabouts. The prisoners will be provided by
my captors with fresh transportation out of Algeria, but before they
are sent on they will be stripped and examined by X ray to insure
that no electronic devices have been concealed in their clothes or
on their bodies.

"If all conditions are met precisely, the seven prisoners will have
forty-eight hours in which to disappear into asylum in a country that
has not been identified to me.

"If there is no indication of betrayal on the part of the United
States or any other government, I will be released twenty-four
hours after the release of the seven prisoners.

"There is one final instruction. The seven prisoners are to be in
their car leaving El Djamila at precisely six o'clock in the evening
—that is eighteen hours by the European clock—on Thursday the
twentieth of January. And I am told to repeat that any attempt to
follow the prisoners' car or to track it electronically will be detected
and will result in my . . . death."

7:45 A.M. EST   ". . . defies the whole purpose of the Constitution,"
Senator Fitzroy Grant said.

Satterthwaite was thinking of Woodrow Wilson's phrase to describe the Senate: *little group of willful men.* . . . He said, "That has
a high moral tone, but would you still say the same thing if Howard
Brewster happened to be a Republican?"

"Yes." The Senate Minority Leader almost snapped it.

"Even though the alternative is Hollander?"

"You're thinking in terms of immediate expediency, Bill. You
always do. I'm thinking of the long haul. I don't think we can
jeopardize the whole meaning of the Constitution for the sake of a
temporary crisis."

"It won't be temporary if Hollander gets to spend four years in the White House. It may be the most permanent thing that's ever happened to this country. If you agree annihilation can be regarded as permanent."

"Let's leave out the sarcasms, shall we?" Grant's voice beat rolling echoes around his office. Past Grant's head through the window Satterthwaite could see the shell of the Capitol with snow on it. The building didn't look much different on the outside from before the bombings. A few construction trailers drawn up against the East Portico, a larger number of guards than there had been a month ago. A bit of absurdity in that, since nobody was inside it except workmen.

Fitzroy Grant's dewlappy face turned slightly and picked up some light from the window; his eyes looked sad. He ran a hand carefully over the neat wave in his white hair. "Look Bill, the majority will vote with you anyway. My vote won't matter."

"Then why not throw in with us?"

The deep slow velvet voice was only faintly ironic. "Call it principle if you like. I realize the truth can't prevail against a false idea whose time has come. But I have to follow my own inclinations."

"Can I ask at least for an abstention?"

"No. I'm going to vote against."

"Even if you turn out to be the swing vote?"

"I'm not that low in the alphabet."

"I'm backpedaling, you can see that. I'm not used to this kind of horsetrading. But it does seem to me there ought to be somewhere where we could meet on common ground. Some kind of compromise."

Grant seemed to smile. "You're not half bad at it, Bill. Don't run yourself down as a politician."

"Well I sure don't seem to be getting anywhere with you."

"Howard Brewster's pushing too hard, Bill. Love me love my ideas. He's put himself on the line—everything he's ever been, everything he's got. One throw of the dice. All right, I realize he's feeling the heat. I don't like Hollander either. But this arrogance from the White House—that's what I can't stand. Frankly I believe we can handle Hollander. Hamstring him. There are ways, if only Congress will show the gumption. Hollander's less of a threat than Howard Brewster, to my mind—because if Brewster puts this over on the country it'll be one more nail in the coffin of the republic. The Roman Caesars came to power by stealing it away from the Senate. Brewster's trying to get Congress to reinstate him in an office he just got through losing in a popular election. It smacks of *coup d'état* to me. I'm afraid I simply haven't got the conscience to back this move. That's all there is to it."

"Fitz, you talked to the President yesterday, and——"

"Let's say the President talked to me."

"——and you told him you couldn't support him. But you agreed to keep the secret until he opened it up. Why?"

"My peculiar brand of personal loyalty I suppose. He made it personal. We've been friends for thirty years."

"Then may I prevail on that friendship for at least this much— that you agree not to campaign actively against the President's move?"

"By actively you mean publicly."

"No. I mean privately as well. While the committee is getting ready to report out the bill will you agree not to perform any of that quiet arm-twisting you're so famous for?"

Fitzroy Grant chuckled amiably. "Funny, I always thought it was Howard Brewster who was famous for that. What do you think you're doing right now if not a little genteel arm-twisting?"

"I'd appreciate an answer."

"Very well, I'll give you one. But it requires a bit of a preamble. With me they always do."

Satterthwaite thought of looking at his watch, thought better of it, waited. He was thinking of the hard-backed chairs over in the Executive Office Building that would be filled in an hour's time by the rumps of two dozen congressional leaders, among whose number the President hoped Fitzroy Grant yet might appear.

"When you look out around you today," Grant said, "you see nothing but the wreckage that's been left by these incredible atrocities and outrages. To my mind that's the inevitable result of our weakness as a people. The libertarian principles have obviously failed. For altogether too long we allowed these goons of the so-called New Left to spread sedition and terror. We stood by and listened while they boasted openly of the violence they were going to do us. Our well-intentioned lawmakers chose to call this treason 'dissent' while the goons were ambushing cops and plotting sabotage and laying the groundwork for insurrection right under our noses. Now it seems to me——"

"Fitz, you're condemning an entire society with guilt by association. There's no proof more than a handful of criminals had any part in these atrocities. Their leaders aren't even Americans."

"I've been hearing that until it's come out my ears."

"You don't believe it?"

"It's totally beside the point. The point is that a society is too permissive, too weak, and too open to further attacks when it allows such things to happen as we've seen happen in the past couple of weeks."

"Yet the alternative is a kind of fascism. That's what Hollander wants—it's also what the radicals want."

"Fascism's a strange word, Bill. It used to mean something specific. It doesn't any longer. It's just an epithet we use to indicate hatred of our enemies. If this country's in any real danger of being taken over by a fascist sort of movement I think that danger exists in the nature of Howard Brewster's effort to bend the Constitution far more than it exists in the senile brain of a weak old man like Wendy Hollander. Hollander's a fool and everybody can see that—that's our means of defense against him."

"Mussolini was a bit of a fool in his later years. It didn't stop him from maintaining the stranglehold on his country."

"Until they killed him."

"You think we ought to kill Hollander then?"

"No. I suppose most of us have thought of it though. I'm sure Howard Brewster has."

"It's been mentioned."

"Why do you suppose he rejected it, Bill?"

"Why do you reject it?"

"Because I'm not a murderer. But then I'm not bucking for a second term in the White House."

"That's slanderous, Senator."

"I expect it is. There's probably some truth in it, however." Grant's chin lifted. His head was silhouetted against the window and Satterthwaite had a poor view of his face but the eyes seemed to gleam out at him. "Bill, that speech I just gave you about the country's lack of strength—about the permissiveness that allows these things to happen. Did that ring a bell with you?"

"Sure. I've heard a lot of people use those arguments. I half believe some of them myself."

"Ever heard Howard Brewster talk that way?"

"On occasion."

"I'm talking about recently. Within the past two or three days."

"No."

"Well I've got news for you, son. Those were almost the exact words he used when he talked to me yesterday in his office."

"It makes sense," Satterthwaite said, half defensively.

"Howard Brewster's kind of sense, you mean. He'd naturally use that sort of conservative spiel with me because he wants my support. Is that what you think?"

"I think it's possible he might have come on a bit strong in that direction for your benefit," Satterthwaite said cautiously. "After all he wouldn't want you to think he was going to be too soft on the radicals."

"Because that might send me scooting right over into Wendy's camp, is that it?"

"Something like that. Hell, we're all adults here. Is that the first time anybody's ever tried to reassure you that way?"

"Hardly. But there's a strange thing about it when you think it over."

"Is there?"

"Think about it, Bill. If he's going to use the same hard line Hollander uses, then why pass over Hollander at all?" And a sudden lunge forward of the handsome senatorial chin. "Could it just be because Howard Brewster wants the satisfaction of stomping the radicals himself? Not to mention his ambition to stay in office four more years?"

"You just said he was a lifelong friend of yours. None of this sounds very friendly to me."

"I'm not feeling too friendly. I stayed up most of the night thinking back on that conversation he had with me yesterday. A few things stuck in my craw. One advantage of knowing a man for thirty years is that you get to know the little signs he puts up when he's just pulling your leg, when he's planning to double-cross you, when he's lying for your benefit. We all do it. If you're a good enough poker player and you play opposite the same people for thirty years you ought to be able to figure out what it means when one of them wiggles his ears."

"I'm not following this completely."

"Bill, he wasn't lying to me yesterday. I know all the signs. I may be one of the handful of living men who do, but I've known the President since the days when he didn't know who sat on which side of the aisle. And I'm telling you the man has every intention of proceeding with measures that aren't very much different from the ones Hollander means to employ. I'm sure he feels honestly that he's got a better chance of putting it over on the country than Hollander has. Hollander's a fool whatever he does; however much Howard Brewster may be disliked nobody faults his intelligence.

He's trying to sweet-talk the Congress of the United States into backing him and so he's playing the public role of man of reason. But to me it's like the Goldwater-Johnson contest in Sixty-four when Johnson stood on a peace platform and then went out and did all the things Goldwater had been stupid enough to announce he'd do if he got elected."

There was a momentary silence. Grant was looking at Satterthwaite, unblinking. "He was telling me the truth, you see, but he wanted me to think he was lying. He tried to make it look like the standard logrolling we all do. But the sincerity showed through."

"Why should he want you to think he was lying?"

"Because if there really wasn't any difference between him and Wendy there was no reason for me to back him."

"You honestly believe there's no difference?"

"Howard Brewster has the capacity to make himself a demagogue in this country. Hollander doesn't. That's the salient difference, Bill. And that's why I won't abide by your request—his request." Grant stood up. "I'm going to fight it publicly *and* privately, Bill. Every way I know how. I've already started—by giving you something to think about."

Satterthwaite walked, almost in relief, to the door. Picked up his armed escort in the corridor and went out to the waiting gray Interagency Motor Pool sedan. On the way to the Executive Office Building he sat in the back seat and held his head as if it weighed half a ton.

Grant's notions were insidious. It was true Brewster was bearing down hard. In essence his argument was *"Aprés moi le déluge."*

According to Grant you had to extend that. You had to start from that premise and look at the evidence and reach the conclusion that Brewster really meant *"L'état c'est moi."*

Satterthwaite closed his eyes. Things were reeling.

He had never been less than intensely loyal. Even when arguing with Brewster he had always played the role of loyal opposition. He had never aligned himself with Brewster's adversaries and he had never differed publicly with the President.

Suddenly he felt himself the man in the middle.

No, he decided abruptly.

It was a mark of his exhaustion that he had let Grant play on his uncertainties. It was ridiculous. Suppose it was true? It still left the choice: Brewster or Hollander. And the choice was still clear.

Satterthwaite had served Brewster long enough to know him. He had observed Hollander for an equal length of time and regardless of Brewster's personal ambitions there really was no comparing the two men. Brewster had stature and conscience; Hollander had neither.

Satterthwaite left the car and headed for the caucus.

3:15 P.M. North African Time　Lime sat in the bar drooling with drunken lechery, clumsily pawing the blonde. His cap was askew at an angle more precarious than rakish. "Hey innkeeper!" he roared at the top of an arrogant American tourist voice. The blonde gave him a blowsy loose smile but Lime wasn't looking at her; he was rearing his head around angrily to locate the bartender, Binaud. "Hey let's get these classes—glasses filled, what's taking you so damn long?" A corner of his vision held Benyoussef Ben Krim crossing the front of the room from the door to the front end of the bar. A big man, fat but not yet obese, limping slightly.

The CIA agent Gilliams had sent the blonde on request and she had brought the Levi's and loud Hawaiian shirt and the yachting cap with its golden anchor embroidered on the crown. Lime provided the rest: the appearance of a flabby dissipated American on a week's holiday from a Saharan oil-company job.

Ben Krim caught Binaud's eye and Lime saw Binaud's careful one-inch nod. Ben Krim stood impatiently while Binaud mixed a drink.

Lime stood up, almost upsetting the chair; patted the blonde and lurched toward the door as if headed for the toilet attached to the outside of the building.

Ben Krim turned to go out the door and Lime managed to collide with him.

"Jesus." Lime started to get angry and then had another look at the size and ferocity of Ben Krim; Lime's face changed, he assumed a cowardly half smile. "Hey, look, I apologize. These freeways are murder aren't they, hey? Good seein' you old buddy."

While he talked he was making drunken efforts to brush Ben Krim's jacket smooth. The Arab stared at him with hooded disgust and Lime stumbled through the door, almost fell off the step, staggered around the corner and poured himself into the toilet chamber.

Through gaps in the boards he had a restricted view along the outside wall of the bar to the road, the pier, the boats and airplane beyond. He saw Ben Krim walk stolidly out onto the pier, putting most of his weight on his left leg, dragging the right foot along. After a moment Binaud appeared and followed Ben Krim onto the pier. A third man got out of a black Citroen 2CV that was drawn up at the near end of the dock and Binaud made a point of inspecting his pilot's papers—Lime assumed that was what they were. Finally an envelope came out of Ben Krim's pocket and Ben Krim counted out money. Binaud counted it too and then put it away in his pants, and ushered the two men down the pier ladder to the dinghy he kept tied up there. Ben Krim followed them down out of sight.

When Lime staggered out of the toilet they were rowing out to the Catalina. He gave them a casual glance and lumbered around to the front door of the bar. Tripped over the step and fell inside.

He picked himself up and stood in the shadows to watch Ben Krim and the pilot climb into the PBY, after which Binaud began to row back toward the pier. Lime walked to the table and removed the yachting cap, handed it to the blonde and said, "Thanks. You did fine."

"Boy do you sober up fast." She smiled and it was genuine this time; it made her look a lot better. "What was that all about anyway?"

"I needed an excuse to bump into him."

"To pick his pocket?"

"Quite the reverse," Lime said. He took two paces into the center of the room to look out through the door. The Catalina's engines were coughing into life and he watched the big-winged plane cast off from its buoy and turn and taxi out on the water.

He followed Binaud into the cruiser's forward cabin. Chad Hill and two agents sat drinking coffee. Hill was saying to Binaud, "You did very well."

"May I have the money now?"

"Let him hold it," Lime said. "Keep two men on him till this is wrapped up." He looked at Hill's camera. "Get some good face shots?"

"I think so."

They might need to be able to identify Ben Krim's pilot later on if things got murky. Lime hadn't got a good look at the man. Too small and fair-skinned to be Corby, but then it wouldn't have been Corby.

Hill put his cup down and yawned. "Time to get back to Algiers, I guess."

The cars were concealed behind the bar. The two-way was blatting when they approached and Lime reached in to unsnap the mike and bring it to his mouth. "Lime here."

"It's Gilliams. Didn't he get there yet?"

"He's already taken off. Haven't you got his bleeper signal?"

"It hasn't moved an inch."

"That's the one on the boat. There were two of them. He took the plane."

"I know. But the signals should have diverged if he's moved. It's still one signal. Standing still." Gilliams' voice came out of the dashboard speaker, poorly defined, heavy with crackling.

Hill said, "Oh shit. The one on the plane isn't working then. It's my fault—I should have tested them."

Lime said into the mike without taking his eyes off Hill, "Gilliams, switch your triangulators over to seventeen hundred. One seven zero zero, got that?"

"One seven zero zero. Hang on a minute."

Chad Hill's puzzled eyes swiveled around to Lime.

Gilliams: "Right, we've got a pulse. It seems kind of weak though."

"It's pretty small and it's inside the plane—it's got a lot of metal around it. Is it strong enough to follow?"

"I guess it is if we stick fairly close to it."

"Then get your aircraft moving."

"They're already moving."

"All right. We're coming into Algiers. Expect us in half an hour. Have the Lear jet standing by. Have you got cars and choppers at Bou Saada?"

"Yes sir. And the Early Birds. Waiting down there with those dart guns."

"I'll see you in half an hour." Lime hung the mike and turned to face Chad Hill. "Pick up the rest of the crew and tell them to follow us in the station wagon."

Chad Hill said, "I'm sorry about the bleeper. But how'd you get that other one on the plane?"

"It's not on the plane. It's on Ben Krim," Lime said. "It's in his pocket."

He went around the car and got into the passenger seat. Hill slid in very slowly, as if he weren't sure the seat would support him.

The sun blasted down, the sand shot painful reflections against the eye. Green hills lifted above the beach. Lime sat back with his arms folded and his face closed up.

They were leaving two men on Binaud; the rest were getting into the station wagon and Chad Hill started the car and drove around the bar to the road.

Once, Hill stiffened, looking at something; Lime looked ahead and saw nothing but the curving road. Whatever it was Hill had identified it and dismissed it; he had relaxed now. He's in better shape than I am, Lime thought; Lime hadn't seen anything at all. His tired eyes stared out of a bottomless disgust.

They boarded the Lear jet to fly to Bou Saada, the "City of Happiness" on the Naïl Plateau. Gilliams' radio direction finders—at Algiers, at El Goléa, and in an airborne tracking station orbiting behind Ben Krim's Catalina—had the target on-screen and it was still moving when the Lear took off and climbed steeply to clear the coastal range. Lime had a one-to-four-million-scale Michelin map across his knees. It showed the whole of north Africa in enough detail to cover every potable waterhole, every jeep track and wadi and fort.

The fertile crowded Tell region lay south of the Atlas Mountains, forming a bulge against the arid plateaus that fell across hundreds of dusty miles toward the Sahara. Putting together what he knew about Julius Sturka and what he had learned about the radius of the Catalina's previous flight, Lime studied the map and came to certain conclusions.

He could rule out the Sahara proper. The plane hadn't gone that far when they'd used it to carry Fairlie. And the Sahara was less a hiding place than a trap—there were too few places to hide. Sturka might be in the outback but he wouldn't be too far from avenues of flight. Somewhere down here in the *bled* within pragmatic distance of a decent road and a place to land and take off in an airplane if you had to. Bedouin country perhaps but not the Tuaregs' desert. Possibly even a farm in the Tell.

The wadi Binaud had pinpointed—the riverbed oasis where he'd picked up the Catalina last week—was east of Ghardaïa and north of Ouargla: arid plains around there, like parts of Arizona and New Mexico—hardpan clay earth that supported boulders and scrub brush, the occasional stunted tree, enough broken ground and cut-banks to conceal armies. Sturka had operated there before with the efficiency of an Apache Indian war chief and he would feel comfortable there.

Lime kept remembering the number of times he had gone looking for Sturka in that country: looking but never finding.

He had one or two advantages now he hadn't had then. Electronic surveillance had become more sophisticated. He didn't have to function in quite so much secrecy now. And he had almost unlimited manpower to draw upon. Gilliams had pulled every CIA man in North Africa into it, from Dakar to Cairo. There was the crew Lime had brought with him and then there were the Early Birds —the A-team killer squads Satterthwaite had sent from Langley. Lime had insisted the Early Birds be armed, in addition to their normal issue, with tranquilizer-dart bullets obtained from a Kenyan game preserve. The darts were fired by standard rifle cartridges; the chemical was M-99, a morphine derivative. The tranquilizer would take effect almost instantly and render the victim unconscious for fifteen or twenty minutes. It was standard procedure in wild-game protection; whether it had ever been used before in a quasi-military operation Lime didn't know and didn't care.

The objective was to get Fairlie out alive; what happened to the kidnappers was secondary but they couldn't afford to leave half a dozen corpses strewn across the Algerian landscape. Algiers wouldn't stand still for that and a fair number of opportunistic capitals—Peking, Moscow, the Third World towns—would join in the condemnations. Rescuing a VIP was one thing, starting a pocket battle on foreign soil was another. If it happened, the United States would survive it as she had survived Laos and the Dominican Republic and dozens of others, but it was better to avoid it if you could.

Lime lacked interest in the complexities of international relations but Satterthwaite had made it fairly clear to him that a gaffe in Algeria might cost the United States the nuclear bases in Spain which both Brewster and Fairlie had been trying mightily to protect before all this idiocy had erupted. Spain was not a NATO member, never had been. Overt American arrogance in Algeria would be too close to home; Perez-Blasco would have to turn away from Washington and that was to be avoided. So it was better to use drugged darts than bullets.

He hoped they were somewhere in the *bled*. It would be so much easier without witnesses. If they were holed up in the middle of one of the towns there would be no way to make it neat.

The chief dilemma was how to get Fairlie away from them. If you attacked them frontally they would use him as a shield.

It had to be played by ear and at any rate he had to find them first.

When they landed at Bou Saada the Catalina was still in the air, still being tracked southward.

"West of El Meghaier," the radio man explained to Lime. "Still maintaining altitude."

Lime left the radio shack and walked across the tarmac to the little gathering of aircraft—the Lear, the charter turboprop with the CIA people aboard, the Early Birds' helicopters.

Lime beckoned Gilliams over and showed him the map. "I think Ben Krim's heading for the same wadi where Binaud picked up the plane last week. Now that Catalina cruises at about a hundred and twenty-five miles an hour. The Lear can do three times that speed. I want to be at that wadi before Ben Krim gets there. I'll want half a dozen of the A-team men with me. The rest of you had better rendezvous at Touggourt and wait for word from me. Have you got a portable scrambler set?"

"Transceiver? There's one in each helicopter."

"Have one put aboard the Lear for me."

"All right Mr. Lime. But what happens if you're guessing wrong? You're out there in some Godforsaken wadi."

"If we don't get there ahead of Ben Krim we've got no way to track his contact. There's a town called Guerara about ten miles from the wadi—I'll have to commandeer a car there."

"If they've got one." Gilliams looked dubious. "You know those *bled* towns. A camel and four jackasses."

"Something else is worrying you. What?"

"Maybe your pilot can land that Lear down there and maybe he can't. But there ain't no for-real airplane runways around there. He'll probably never take it off."

"Then we've cost ourselves an airplane haven't we."

The killer boys were trooping on board the jet with their rifles and knapsacks. Lime collected Chad Hill and went up the boarding stairs. Somebody closed the door after them and as Lime was buckling into his seat he felt the engines begin to whine and vibrate.

The Lear had oil company markings and he hoped that would appease Sturka's bunch if they saw it go by overhead. He had a strong feeling they were right down there somewhere—almost near enough to touch.

There was a road outside Guerara, a paved secondary road that went in an absolutely straight line across seventy miles of plateau to the main highway at Berriane. It made a fine landing strip for the Lear; they buzzed it once to make sure there was no traffic and the pilot set down easily on the pavement, wandering with a bit of wind drift because the road had a high crown.

The chief of the A-team unpacked the fold-up motorbike from the seemingly endless stockpile of gadgetry the CIA teams always carried, and went putt-putting off with an agent riding behind him on the fender, east toward Guerara, a palmtree-shadowed village a mile away. From the air they had spotted half a dozen vehicles there and Lime had specified two of them he wanted: a Land Rover and a truck.

Twenty minutes. The sun went down with a splash of color and the Land Rover came up over the rise into view. The truck was a two and one half ton Weyland with hooped canvas over its rear bed; it was war surplus—something Monty's army had left behind in wreckage after El Alamein.

Lime didn't ask the CIA chief how he had obtained the two vehicles and the CIA chief didn't volunteer the information. His name was Orr, he was a wiry Texan with close-cropped iron-gray hair, and there wasn't a doubt in the world he had once been in the paratroops or the Green Berets.

Lime spread the map on the hood of the Land Rover, on top of the spare tire, and talked for five minutes. Orr listened and nodded. When Lime got into the Land Rover with one of the agents for a driver, Orr gathered the rest of his men in the truck and they set out eastward in close-formation convoy. In the road behind them the Lear was taxiing off to the side to wait in case Lime needed it again.

They drove through the village and the stares of Arabs followed them until they were beyond the palms. Lime twisted around in the seat to crank up the battery-powered scrambler transceiver they had manhandled off the plane. It took him three or four minutes to make contact.

"Gilliams?"

"Yes sir, sir." Gilliams sounded in good spirits.

"He still in the air?"

"Yes sir he sure is. Starting his descent just a few minutes ago. Right where you guessed he'd go."

"We're on the ground. It should take us ten minutes or so to get there, another five or ten minutes to get in position. Have we got enough time?"

"I imagine you have. He's still got thirty-five miles to cover and it'll take him some time to feel his way down. It'll be dusk by then, pret' near dark. I doubt he'll have much by way of landing lights."

"A pair of headlights I imagine," Lime said. "Don't make any more calls on this frequency until I get back to you."

"Step it up a little," he told the driver.

"Can I use the headlights?"

"God no."

Lime and Orr were belly-down in the brush along the wadi bank when the PBY came lumbering down onto the *piste*, the jeep dirt track that ran alongside the dry river. A car sat in the road with its headlights stabbing forward; Ben Krim's pilot was guiding by the headlights but it was a tricky maneuver because the closer he got to the ground the more blinding the headlights would be in his eyes. But the pilot would be good. Sturka used only experts.

Two of Orr's commandos had slithered toward the car that was lighting up the plane's landing strip. If the driver was sitting in the car they were to wait; if he was outside they were to plant the bleeper on the car. He would have to get out to meet Ben Krim and turn over the parcel.

That would be Corby or Renaldo in the car. He'd have with him one of those tape-recorder-transmitter devices to broadcast the next set of instructions to the Americans—where to deliver the Washington Seven.

It was Ben Krim's job to report to Sturka's man—give him the firsthand report on the landing of the Seven in Geneva—and collect the recorder-transmitter, and fly back to El Djamila to deposit the Catalina, and drive to Algiers, and book a flight to Madrid or Paris or Berlin where he would set up the transmitter on another tiresome little clock device so that Ben Krim would be halfway back to Algiers by the time the thing broadcast its message to the world.

Lime was only mildly interested in what the instructions would be. At any rate Ben Krim would be picked up when he flew back to El Djamila and Gilliams' people would analyze the tape.

In the meantime the car was bugged and Lime would be following Corby or Renaldo back to Sturka's lair.

It was going to work. He felt it for the first time: the positive knowledge that he had Sturka.

In the night silence he watched the PBY make its superb landing-roll to a stop within a hundred feet of the waiting headlights. The lights clicked off. Someone got out of the car and walked toward the airplane, and Benyoussef Ben Krim climbed down from the dimly lit cockpit to meet the courier. Through the Mark Systems glasses Lime watched the two shadows flow together in the dusk.

The meeting was brief. There was enough light to make out silhouettes, and Lime was fairly sure that was Cesar Renaldo. Not big enough for Corby nor lean enough for Sturka himself.

A curious question occurred to him. What if it had been Sturka? Arrest him on the spot and search for the others? Or, having him in hand, let him go so he could lead you back to them? With Renaldo Lime didn't care, would let him go; Lime didn't want Renaldo, not personally. *But suppose it had been Sturka?*

Renaldo get back in the car, started it up, switched on his lights, drove along the *piste* making a little curve to get around the PBY, drove almost a mile and stopped in the distance to make a U-turn, his headlights glaring with starlike twinkles across the flat clarity of the *bled*. Ben Krim was back in the plane and the pilot had one engine running; using a lot of rudder brakes he was turning the ungainly craft around in its own length on the ground. The plane stood still for a moment while the second engine burst into chatter and then it began to roll, searchlights booming from the nacelles, red and white wingtip lights winking.

Lime was looking at the place where Renaldo's car had been sitting and his brain was working again. A car, he thought. Not a jeep, not a Land Rover. A car. One of those old diesel-powered Mercedes sedans, it was. Humpbacked and round.

So they were holed up on or near a road. Not a *piste*. It confirmed another expectation.

Lime watched the plane go away and the car drive up the desert track to the northeast, and then he tapped Orr on the shoulder and said, "Okay, let's go."

"We going to follow him? I mean he'll see our lights. It's getting too dark to travel without lights."

"No need to follow him," Lime said.

"Because he's bugged?"

"Because I know where he's going."

They walked to the Land Rover and Lime cranked up the scrambler. "Gilliams?"

"Yes sir."

"Get me a caravan."

"*What?*"

It was one of the advantages of having limitless dollars and limitless armies to command.

The camel caravans of North Africa were a tradition going back a thousand years; they were more than a method of transportation: they were a way of life, a self-perpetuating institution. Each caravan numbered anywhere from a dozen to two hundred camels and made one trip a year but the trip was of a year's duration: they started somewhere along the Niger with a cargo of pelts and salt and dried meat and handicrafts, they traveled slowly north trading on the way—trading cargo and camels as well—and six months later they reached the Atlas Mountains and picked up a new cargo of manufactured things, dates, kerosene, gunpowder; then they turned around and went back. A caravan was a home: you were born and lived and died in the caravan.

There was usually a caravan around here. It was near the northern terminus. No matter what route they had taken to get here from the south they all converged on the string of foothill towns south of Algiers. It was no great feat for Gilliams to locate one west of Touggourt, and no difficulty to hire its services. Everything was for sale or for hire.

The caravan was in motion less than two hours after Lime's call. At the same time Lime's little convoy of Land Rover and truck set out overland, heading across the *bled* to rendezvous with it.

The fact that Renaldo was driving an ordinary automobile had pinpointed the hiding place for Lime. There was only one passable road from the wadi. It went northeast as far as the old Foreign Legion post at Dzioua and then turned due east to cross ninety miles of broken country to Touggourt and the main highway to Biskra.

The Legion fort was still in use as a district admin headquarters. But for every full-dress fortress there had once been a string of outpost *bomas* at one-day's-ride intervals. Thirty miles southeast of Dzioua was a small *boma* which had been abandoned after World War II. Once or twice in the fifties Lime had visited the place and found evidence someone had been there: bandit *fellagha* or FLN guerrillas. Conceivably Sturka had used it as a rallying point even in those days. It sat on a two-hundred-foot height and commanded an excellent field of view—or of fire—and it was within a few hundred feet of the present road. It was an ideal place to hold Fairlie —impossible to approach unseen.

The American planeloads and helicopter-loads of personnel had landed at Touggourt, sixty miles from the *boma,* and they would be ready by the time Lime joined the camel train. There was a doctor, there were several pints of AB-negative blood, there were dozens of sharpshooters and communications people and gadgets. Lime was going to need speed and firepower. He couldn't sneak inside Sturka's fortress by stealth or subterfuge.

The risk was enormous: the risk to Fairlie. If it failed Lime would be condemned as a murdering blunderer. Probably they would find a way to put him away for the rest of his life, if they let him live. But everything entailed risk. He could leave Sturka strictly alone and see what happened if he cooperated in turning the Washington Seven loose into asylum. But there was no way to force Sturka to keep his word and release Fairlie; so that risk was equally high. In a way it was better odds to attack—because the people with Sturka weren't professionals, they weren't trained to kill without thought, and all he really had to worry about was keeping Sturka away from Fairlie until he could get to Fairlie. The rest of them wouldn't instinctively know what to do and in their confusion he had a good chance to break through.

The Land Rover bounced across rocks and gullies, its headlights heaving wildly around; Lime gripped his seat and smoked furiously and began to sweat.

WEDNESDAY, JANUARY 19

4:15 A.M. North African Time   She was lying in a rowboat drifting on a placid lake. A blue sky and a pleasantly warm sun, glass-calm water with only enough current to keep the boat moving gently along. There was no one else; everything was soundless. She didn't raise her head to look but she knew that the lake emptied into a deep tunnel and that sooner or later the boat would drift into that tunnel and carry her cozily into its warm darkness.

". . . Peggy. Hey."

"Whum?"

"Come on come on. Do I got to slap your face?"

"All right—all right." She was awake now; she threw the blanket back. "Time's it?"

"Little after four."

"Four in the morning?"

"Sometheen wrong with the pig. You got to look at him."

The words brought her sharply to her senses. "What's the matter with him?" She was reaching for the veil and robe.

"I don' know. He just doesn't look too good."

She remembered her watch and took it downstairs with her into the cellar corridor.

Alvin had a worried face. He had the door open and Peggy eeled in past him.

Fairlie looked like a corpse. She held the watch crystal to his nostrils and after a moment the crystal fogged slightly. Tested his pulse—it was down, way down.

Oh shit. "You'd better get Sturka."

Cesar left. She heard his heavy tread on the stair. Not that Sturka could do anything, she thought. She beckoned to Alvin. "I think we ought to try to get him on his feet. Walk him back and forth."

"You mean like when people take an overdose of sleeping pills?"

"I don't know anything else to do. Is there any coffee?"

"I'll have a look. You want me to make some?"

"Yes."

Alvin left and she heaved Fairlie into a sitting position: slid his feet off the cot and turned him, got her shoulder under his arm and tried to lift him to his feet. But the angles were wrong and she fell asprawl across him and got untangled and tried it again.

It still didn't work. He was limp and it was going to take two of them to walk him. She left him propped against the wall and waited for the others.

Alvin returned with half a cup of coffee. "I put some more on. This is cold."

"That's all right. Let's try and get it down him. You hold his head."

She didn't have to open his mouth; his jaw hung slack. She tipped his head back. "Hold him that way." Poured a little coffee in to see if he would swallow it.

Sturka's voice made her jump. "What's the matter with him?"

"Bad reaction to the drugs," she said. She looked over her shoulder, filled with anger. "Too much drugs."

"Well never mind that right now. I think we have visitors."

Cesar appeared in the doorway behind Sturka. Alvin said, "What kind of visitors?"

Peggy was trying to get coffee down Fairlie. "Hold his head still damn it."

Cesar said, "Some kind of camel caravan."

Alvin was suspicious. "Traveling at night?"

"Sometimes they do," Sturka said. "But I don't trust it. Let's go." He pointed to Cesar. "You out to the back. You know your post."

Cesar went. Peggy watched Fairlie's Adam's apple move up and down when he swallowed. It was a good sign she thought. Then she heard Sturka say, "Bring him upstairs."

Alvin said dubiously, "We'll have to carry him."

"Then carry him." Sturka had an ugly AK submachine gun slung across his back; he flicked it into his hand and went nimbly into the corridor. Peggy heard him go up the stairs—softly and quickly, two steps at a time.

The movement wouldn't hurt Fairlie but she wanted to get the rest of the coffee into him first. She motioned Alvin to hold his head again and lifted the cup to Fairlie's pale lips.

4:28 A.M. North African Time   Lime edged through the rubble feeling his way with his feet before he put his weight on them. Starlight fell on the pale crumbled walls; he kept to the deep shadows. When he looked back he couldn't see the four men behind him and that was good.

He heard someone moving through the wreckage beyond the stucco wall that stood more or less intact against the sky. It loomed just ahead of him, one corner broken off raggedly by a forgotten Italian bomb. It was significant that he could hear the man's approach; it meant the man didn't really expect anyone to be out here. The rest of them would be at the opposite end of the building looking out through rifle slits, watching the camel train wind past. Sturka had sent one man to the back because of the possibility the camel train was a diversion—which it was.

There was only one way to do this kind of thing: fast and simply. Get up as close as possible and then rush them, overrun them before they could react against Fairlie.

No subtleties, no elaborate schemes. Just attack. He had to assume Sturka had only three or four comrades; he was relying on his hostage, not his military strength. Lime had to assume there weren't more than half a dozen of them and that he could overwhelm that many instantly.

He stood with his back to the stucco wall and listened to the man approach the doorway beside him. At the back of his neck the short hairs prickled. He had the sound of his heartbeat in his ears. He let his breath trickle out slowly through his mouth; he fought a cough down.

The man had stopped just inside the door. Lime couldn't wheel into sight to silence the man without alarming him. It was probably Corby or Renaldo and either of them might be able to sense the presence of alien beings in the silent wreckage. If so it would draw the man outside and that was what Lime needed. . . .

The pulse throbbed at his throat. Distantly he could hear the caravan trudging past, the flipflop of camel hoofs across the stones down below the hill.

Stupid bravado, he thought. It would have made sense to send a younger man on point. But Chad Hill was an innocent and he didn't know any of the others, they were strangers and if mistakes were made it was better to make them himself. . . .

His elbows and knees were abraded raw: he had come the last two hundred yards on his belly. He settled the knife in his fist.

Movement: the shift of a leather sole on gritty earth. The man was coming out. Lime could hear his breathing.

He stood poised, motionless, down to his raw quivering nerve ends.

He sensed it before he saw it. He timed the man's breathing; he waited for the man to exhale a breath and then he wheeled into the doorway. Clapped his hand over the man's mouth and used the knife. Once in Oran he had stabbed into a man who had just taken a deep breath and the scream had echoed a mile.

The man's body went taut. Lime released the knife and got a grip on the man to keep him from turning.

Renaldo, he thought.

He lowered the body without sound. Stepped outside and made hand motions.

Stealth now, but there would be discovery and soon they would have to move ever so fast. The four sharpshooters slipped in past him, stepped across Renaldo's body, went prowling ahead like sharks, rifles out ahead of them. Lime fell in behind Orr, lifting the .38 out of the clamshell. Lime was the only one armed with lethal ammunition. It had to be that way. Total authority, and total responsibility. Nobody got killed unless Lime did the killing.

There had been lights before—probably kerosene lamps—but there were none now. That was to be expected; Sturka would have extinguished all lamps.

Sturka was probably at one of the gunports in the front wall watching the passage of the caravan. He would have Fairlie with him or close to him: Fairlie was his shield against trouble.

Lime had given the shooters the classic order: *Shoot anything that moves.* Their ammunition was tranquilizer darts; they would be able to sort out friend and foe afterward.

They moved forward in silence through the tumbled corridors of the old outpost. The roofs were half caved in and there was a little light, enough to see by. An old splintered door stood half off its hinges at the end of the corridor, ajar two feet, giving access to the room beyond but blocking view of it. They crowded up close to the door, staying behind it; the others waited for Lime's signal and Lime waited for his ears to tell him whether the room beyond the door was where Sturka stood with Fairlie. He was trying to reconstruct the architecture in his mind, trying to remember the plan of the place. Fifteen years. . . .

4:35 A.M. North African Time   Alvin was walking Fairlie back and forth. Peggy went across to the deep shadows of the front corner to look out one of the windows. Through the deep slit she saw the slow procession of camels and riders at the foot of the hill, hooded silent figures in the starlight. Sturka was at the window fifteen feet to her right—watching, more tense than she had ever seen him. She saw no danger but Sturka sensed something. He didn't communicate it to the rest of them except by the taut line of his back, the high set of his head.

A sound.

Somewhere in back. She turned her head, trying to identify it. The scrape of a foot? But Cesar was back there.

It was probably Cesar then, or a rodent in the walls.

But Alvin had heard it too and had stopped in the center of the room with Fairlie draped against him, Fairlie's arm over his shoulders. Alvin had his left arm around Fairlie's waist and a revolver in his right hand. Sturka had been explicit, the brief sibilant command on the stairs: *If there's any trouble at all—shoot him and then worry about yourself.*

Fairlie wasn't quite conscious; neither was he comatose. His legs functioned after a fashion but if let go he would fall. Like a drunk.

Sturka turned and stared at the back door. Cesar had shut it when he'd gone to the back. It stood closed, mute—but something had drawn Sturka. Beyond was a half-demolished barrack room; then a door lodged askew, a corridor past the ruins of officer quarters, another door, finally wrecked ruins of rock and stucco too destroyed to indicate its previous use.

Sturka was scowling; he had thrown the Arab hood back off his head. He made a hand motion to Alvin.

But Alvin hadn't time to move. Peggy saw the door crash open and abruptly the room was filled with men firing rifles. . . .

It was dim. Probably a very bad light for shooting. Her eyes were used to it but still she wasn't sure what happened. The eruptive flashes stung her eyes. The racket was earsplitting.

Alvin was in the center of her vision and she saw that part of it most clearly: Alvin firing instinctively into the attackers, his revolver bucking. But Alvin waited to watch his target fall and that gave the rest of them plenty of time. Someone shot Alvin and the force of the blow knocked him into a spin.

She watched in disbelief. Her head turned dreamily and she saw Sturka, his rough pitted face lifted, his eyes unrevealing, bracing the submachine gun to fire. To fire not at the attackers but at Fairlie who was already falling to the floor. . . .

A big man with a revolver was firing as if he were on a target range somewhere: holding the revolver at arms' length in both hands and shooting with a horrible rhythmic intensity, shooting and shooting until the gun was empty and the hammer clicked drily. . . .

She saw Sturka fall and she thought suddenly *They haven't seen me yet it must be too dark here* and she felt the weight of the pistol Sturka had pressed into her hand; she saw Fairlie stirring on the floor and she thought *They haven't killed him, it's up to me to kill him isn't it?* But she didn't lift the pistol. She only stood in the corner's deep shadows and watched while one of the attackers discovered her and lifted his rifle.

She saw the orange flame-tip when he fired.

4:39 A.M. North African Time　Lime had a stitch in his ribs. He stood soaked in his own juices.

Sturka had six wounds, caliber .38 inches and any one of them might have killed him. Lime had fired with deliberation, knowing there was time to get the others out, knowing Sturka was the one he had to kill.

Sturka died at Lime's feet. Lime saw his face crumple in death but there was no recognition in Sturka's eyes and no sign he realized anything: Sturka died in sulky silence without last words. He lay seeping blood into the stone floor and when the blood stopped flowing Lime went across the floor to where Clifford Fairlie lay.

Fatigue was gritty in his eyes. He could smell already the sickening pungency of death in the room. Sturka was dead and Corby had killed one of the Early Birds. The Astin girl lay in a crumpled heap, stunned by the force of the dart that had struck her in the chest; the tranquilizer would keep her unconscious for a bit.

And Fairlie. Orr had a flashlight, he was shaking it to strengthen its beam. Perhaps it was the quality of that light, but Fairlie had the pallor of death. Lime dropped to his knees beside the President-elect. He heard Orr say, "Get the doctor, Wilkes," and one of the sharpshooters ran out front to signal the caravan.

When the doctor arrived Fairlie had stopped breathing.

"We'll need an autopsy to be sure."

Lime was too drained to reply. He only stared at the doctor out of a dulled agony.

"Probably they had him doped up to keep him docile," the doctor said.

"And that killed him?"

"No. Your tranquilizer bullet killed him. On top of what was already in his system it became an overdose. Look, you had no way to anticipate this. I'll testify to that."

Lime had no interest in trying to shift the blame. It was beside the point. There was only one point. He had made a mistake and it had cost Fairlie's life.

"You did everything right," Orr was saying inaccurately. "None of them touched Fairlie with so much as a finger. We took them all out before they had a chance at him. Look it wasn't your fault. . . ."

But Lime was walking away. One of the men was on the walkie-talkie summoning the convoy and Lime went outside to meet it and waited in the night repressing all feelings and all thought.

"I'm sorry. I'm so Goddamned sorry sir."

Lime accepted Chad Hill's sorrow with a vague nod of his head. "I'll have to talk to somebody on that scrambler. See if you can raise Washington for me."

"The President?"

"Whoever you can get."

"You want me to do it sir?"

He felt remote gratitude and he touched Chad Hill's arm. "Thank you. I guess it's up to me."

"I mean I could——"

"Go on Chad."

"Yes sir."

He watched the youth lope down the hillside to the Land Rover.

He followed more slowly, moving like a somnambulist, tripping over things.

Eighteen or twenty riflemen stood around watching him with aggrieved compassion. He walked through their little knot and they made way for him. He reached the Land Rover and wasn't sure he could stay on his feet; he pulled the tailgate down and sat on it. Chad Hill handed him the telephone-style handset. "It's Mr. Satterthwaite in the war room."

There was a lot of racket. Static, or the scrambler operating imperfectly, or perhaps just the busy noise of the war room.

"Lime here."

"David? Where are you?"

"I'm in the desert."

"Well?"

". . . He's dead."

"What? Who's dead?"

"Clifford Fairlie."

Silence against the background noise.

Finally: "Dear sweet God." A voice so weak Lime hardly caught it.

"We got them all if it matters. Sturka and Renaldo bought the farm." My God. Bought the farm. An expression he hadn't heard or used in fifteen years.

Satterthwaite was saying something. Lime didn't catch it. "What?"

"I said that puts President Brewster back in office for four more years. The Senate voted cloture on Hollander's filibuster a couple of hours ago. They've amended the Act. It's on the President's desk for signature."

"I don't know what you're talking about. I'm not sure I care."

"I think," and Satterthwaite's voice was very low and very slowly distinct, "I have to know how and why Fairlie died, David."

"He died of an overdose of tranquilizers. I suppose you could say I killed him. I suppose you could say that."

"Go on. Tell me all of it."

Lime told him. And then asked, "What do you want me to do?"

"I don't know. We'll have to see. Don't say anything to anyone just yet. Keep all your people together, bring them all home. You'll fly Fairlie's body into Andrews—I'll meet you or have someone meet you. There'll have to be a debriefing—make sure you keep all your people incommunicado."

"No announcement at all?"

"Not from you. We'll have to release the news at this end. Actually I suppose it's up to the President to make the announcement."

Lime fumbled for a cigarette. "You may as well recall those seven prisoners. There won't be any exchange now."

"I will. All right, David, I'll see you," Satterthwaite said lamely and broke the connection.

Lime tossed the handset into the bed of the Land Rover and began jabbing his pockets to find his cigarette lighter.

12:20 A.M. EST   It looked like snow again. Satterthwaite stood in a small bare room on the top floor of the Executive Office Building. He hadn't switched any lights on. The city beyond the window threw in a little light. He had been standing alone in the dimness for some time. Just standing there.

Everybody had gone home. The war room had been dismantled. He had sat in it alone until the clean-up crews had come to clear up the mess; then he had come up here to think.

The Southern bloc had fought for Hollander but it had been no real contest. Brewster's supporters had played on the senility issue; nothing overt had been said on the Senate floor about Hollander's political leanings. That would have been too raw. In fact very little had been said about Hollander at all, except by his supporters. The issue—the pretended issue—was experience and qualifications. *Mr. President, I gladly avail myself of the privilege of offering my support to the able and distinguished Senator from Montana in affirming that in national crises when time is of the essence, the laws of succession to the Presidency of the United States must take into account the realities of today's complex administrative problems. We cannot and should not expect anyone to have to assume the burdens of this office without adequate preparation and introduction—that is to say briefings—on the multitude of critical ongoing problems which inevitably hang in the balance between changing administrations. Under the present circumstances where there is quite obviously no time at all to hand over the reins of government to a newcomer in an orderly fashion, is it not clear that we have but one intelligent course to follow? . . .*

Of course it was all poppycock, everyone knew it: Brewster could easily stay on as a guest in a White House wing for long enough to brief the new President if that were the only difficulty. Hollander's supporters had pointed out such things with biting scorn and thundering anger but there had been no stemming the pressure for Brewster. Everyone remembered how close the popular election had been. The accusations against Los Angeles and other cities, the recounts, the solid Democratic majority in both houses which secretly applauded Brewster's move because it vindicated the party.

But all these were minor; there was only one real issue and that was Wendell Hollander. His senile paranoia, his political dementia. Hollander had the unique ability to terrify almost everyone in Congress. And those who knew him best were those whom he terrified most.

Against that terror the anti-Brewster arguments, no matter how legion and logical, had carried no weight. It was true Brewster had usurped the prerogatives of the electorate: having lost the popular election he was overruling its results by act of Congress. It was true as Fitzroy Grant insisted that Brewster's action was in defiance of every reasonable interpretation of the spirit of the Constitution's safeguards. Maybe it was true also that Brewster's ability to acquire power far exceeded his ability to exercise it wisely; at least Fitz Grant suspected as much.

Yet what Brewster had done was not illegal, not unconstitutional, not technically refutable. He had seized upon the law—or a loophole in it—and had won because Congress had seized on an emotional loophole. The legislators had accepted the emergency plan primarily because it covered an emergency they had hoped and expected not to have meet. Like everyone else they had convinced themselves that Fairlie would be recovered alive. The irony was, they probably wouldn't have voted for the measure if they had known Fairlie was about to die—and so Hollander would have been President after all.

The Senate's opposition had been led by Grant, who was respected even if unheeded; over in the House the resistance had been led by a handful of hysterical far-right Congressmen who had quite literally been hooted off the floor. Ways and Means had reported out the House resolution within hours of the President's appeal and the roll-call vote had been taken with the relentless speed of a panzer blitz. The Acting Speaker, Philip Krayle of New York, had directed Ways and Means to form a subcommittee ready to meet on ten minutes' notice with the Senate's companion committee the instant the Senate bill had been ratified. It had all taken place with guilty haste and scores of them had slipped away furtively the instant their work had been done.

Satterthwaite hated equally Brewster's lunatic confidence and Fitz Grant's lunatic misgivings. Congress had taken the better of two choices. No denying that. But to prevent one form of tyranny they had created another.

Abruptly Satterthwaite stopped in front of the window. He made a number of grunts, audible punctuation to his thoughts. He was staring out at the city with the intense concentration of a lecher watching a woman disrobe but he wasn't seeing much of anything: his mind was turned inward and abruptly he shot out of the room and hurried toward the elevators.

The clean-up crew still mopped in the war room. Satterthwaite popped across the hall into the conference room and reached for the telephone and the federal directory. He found Philip Krayle's number and dialed.

It rang a dozen times. No answer. Well of course that would be Krayle's office. It was one o'clock in the morning. Satterthwaite spoke an oath, looked in the city phone book. No number for Representative Krayle.

Unlisted. Damn the son of a bitch. Satterthwaite pounded his fist on the table.

Finally he dialed a number he knew: Liam McNeely's home phone.

McNeely answered on the second ring.

"It's Bill Satterthwaite, Liam."

"Hello Bill." A voice utterly devoid of everything. Well it was understandable: McNeely had been Fairlie's closest political advisor and friend and had only learned of Fairlie's death within the past couple of hours. The President had gone on television at eleven to make two announcements. Someone—possibly Perry Hearn—had thought to call McNeely because McNeely had called Satterthwaite to ask for details. Satterthwaite had stuck to the prepared script: Fairlie had been dead before the rescuers arrived, the kidnappers had injected him with an overdose of drugs.

"Liam, I'm sorry to bother you at a time like this but it's vital. I need to reach Philip Krayle. I thought you might have his home number."

"Well I——"

Satterthwaite waited for McNeely to wrench his thoughts onto the new subject. In the end McNeely said, "Hang on a minute, I'll get it," in a faraway tone.

In a short while McNeely was back on the line. He spoke seven digits and Satterthwaite wrote them down on the cover of the directory by the phone.

"That all you wanted Bill?"

"Yes, thanks. I'm sorry I disturbed you."

"It's all right. I wasn't about to sleep tonight."

"I'm—wait a minute, Liam, I think you can help me."

"Help you do what?"

"I can't talk on the phone. Are you dressed?"

"Yes."

"I'm in the Executive Office Building. The conference room across the hall from the NSC boardroom. Can you get over here right away? I need someone to help me do some telephoning. A lot of calls to make."

"I don't know if I'd be much good talking to anyone tonight, Bill. I hate to cop out on you but——"

"It's for Cliff Fairlie," Satterthwaite said, "and it's important."

By the time McNeely arrived—improbably natty in a mohair suit and Italian shoes—the clean-up crew had finished in the boardroom. Satterthwaite took him inside and closed the door. "I'm glad you could come."

"Very mysterious. What the hell have you got in mind?"

They were not exactly friends although they had had a great deal of contact since the election. It had been taken for granted McNeely would assume Satterthwaite's role in the new administration.

"You've been thinking about Fairlie I'm sure."

"Yes."

"There'll be rumors Brewster had him killed."

"I suppose there will. There always are, when one man benefits from another's death."

"Those rumors will have no basis in fact," Satterthwaite said. "I have to clear that up with you before we go on."

McNeely's one-sided smile was merely polite. "We called him a lot of names in the campaign but I don't think any of them was murderer."

"He's a surprisingly honest man, Liam. To use an archaic turn of phrase he's a man of goodwill. I realize from your point of view he's

LINE OF SUCCESSION   327

too much a prisoner of old-fashioned political values, but you've got to credit his integrity."

"Why are you saying all this to me?"

"Because more and more I've become convinced it's wrong that a President who's been defeated should be permitted to succeed himself."

"Come again?"

"Sit down, take your coat off. I'll explain it as best I can."

Krayle arrived at twenty before two, a lumpy man in a rumpled topcoat. "What is it, Bill?"

"You know Liam McNeely of course."

"Sure. We campaigned together."

"I'm no expert on congressional regulations," Satterthwaite said. "I need facts from you about the breakdown—the table of organization. The chief officer in the House is the Speaker, is that right?"

"Sure, sure." Krayle looked very tired. He moved to a chair and rubbed his face and propped an elbow on the long table.

Satterthwaite glanced at McNeely. The slim New Yorker was watching them both with keen intensity.

"This could be damned important to all of us," Satterthwaite said. "When Milton Luke died why wasn't a successor elected immediately? Why were you installed as Acting Speaker?"

Krayle shook his head. His mouth made a wry shape. "I see what you're getting at. You're a strange one to ask me that question—one of Brewster's own boys?"

"Go on then," Satterthwaite said.

"Well I'm a little new to the job of course. They needed somebody to fill the interim post and I was handy. I'm not really qualified for it. I haven't got much seniority—there are a lot of people ahead of me. Mostly Southerners."

"Why didn't they elect a permanent successor to Luke?"

"Two reasons. First we don't have a full head count. We lost a lot of people in the various bombings if you recall." Very dry. Krayle didn't have a reputation for caustic sarcasms; it must have been his way of throwing up defenses against the chain of traumatic shocks that had affected them all.

"Maybe you don't know everything that's happened in the last twenty-four hours," Krayle said. "We had to drag a hundred Congressmen back to Washington. A lot of them went home for the funerals of their friends. Until this evening we didn't have a quorum in the chamber. We've lost seventy-two Congressmen. Fourteen others are still in the hospitals. Thank God none of them's still on the critical list. But the point is, we're eighty-six bodies short—and the majority of the dead ones were Democrats. You get my point?"

"You mean the Democrats couldn't scrape up a majority if you tried to seat a new Speaker right now."

"Something like that. There's been a lot of agitation. Some of the Southerners seem quite willing to switch sides of the aisle unless we agree to compromise on a Dixiecrat for Speaker. A group of us talked it over—both parties but Northerners mainly. We decided it would be better to wait until special elections have been held or governors' appointments made, to fill the vacant seats. Presumably that would more or less restore the solid Democratic majority from before. Also it would prevent anybody from accusing us of railroading something through while we didn't have a full contingent on hand."

"That didn't seem to stop you from reelecting Howard Brewster last night," McNeely said.

"My God nobody believed Fairlie would die—and besides, you know what the alternative was."

Satterthwaite said, "You still haven't explained it to my satisfaction. The Speaker of the House, if there were one right now, would be next in line for the Presidency. Ahead of Hollander, even ahead of Brewster. So why didn't you elect a new Speaker and let him become President?"

"That was the first thing we thought of. But the law doesn't work that way. The line of succession applies only to officers who've held office—and let me quote—'prior to the time of death, resignation, removal from office, inability, or failure to qualify.' I mean you can see the point. You simply can't go and appoint a new Speaker of the House who's really being appointed to the Presidency after the fact. The only Speaker of the House who was fully entitled to take Cliff Fairlie's place was the man who held that office prior to the time when Fairlie was kidnapped. That was Milton Luke and of course he's dead."

McNeely said, "That doesn't make sense to me."

Krayle looked at him. "Why not?"

"Because I don't know of any law that says you can't elect a new Speaker whenever an old Speaker dies or retires. You don't have to wait for the beginning of the next session of Congress to do that."

"It's true we can elect a new Speaker any time we want to, but whoever we elect now is someone who will have been elected to the Speakership *after* the fact. Don't you see? Fairlie's already dead. The law says 'prior to the time of death,' etcetera etcetera."

"But Fairlie isn't the President. Never has been."

"The law applies equally to a President-elect. Section Three, Twentieth Amendment to the Constitution. Also the Presidential Succession Act, Three U.S.C. Nineteen seventy-one. Don't think we haven't done our homework."

McNeely collapsed into a chair. He waggled a hand toward Satterthwaite. "Well it was worth a try."

"You should have known that idea would have occurred to a lot of other people besides you," Krayle said. "What the hell."

Satterthwaite said, "I'm not ready to give it up. It appears to me the law applies to people who hold office at the time when the vacancy occurs in the Presidency. There's no vacancy until noon tomorrow when Brewster's term ends."

"There's one trouble with that position," Krayle said wearily. "The laws are worded so that the President-elect occupies a sort of quasi-office. When he dies the Vice-President-elect becomes President-elect. When *he* dies the incumbent Speaker becomes President-elect for all practical purposes. That takes place at the time of death, not the time of vacancy in the White House. I'm not trying to pretend it's simple or even cut-and-dried, but that's the way it appears to work. The minute Dexter Ethridge died, Milton Luke was for all practical purposes the President-elect of the United States. That's the law."

"I don't see how you can have it both ways. If what you say is true, then the minute Luke died, Wendell Hollander became President-elect. If that's true then Brewster can't supersede Hollander—you can't make that kind of law retroactive."

Krayle's droopy eyes slowly changed shape. "You might have a point there. I don't think that occurred to any of us."

"Suppose it occurs to Hollander sometime in the next four years? We could have a hell of a mess—the Presidency up for grabs."

"What is it you're getting at?"

Satterthwaite felt the Congressman's hard stare. Krayle's eyes burned like gems. McNeely, slumped low in his chair, watched with avid fascination.

Satterthwaite said, "There's confusion in the laws, that's obvious. Nobody ever anticipated the unique situation we're in today—how could they? So no matter what solution is found, someone's going to find a legal objection to it."

"Yes. Go on."

"I'm willing to accept your interpretation of the laws of succession. Evidently just about everyone agrees with it. But you've got to be willing to accept the possibility that if you did go ahead and elect a new Speaker right now, he'd have a legitimate claim on the Presidency."

"You mean if we elected a new Speaker before noon tomorrow."

"Of course."

"Well it would be a disputed claim. It would only make things worse."

"But such a claim would have a certain legitimacy, wouldn't it?"

"I suppose you could say that. It's possible to read the law that way. A lot of people would dispute it."

"But the alternative is to allow Brewster to continue in office for four years in spite of the fact that he's obviously flouting the whole purpose of the Constitution."

"Electing a new Speaker would flout it just as much." Krayle shook his head. "I can't go along with you. The point you're ignoring is that Brewster would fight it tooth and nail—and Brewster's got the mass popular backing to make an awful fight of it, unlike old Wendy Hollander."

Liam McNeely said, "I think a lot of that mass popular backing would dwindle away in the flick of an eye if you gave the mass populace an attractive alternative."

Krayle didn't accept it. "If you think the country's ready to explode now, what do you think would happen after we got done dividing it up with this fight you're proposing? And anyhow I'll tell you something—Congress has been pushed around enough. They won't stand for more railroading from your direction. If you were going to switch sides against Brewster why didn't you do it a lot earlier?"

"Because I hadn't thought of a viable alternative to Hollander. Neither had anybody else. Look, I'm not *against* Howard Brewster, I'm only against going through with a hell of a dangerous precedent. I think we have to avoid that if we can."

"We can't. It's too late."

"I don't believe that," Satterthwaite said.

"The thing is," McNeely said, "Brewster might let go voluntarily. Especially if it's to defer to a popular choice. He knows if he tries to keep office for another four years his hold on the country will be tarnished. Nobody will ever forget the way he got his second term. It'll rankle. The dissidents hate him already—and a lot of people will join them."

Satterthwaite let the air settle before he spoke; when he did it was with quiet emphasis. "I know Howard Brewster. He doesn't want to be hated. I think we may be able to persuade him to support a move to nominate a new Speaker of the House."

Krayle sighed. "You'll have to forgive my skepticism."

"I'm sure it's justified. But grant us the possibility, will you?"

"In politics just about anything's possible, Bill."

"Good enough. Which brings us to the reason we wanted to talk to you. We can't have the House members scattering again. Can you corral the membership and keep them on tap for the time between now and Thursday noon?"

Krayle tipped his head back to study him narrowly. "I suppose you've even got a candidate all picked out for us too."

"Of course."

"Yes?"

"The man who almost got the nomination. The man Fairlie wanted on his own ticket—the man Dex Ethridge designated as his Vice-President."

"Andrew Bee," Krayle breathed. "Jesus Christ, Bill, I think you've damn well got something there."

9:45 A.M. EST   The big jet landed at Andrews and when it taxied to a stop Lime unbelted himself and left the plane, unrefreshed by the six hours' sleep above the Atlantic. The scrambler call from Satterthwaite had reached him at Gibraltar and he had obeyed instructions, coming on ahead of the others in a virtually empty plane, leaving Chad Hill in charge to bring all the bodies home, living and dead.

There was no sun. The runway was a little misty, the pavement slick. It was a day filled with gray gloom. An Air Force FOLLOW ME jeep came hissing along to the plane and Satterthwaite was in the passenger seat.

They reached the White House at ten-thirty. The Secret Service people nodded to Satterthwaite and greeted Lime with grave welcomes. Their movements were tracked by many alert eyes while they made their way to the President's sanctum. Here and there a crate stood in a quiet corner: Brewster had packed weeks ago and it would have been unseemly to begin unpacking again.

Margaret kept them cooling their heels for nearly twenty minutes before they were admitted. Whoever had shared the President's company in the interval had departed by the side door.

Brewster greeted them with ill-controlled anger. Lime, closing the door after Satterthwaite, looked at the President and was struck by the sheer physical size of the man as he had been struck by it before. On his feet Brewster loomed, he filled the big office the way a caged tiger filled his cell.

"What's all the mystery, Bill?"

"We have to talk to you, Mr. President."

"About this Andy Bee business I assume?"

Satterthwaite couldn't help a little smile. "How long have you known?"

"Several hours. I've got a lot of ears—you of all people ought to know that." The President's eyes flicked briefly across Lime's face: quite obviously he wanted to know what Lime was doing here, why he was with Satterthwaite. Quickly Brewster's attention went back to Satterthwaite: "I suppose it's an appropriate time for me to make a little 'Et tu Brute' speech. It *was* you, wasn't it? Or did my sources foul that up?"

"It was me."

Brewster nodded; the big head shifted, the eyes examined Lime and Satterthwaite in turn. Lime felt the force in them; he met the President's stare uneasily.

Brewster said, "And now I suppose you're ready to explain to me all the reasons why I should step aside and yield to Andy Bee."

The conversation had very little reality for Lime. He was tired, he wasn't a political animal; out of place, he only watched and awaited his cue.

The President said, "I guess you've been letting Fitz Grant bend your ear."

"Fitz believes you intend to crack down on thousands of radicals."

"I might have had that in mind. It's a human reaction, Bill."

"And now?"

"I'm still thinking on it."

"It'd be a mistake the country would never recover from."

"It might," the President said, "but not for the reason you think it would."

"No?"

"They need cracking down on, Bill. God how they need it. If we can't hold up our heads in this country and fight back at the subversives who want to destroy us—Christ, if you won't fight you deserve to lose. But I'm in a pickle now. I wish I'd foreseen it. I campaigned against Wendy Hollander on a ticket of moderation and tolerance. If I turned around and destroyed the radicals the way I should, the country'd have my hide in strips." An odd smile, a quick hand gesture. "Puts me in a corner, don't it."

"Fitz Grant did say something like that. You'd end up looking like Johnson to Hollander's Goldwater."

"All right. But that's not what you're here to talk about. Is it."

"There are reasons," Satterthwaite said—and Lime felt the bitter reluctance—"why you must stand aside and support the Bee nomination."

"Are there?"

"Several. For one thing there's a legal technicality. I won't go into detail at this point but we're fairly certain Wendy Hollander has a basis to challenge you if you leave things stand as they are. He can maintain that according to the law he became President-elect the minute Milton Luke died, and that the amendment you passed in Congress was not binding because it would have had to be retroactive."

"He'd have a hell of a time making that stick."

"Mr. President, he could tear the country apart on that issue."

"He could try. I'd be willing to fight it."

"All right. Then consider the flimsy position you're in with the public. They'll call you a despot and a dictator and a lot of other names. They'll insist you've flouted the Constitution and the will of the electorate. They'll be calling for your resignation—in fact I wouldn't put it past some of them, not only the leftists but the Hollander wing as well, to start impeachment proceedings."

"They wouldn't get far."

"Far enough to whip the public into a frenzy. Do you want battle lines drawn up in the streets?"

"You're forecasting civil war. That's fanciful."

"No, Mr. President, I don't think it is. Because your opposition will have a piece of ammunition you won't be able to defend yourself against." Satterthwaite whipped around to Lime. "David, I want you to tell the President exactly what happened to Clifford Fairlie."

The President was taken aback for the first time. Lime saw it; he had been watching the man steadily.

Lime told it straight. "You could call it an accident," he concluded, "but any way you cut it, he was killed by agents of the American Government, not by his kidnappers."

"Well yes, but——"

"There were half a dozen of us in the room at the time that dart was fired, Mr. President. There must have been twenty of us in the place by the time the doctor announced his findings. We're holding them incommunicado but you can't do that forever. With that many people involved in the secret, the truth will get out."

Satterthwaite raised a hand, palm out. Lime's part of it was concluded and Satterthwaite picked up the ball. "They'll claim we did it deliberately of course. They'll say you wanted Fairlie dead to perpetuate yourself in office."

The President drew himself up. "Bill, you don't walk into the office of the President of the United States with a cheap attempt at blackmail. For the love of——"

"No sir. You misunderstand. David and I aren't threatening you. If the accusations are made—and believe me they will be—we'll both back you to the hilt. We'll tell the absolute truth. Don't forget David and I are implicated just as deeply as you are, if not more so. We'll have to defend ourselves and of course we'll do it with the truth. You didn't murder Fairlie. Nobody murdered him. It was a freak accident, the result of our ignorance of one fact—the fact that Fairlie had been doped up so heavily before we reached him."

Satterthwaite took a ragged breath. "But who's going to believe us, Mr. President?"

Brewster's face was suffused with a rush of blood. "I don't like being bulldozed, Bill. There've been ridiculous rumors and accusations before."

"Not like these."

"Don't you remember the slanders against Lyndon Johnson after the Kennedy assassination?"

"It wasn't the same, Mr. President. Kennedy was not killed by known agents of the Administration. Johnson hadn't just lost an election to the dead man. And if I can be blunt about it Johnson didn't have the kind of enemies you have now. Hollander on the right, everybody on the far left, and a vast body of uncertain people in the center."

"From what you say there'll be rumors whether or not I remain in this seat. That's the weakness in your strategy, Bill."

"No sir. If you step down now it'll prove you had nothing to gain by Fairlie's death. It won't stop the rumors but it'll take the force out of them. Their target will be a retired politician, not the incumbent President of the United States. There's a world of difference."

Howard Brewster reached for a cigar but did not light it. He studied it for a very long time. Lime felt the busy hum of the White House through the soles of his shoes.

Finally the President spoke. "The idea of nominating Andy Bee to the Speakership—was that your notion, Bill?"

"A lot of them thought of it, or something like it. Naturally. But they didn't act on it because they weren't sure it would work—they all assumed you'd fight it bitterly and none of them had the strength left for another battle. They're scared, Mr. President. We're all scared."

"But you put them up to it."

"You could say that. It's still uncertain. If you decide to fight it they may not even introduce the measure. You've got enough loyal supporters to maintain a filibuster from here to tomorrow noon."

"Putting me exactly where Hollander was twenty-four hours ago, hey?"

"It's not quite the same. But close enough."

Suddenly Lime felt the presidential eyes drill into him. "You sir. What do you think?"

"I don't count, Mr. President. I'm just a gumshoe."

"You've got a brain in your head. A good one. Tell me what it thinks."

"I think you've been a pretty good President, sir. And I think the people voted you out of office last November."

"Thank you for your candor, Mr. Lime."

The President's attention dropped to the cigar in his fingers and Lime glanced at Satterthwaite. They were both thinking the same thing, Lime felt. The President hadn't really been seeking advice from him; he'd been looking for something deeper—a clue to the realities that lay outside this room. He knew he still had the authority to say "Frog" but he was no longer certain which way the people would jump in response.

Brewster was in fact awesomely close to Hollander's position of yesterday and he knew it, visibly. Once again, dizzily, the country had a choice. Andrew Bee was the closest thing to Fairlie it was possible to offer. Bee would be acceptable to the left because of his politics; paradoxically he might be equally acceptable to the right because he did have a lawful claim to the office, he represented everything the voters had mandated, and his position would appeal to the sympathies of those who held to strict adherence to law and Constitution. Only the blessing of one man was needed—a man who sat in a historically unique position because he alone had the power to decide which of two men should become President of the United States.

THURSDAY,
JANUARY 20

12:00 noon EST "Hold up your right hand and repeat after me."
The cameras zoomed in close on the face of the next President.
Lime reached for a cigarette without taking his eyes off the screen.
On the couch Satterthwaite stirred his coffee. Bev stood behind
Lime's chair watching the television screen, massaging the back of
Lime's neck.

". . . do solemnly swear that I will faithfully execute the office of
President of the United States, and will to the best of my ability
preserve, protect and defend the Constitution of the United States.
So help me God."

Satterthwaite bounded off the couch and strode to the set to turn
the sound down. His burning magnified eyes rode around to Lime.
"He could have told us the minute you and I walked into the office
yesterday. I feel like a prize ass."

"Uhn."

"You figured it out before I did. Didn't you."

"Maybe," Lime said. "I guessed; I wasn't sure."

"But you didn't tell me. You could have warned me to pull in my
horns. You didn't."

"I thought it was up to him to do that." Lime stretched drowsily;
tipped his face back and peered into Bev's smiling upside-down
eyes.

"Not telling me," Satterthwaite muttered, "that was his way of
punishing me for losing the faith."

Bev from her experiential wisdom of years in the Speaker's office
said, "Andy Bee's a Republican of course," as if that explained
everything.

Perhaps it did. Brewster was an old-line Democrat and that was why it hadn't occurred to him until Krayle had got him out of bed yesterday to tell him Satterthwaite's scheme.

On the screen President Andrew Bee was launching into a low-keyed Inaugural Address and the camera pulled back to show the others on the dais with him: Howard Brewster prominently at his right elbow, looking attentive and content—almost smug. It brought to mind the smile Brewster had shown yesterday when finally he had said to Satterthwaite, "Have Perry set up the television room."

"Yes?"

"I made my decision hours ago, Bill. I'm afraid you're too late to change my mind. I tried to reach you quite a while ago but I suppose you must have been out at Andrews to meet Mr. Lime. Nobody knew where to reach you."

Satterthwaite had reddened. "And you've just been letting me shoot my face off."

"It helped. It wasn't an easy decision—I'm glad to have had confirmation from both of you. Bill, I'm sorry the idea of nominating Bee to the Speakership didn't occur to me before it occurred to someone else. It's the only answer—the only way out of this bog we're mired in."

Lime had caught Satterthwaite's wry tail-of-the-eye glance. They had expected appeals to loyalty, friendship; attempts to reason, to fight; threats and pleas. Now it was like throwing a fist against an opponent who had obligingly fallen to the floor a split second before you tried to hit him. And the President was taking pleasure in it.

The Brewster smile broadened. "Haven't you ever known me to give in graciously?"

"Not where your whole political career was at stake."

"My political career ended last November at the polls, Bill."

"And you're giving up without a fight." Satterthwaite's tone was laced with disbelieving skepticism.

"I never refused to fight," the President said. "I fought pretty well, I think. I just lost, that's all. You fight, you lose, you go home and lick your wounds. That's the biological law. The arguments you've been raising here this morning—I'd be a prize fool if I hadn't thought of them long before you proposed them to me. Now if there's nothing else I'd suggest you set up the news conference, Bill. And get Andy Bee on the wire for me."

After that there had been the frantic telephoning and organizing and caucusing. It took pressure and persuasion to bring some of the leaders around: they got balky because they felt they were being treated cheaply. First Brewster had railroaded his "emergency measure" through. Now Fairlie was dead, the emergency measure stood ready to fill the gap, and suddenly Brewster didn't want to use it—he wanted something else instead.

In the end he had got what he wanted, but not because it was his wish. The House voted to seat Bee simply because he was an alternative to Brewster as Brewster had been to Hollander. But it had taken herculean work from Krayle and all the others and even so it had barely squeaked through, more as a protest against Brewster's high-handedness than as a gesture of support for him. The vote had come through at seven-fifty this morning.

Bev said, "Hadn't you better go home to your wife?"

Lime jerked upright and only then realized she was talking to Satterthwaite.

"I probably will. No place else to go anymore." Satterthwaite gave them a benign look, got up and reached for his coat.

Bev's strong fingers kneaded Lime's back. Satterthwaite was moving to the door; Lime kept him in view.

Satterthwaite waved his coat grandly. "It's pretty funny when you think about it, David. You and I have changed the history of the planet and what do we have to show for it? We're both out of a job."

Lime neither spoke nor smiled. Satterthwaite had his hand on the knob. "What sort of unemployment compensation do you suppose you have for people who saved the world for democracy?" His laughter, very off key, rang behind him after he had left.

Lime put his cigarette in the ashtray and closed his eyes. He felt Bev's strong ministrations and heard faintly the mutter of Andrew Bee's steady reassuring voice.